Also From Joe Books

Disney Princess Comics Treasury
Disney Frozen Cinestory Comic
Disney Cinderella Cinestory Comic
Disney 101 Dalmatians Cinestory Comic
Disney Descendants Wicked World Cinestory Comic Volume One
Disney Descendants Wicked World Cinestory Comic Volume Two
Disney Descendants Wicked World Cinestory Comic Volume Three
Disney Alice in Wonderland Cinestory Comic
Disney Star vs the Forces of Evil Cinestory Comic
Disney Princess Comic Strips Collection Volume One
Disney Star Darlings Cinestory Comic: Becoming Star Darlings
Disney Moana Comics Collection
Disney Elena of Avalor Cinestory Comic: Ready to Rule
Disney Tangled Cinestory Comic
Disney Beauty and the Beast Cinestory Comic

Don't Miss Our Monthly Comics...

Disney Frozen
Disney Princess

Disney Tangled
Before Ever After

Cinestory Comic

JOE BOOKS LTD

Published simultaneously in the United States and Canada by Joe Books
Ltd, 489 College Street, Toronto, ON M6G 1A5

www.joebooks.com

First Joe Books edition: May 2017

Print ISBN: 978-1-77275-447-6
ebook ISBN: 978-1-77275-555-8

"WIND IN MY HAIR"
Music by Alan Menken, Words by Glenn Slater
© 2016 Wonderland Music Company, Inc. (BMI) /
Walt Disney Music Company (ASCAP)
All Rights Reserved. Used With Permission

"LIFE AFTER HAPPILY EVER AFTER"
Music by Alan Menken, Words by Glenn Slater
© 2016 Wonderland Music Company, Inc. (BMI) /
Walt Disney Music Company (ASCAP)
All Rights Reserved. Used With Permission

"MORE OF ME"
Words and Music by Andy Dodd and Dewain Whitmore Jr.
© 2016 Walt Disney Music Company (ASCAP)
All Rights Reserved. Used With Permission

Joe Books™ is a trademark of Joe Books Ltd. Joe Books® and the
Joe Books Logo are trademarks of Joe Books Ltd, registered in
various categories and countries. All rights reserved.

Adaptation, design, lettering, layout, and editing by First Image.

Library and Archives Canada Cataloguing in Publication
information is available upon request.

Printed and bound in Canada
1 3 5 7 9 10 8 6 4 2

DISNEY
Tangled
Before Ever After

— Tangled Before Ever After Part I —

DIRECTED BY
Tom Caulfield

PRODUCED BY
Chris Sonnenburg and Shane Prigmore

WRITTEN BY
Jase Ricci

— Tangled Before Ever After Part II —

DIRECTED BY
Stephen Sandoval

PRODUCED BY
Chris Sonnenburg and Shane Prigmore

WRITTEN BY
Jase Ricci

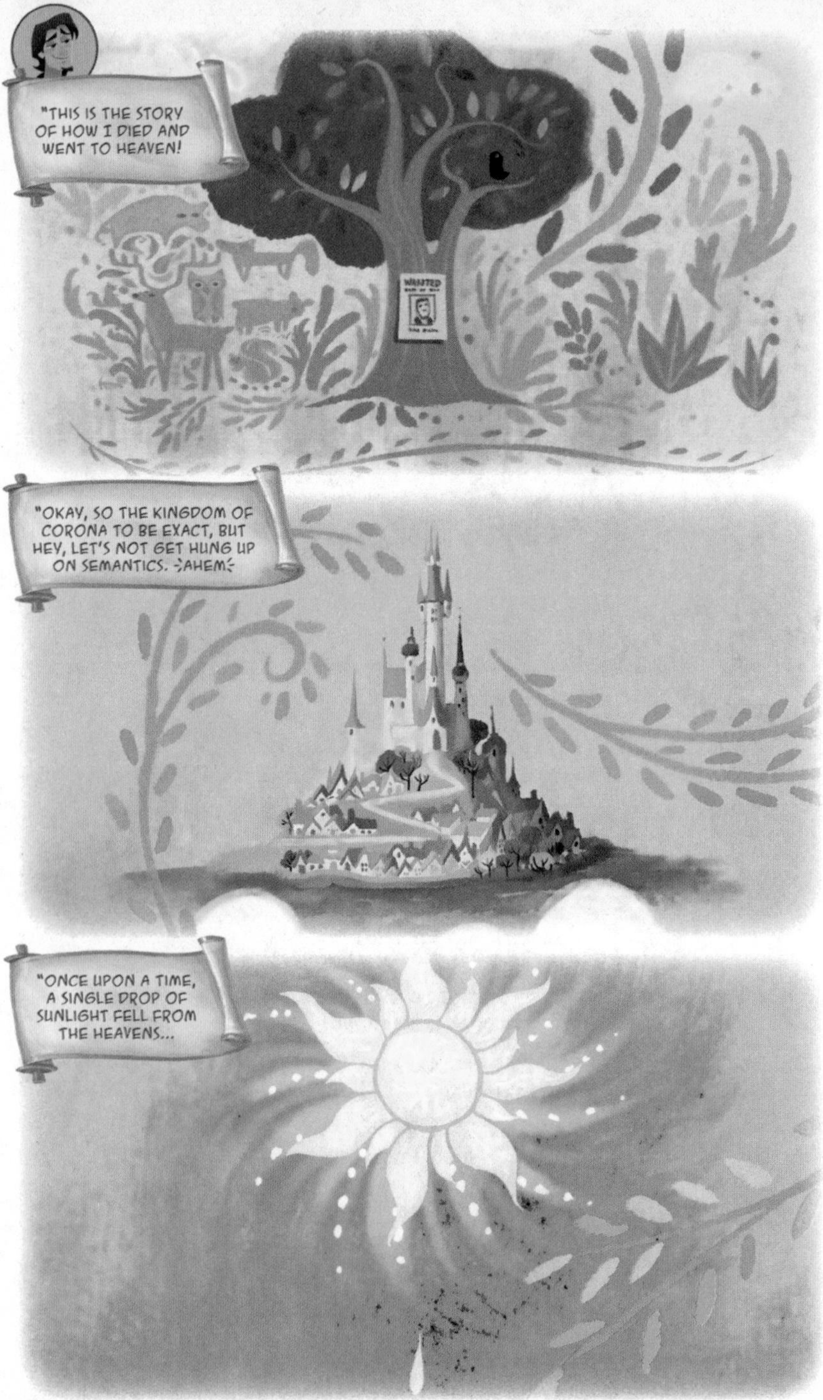
"THIS IS THE STORY OF HOW I DIED AND WENT TO HEAVEN!
"OKAY, SO THE KINGDOM OF CORONA TO BE EXACT, BUT HEY, LET'S NOT GET HUNG UP ON SEMANTICS. AHEM
"ONCE UPON A TIME, A SINGLE DROP OF SUNLIGHT FELL FROM THE HEAVENS...

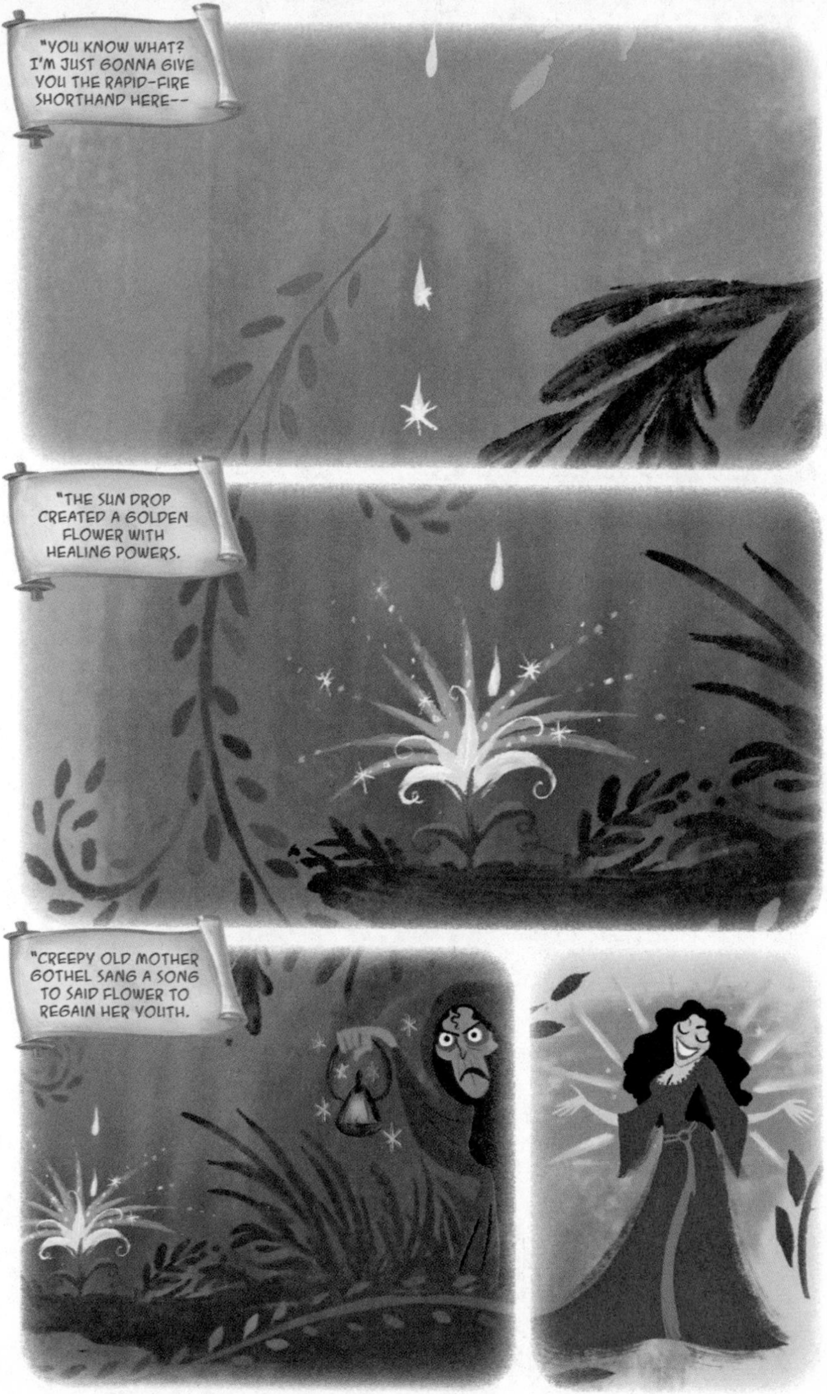
"YOU KNOW WHAT? I'M JUST GONNA GIVE YOU THE RAPID-FIRE SHORTHAND HERE--
"THE SUN DROP CREATED A GOLDEN FLOWER WITH HEALING POWERS.
"CREEPY OLD MOTHER GOTHEL SANG A SONG TO SAID FLOWER TO REGAIN HER YOUTH.

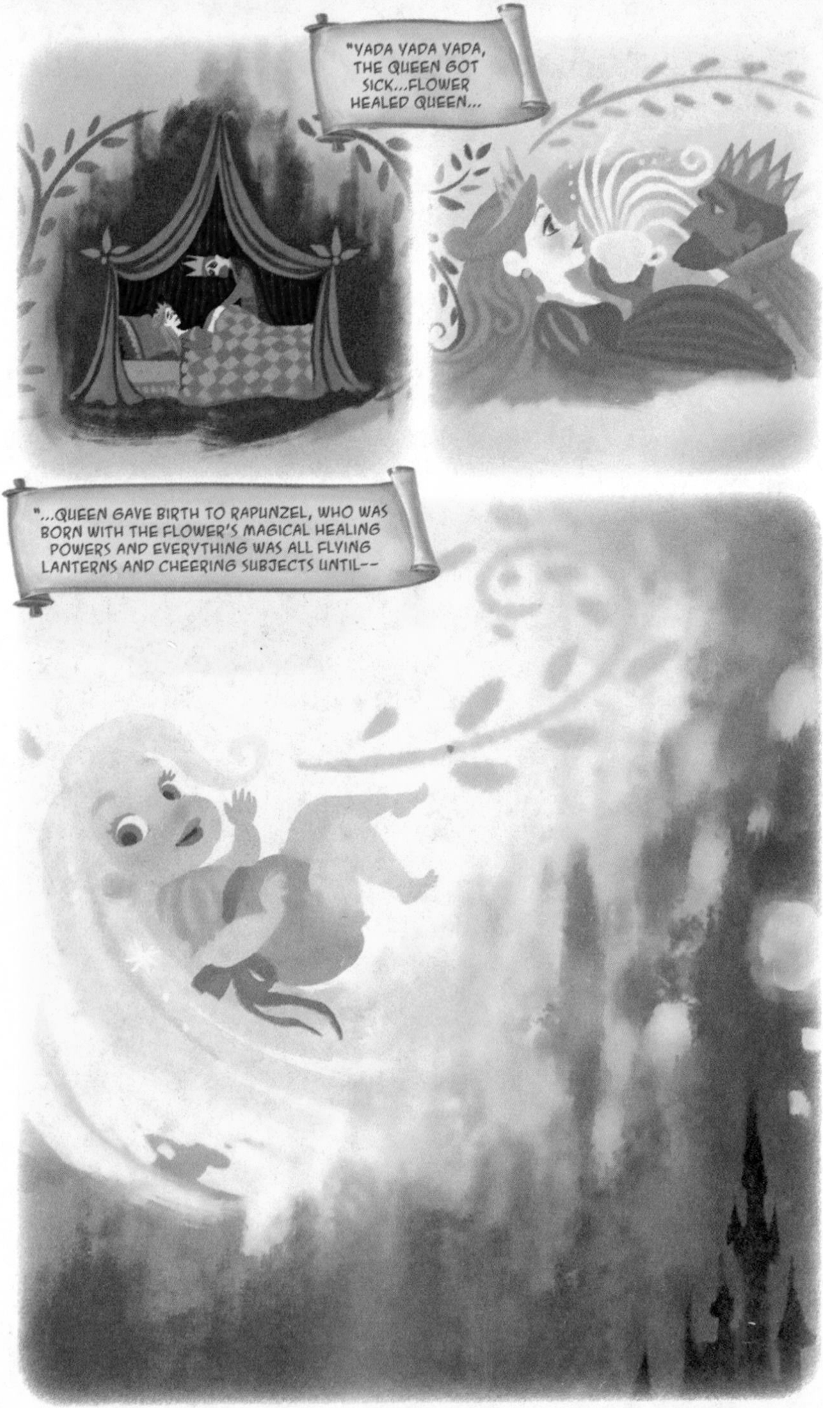
"YADA YADA YADA, THE QUEEN GOT SICK...FLOWER HEALED QUEEN...
"...QUEEN GAVE BIRTH TO RAPUNZEL, WHO WAS BORN WITH THE FLOWER'S MAGICAL HEALING POWERS AND EVERYTHING WAS ALL FLYING LANTERNS AND CHEERING SUBJECTS UNTIL--

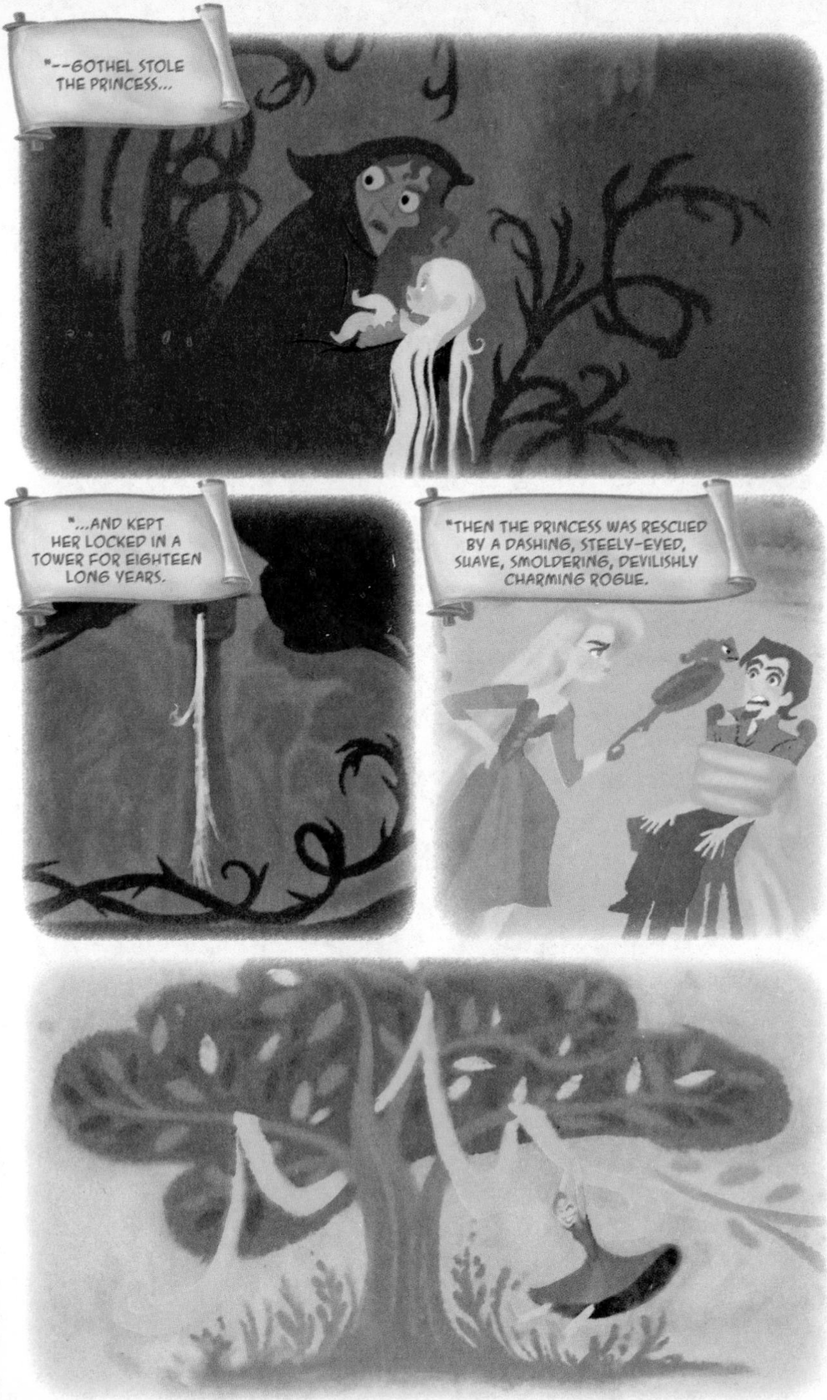
"--GOTHEL STOLE THE PRINCESS...
"...AND KEPT HER LOCKED IN A TOWER FOR EIGHTEEN LONG YEARS.
"THEN THE PRINCESS WAS RESCUED BY A DASHING, STEELY-EYED, SUAVE, SMOLDERING, DEVILISHLY CHARMING ROGUE.

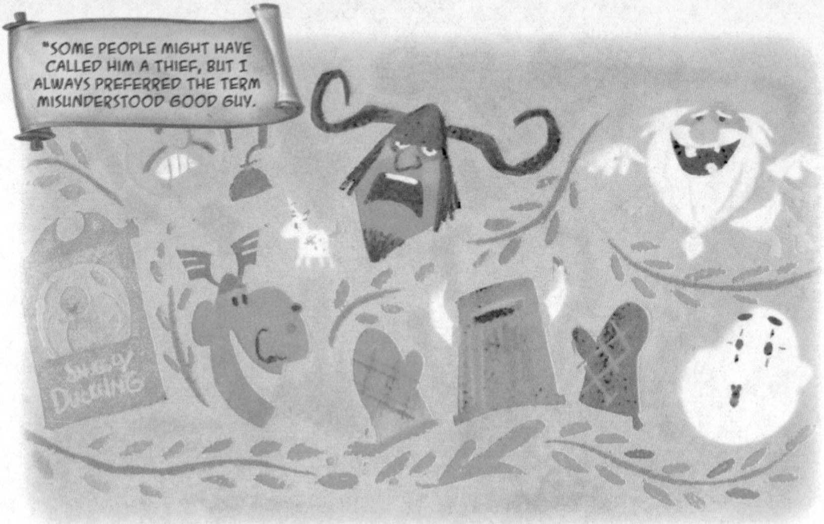
"SOME PEOPLE MIGHT HAVE CALLED HIM A THIEF, BUT I ALWAYS PREFERRED THE TERM MISUNDERSTOOD GOOD GUY.
Snuggly Duckling

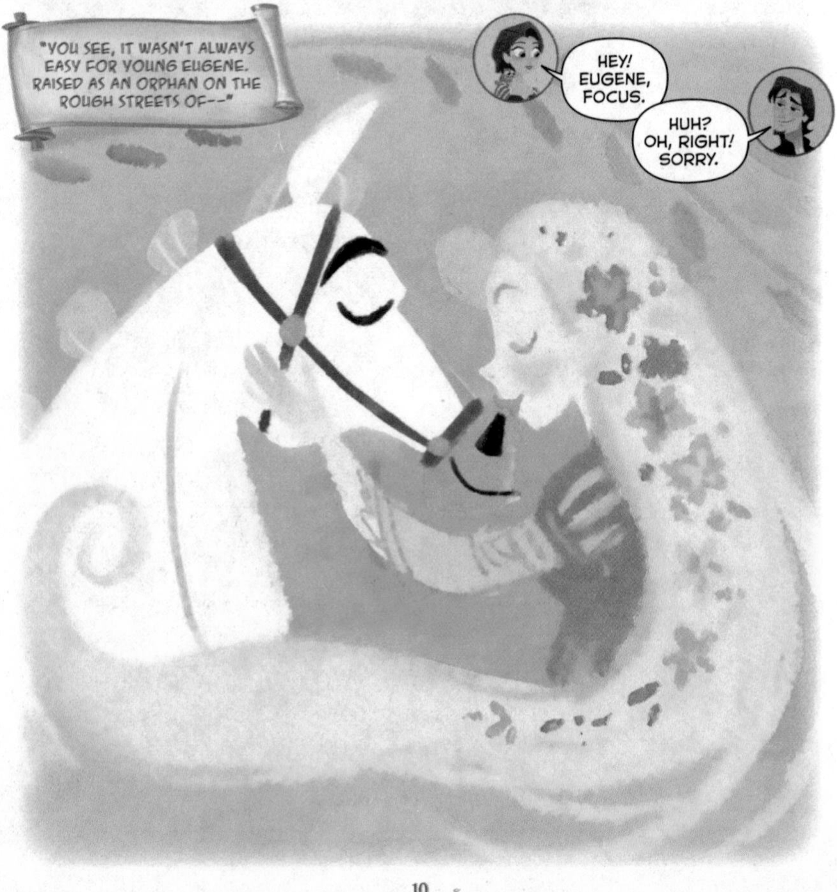
"YOU SEE, IT WASN'T ALWAYS EASY FOR YOUNG EUGENE. RAISED AS AN ORPHAN ON THE ROUGH STREETS OF--"
HEY! EUGENE, FOCUS.
HUH? OH, RIGHT! SORRY.

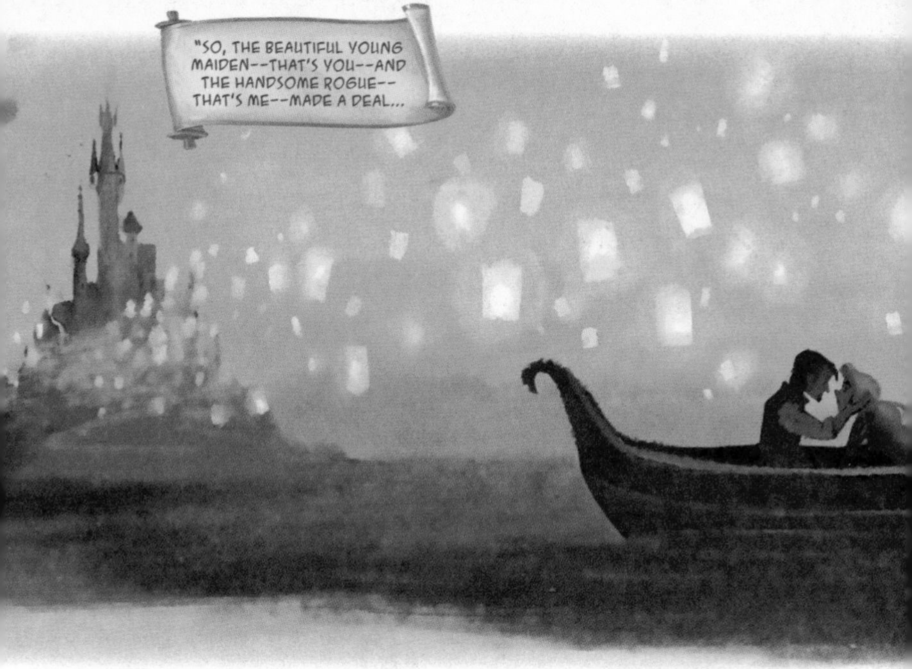
"SO, THE BEAUTIFUL YOUNG MAIDEN--THAT'S YOU--AND THE HANDSOME ROGUE--THAT'S ME--MADE A DEAL...

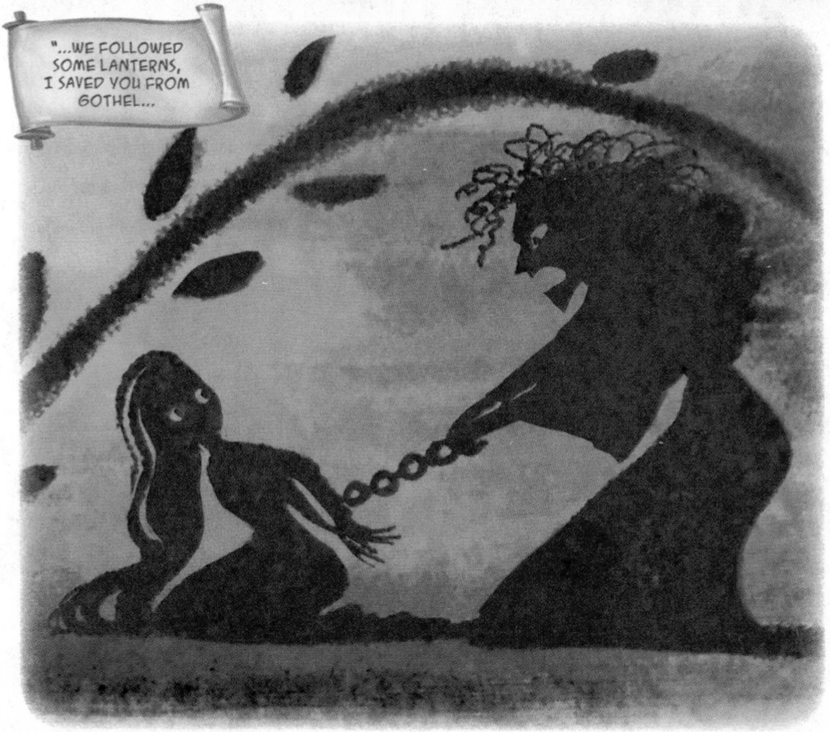
"...WE FOLLOWED SOME LANTERNS, I SAVED YOU FROM GOTHEL...

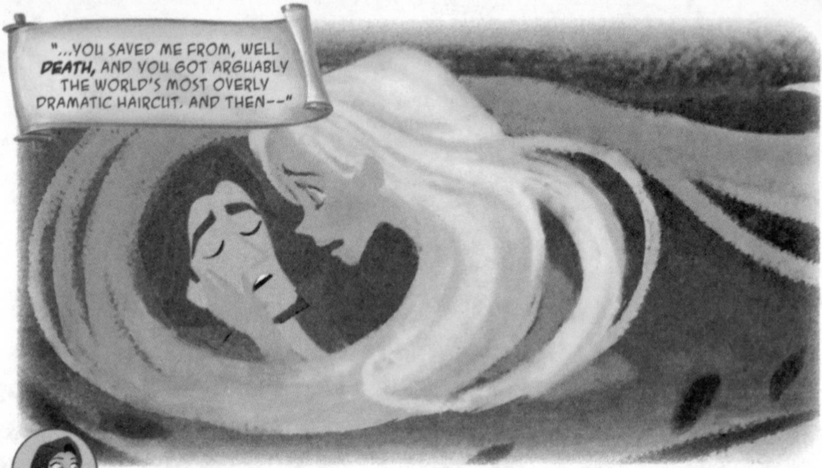
"...YOU SAVED ME FROM, WELL **DEATH,** AND YOU GOT ARGUABLY THE WORLD'S MOST OVERLY DRAMATIC HAIRCUT. AND THEN--"

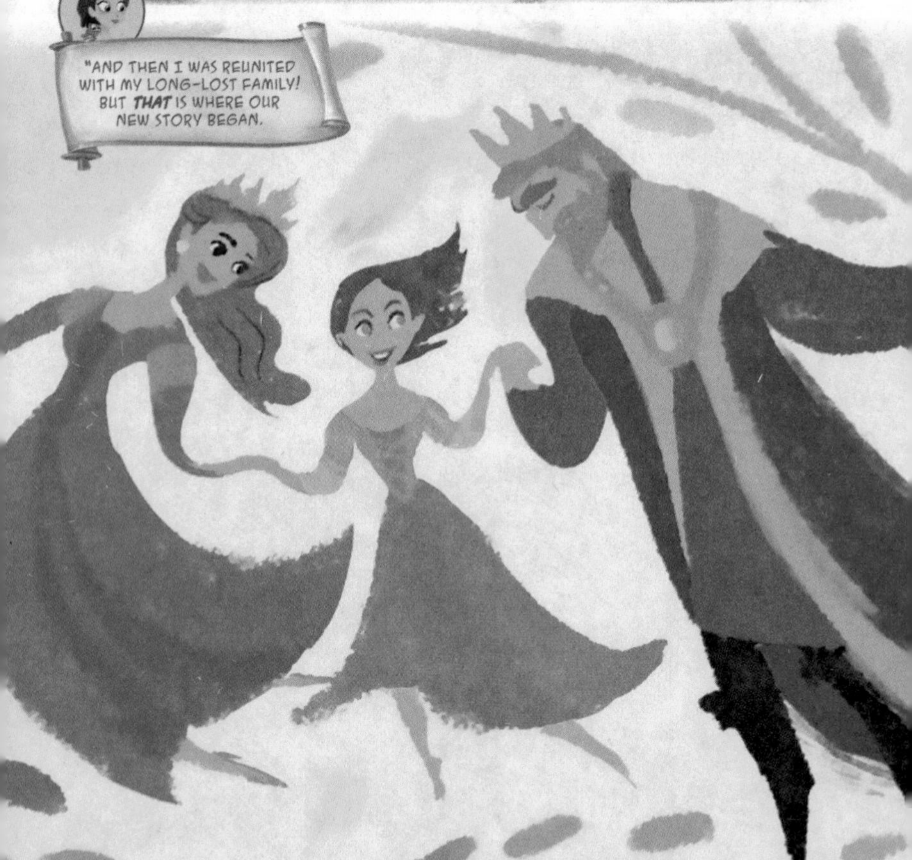
"AND THEN I WAS REUNITED WITH MY LONG-LOST FAMILY! BUT **THAT** IS WHERE OUR NEW STORY BEGAN.

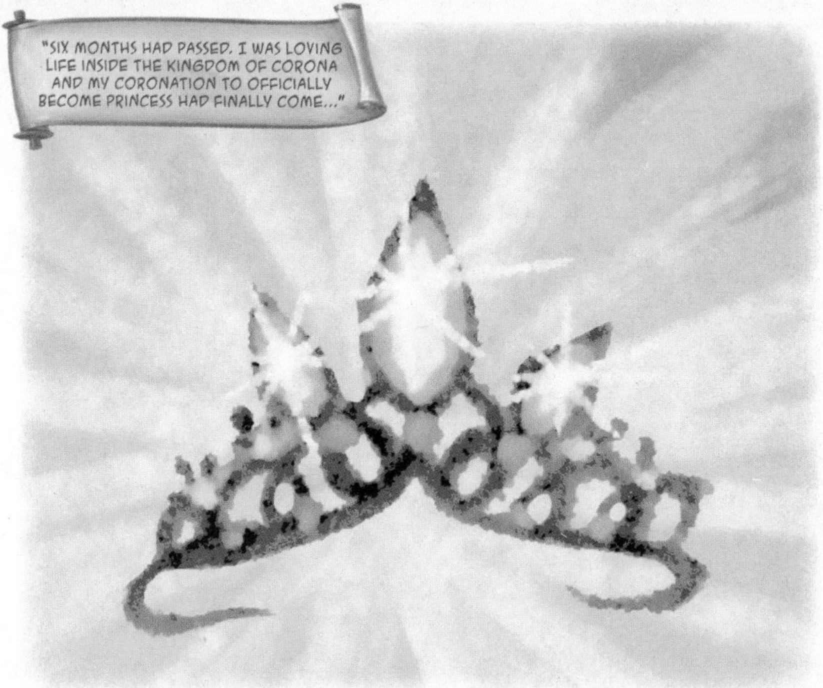
"SIX MONTHS HAD PASSED. I WAS LOVING LIFE INSIDE THE KINGDOM OF CORONA AND MY CORONATION TO OFFICIALLY BECOME PRINCESS HAD FINALLY COME..."

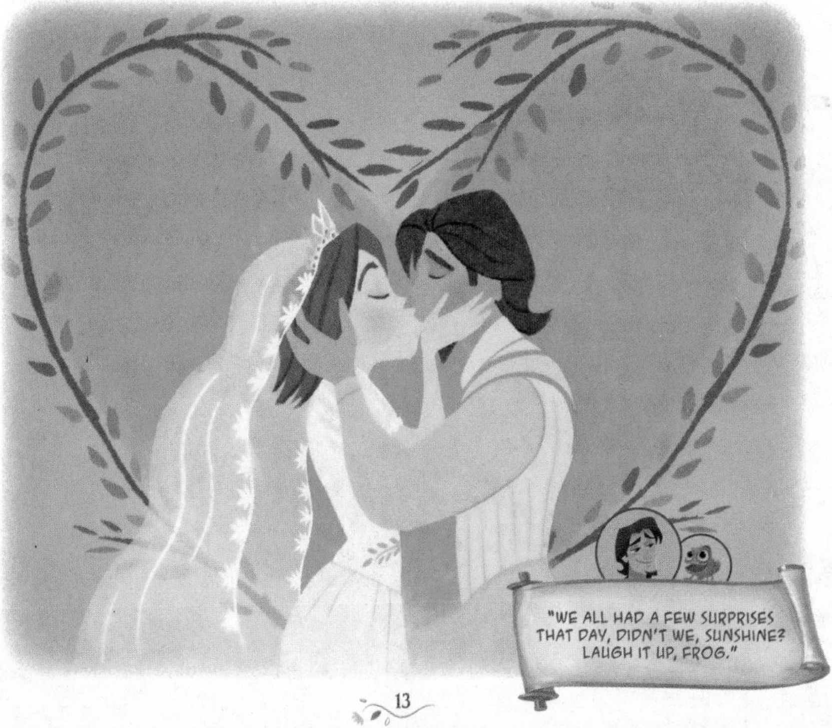
"WE ALL HAD A FEW SURPRISES THAT DAY, DIDN'T WE, SUNSHINE? LAUGH IT UP, FROG."

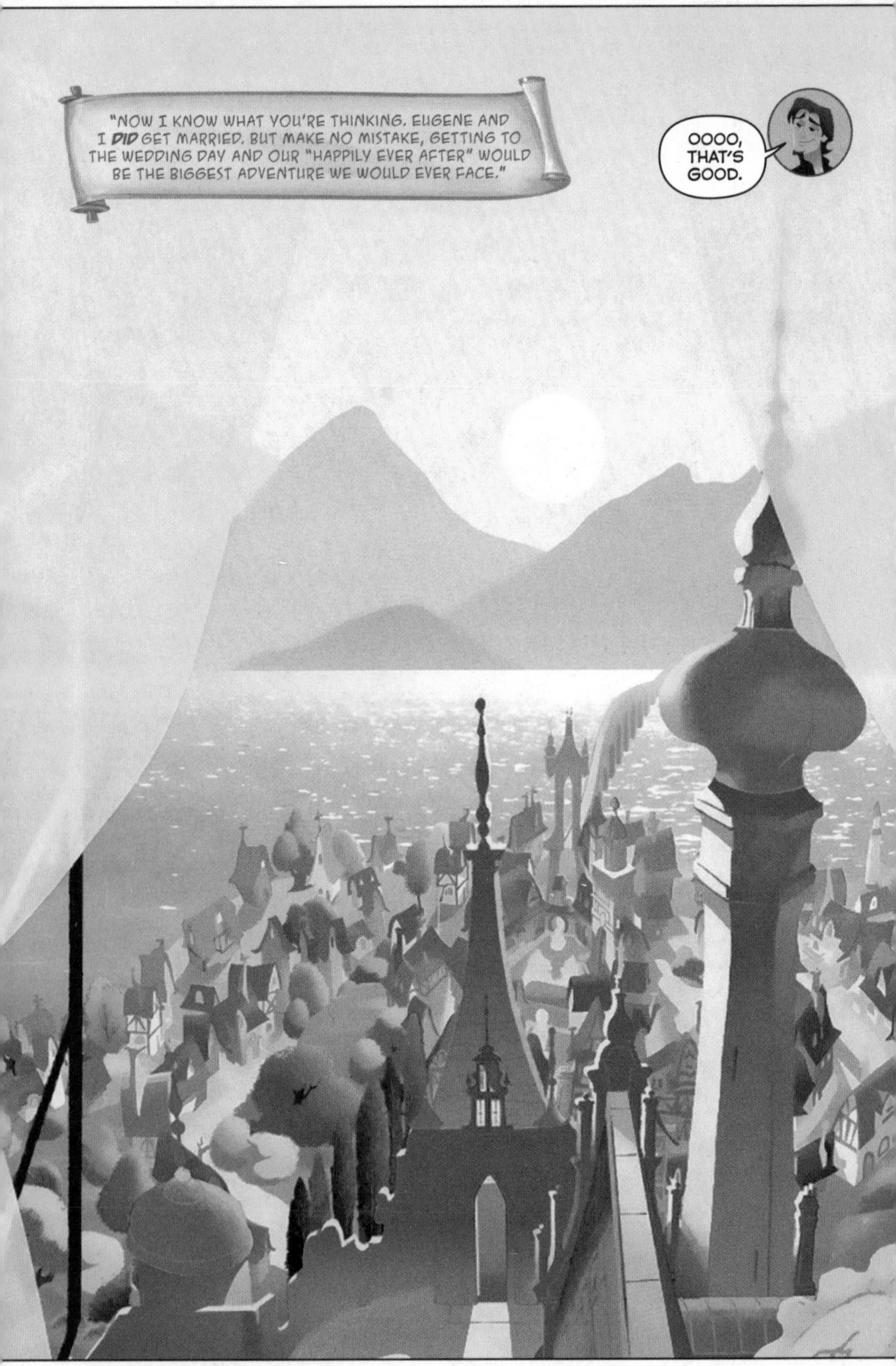
"NOW I KNOW WHAT YOU'RE THINKING. EUGENE AND I ***DID*** GET MARRIED. BUT MAKE NO MISTAKE, GETTING TO THE WEDDING DAY AND OUR "HAPPILY EVER AFTER" WOULD BE THE BIGGEST ADVENTURE WE WOULD EVER FACE."
OOOO, THAT'S GOOD.

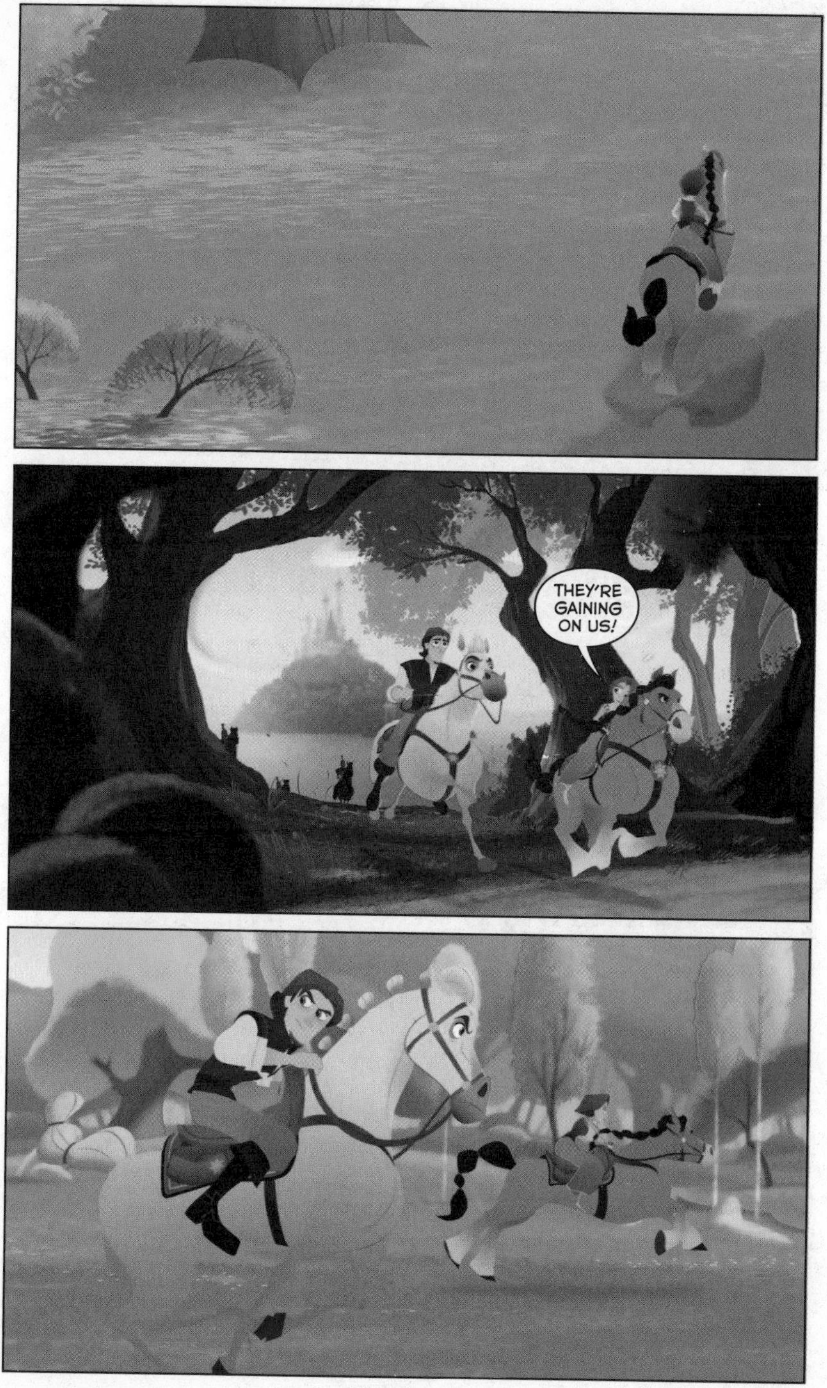
THEY'RE GAINING ON US!

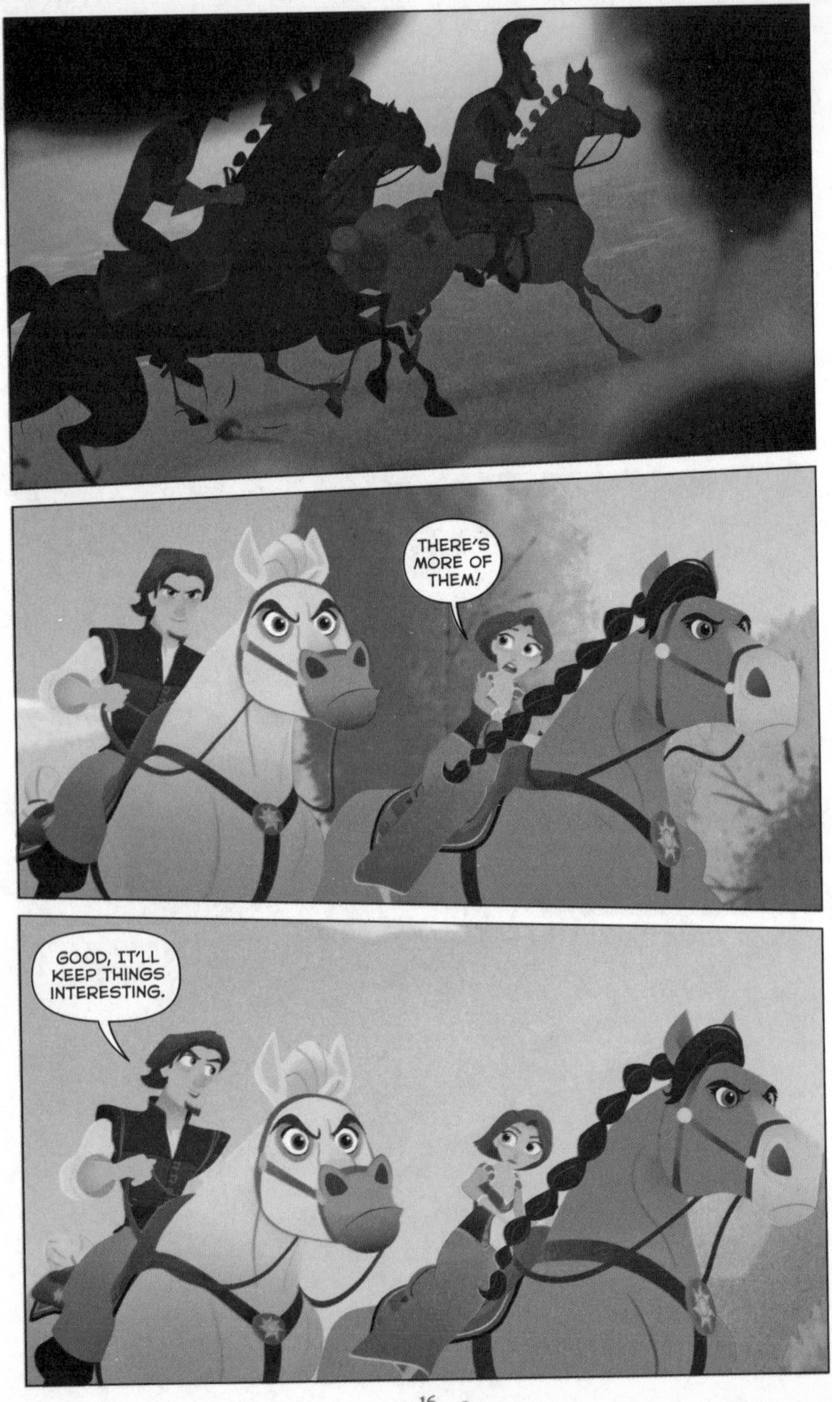
THERE'S MORE OF THEM!
GOOD, IT'LL KEEP THINGS INTERESTING.

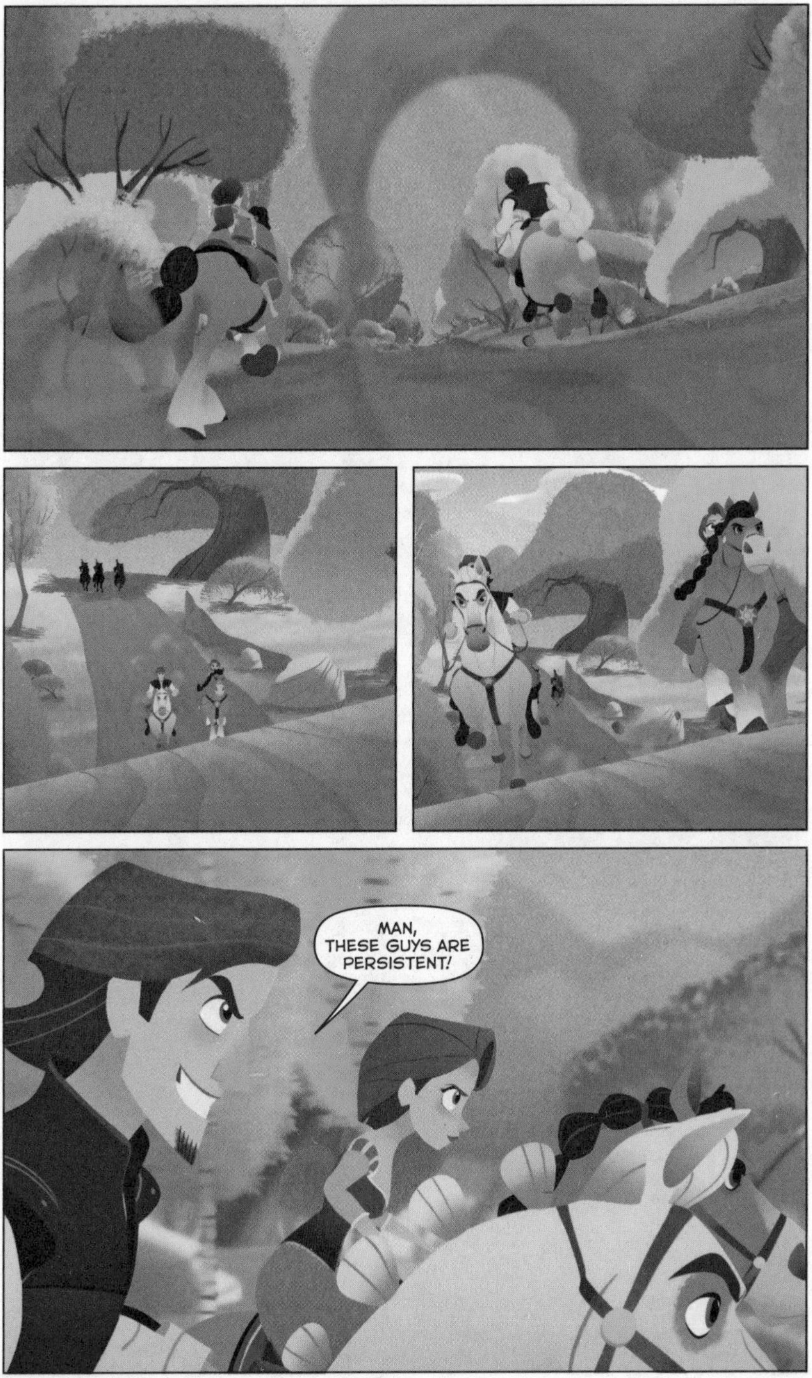
MAN,
THESE GUYS ARE
PERSISTENT!

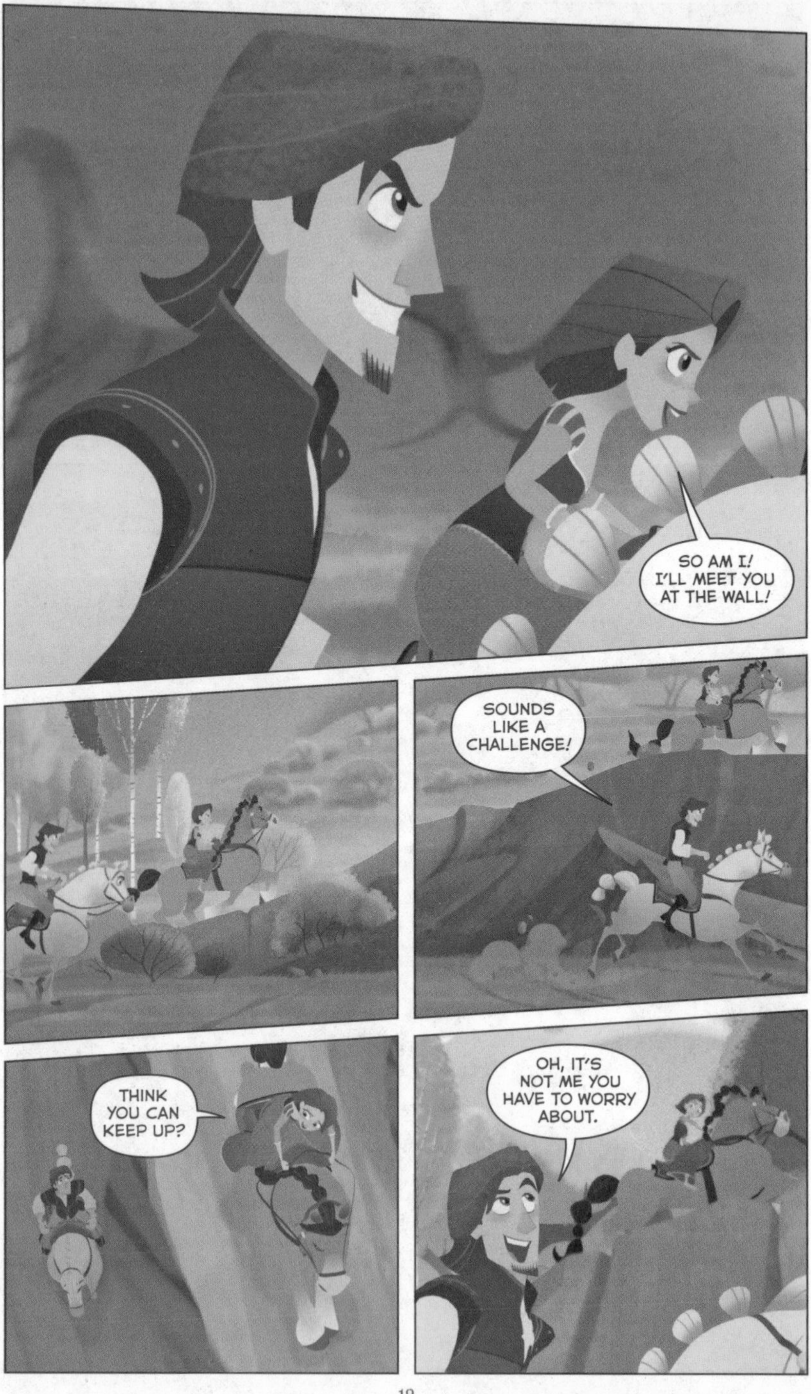
SO AM I! I'LL MEET YOU AT THE WALL!
SOUNDS LIKE A CHALLENGE!
THINK YOU CAN KEEP UP?
OH, IT'S NOT ME YOU HAVE TO WORRY ABOUT.

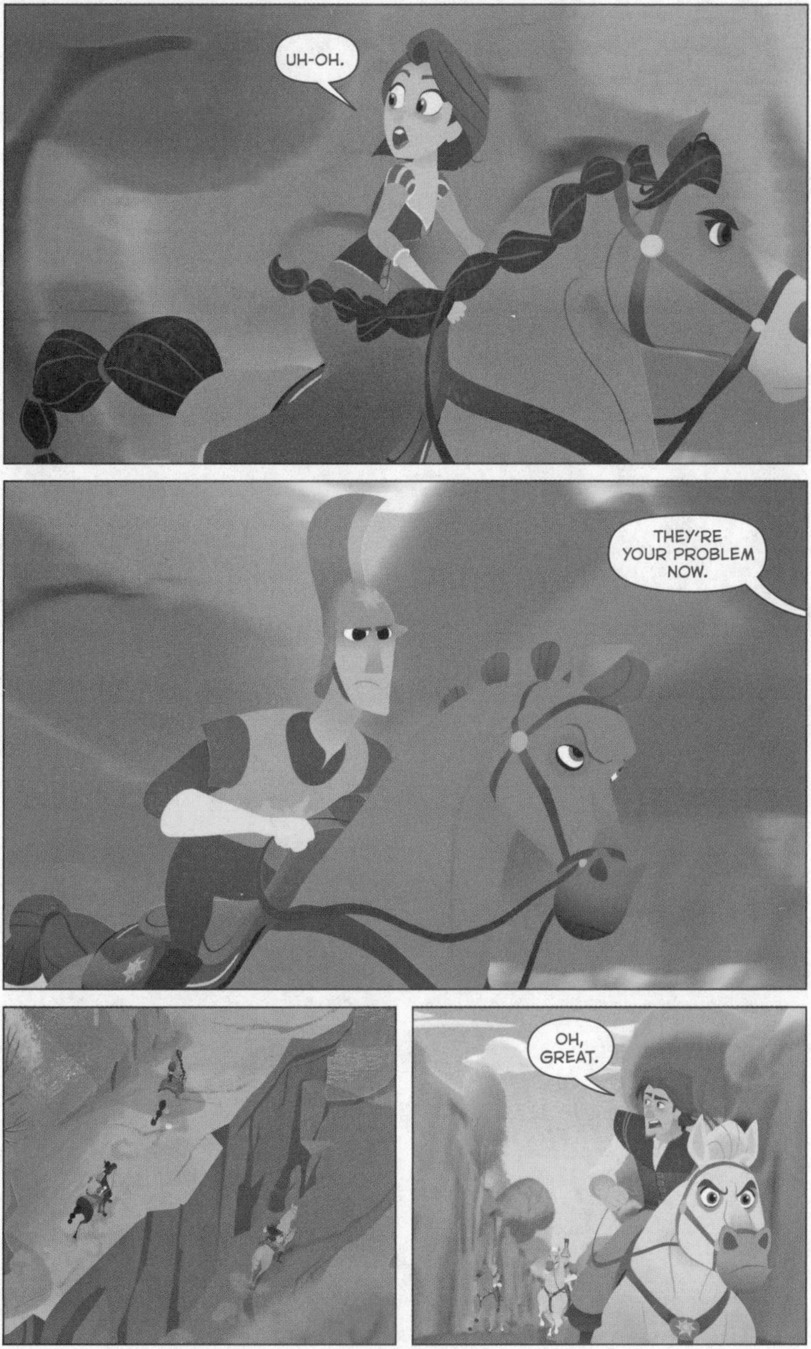
UH-OH.
THEY'RE YOUR PROBLEM NOW.
OH, GREAT.

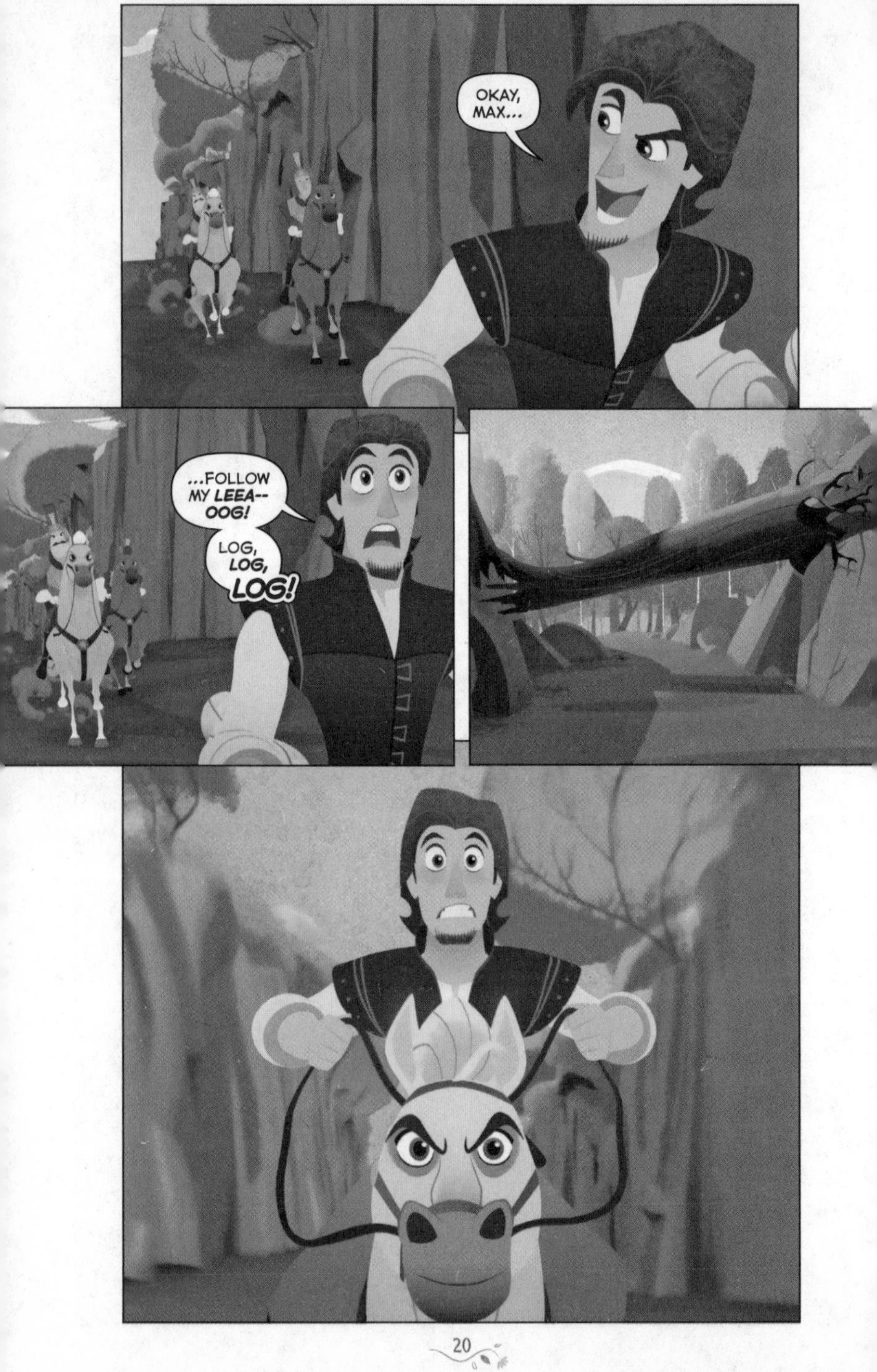
OKAY, MAX...
...FOLLOW MY LEEA--OOG!
LOG, LOG, LOG!

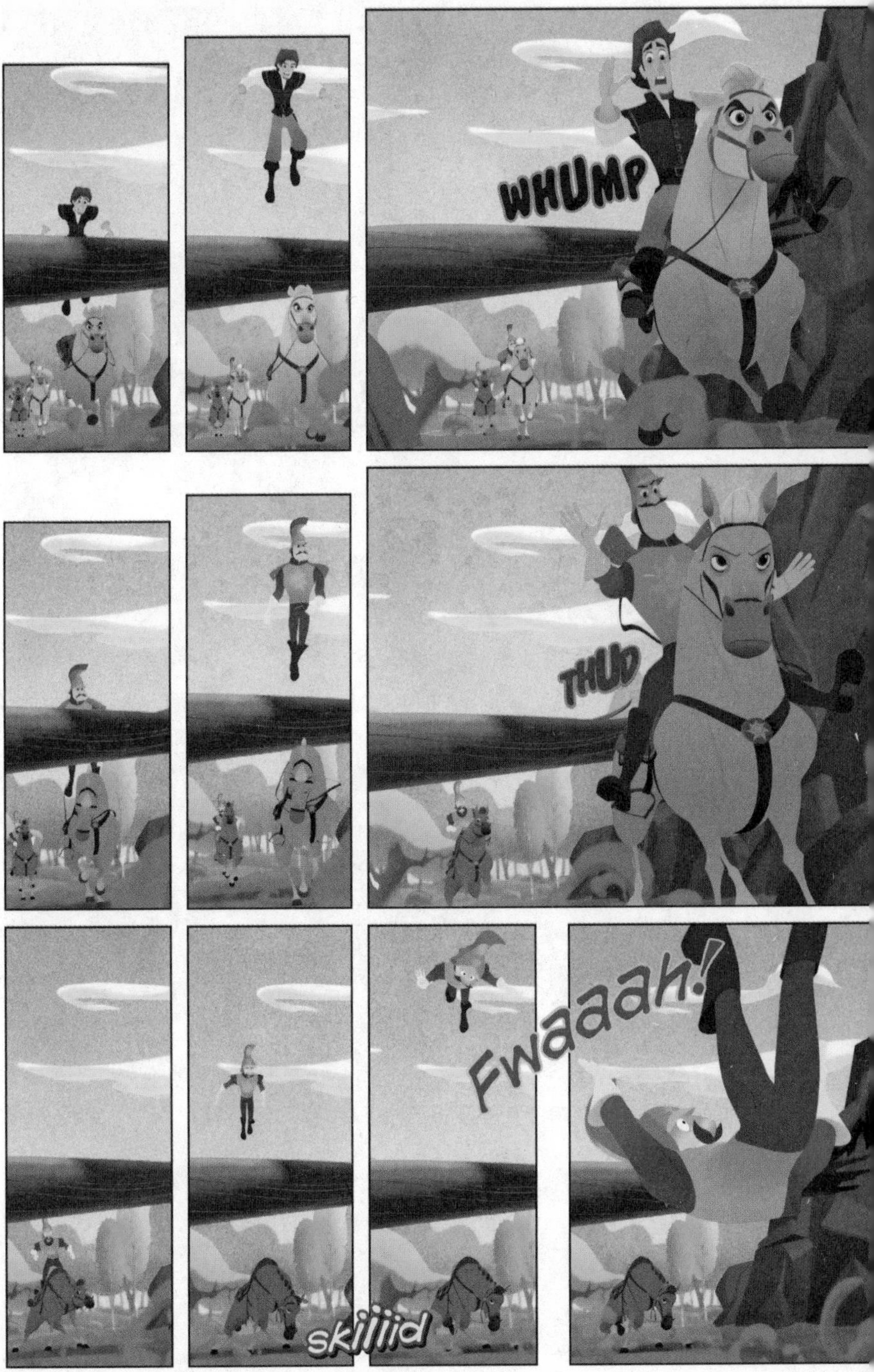
WHUMP
THUD
Fwaaah!
skiiiid

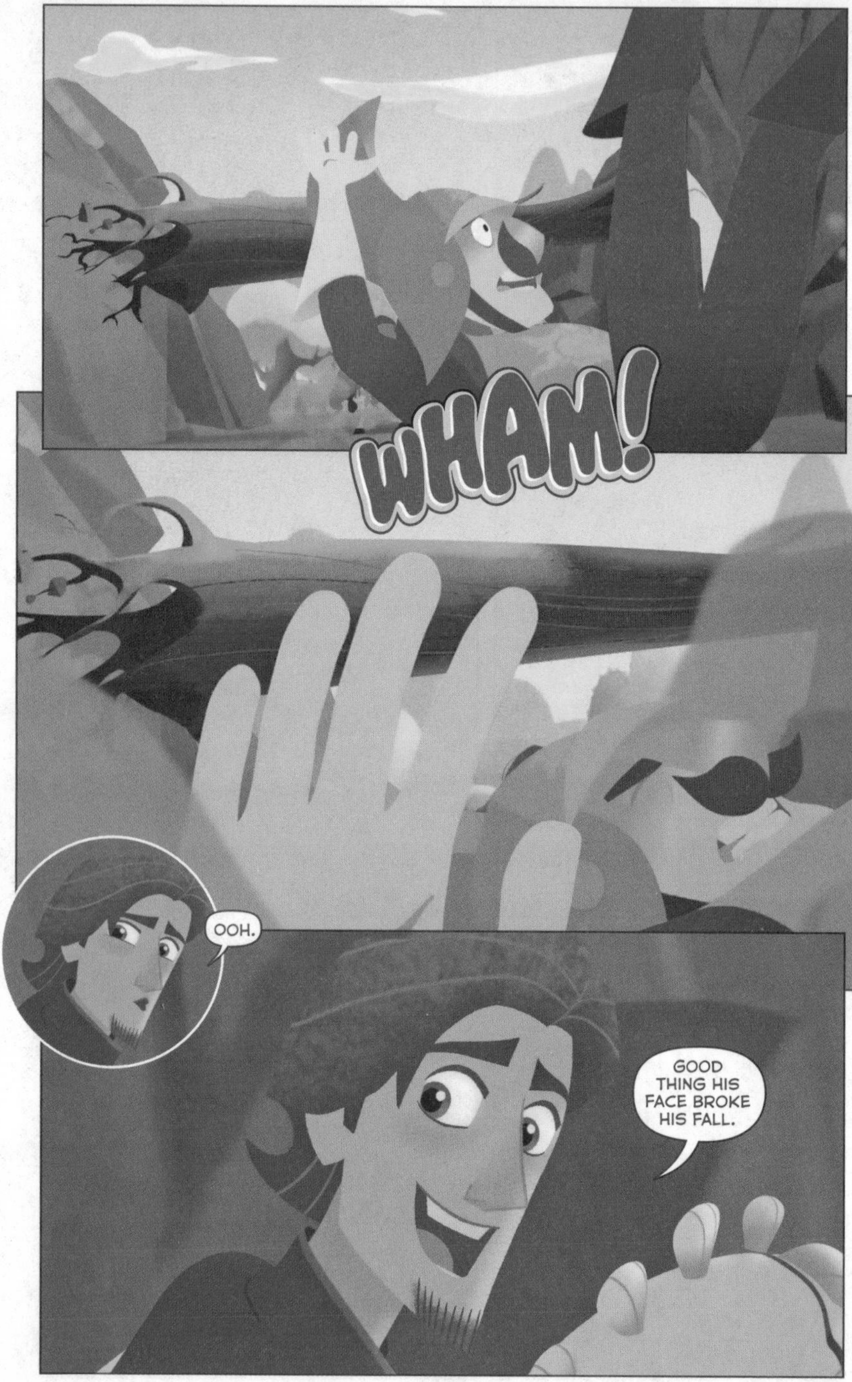
WHAM!
OOH.
GOOD THING HIS FACE BROKE HIS FALL.

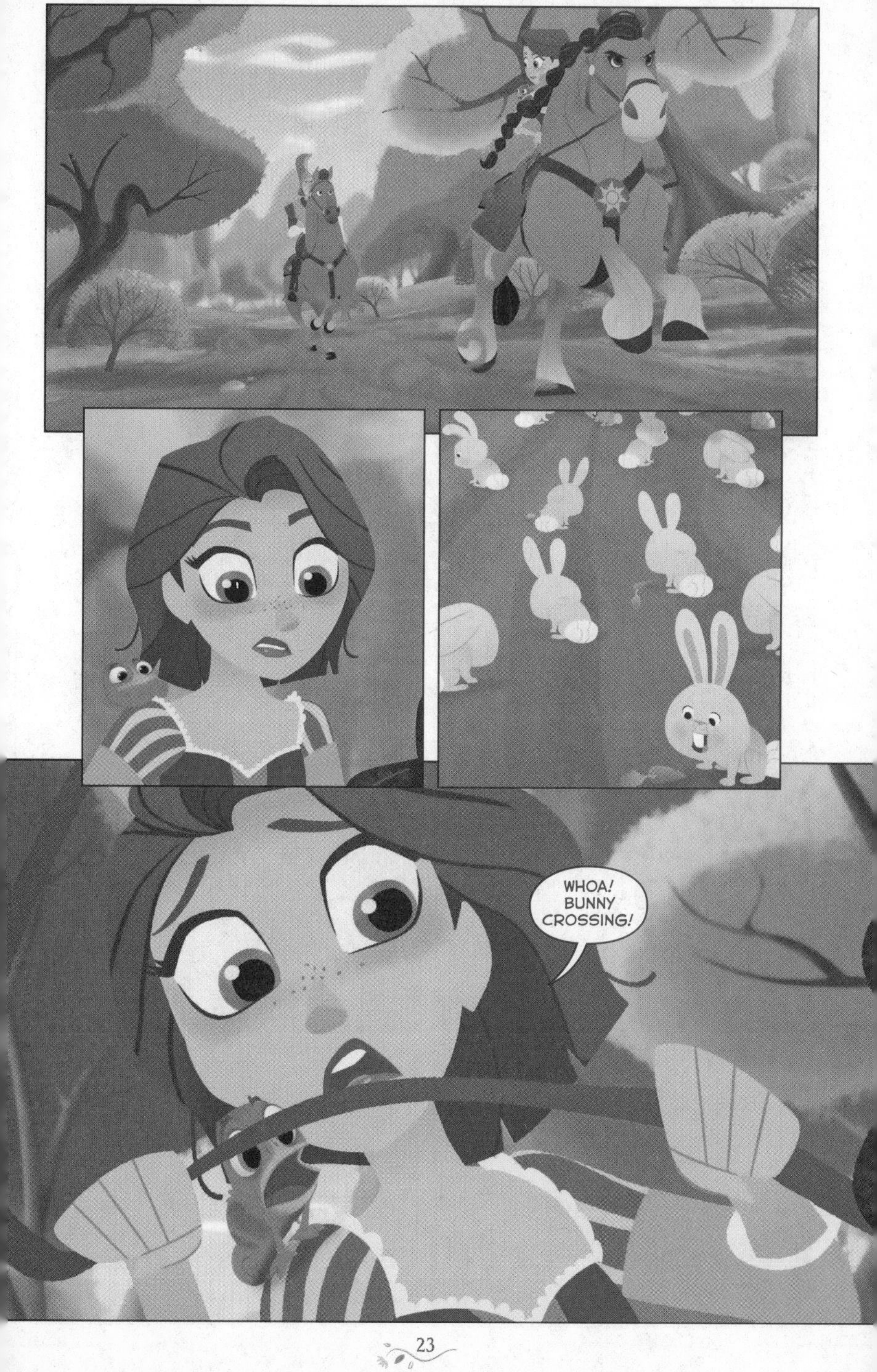
WHOA!
BUNNY
CROSSING!

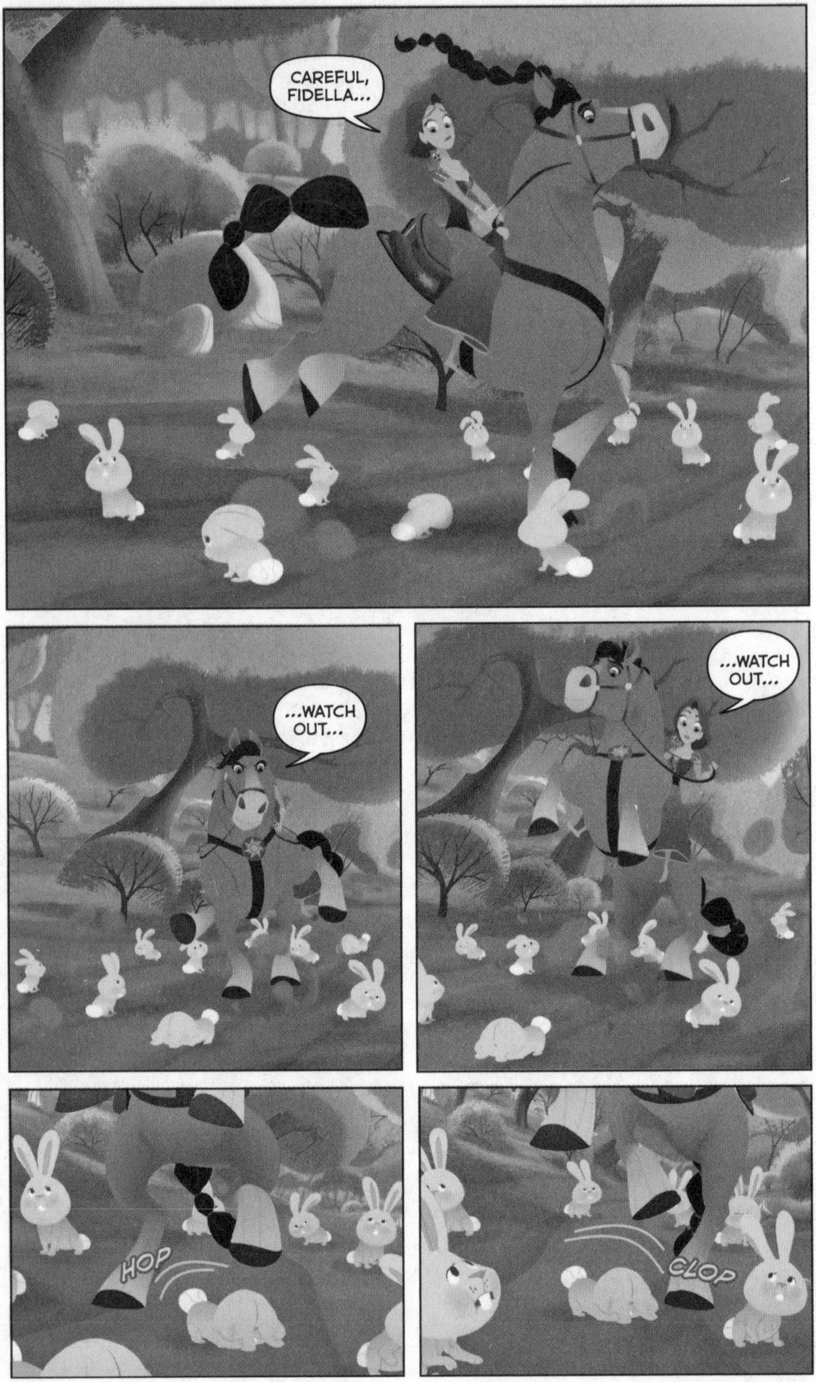
CAREFUL, FIDELLA...
...WATCH OUT...
...WATCH OUT...
HOP
CLOP

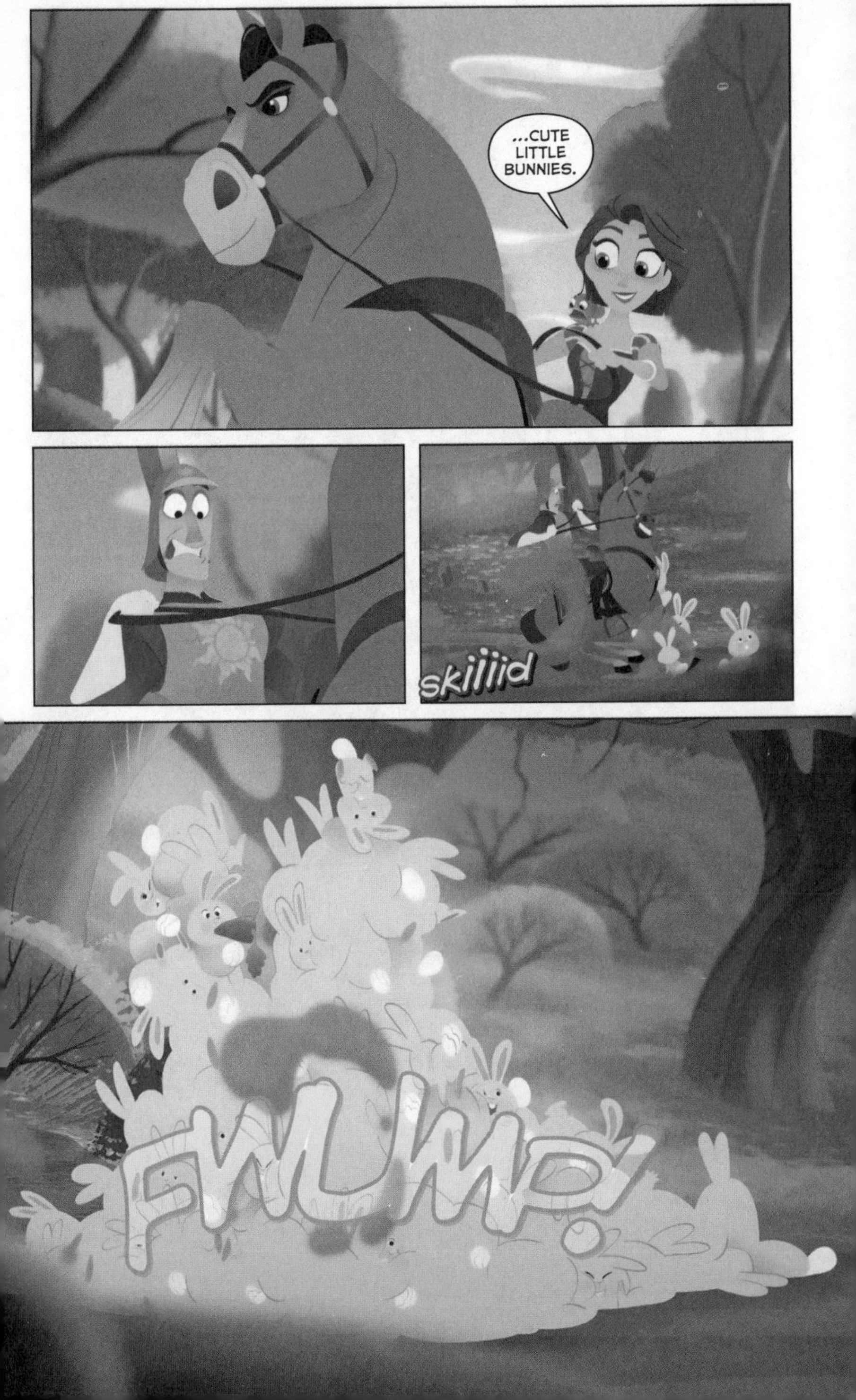
...CUTE LITTLE BUNNIES.
skiiiid
FWUMP!

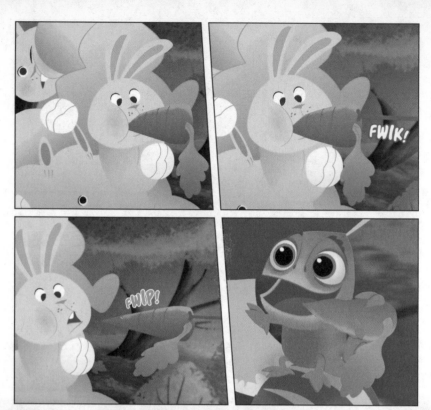

FWIK!

FWIP!

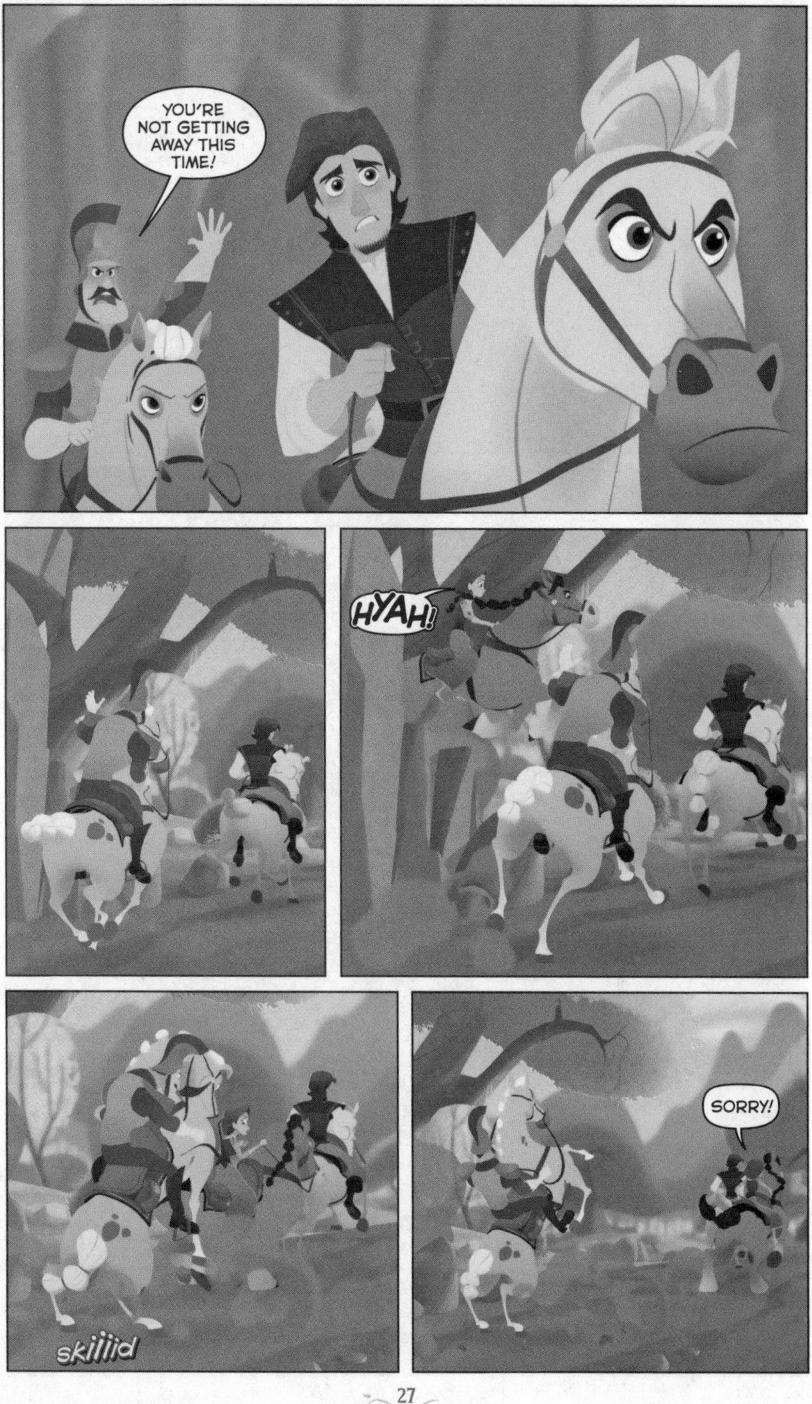
YOU'RE NOT GETTING AWAY THIS TIME!
HYAH!
skiiiid
SORRY!

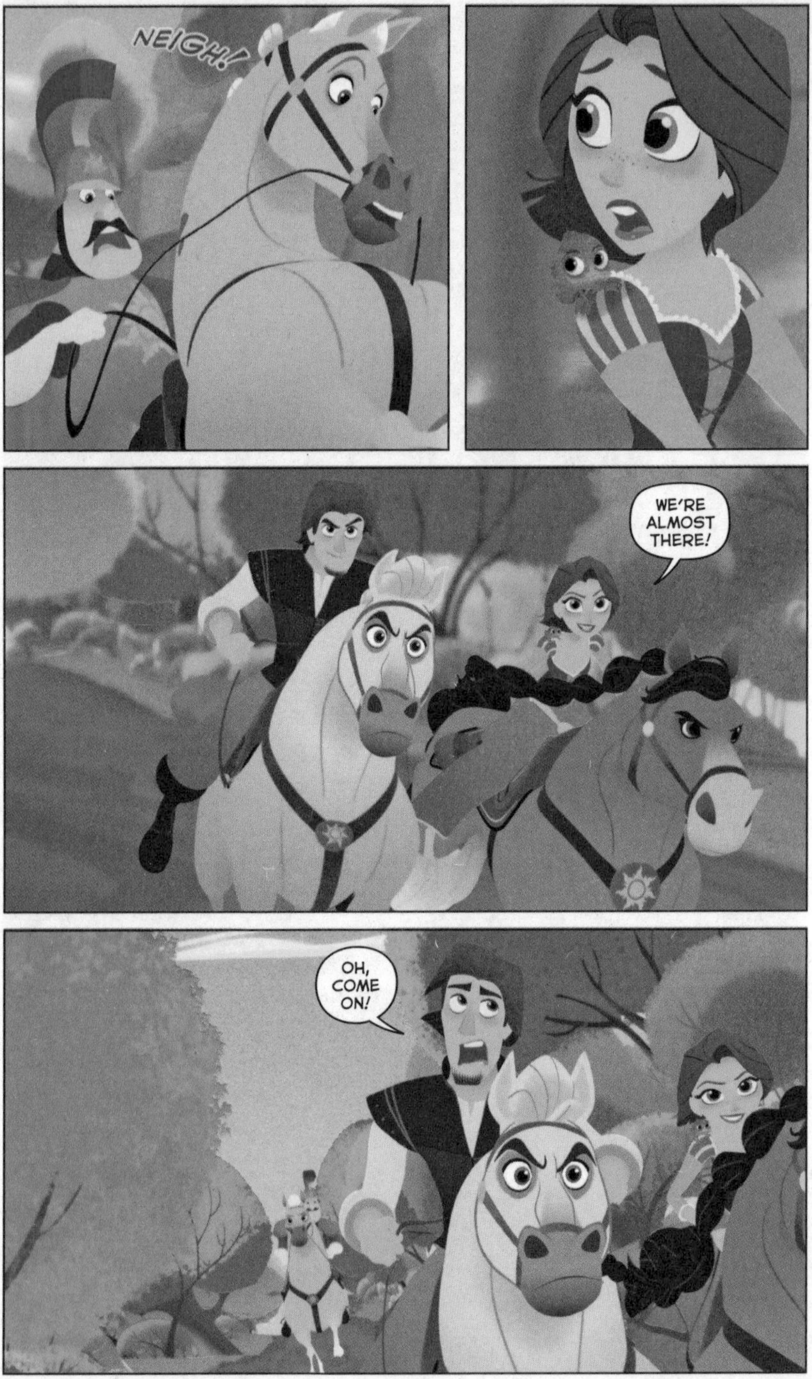
NEIGH!
WE'RE ALMOST THERE!
OH, COME ON!

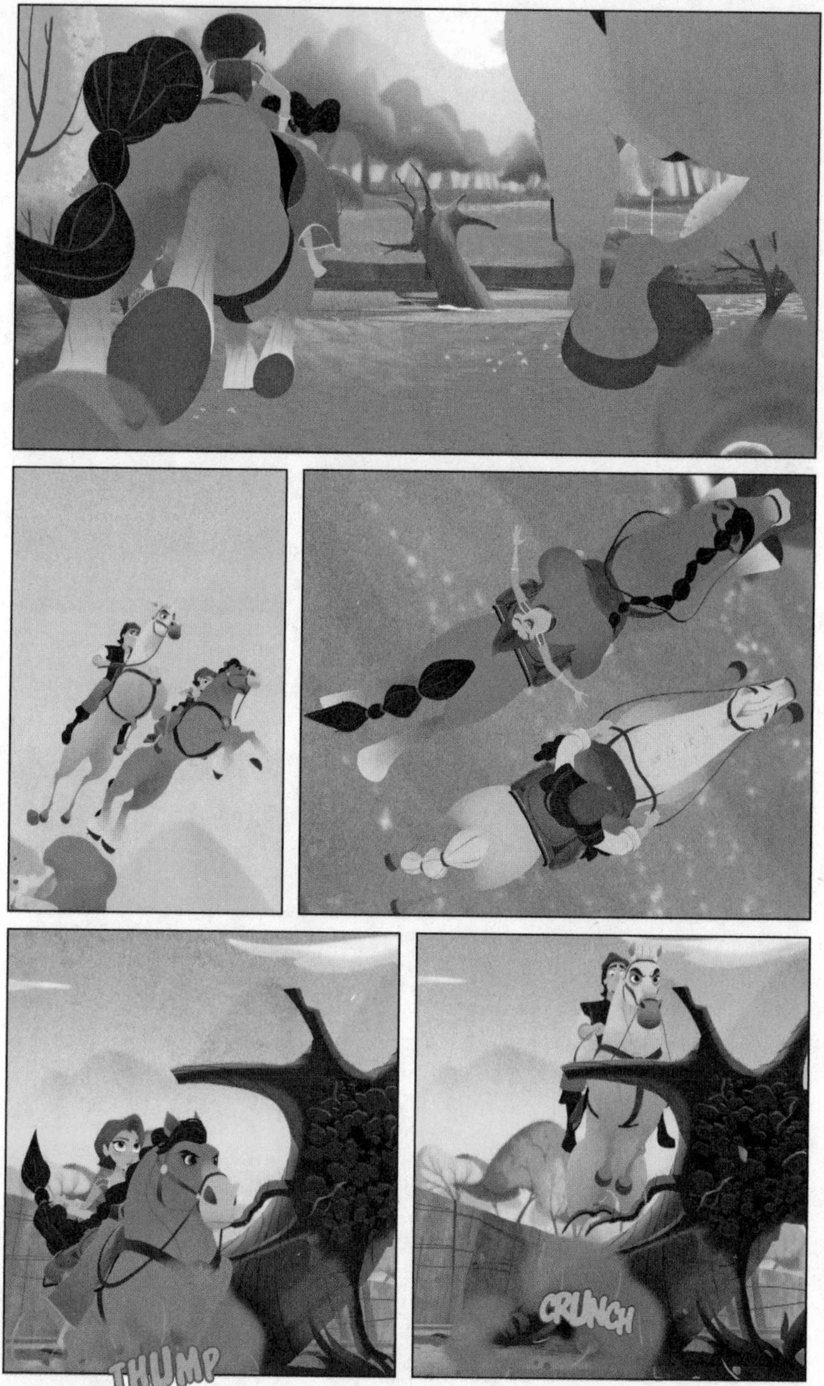
THUMP
CRUNCH

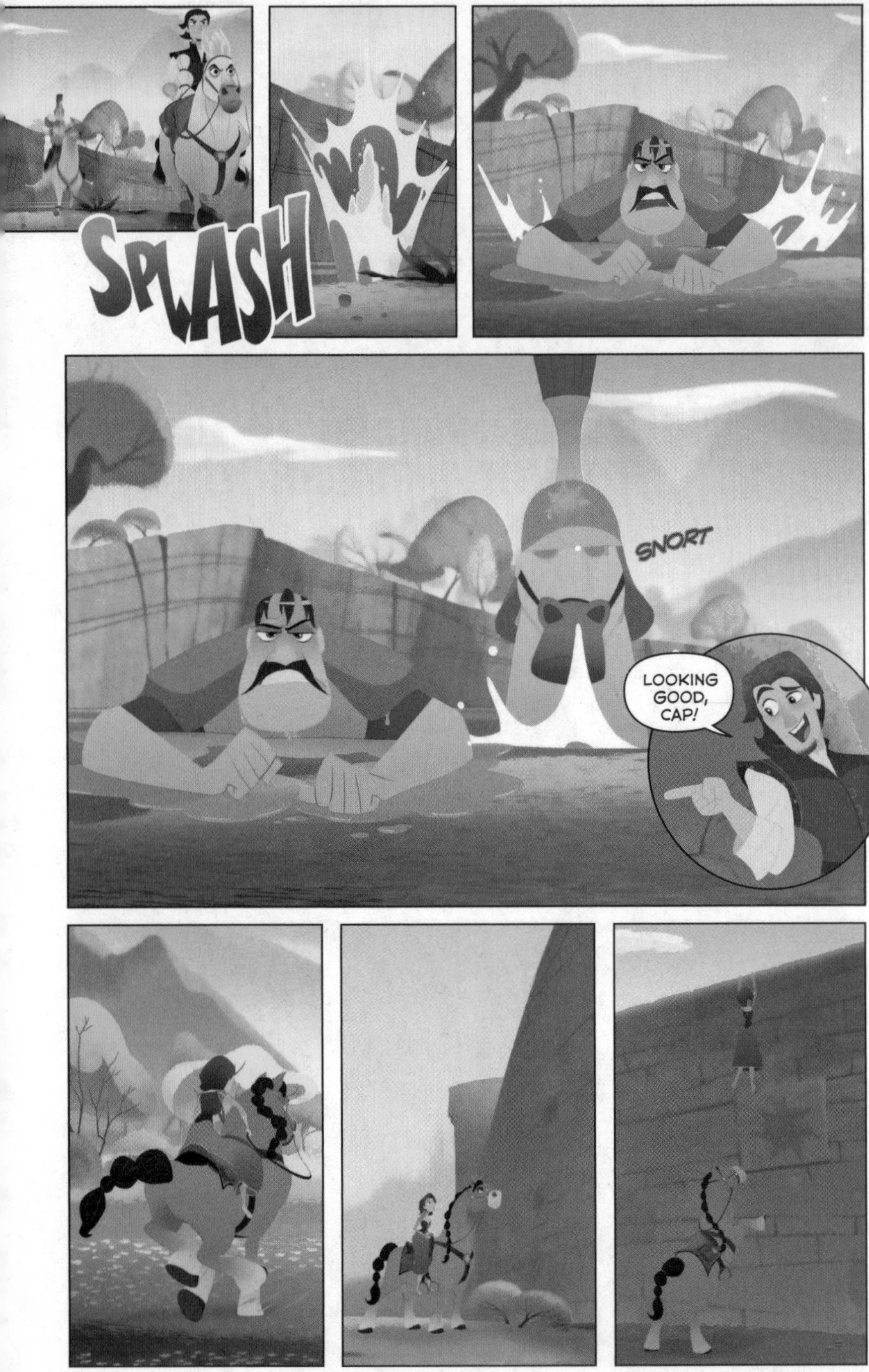
SPLASH
SNORT
LOOKING GOOD, CAP!

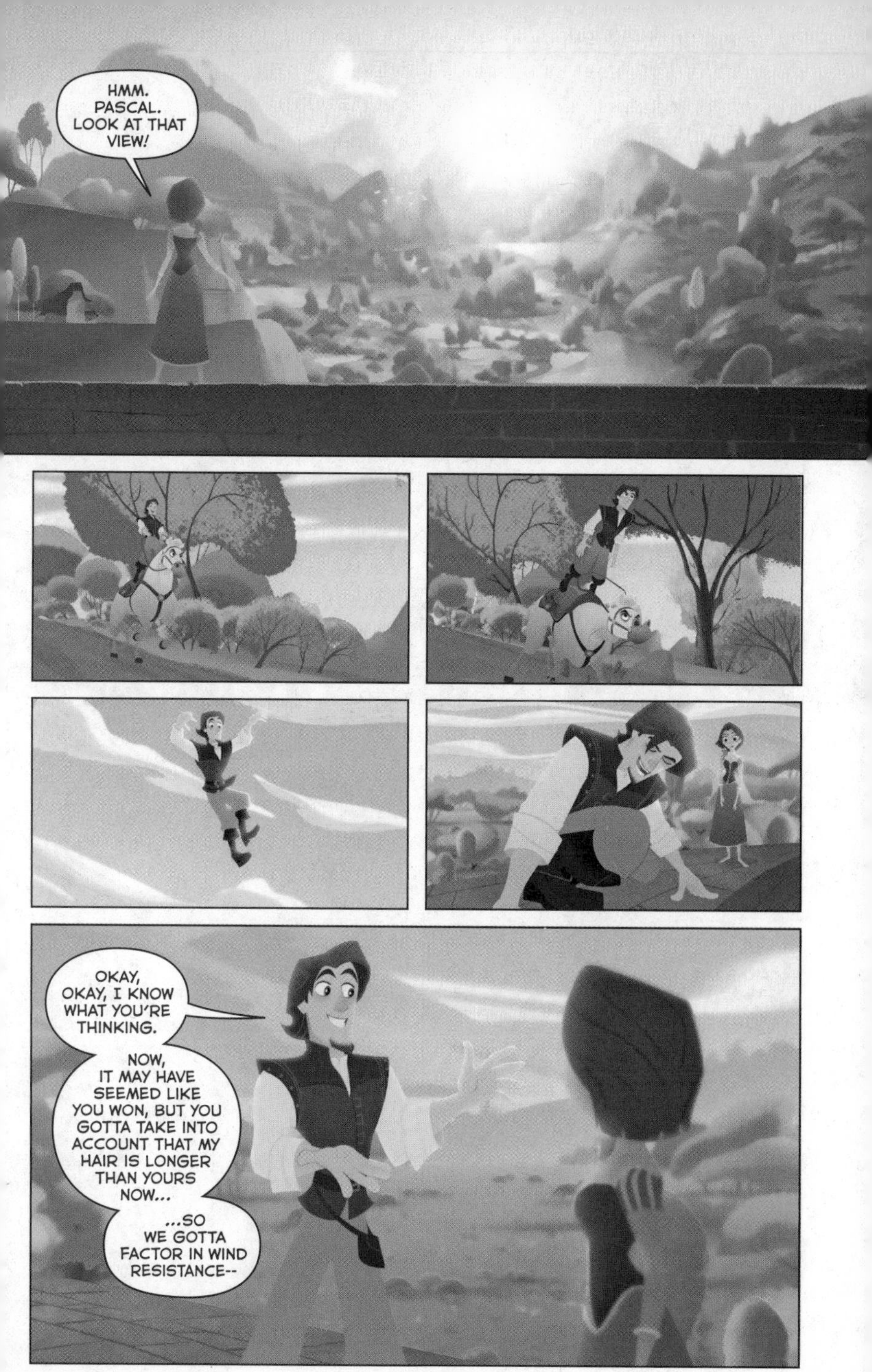
HMM. PASCAL. LOOK AT THAT VIEW!
OKAY, OKAY, I KNOW WHAT YOU'RE THINKING.
NOW, IT MAY HAVE SEEMED LIKE YOU WON, BUT YOU GOTTA TAKE INTO ACCOUNT THAT MY HAIR IS LONGER THAN YOURS NOW...
...SO WE GOTTA FACTOR IN WIND RESISTANCE--

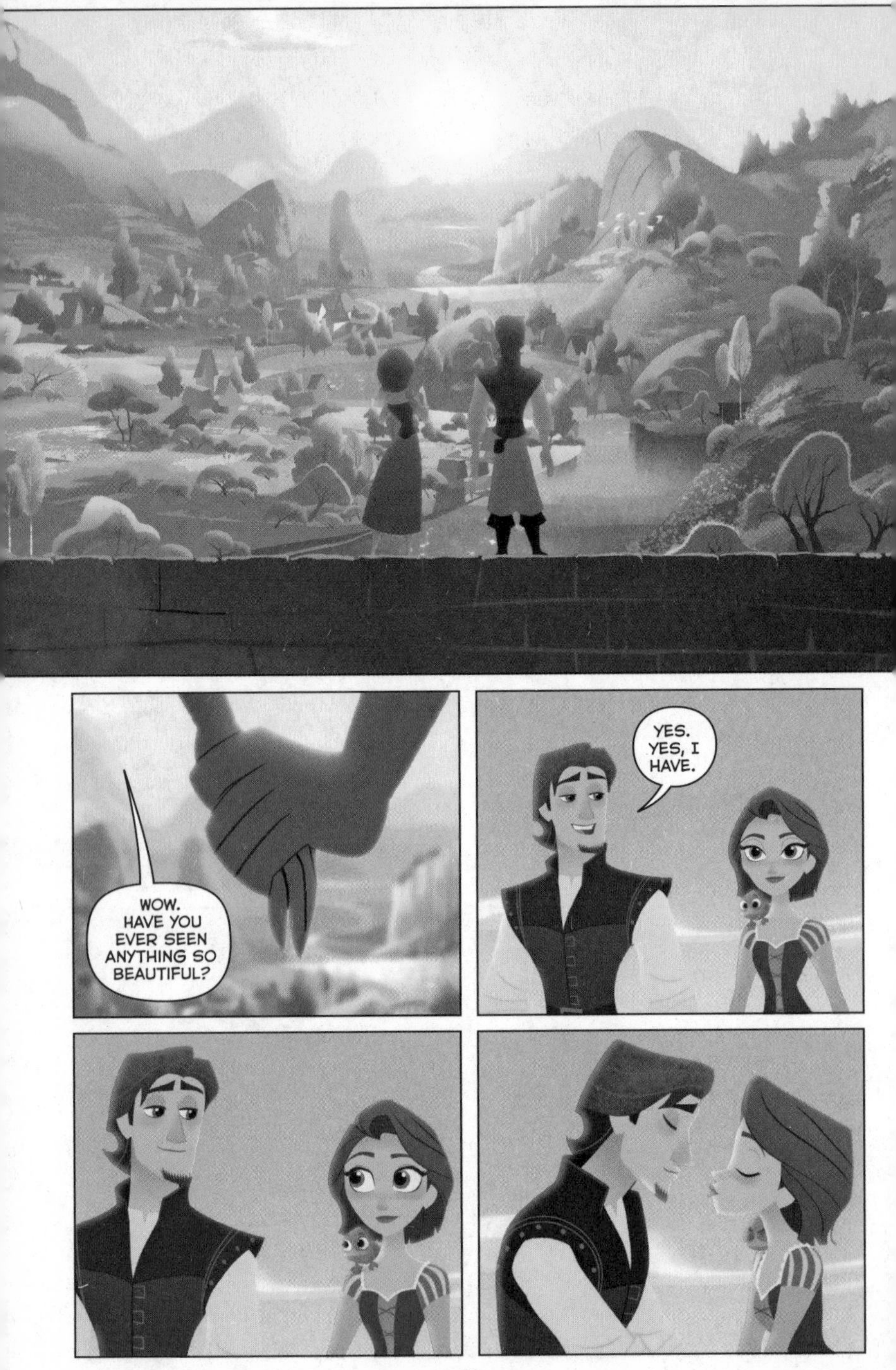
WOW. HAVE YOU EVER SEEN ANYTHING SO BEAUTIFUL?
YES. YES, I HAVE.

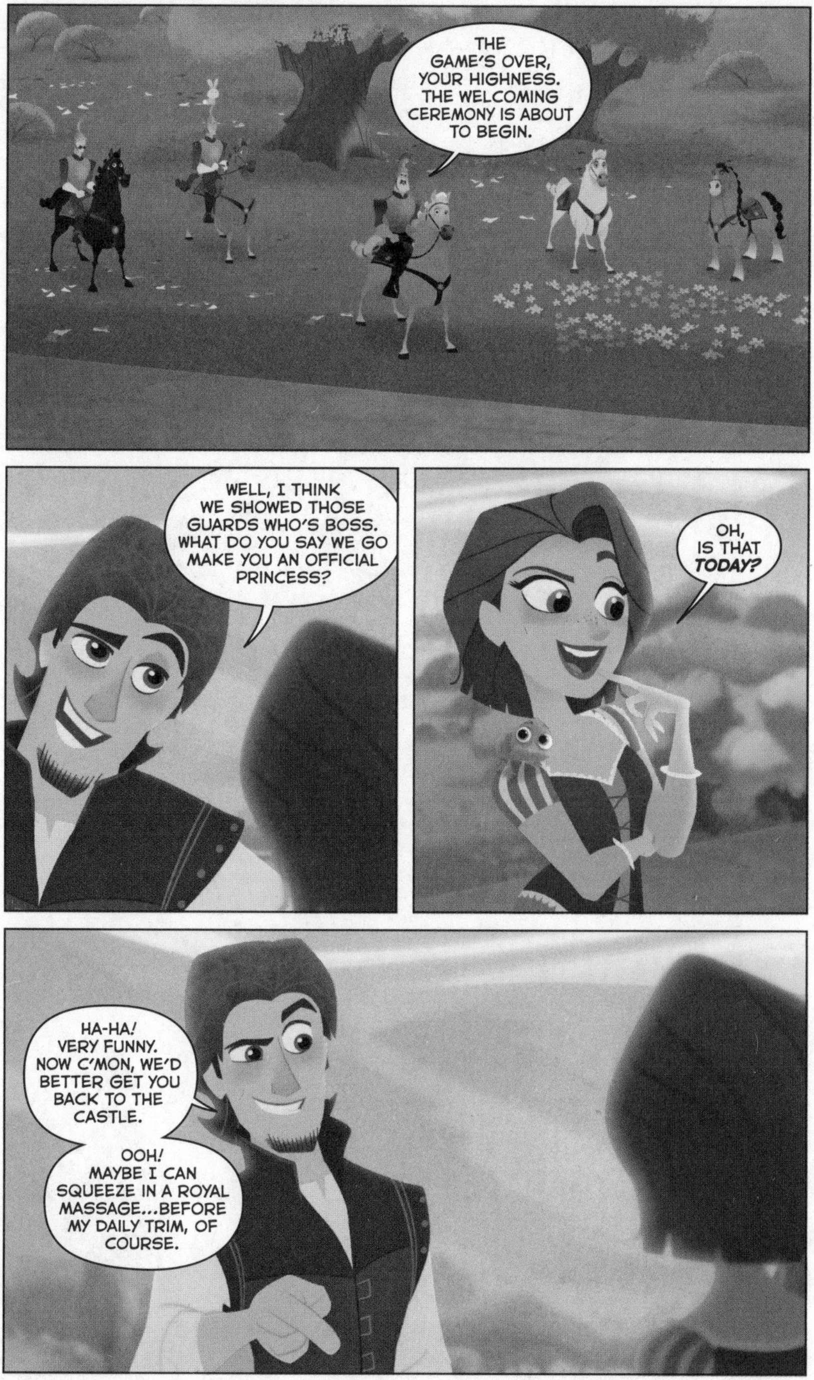
THE GAME'S OVER, YOUR HIGHNESS. THE WELCOMING CEREMONY IS ABOUT TO BEGIN.
WELL, I THINK WE SHOWED THOSE GUARDS WHO'S BOSS. WHAT DO YOU SAY WE GO MAKE YOU AN OFFICIAL PRINCESS?
OH, IS THAT *TODAY?*
HA-HA! VERY FUNNY. NOW C'MON, WE'D BETTER GET YOU BACK TO THE CASTLE.
OOH! MAYBE I CAN SQUEEZE IN A ROYAL MASSAGE...BEFORE MY DAILY TRIM, OF COURSE.

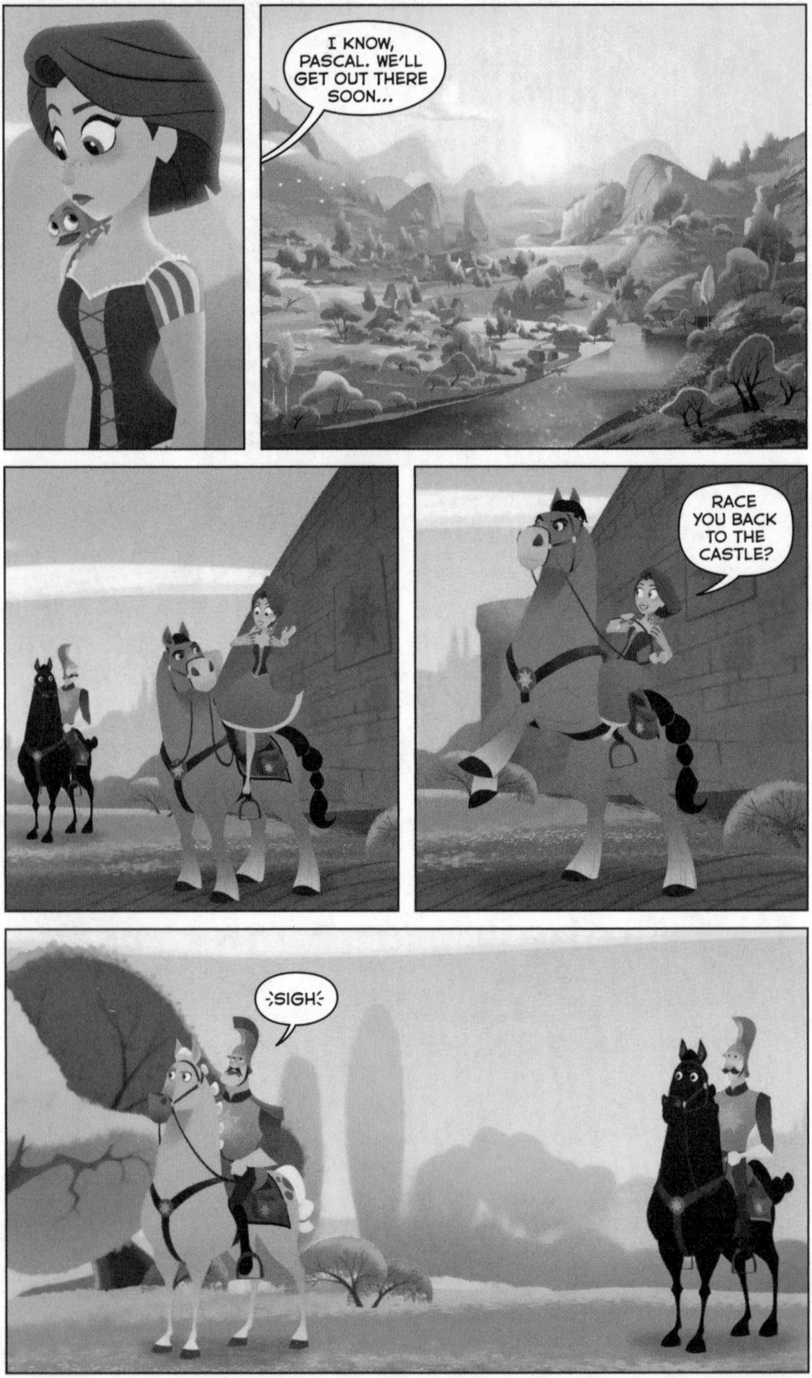
I KNOW, PASCAL. WE'LL GET OUT THERE SOON...
RACE YOU BACK TO THE CASTLE?
SIGH

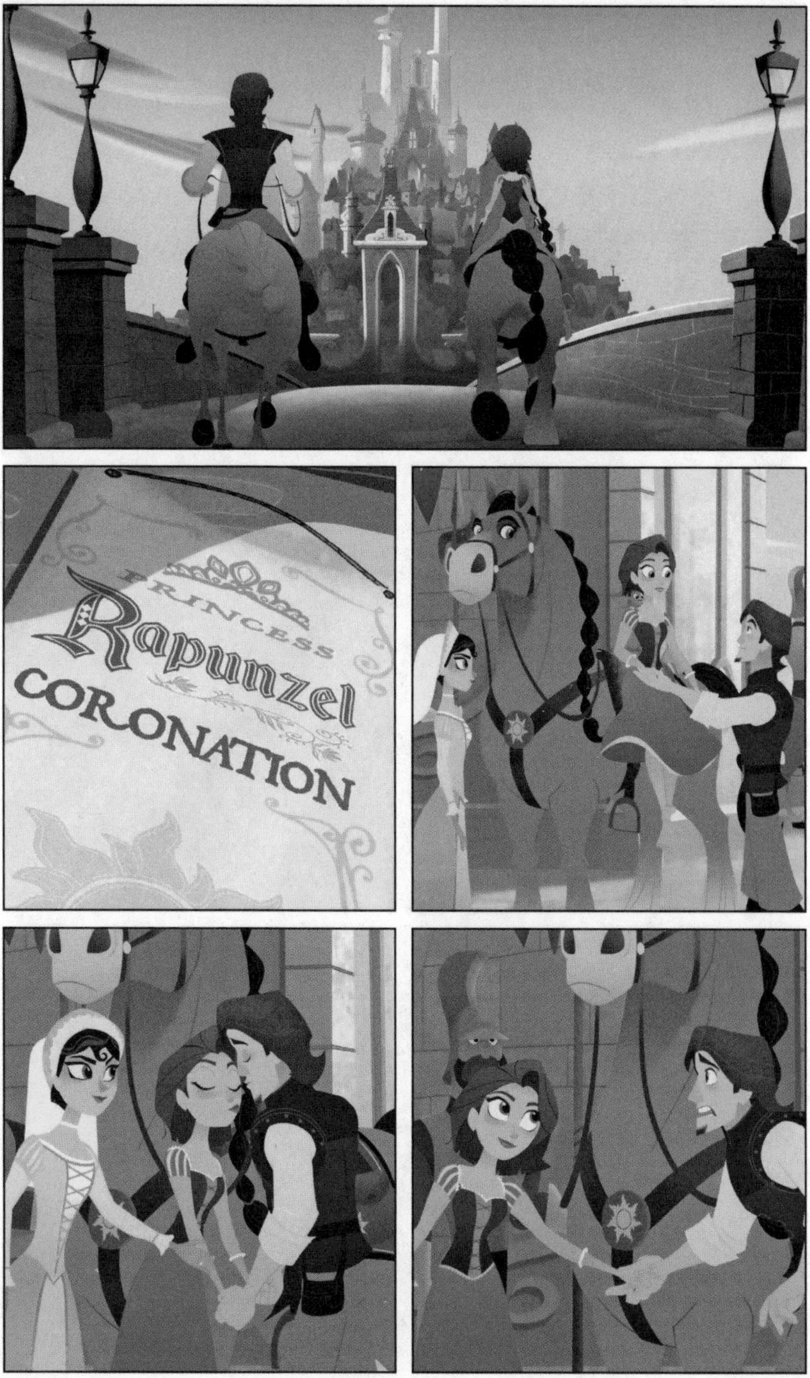
PRINCESS
Rapunzel
CORONATION

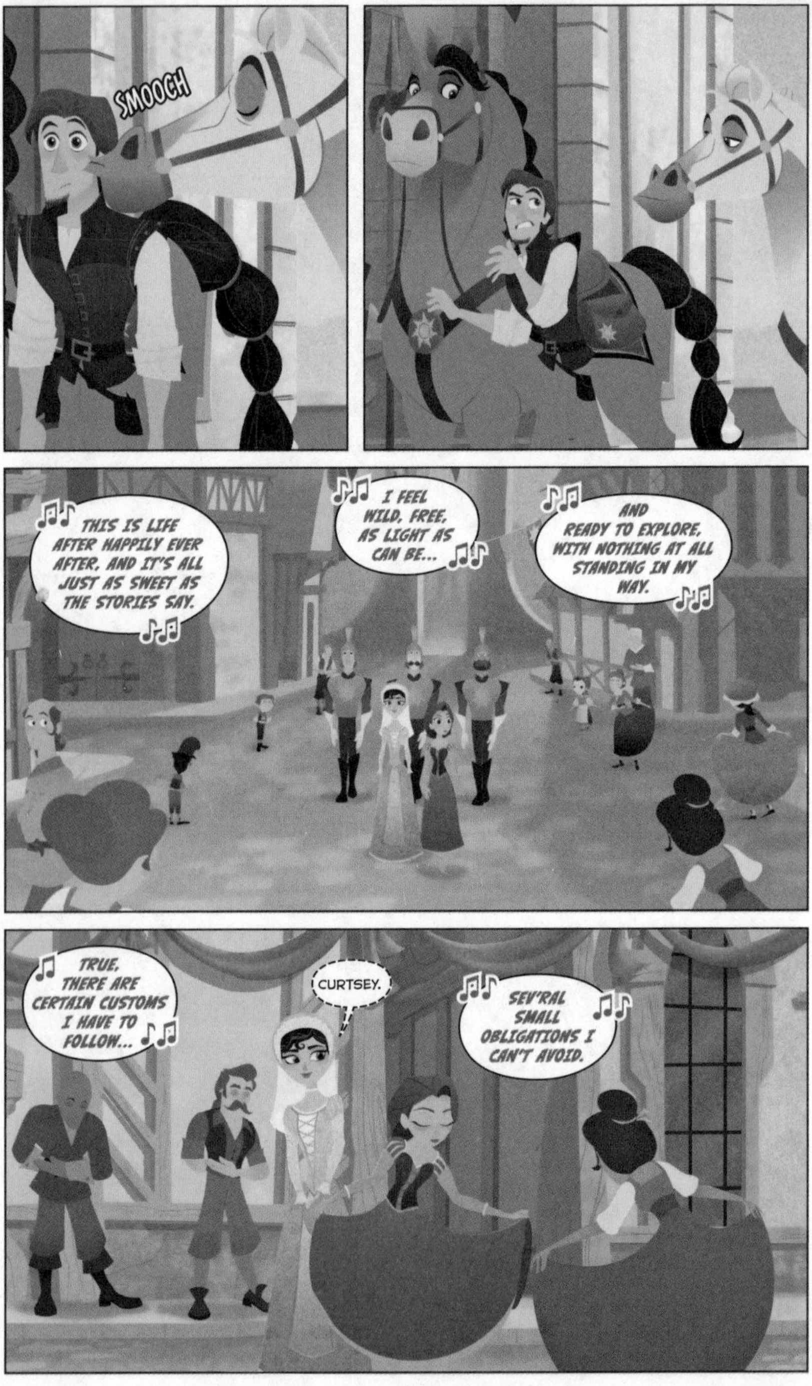
SMOOCH
THIS IS LIFE AFTER HAPPILY EVER AFTER, AND IT'S ALL JUST AS SWEET AS THE STORIES SAY.
I FEEL WILD, FREE, AS LIGHT AS CAN BE...
AND READY TO EXPLORE, WITH NOTHING AT ALL STANDING IN MY WAY.
TRUE, THERE ARE CERTAIN CUSTOMS I HAVE TO FOLLOW...
CURTSEY.
SEV'RAL SMALL OBLIGATIONS I CAN'T AVOID.

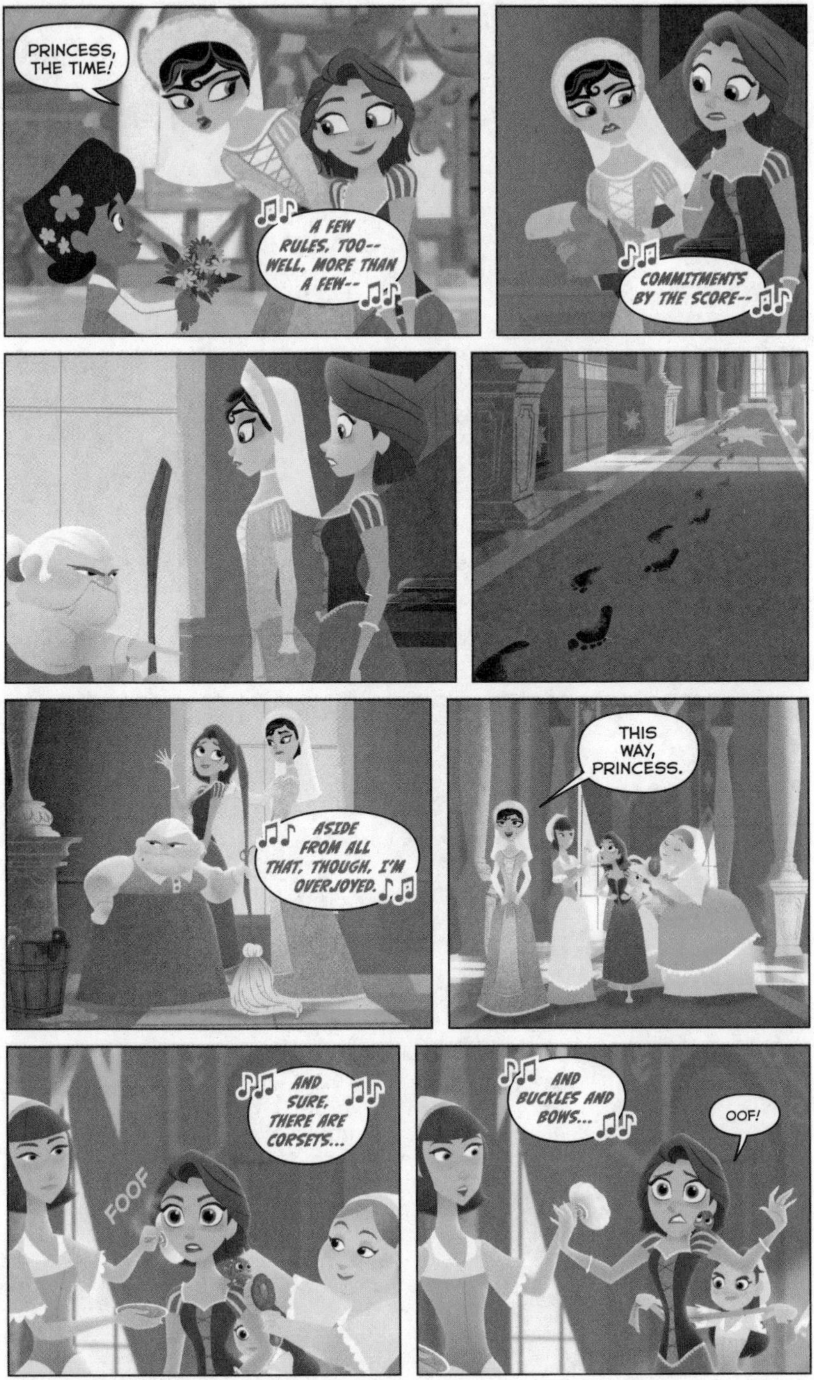
PRINCESS, THE TIME!
A FEW RULES, TOO-- WELL, MORE THAN A FEW--
COMMITMENTS BY THE SCORE--
ASIDE FROM ALL THAT, THOUGH, I'M OVERJOYED.
THIS WAY, PRINCESS.
AND SURE, THERE ARE CORSETS...
FOOF
AND BUCKLES AND BOWS...
OOF!

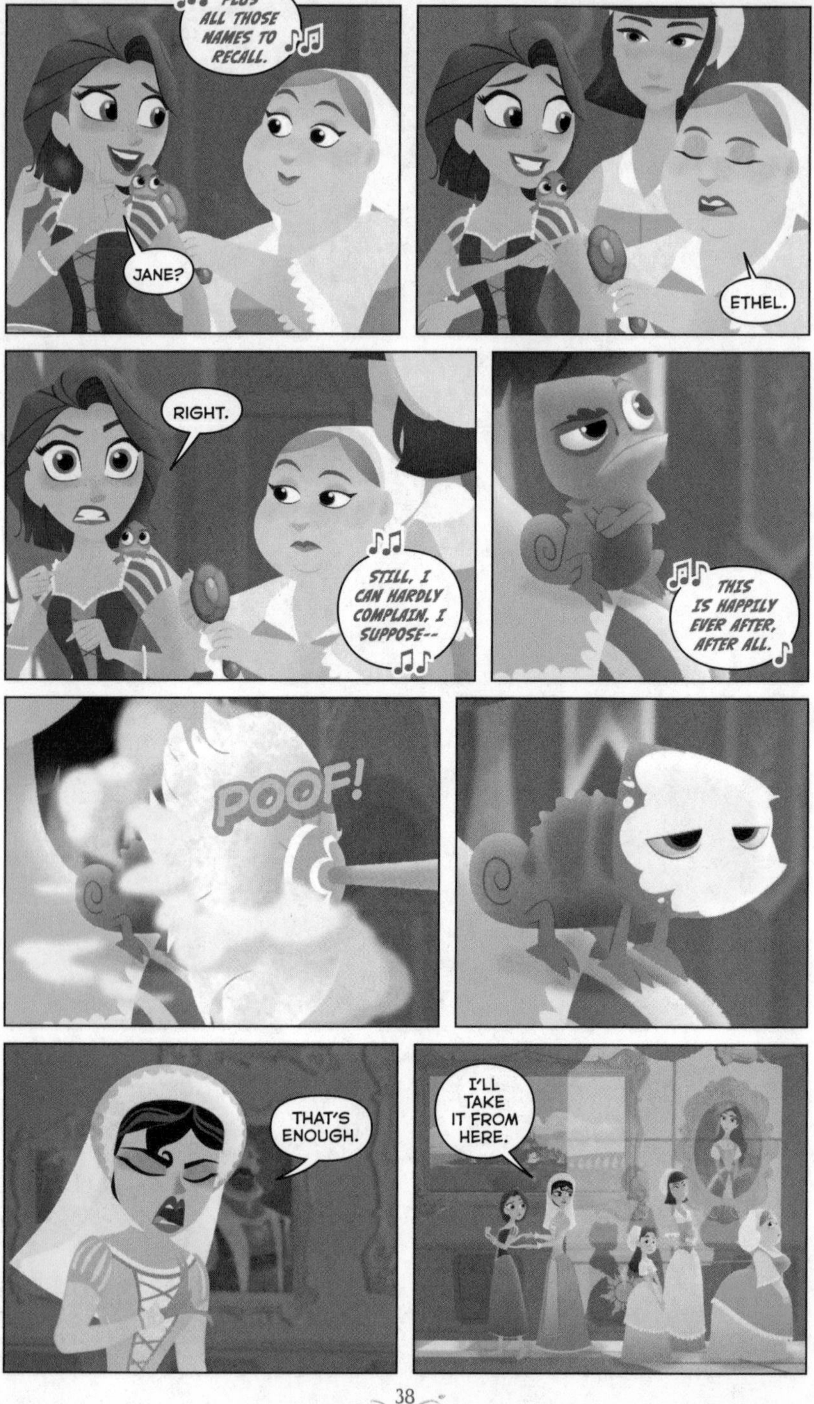
PLUS ALL THOSE NAMES TO RECALL.
JANE?
ETHEL.
RIGHT.
STILL, I CAN HARDLY COMPLAIN, I SUPPOSE--
THIS IS HAPPILY EVER AFTER, AFTER ALL.
POOF!
THAT'S ENOUGH.
I'LL TAKE IT FROM HERE.

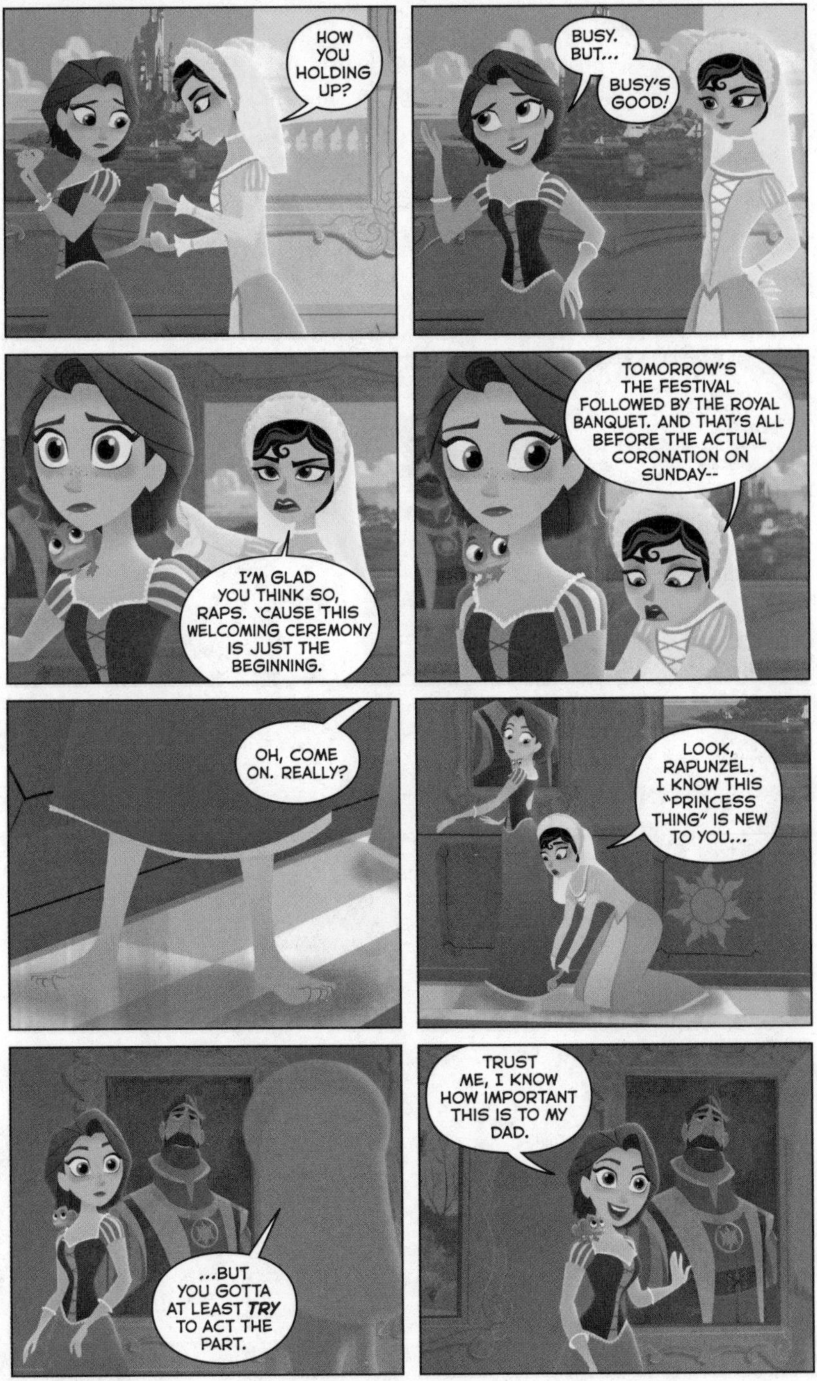
HOW YOU HOLDING UP?
BUSY. BUT...
BUSY'S GOOD!
I'M GLAD YOU THINK SO, RAPS. 'CAUSE THIS WELCOMING CEREMONY IS JUST THE BEGINNING.
TOMORROW'S THE FESTIVAL FOLLOWED BY THE ROYAL BANQUET. AND THAT'S ALL BEFORE THE ACTUAL CORONATION ON SUNDAY--
OH, COME ON. REALLY?
LOOK, RAPUNZEL. I KNOW THIS "PRINCESS THING" IS NEW TO YOU...
...BUT YOU GOTTA AT LEAST *TRY* TO ACT THE PART.
TRUST ME, I KNOW HOW IMPORTANT THIS IS TO MY DAD.

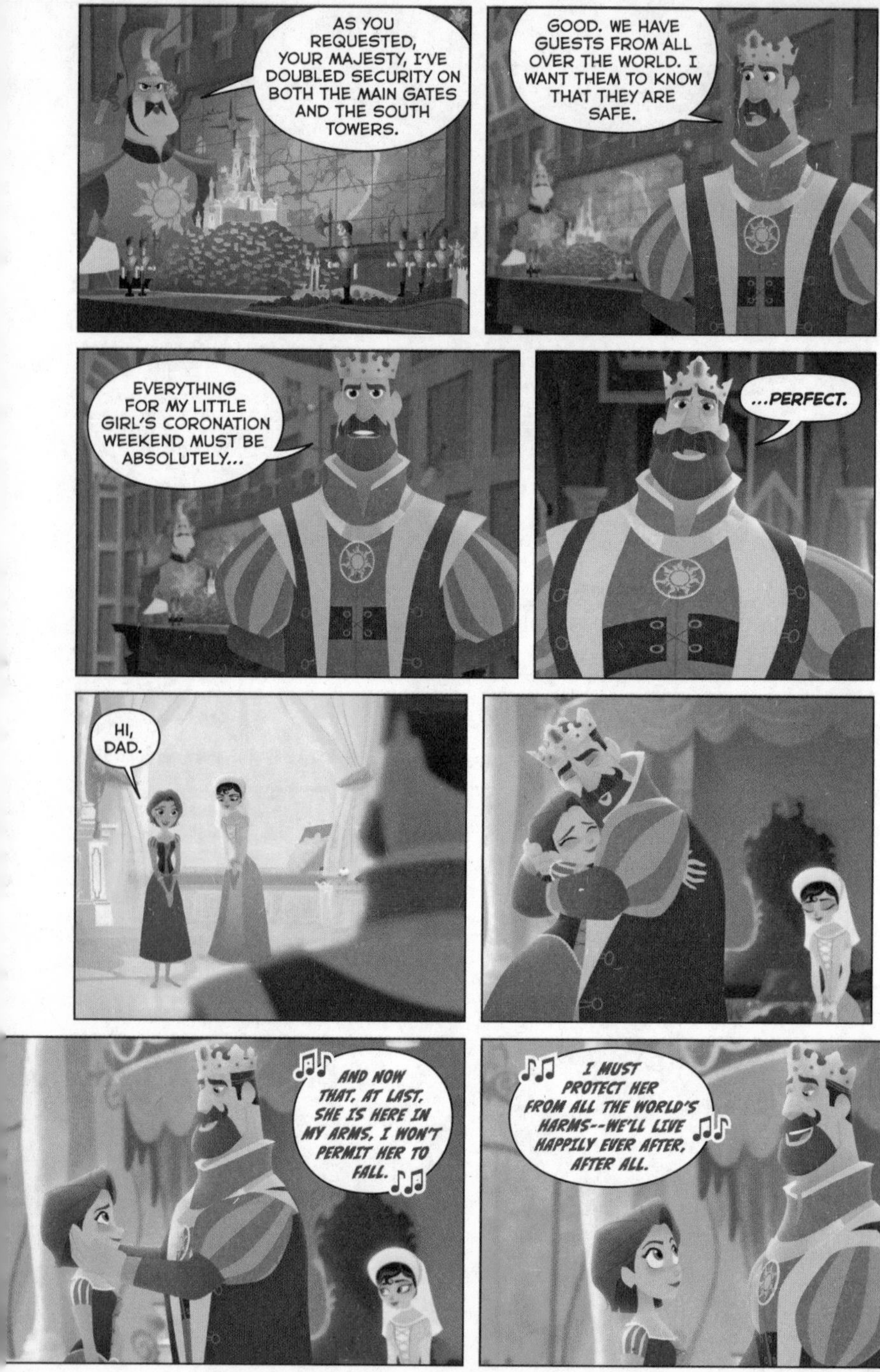
AS YOU REQUESTED, YOUR MAJESTY, I'VE DOUBLED SECURITY ON BOTH THE MAIN GATES AND THE SOUTH TOWERS.
GOOD. WE HAVE GUESTS FROM ALL OVER THE WORLD. I WANT THEM TO KNOW THAT THEY ARE SAFE.
EVERYTHING FOR MY LITTLE GIRL'S CORONATION WEEKEND MUST BE ABSOLUTELY...
...PERFECT.
HI, DAD.
AND NOW THAT, AT LAST, SHE IS HERE IN MY ARMS, I WON'T PERMIT HER TO FALL.
I MUST PROTECT HER FROM ALL THE WORLD'S HARMS--WE'LL LIVE HAPPILY EVER AFTER, AFTER ALL.

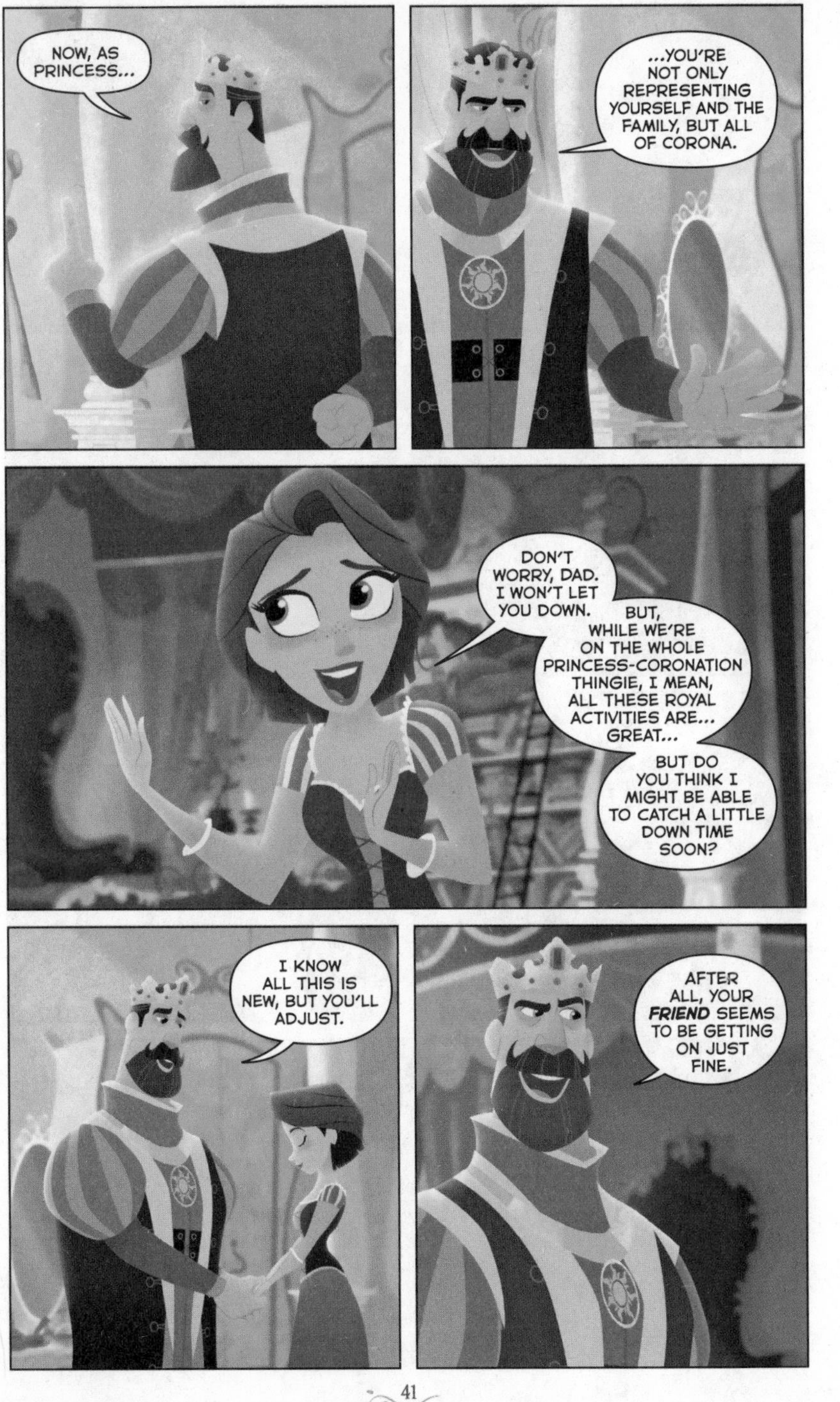
NOW, AS PRINCESS...
...YOU'RE NOT ONLY REPRESENTING YOURSELF AND THE FAMILY, BUT ALL OF CORONA.
DON'T WORRY, DAD. I WON'T LET YOU DOWN.
BUT, WHILE WE'RE ON THE WHOLE PRINCESS-CORONATION THINGIE, I MEAN, ALL THESE ROYAL ACTIVITIES ARE... GREAT...
BUT DO YOU THINK I MIGHT BE ABLE TO CATCH A LITTLE DOWN TIME SOON?
I KNOW ALL THIS IS NEW, BUT YOU'LL ADJUST.
AFTER ALL, YOUR ***FRIEND*** SEEMS TO BE GETTING ON JUST FINE.

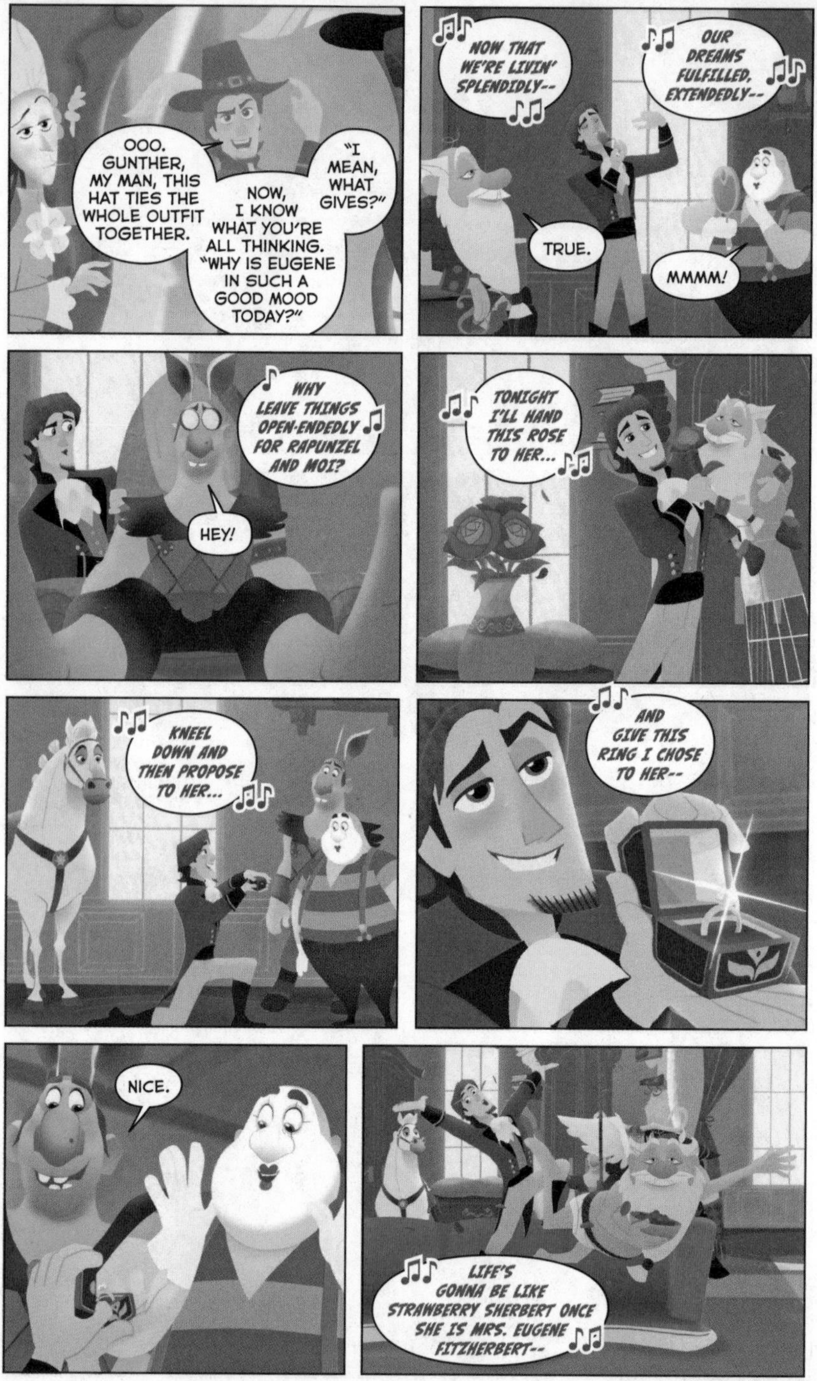
OOO. GUNTHER, MY MAN, THIS HAT TIES THE WHOLE OUTFIT TOGETHER.
NOW, I KNOW WHAT YOU'RE ALL THINKING. "WHY IS EUGENE IN SUCH A GOOD MOOD TODAY?"
"I MEAN, WHAT GIVES?"
NOW THAT WE'RE LIVIN' SPLENDIDLY--
TRUE.
OUR DREAMS FULFILLED, EXTENDEDLY--
MMMM!
WHY LEAVE THINGS OPEN-ENDEDLY FOR RAPUNZEL AND MOI?
HEY!
TONIGHT I'LL HAND THIS ROSE TO HER...
KNEEL DOWN AND THEN PROPOSE TO HER...
AND GIVE THIS RING I CHOSE TO HER--
NICE.
LIFE'S GONNA BE LIKE STRAWBERRY SHERBERT ONCE SHE IS MRS. EUGENE FITZHERBERT--

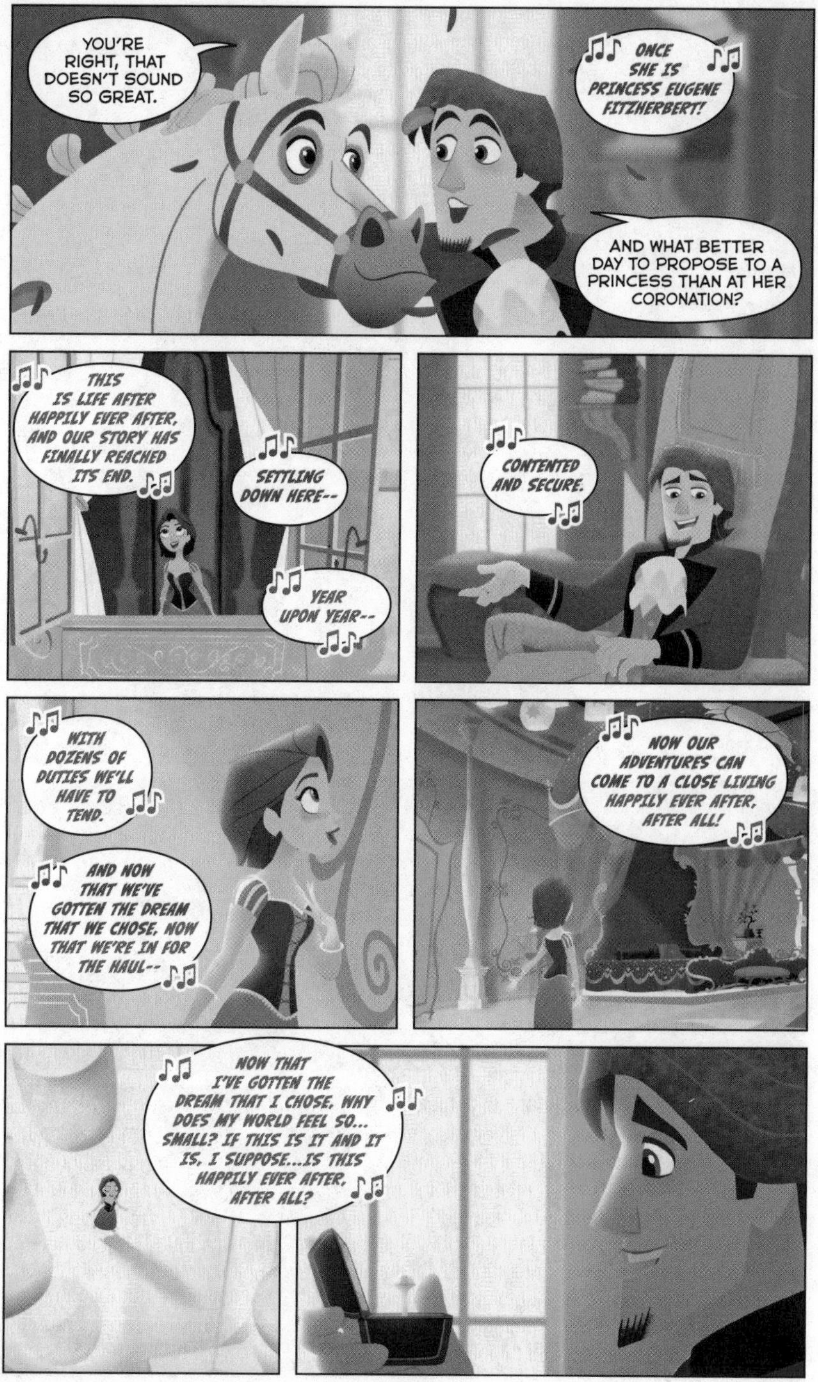
YOU'RE RIGHT, THAT DOESN'T SOUND SO GREAT.
ONCE SHE IS PRINCESS EUGENE FITZHERBERT!
AND WHAT BETTER DAY TO PROPOSE TO A PRINCESS THAN AT HER CORONATION?
THIS IS LIFE AFTER HAPPILY EVER AFTER, AND OUR STORY HAS FINALLY REACHED ITS END.
SETTLING DOWN HERE--
YEAR UPON YEAR--
CONTENTED AND SECURE.
WITH DOZENS OF DUTIES WE'LL HAVE TO TEND.
AND NOW THAT WE'VE GOTTEN THE DREAM THAT WE CHOSE, NOW THAT WE'RE IN FOR THE HAUL--
NOW OUR ADVENTURES CAN COME TO A CLOSE LIVING HAPPILY EVER AFTER, AFTER ALL!
NOW THAT I'VE GOTTEN THE DREAM THAT I CHOSE, WHY DOES MY WORLD FEEL SO... SMALL? IF THIS IS IT AND IT IS, I SUPPOSE...IS THIS HAPPILY EVER AFTER, AFTER ALL?

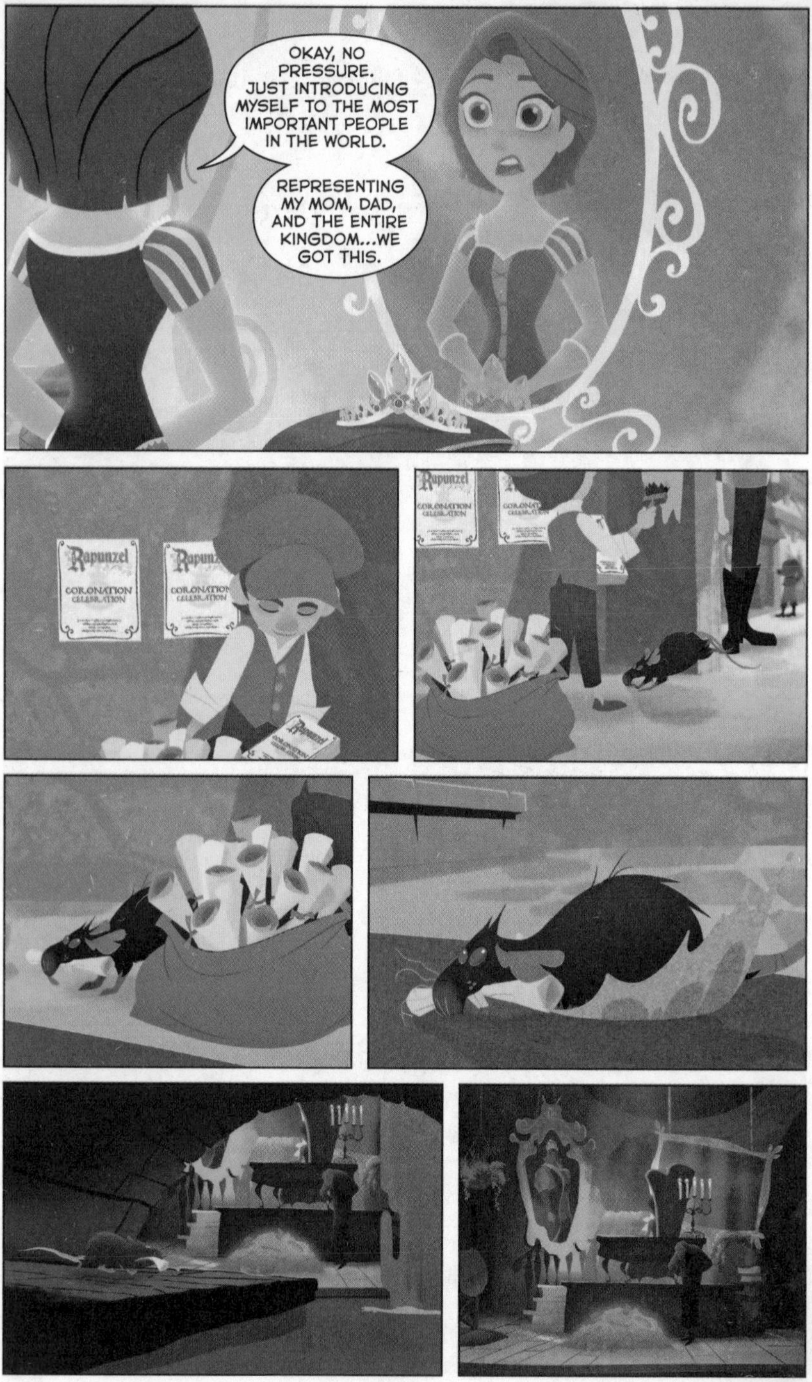
OKAY, NO PRESSURE. JUST INTRODUCING MYSELF TO THE MOST IMPORTANT PEOPLE IN THE WORLD.
REPRESENTING MY MOM, DAD, AND THE ENTIRE KINGDOM...WE GOT THIS.
Rapunzel
CORONATION CELEBRATION

LADY CAINE...WHAT IS IT?
Rapunzel
CORONATION CELEBRATION
TIME TO PAY OUR RESPECTS TO OUR BELOVED ROYALS.

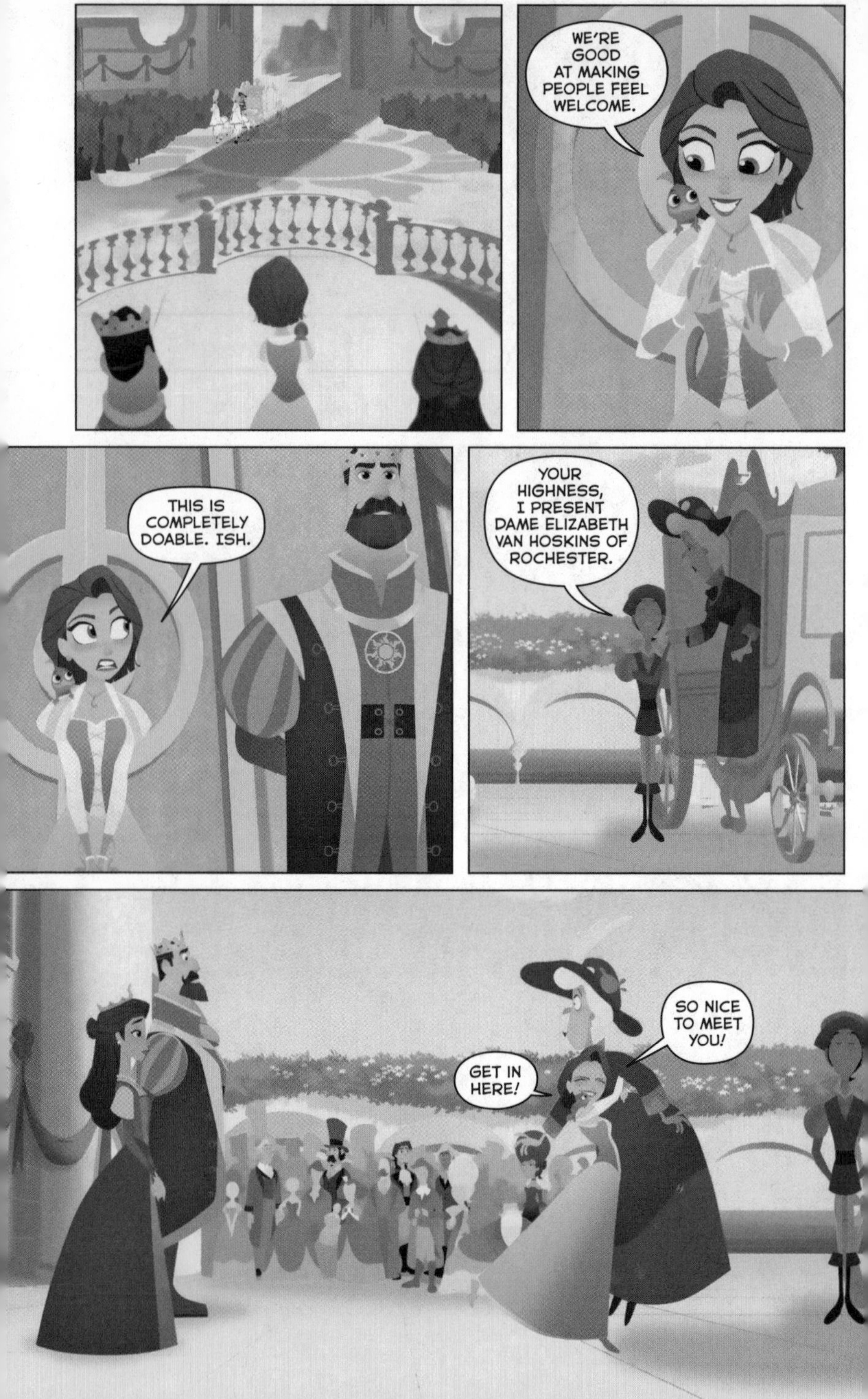
WE'RE GOOD AT MAKING PEOPLE FEEL WELCOME.
THIS IS COMPLETELY DOABLE. ISH.
YOUR HIGHNESS, I PRESENT DAME ELIZABETH VAN HOSKINS OF ROCHESTER.
SO NICE TO MEET YOU!
GET IN HERE!

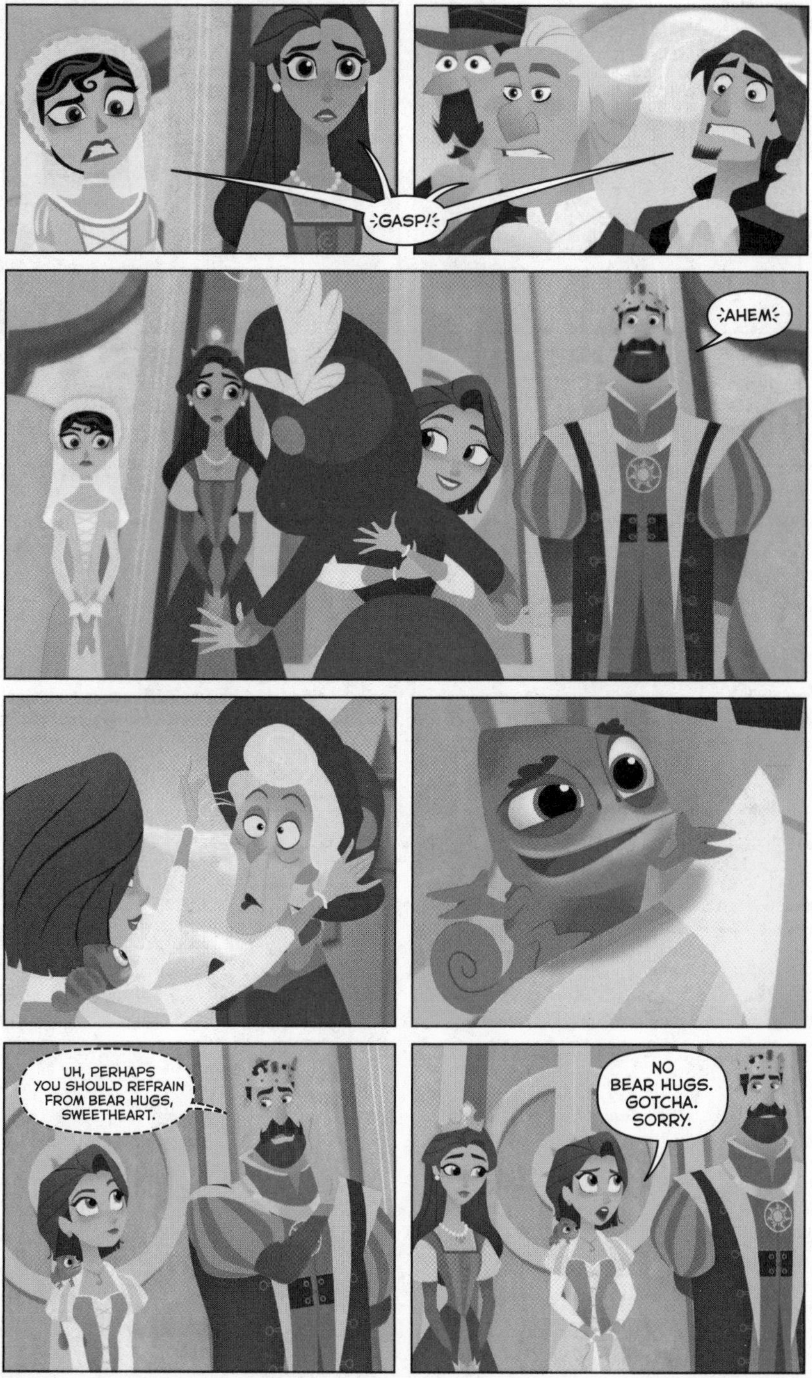
GASP!
AHEM
UH, PERHAPS YOU SHOULD REFRAIN FROM BEAR HUGS, SWEETHEART.
NO BEAR HUGS. GOTCHA. SORRY.

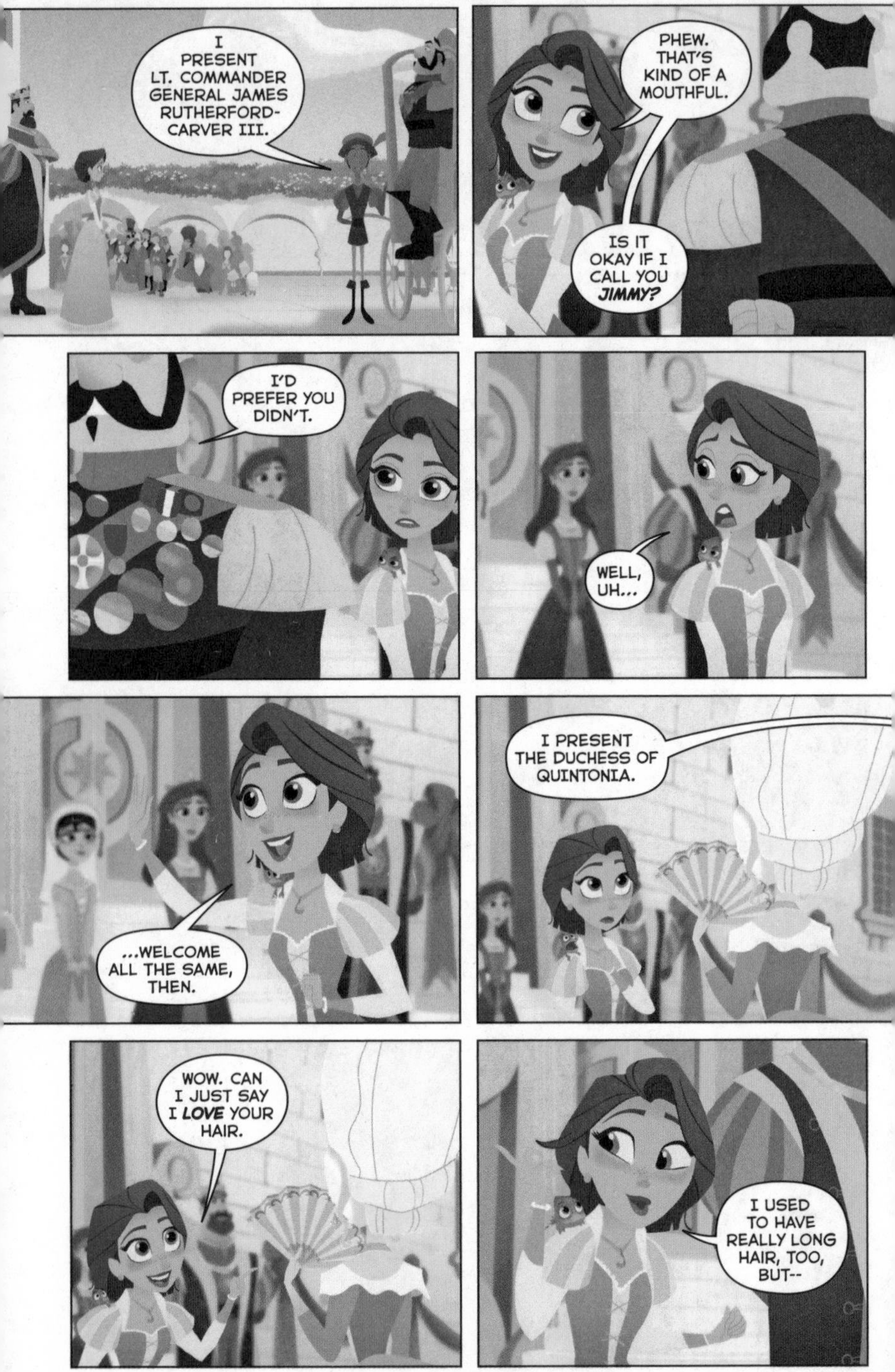
I PRESENT LT. COMMANDER GENERAL JAMES RUTHERFORD-CARVER III.
PHEW. THAT'S KIND OF A MOUTHFUL.
IS IT OKAY IF I CALL YOU *JIMMY?*
I'D PREFER YOU DIDN'T.
WELL, UH...
...WELCOME ALL THE SAME, THEN.
I PRESENT THE DUCHESS OF QUINTONIA.
WOW. CAN I JUST SAY I **LOVE** YOUR HAIR.
I USED TO HAVE REALLY LONG HAIR, TOO, BUT--

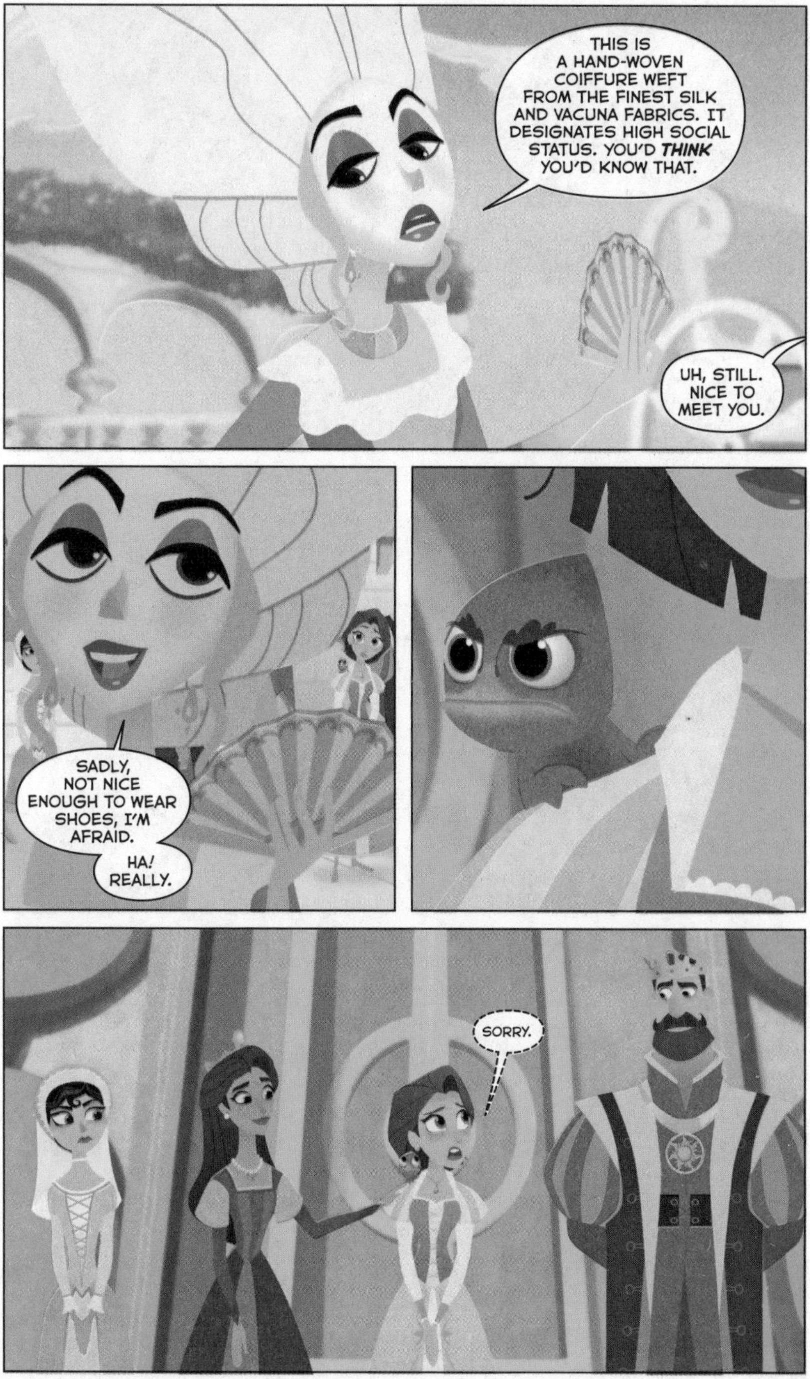
THIS IS A HAND-WOVEN COIFFURE WEFT FROM THE FINEST SILK AND VACUNA FABRICS. IT DESIGNATES HIGH SOCIAL STATUS. YOU'D *THINK* YOU'D KNOW THAT.
UH, STILL. NICE TO MEET YOU.
SADLY, NOT NICE ENOUGH TO WEAR SHOES, I'M AFRAID.
HA! REALLY.
SORRY.

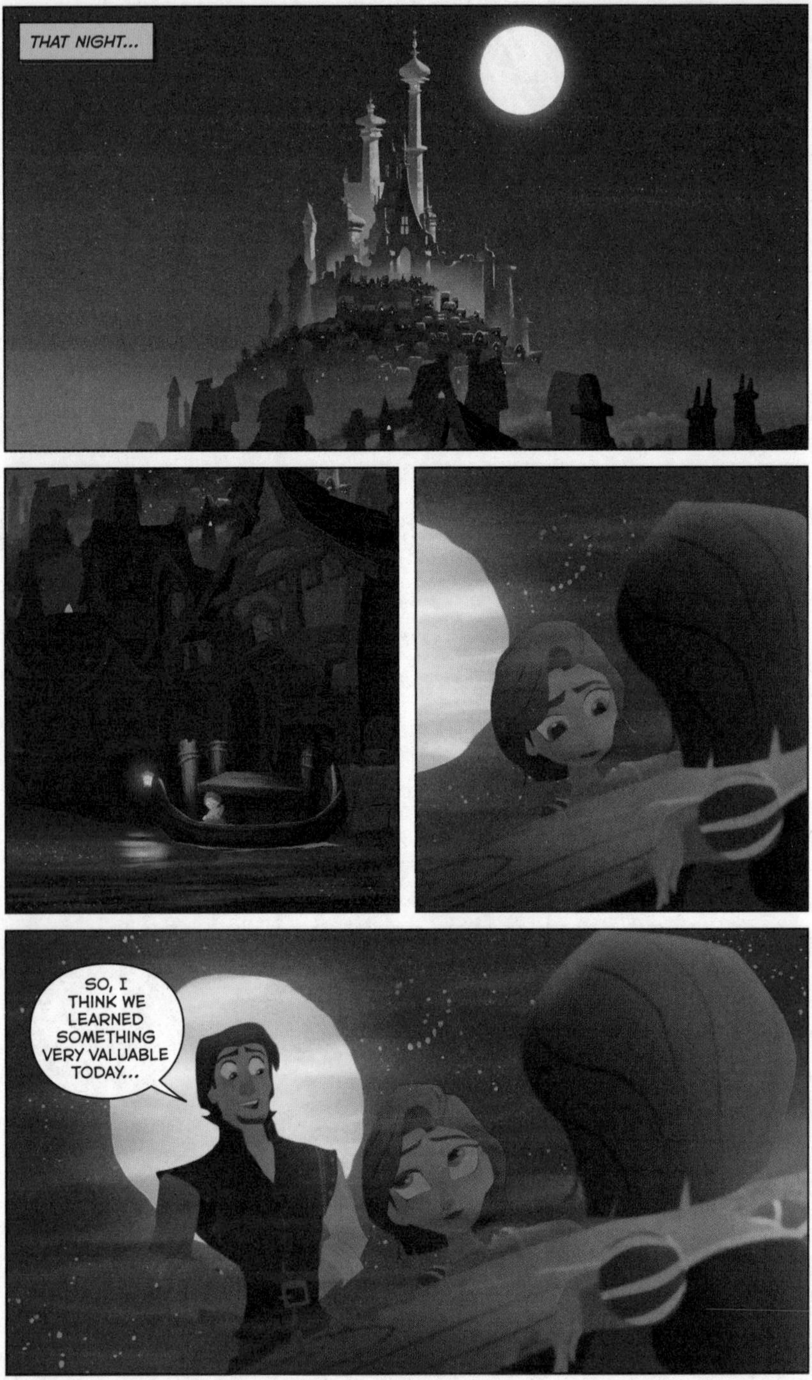
THAT NIGHT...
SO, I THINK WE LEARNED SOMETHING VERY VALUABLE TODAY...

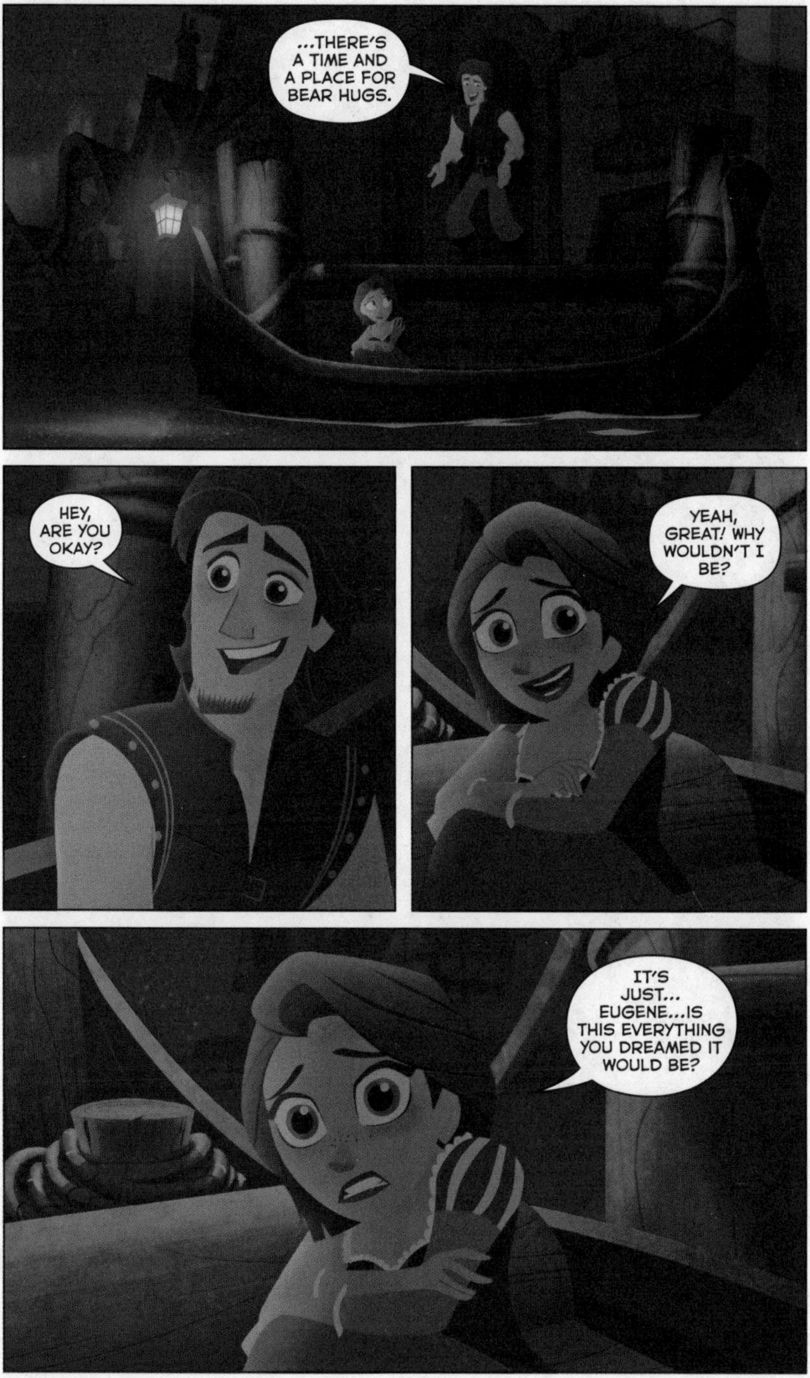
...THERE'S A TIME AND A PLACE FOR BEAR HUGS.
HEY, ARE YOU OKAY?
YEAH, GREAT! WHY WOULDN'T I BE?
IT'S JUST... EUGENE...IS THIS EVERYTHING YOU DREAMED IT WOULD BE?

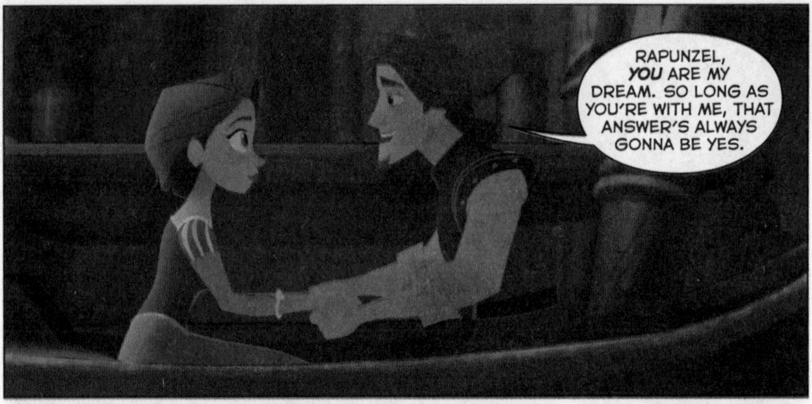
RAPUNZEL, YOU ARE MY DREAM. SO LONG AS YOU'RE WITH ME, THAT ANSWER'S ALWAYS GONNA BE YES.

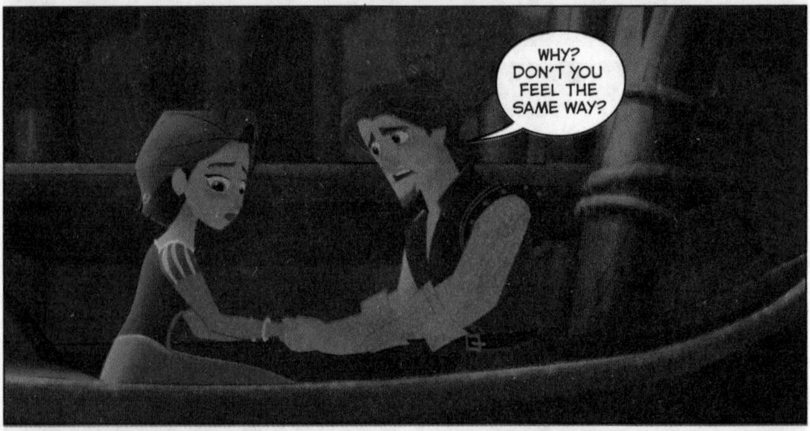
WHY? DON'T YOU FEEL THE SAME WAY?

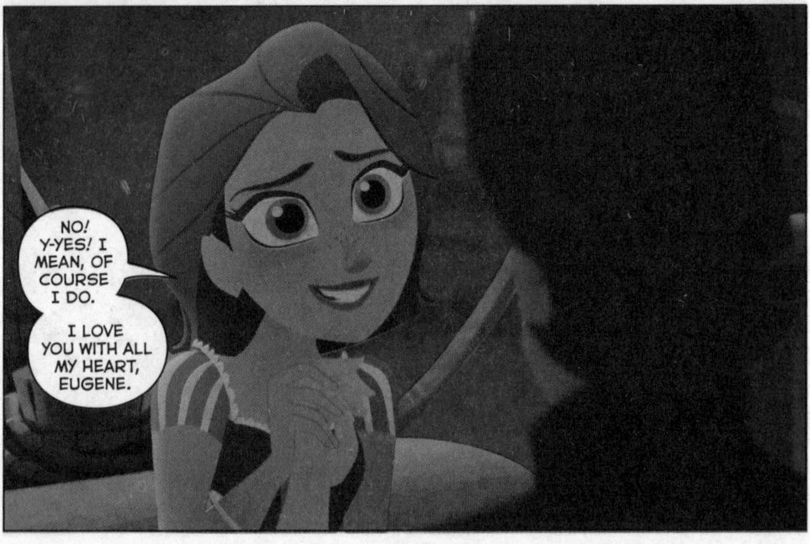
NO! Y-YES! I MEAN, OF COURSE I DO.
I LOVE YOU WITH ALL MY HEART, EUGENE.

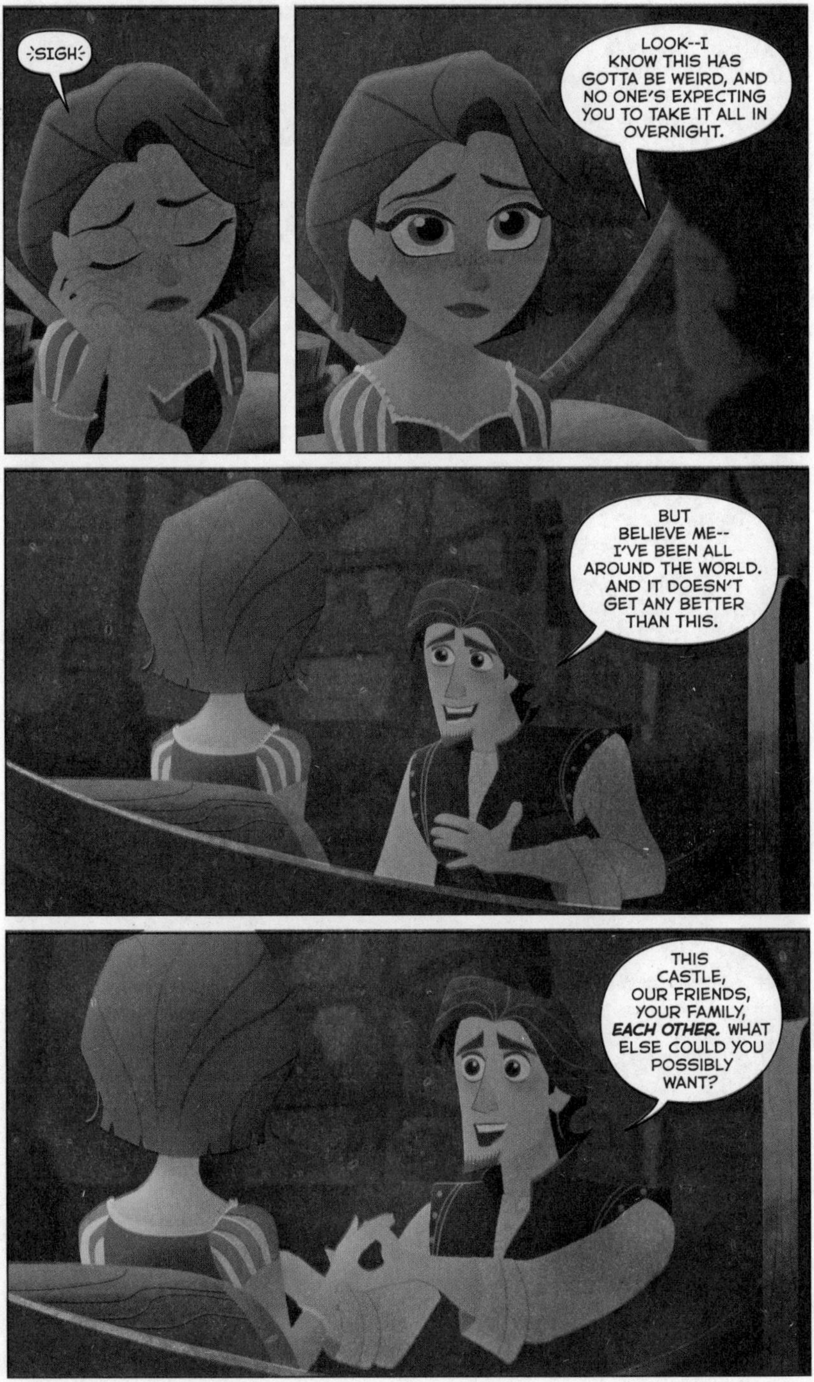

SIGH
LOOK--I KNOW THIS HAS GOTTA BE WEIRD, AND NO ONE'S EXPECTING YOU TO TAKE IT ALL IN OVERNIGHT.
BUT BELIEVE ME-- I'VE BEEN ALL AROUND THE WORLD. AND IT DOESN'T GET ANY BETTER THAN THIS.
THIS CASTLE, OUR FRIENDS, YOUR FAMILY, ***EACH OTHER.*** WHAT ELSE COULD YOU POSSIBLY WANT?

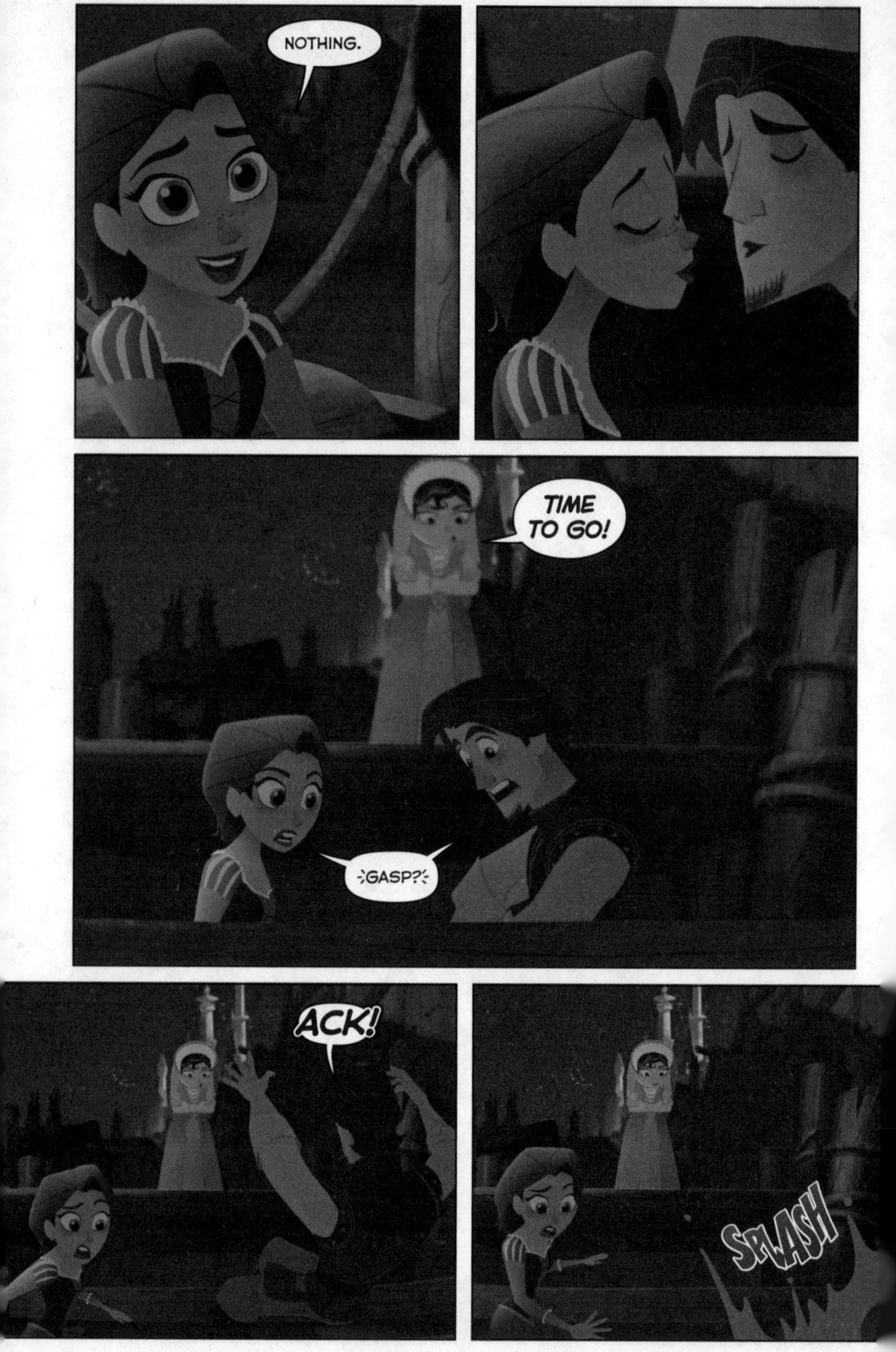
NOTHING.
TIME TO GO!
GASP?
ACK!
SPLASH

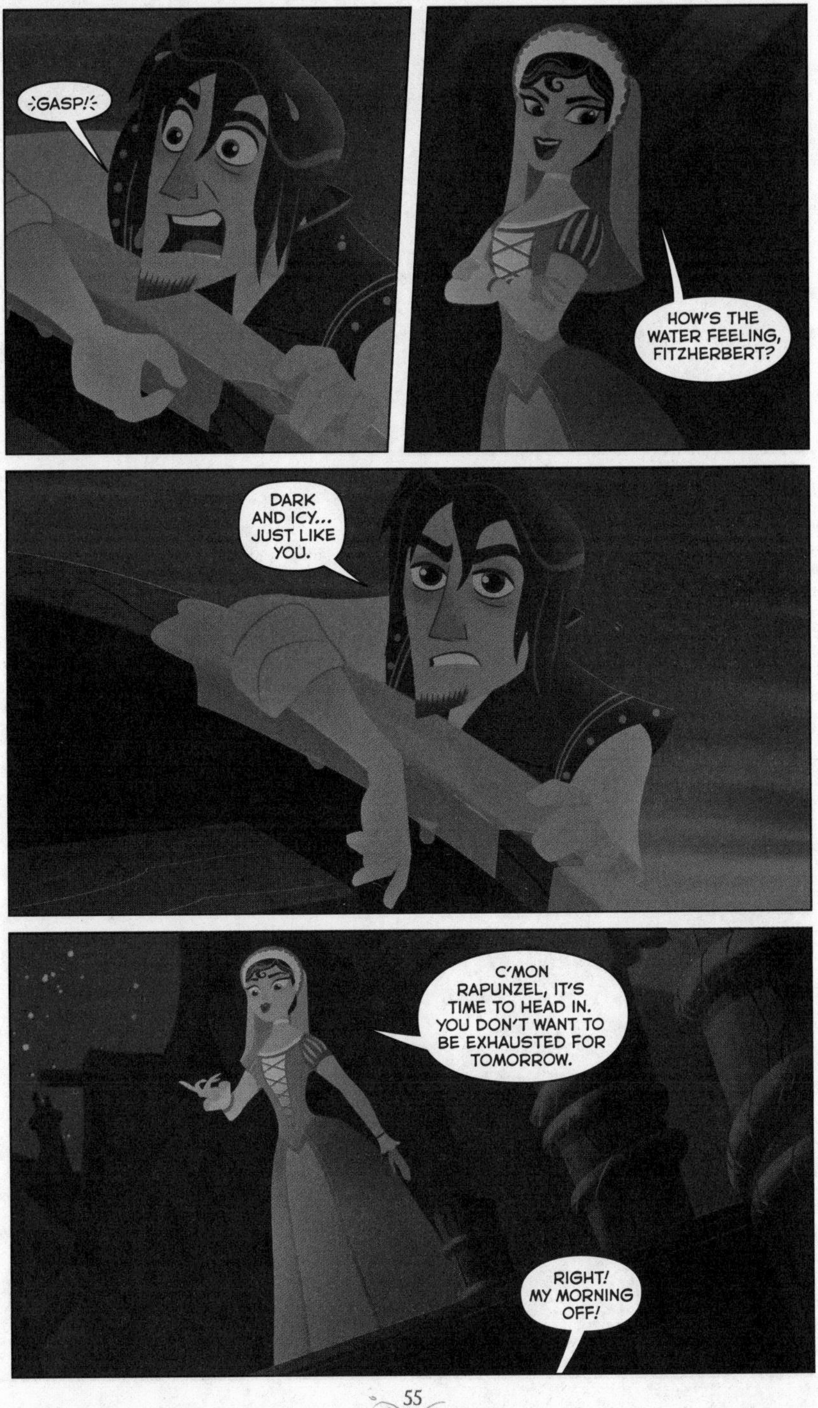

:GASP!:
HOW'S THE WATER FEELING, FITZHERBERT?
DARK AND ICY... JUST LIKE YOU.
C'MON RAPUNZEL, IT'S TIME TO HEAD IN. YOU DON'T WANT TO BE EXHAUSTED FOR TOMORROW.
RIGHT! MY MORNING OFF!

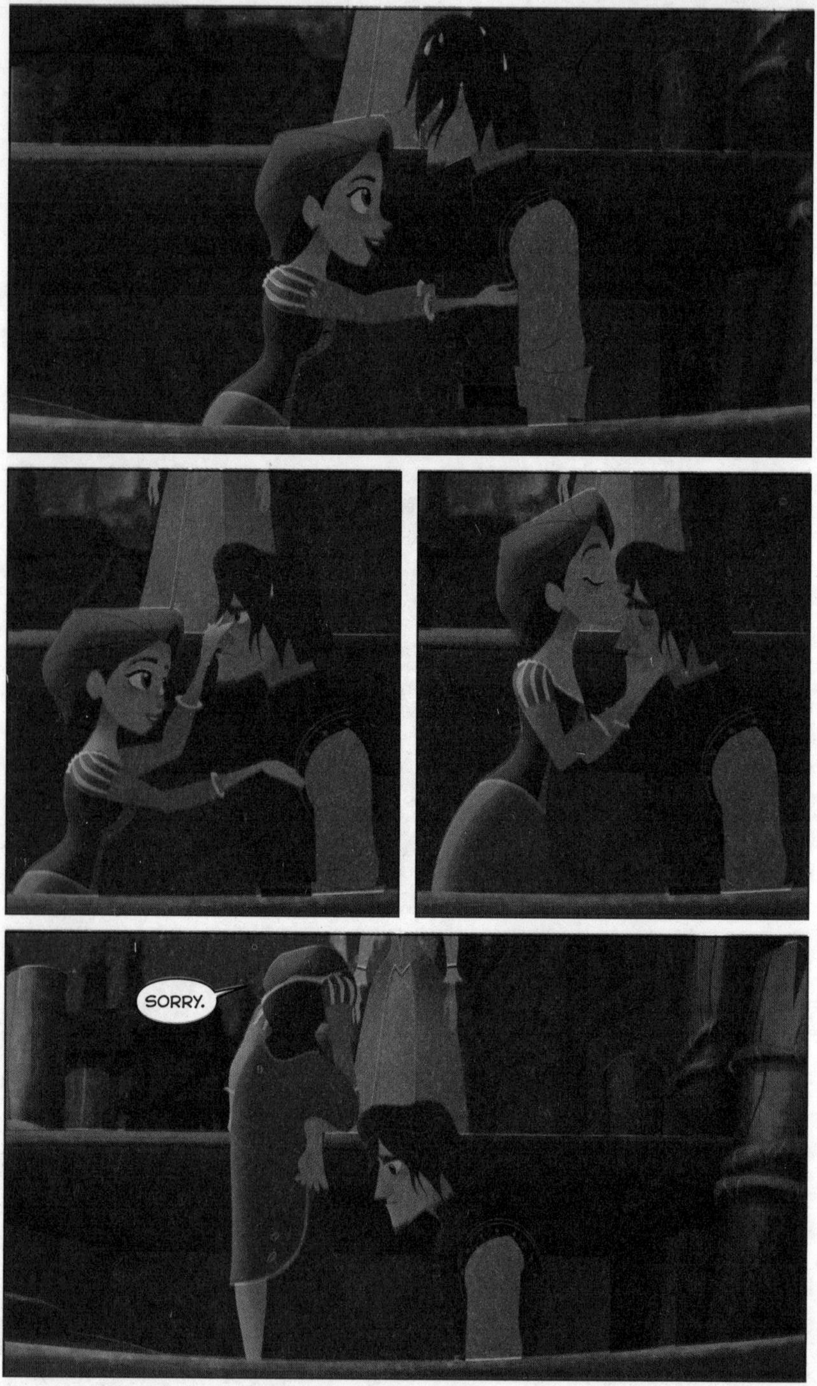
SORRY.

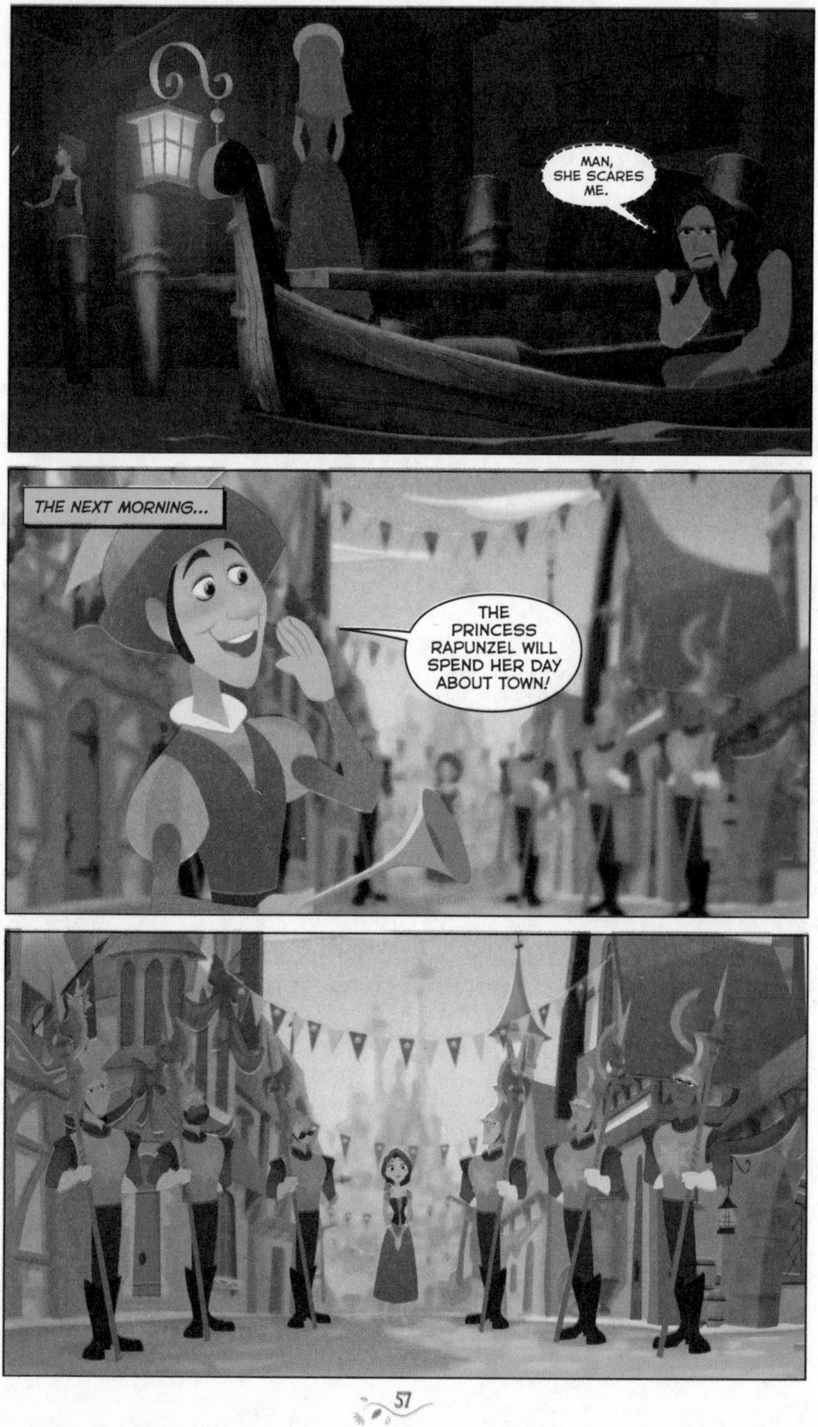
MAN, SHE SCARES ME.
THE NEXT MORNING...
THE PRINCESS RAPUNZEL WILL SPEND HER DAY ABOUT TOWN!

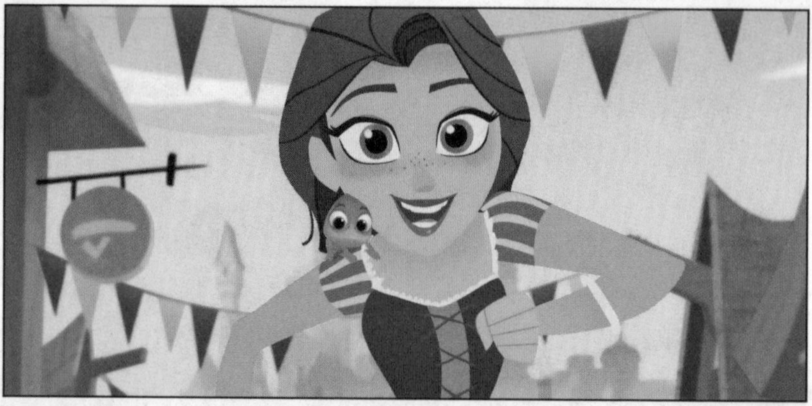

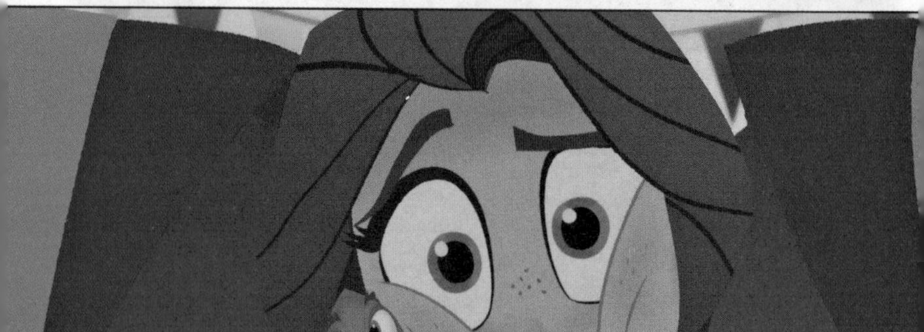

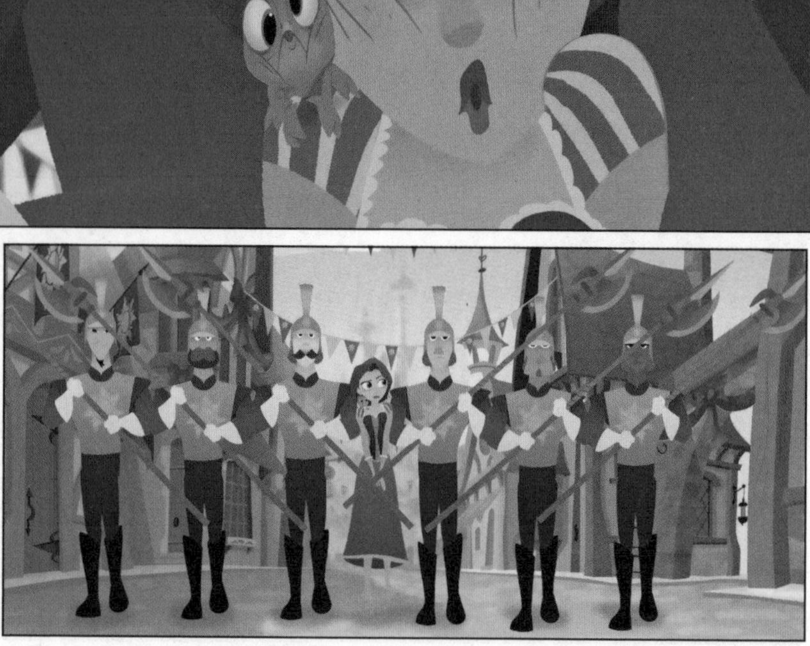

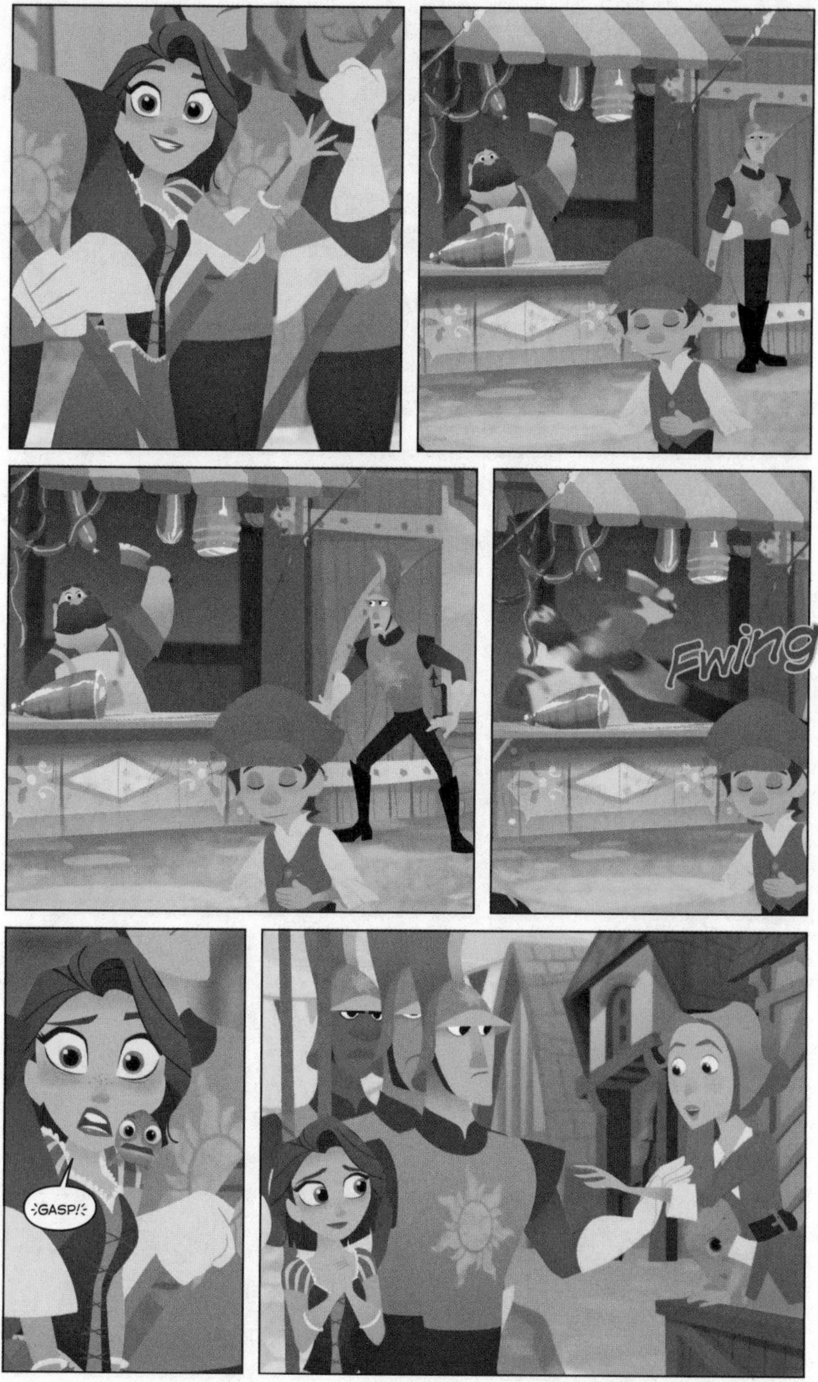
Fwing!
GASP!

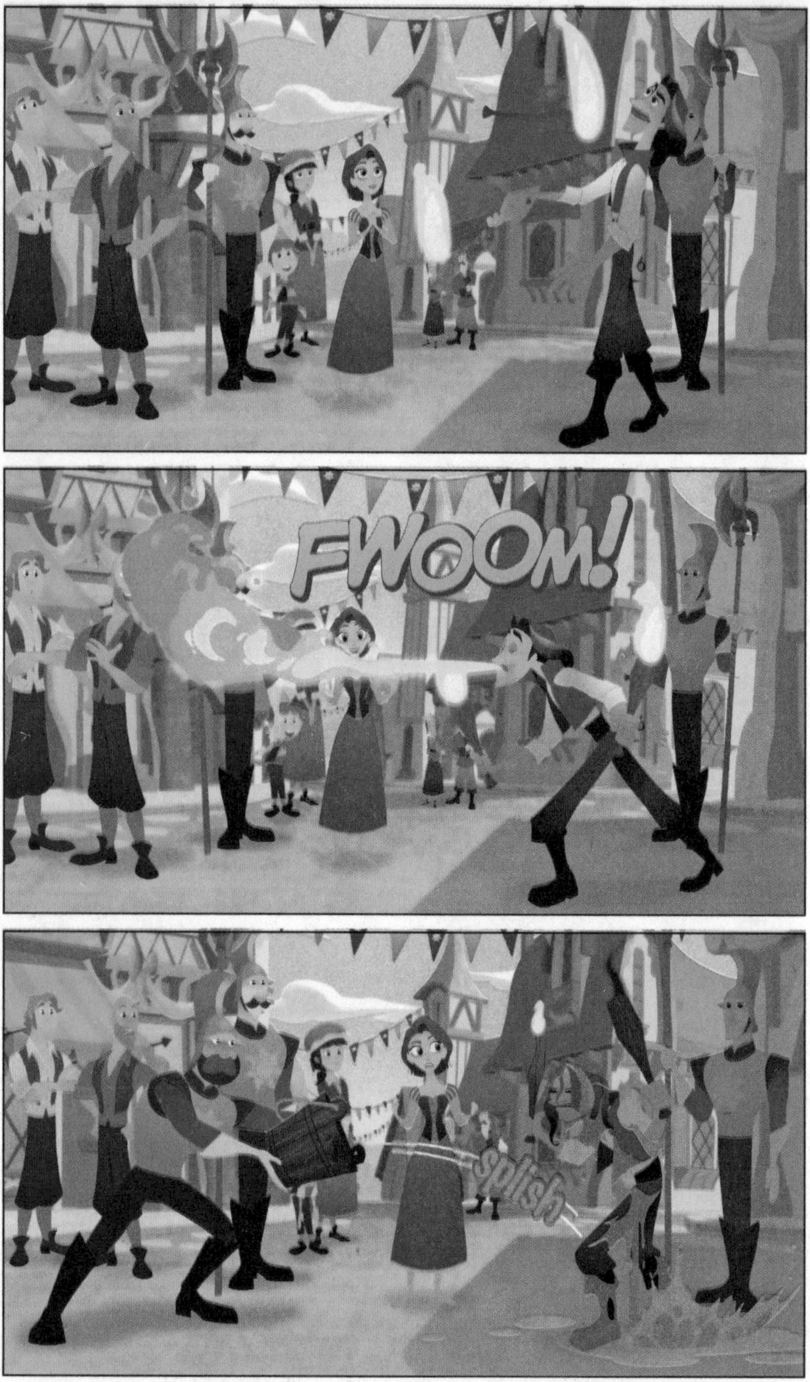
FWOOM!
splish

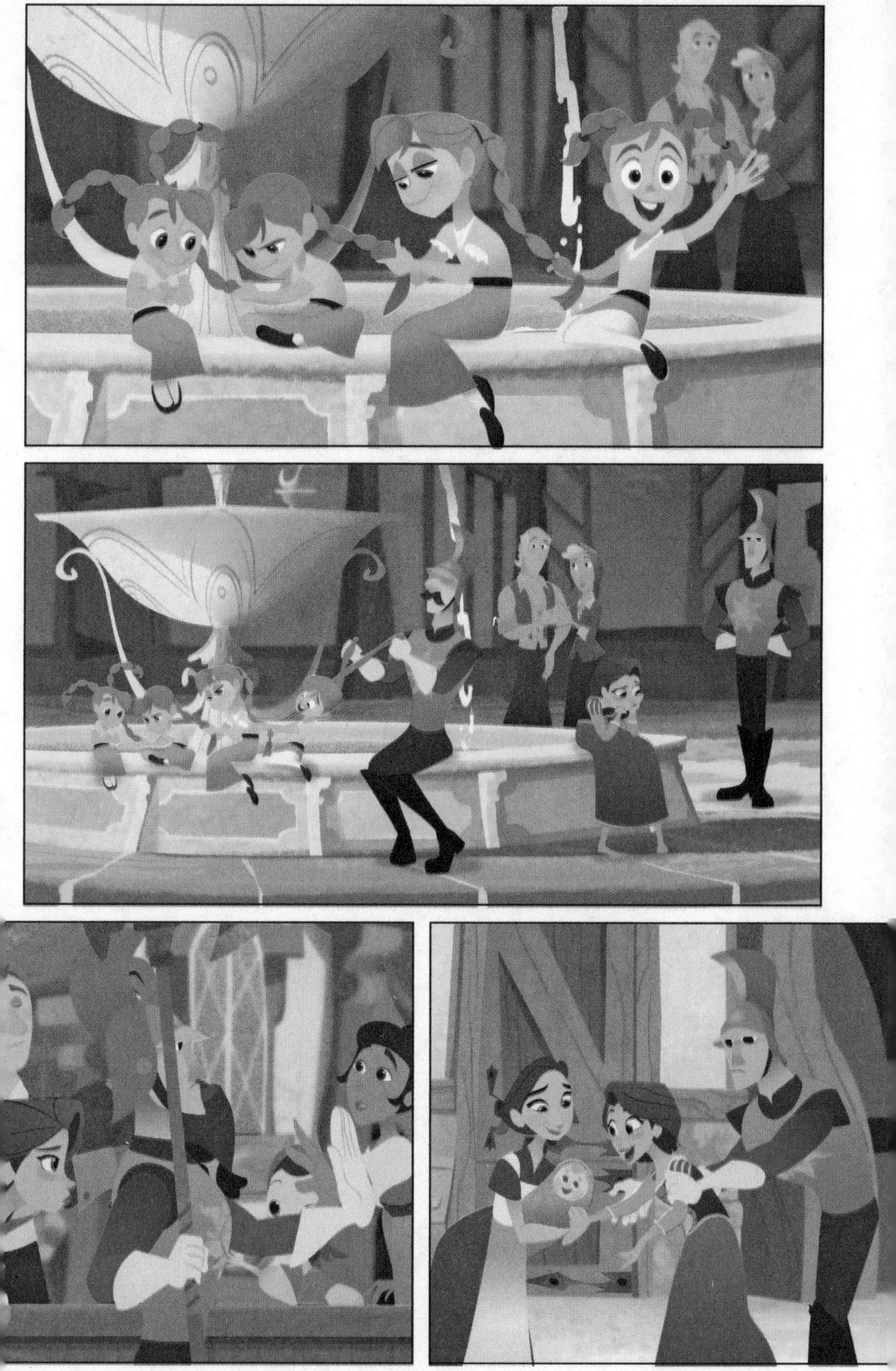

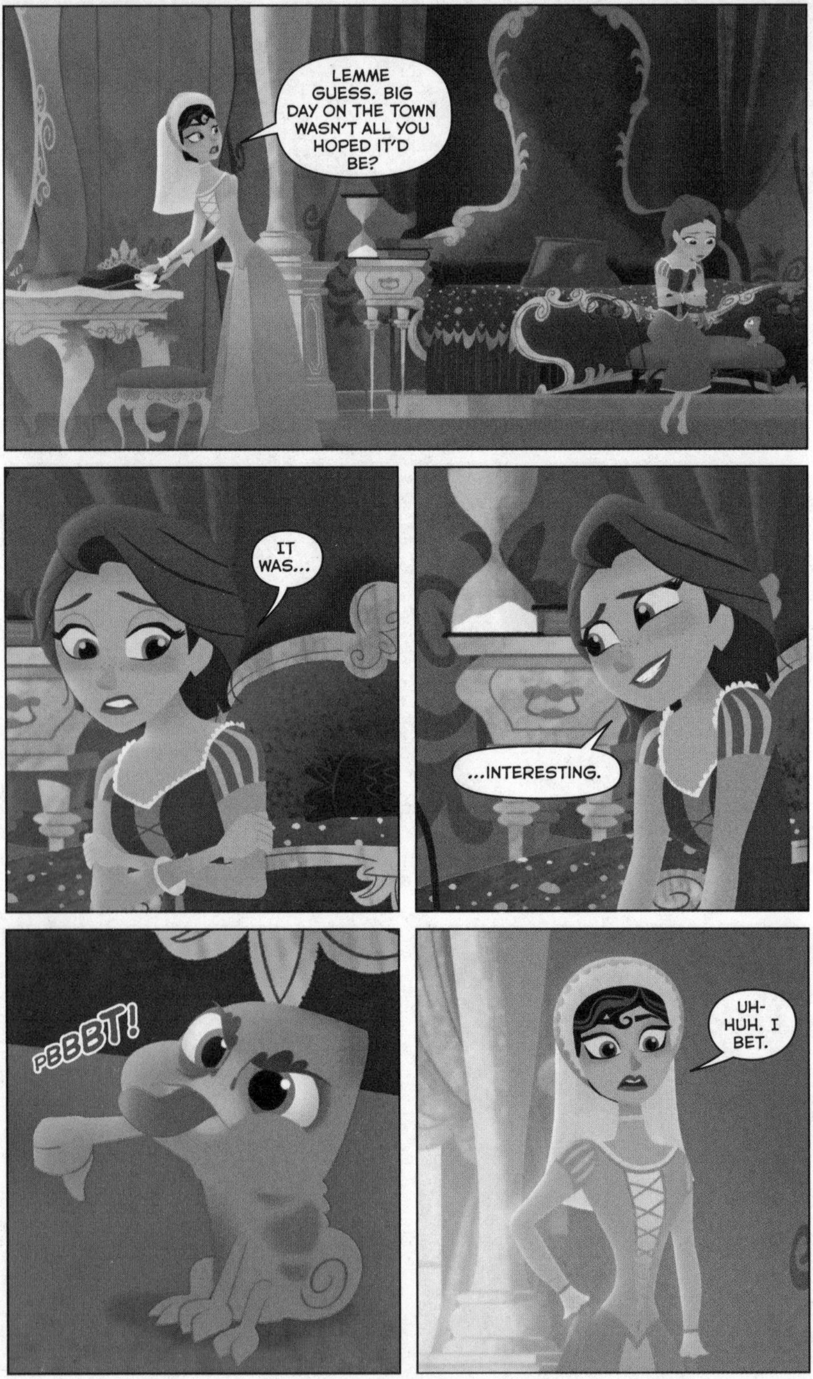
LEMME GUESS. BIG DAY ON THE TOWN WASN'T ALL YOU HOPED IT'D BE?
IT WAS...
...INTERESTING.
PBBBT!
UH-HUH. I BET.

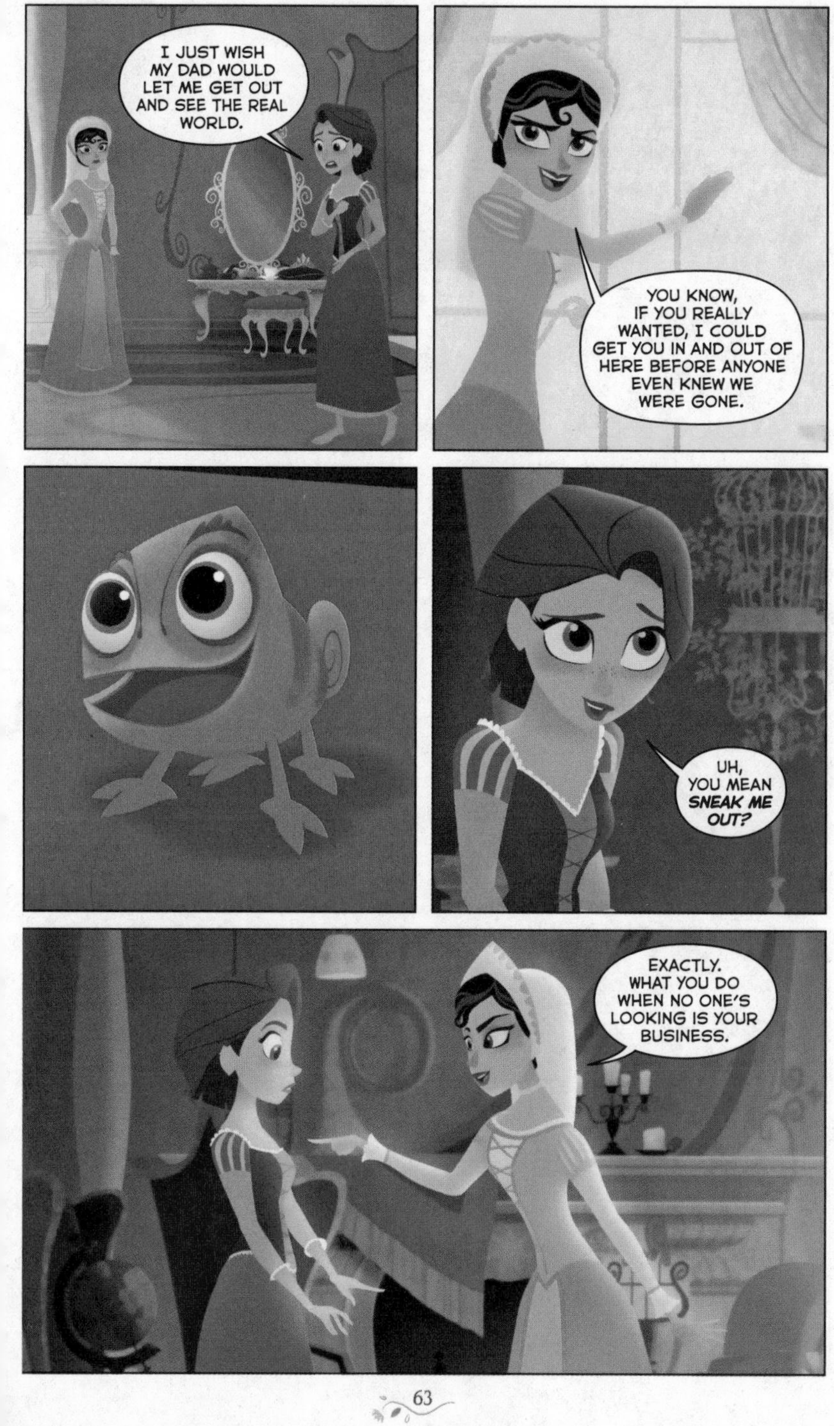
I JUST WISH MY DAD WOULD LET ME GET OUT AND SEE THE REAL WORLD.
YOU KNOW, IF YOU REALLY WANTED, I COULD GET YOU IN AND OUT OF HERE BEFORE ANYONE EVEN KNEW WE WERE GONE.
UH, YOU MEAN ***SNEAK ME OUT?***
EXACTLY. WHAT YOU DO WHEN NO ONE'S LOOKING IS YOUR BUSINESS.

KNOCK KNOCK

THE ROYAL BANQUET IS READY TO RECEIVE THE PRINCESS NOW.

CHEER UP, RAPS. HEY, MAYBE YOUR DAD GOT SOMEONE TO CHEW YOUR FOOD FOR YOU.

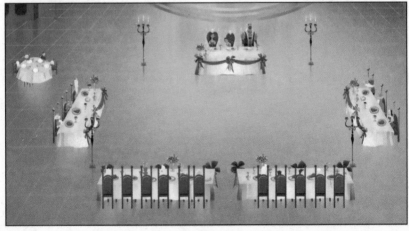

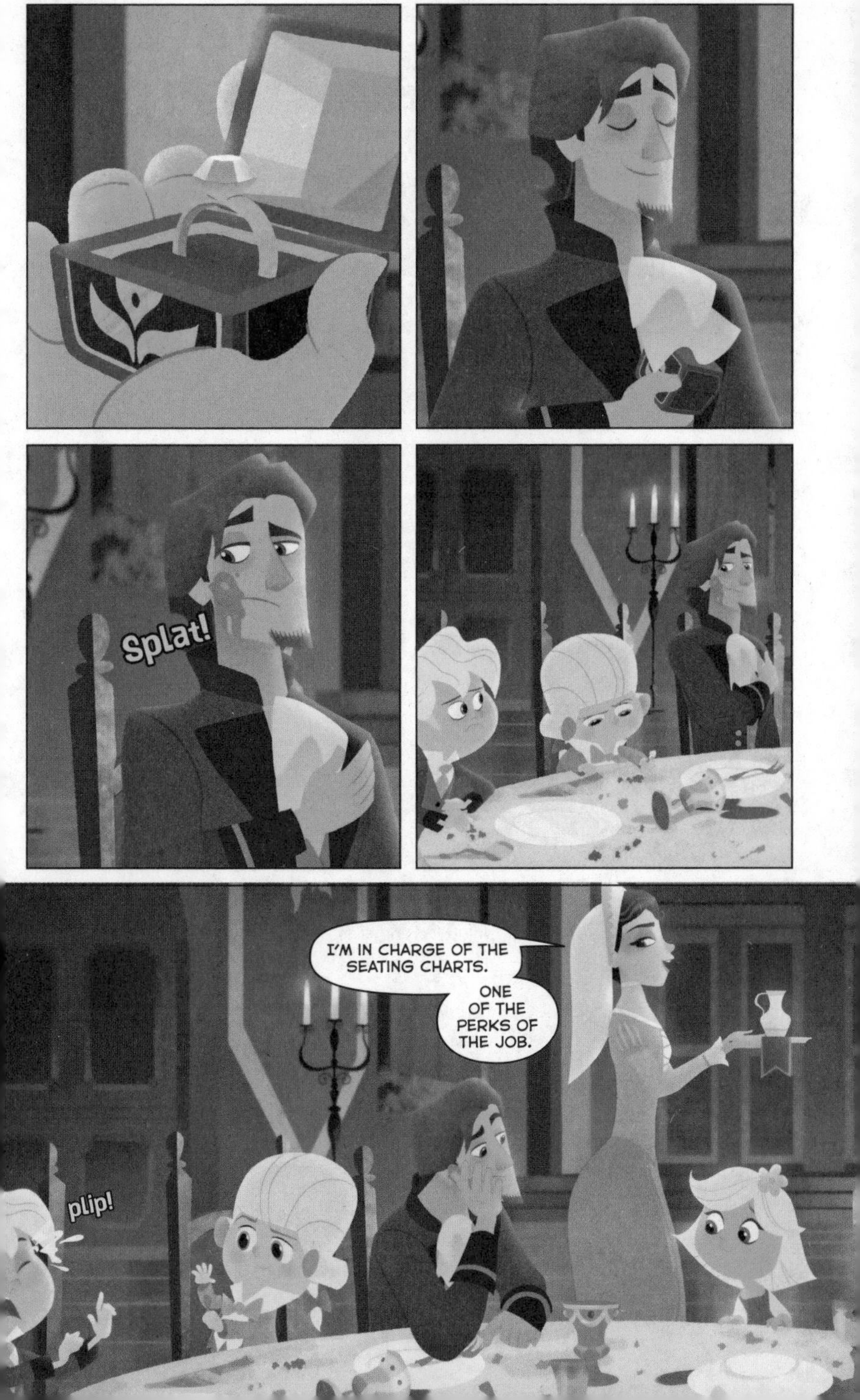
Splat!
I'M IN CHARGE OF THE SEATING CHARTS.
ONE OF THE PERKS OF THE JOB.
plip!

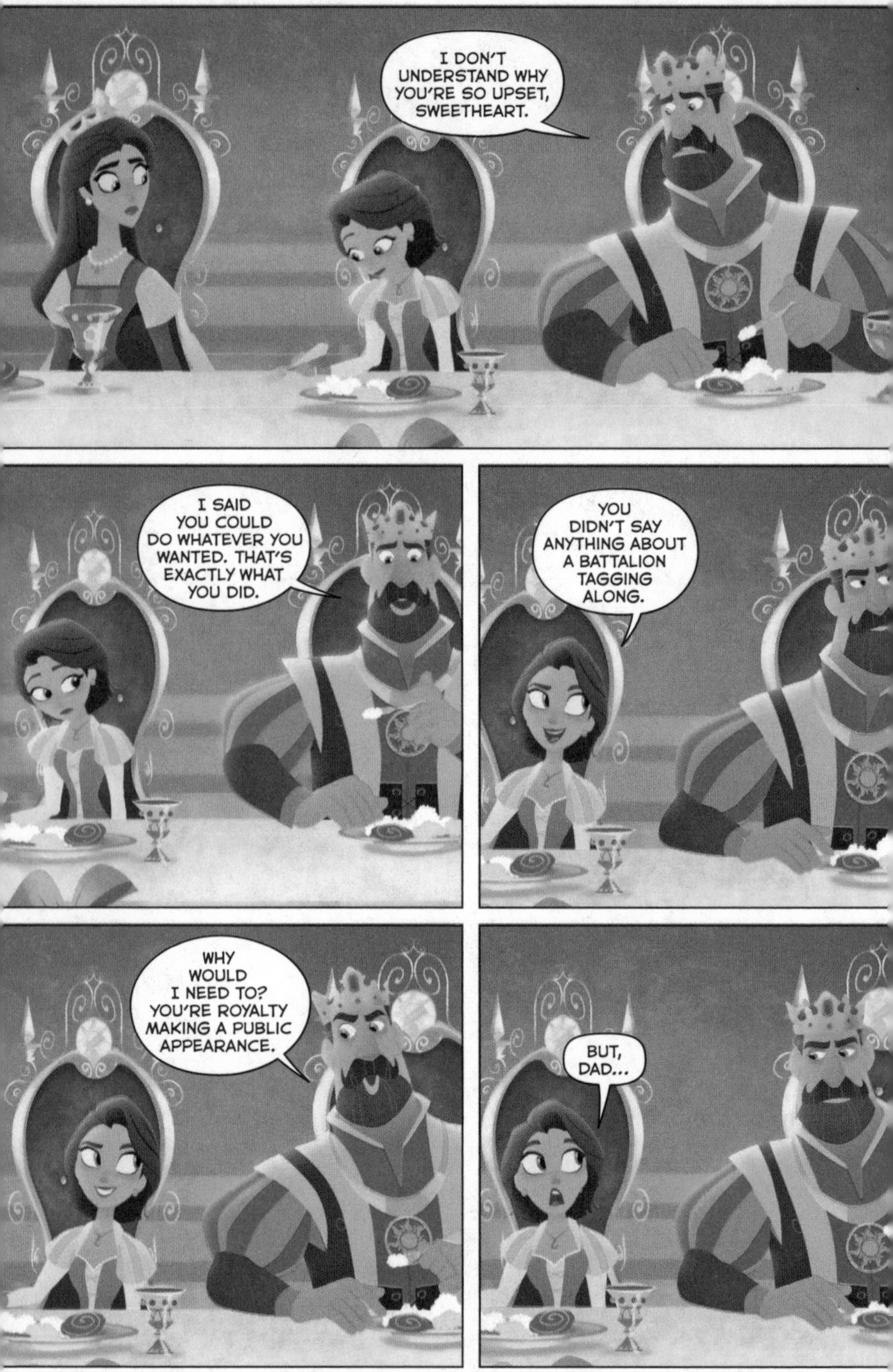
I DON'T UNDERSTAND WHY YOU'RE SO UPSET, SWEETHEART.
I SAID YOU COULD DO WHATEVER YOU WANTED. THAT'S EXACTLY WHAT YOU DID.
YOU DIDN'T SAY ANYTHING ABOUT A BATTALION TAGGING ALONG.
WHY WOULD I NEED TO? YOU'RE ROYALTY MAKING A PUBLIC APPEARANCE.
BUT, DAD...

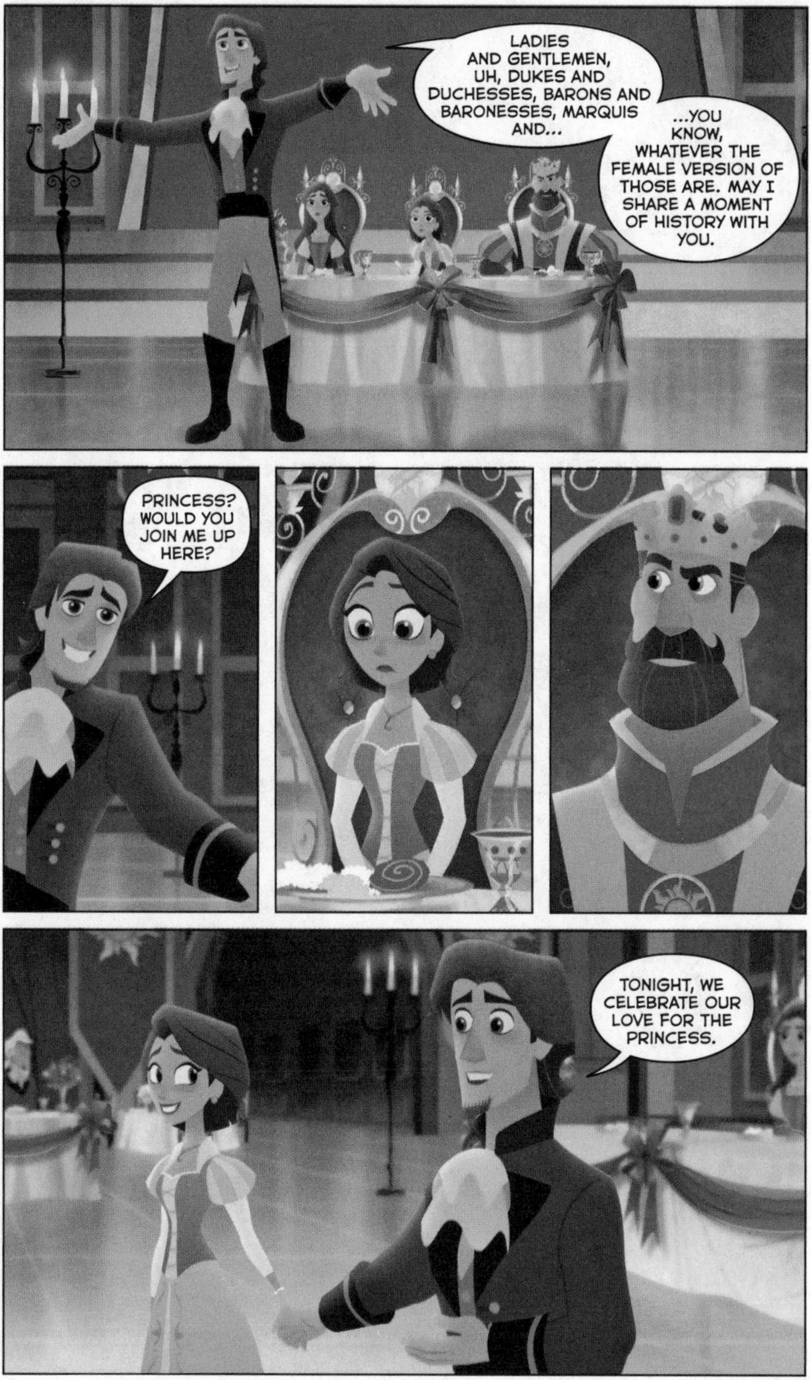
LADIES AND GENTLEMEN, UH, DUKES AND DUCHESSES, BARONS AND BARONESSES, MARQUIS AND...
...YOU KNOW, WHATEVER THE FEMALE VERSION OF THOSE ARE. MAY I SHARE A MOMENT OF HISTORY WITH YOU.
PRINCESS? WOULD YOU JOIN ME UP HERE?
TONIGHT, WE CELEBRATE OUR LOVE FOR THE PRINCESS.

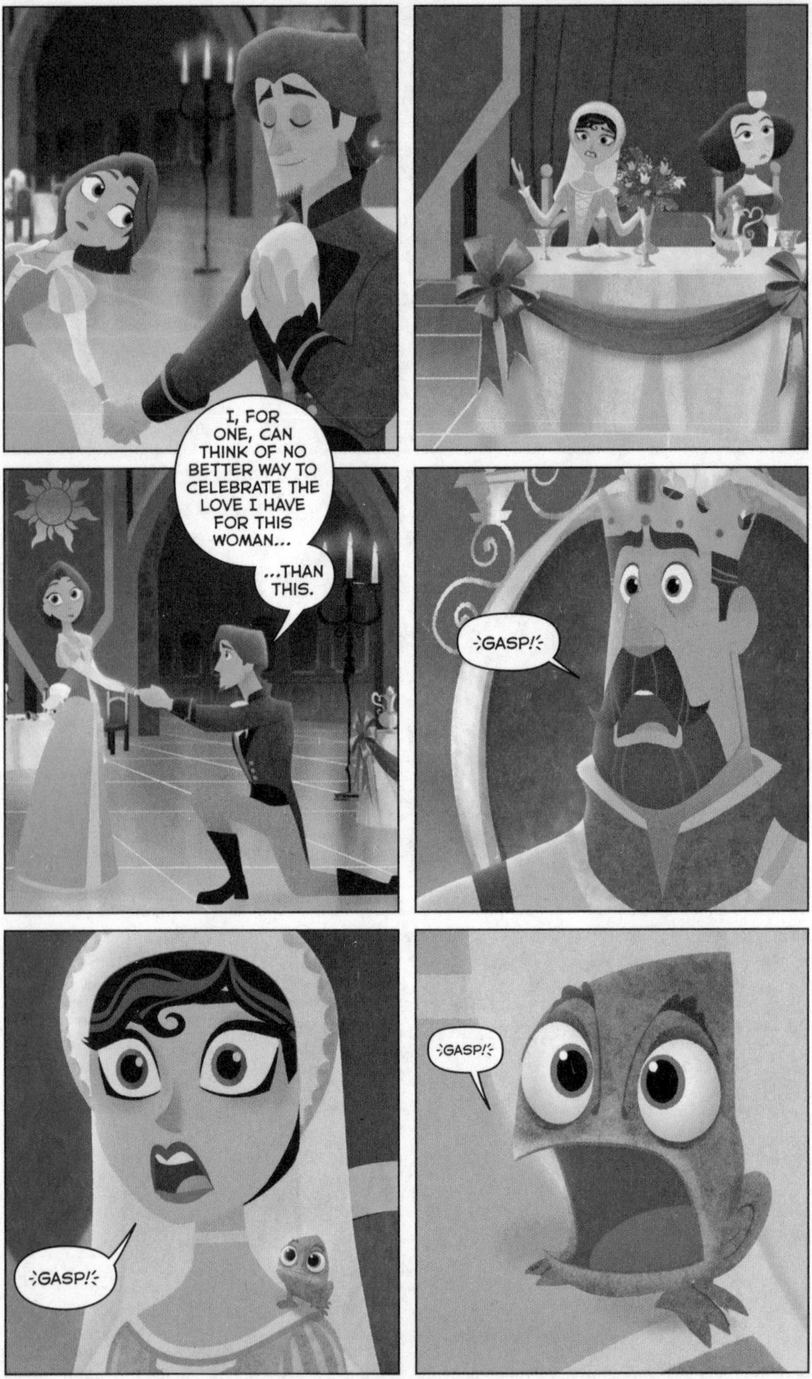
I, FOR ONE, CAN THINK OF NO BETTER WAY TO CELEBRATE THE LOVE I HAVE FOR THIS WOMAN...
...THAN THIS.
GASP!
GASP!
GASP!

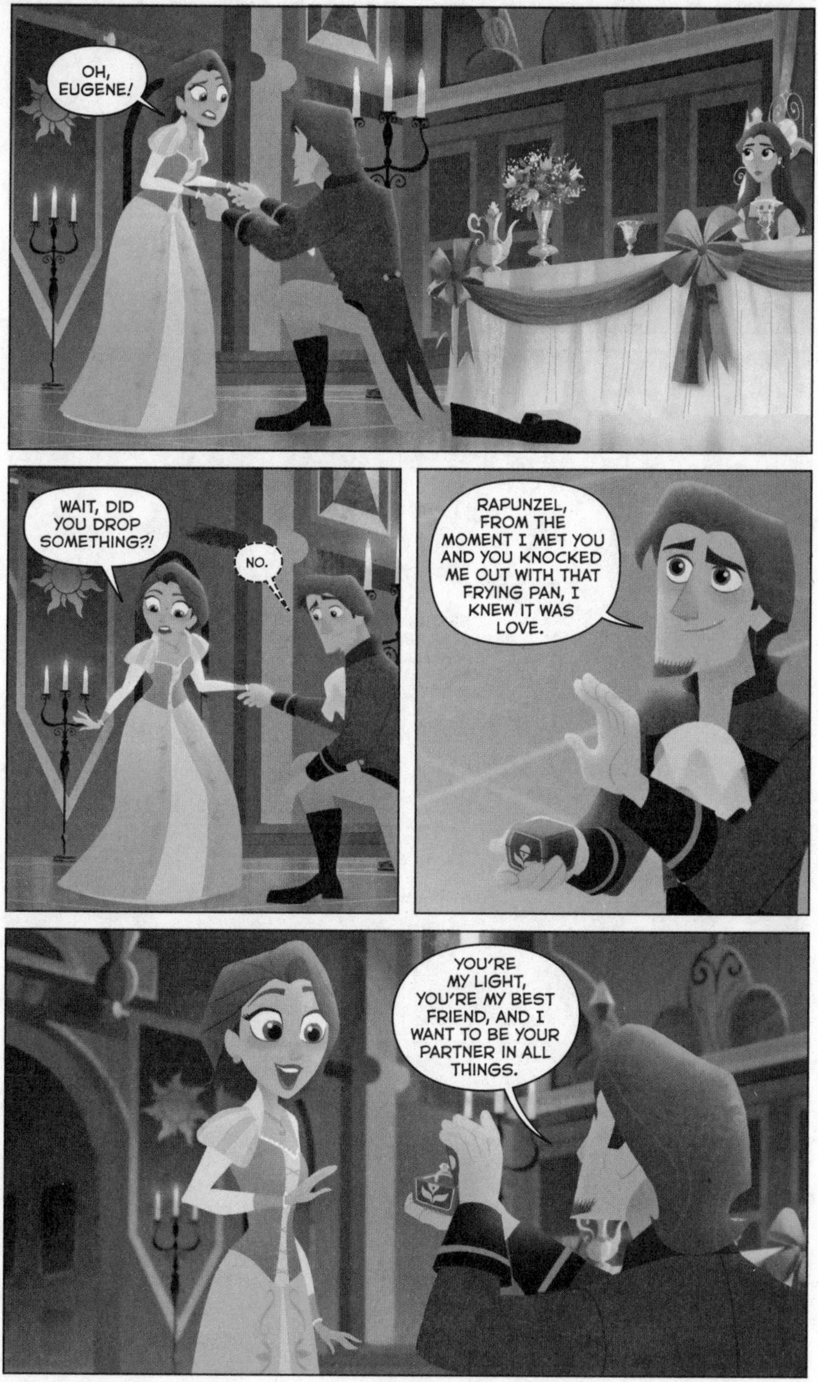
OH, EUGENE!
WAIT, DID YOU DROP SOMETHING?!
NO.
RAPUNZEL, FROM THE MOMENT I MET YOU AND YOU KNOCKED ME OUT WITH THAT FRYING PAN, I KNEW IT WAS LOVE.
YOU'RE MY LIGHT, YOU'RE MY BEST FRIEND, AND I WANT TO BE YOUR PARTNER IN ALL THINGS.

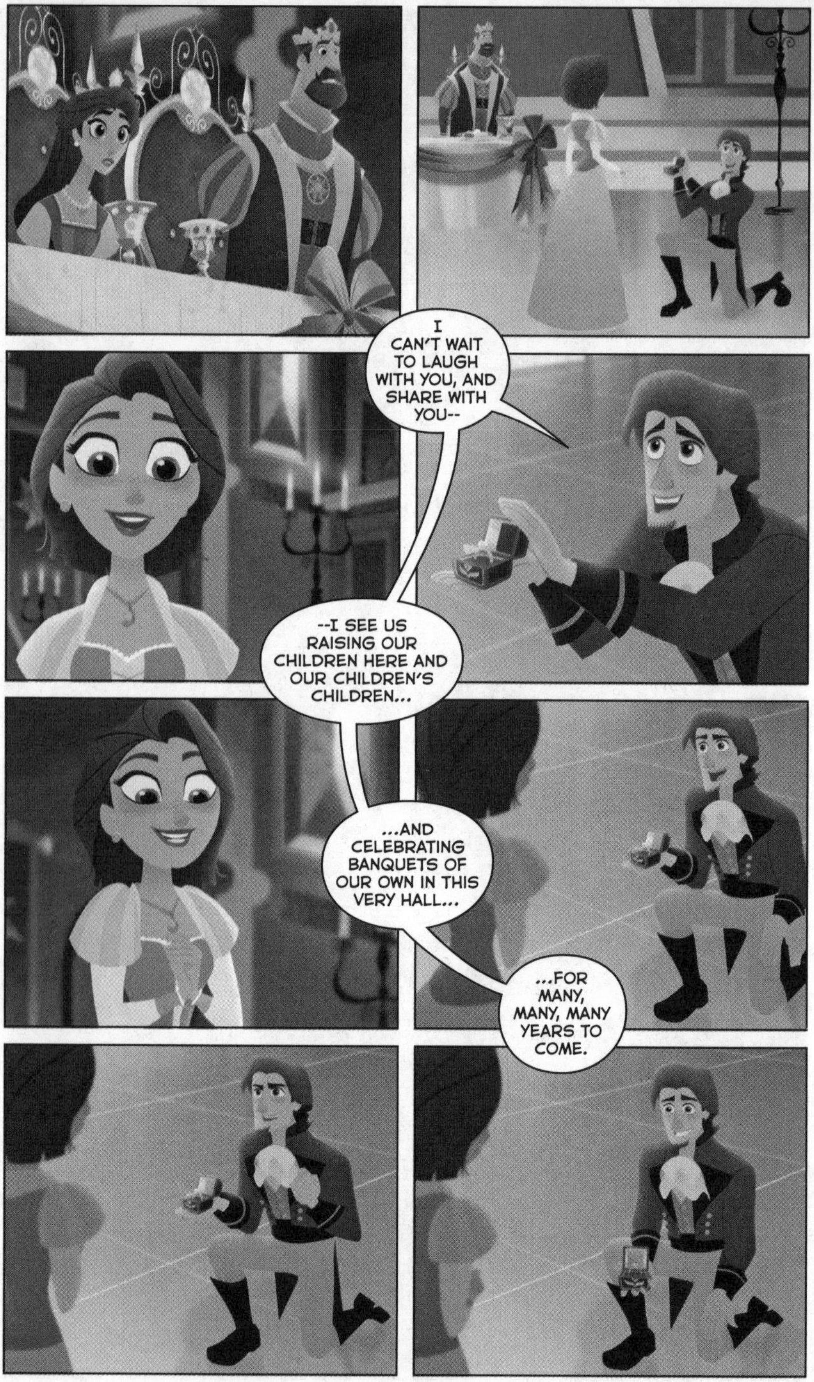
I CAN'T WAIT TO LAUGH WITH YOU, AND SHARE WITH YOU--
--I SEE US RAISING OUR CHILDREN HERE AND OUR CHILDREN'S CHILDREN...
...AND CELEBRATING BANQUETS OF OUR OWN IN THIS VERY HALL...
...FOR MANY, MANY, MANY YEARS TO COME.

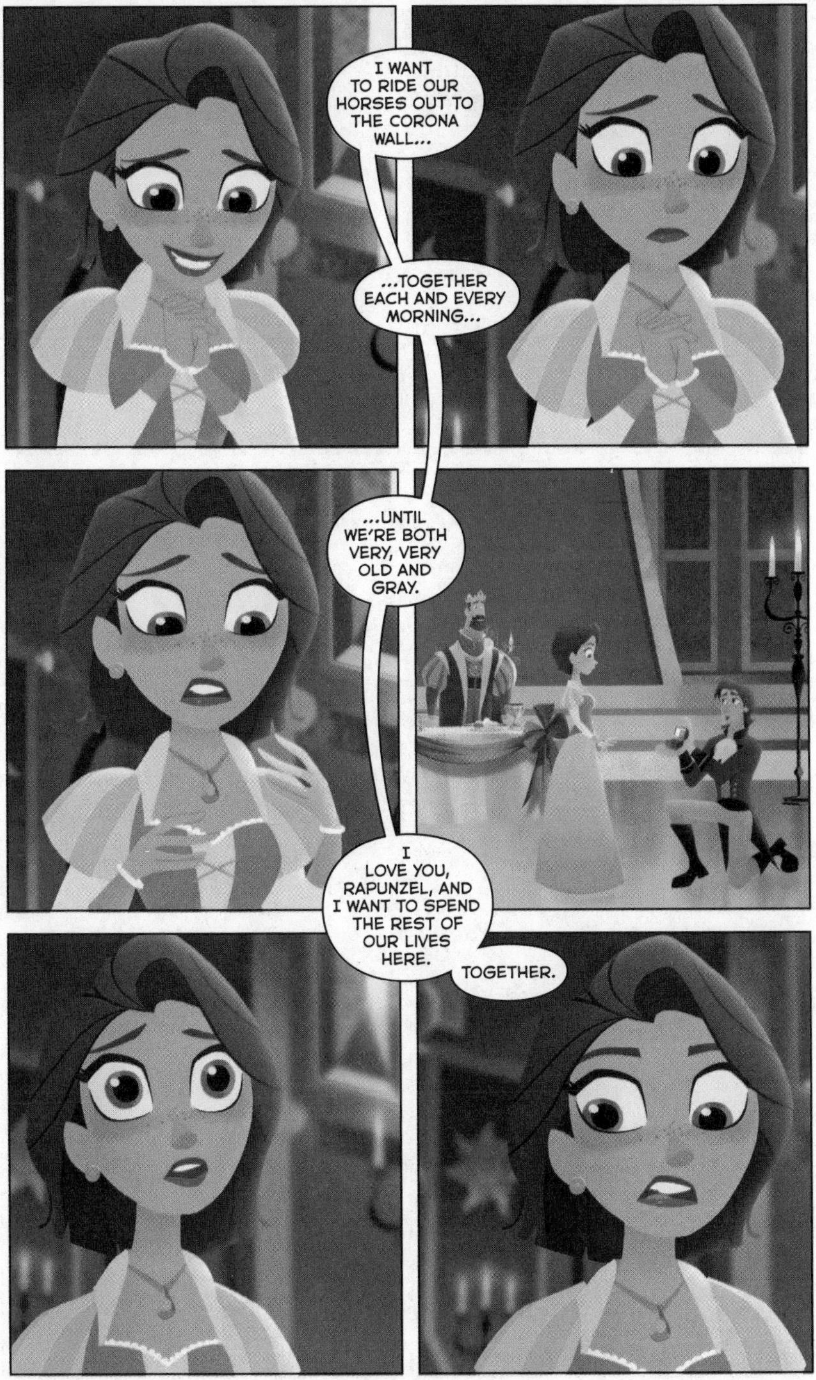
I WANT TO RIDE OUR HORSES OUT TO THE CORONA WALL...
...TOGETHER EACH AND EVERY MORNING...
...UNTIL WE'RE BOTH VERY, VERY OLD AND GRAY.
I LOVE YOU, RAPUNZEL, AND I WANT TO SPEND THE REST OF OUR LIVES HERE.
TOGETHER.

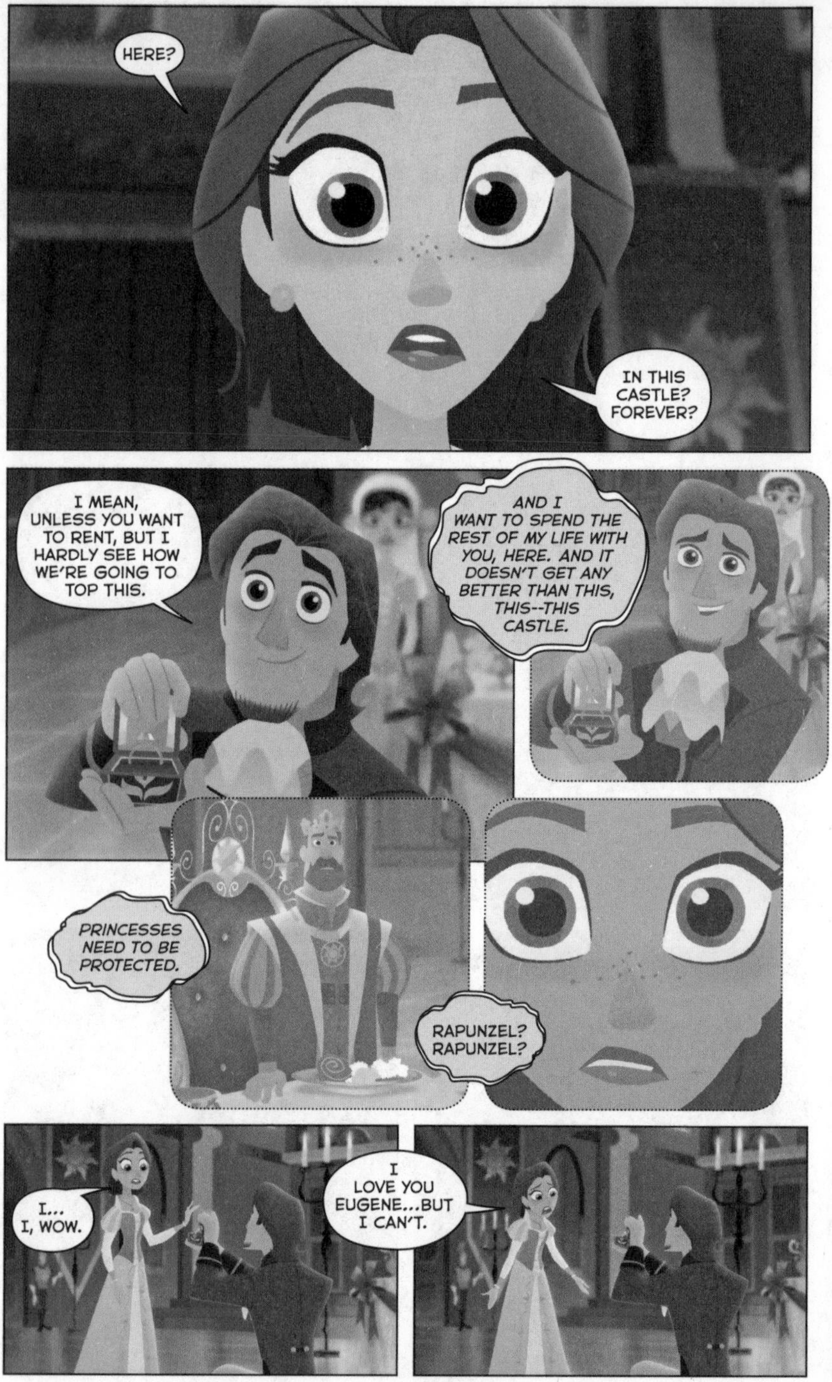
HERE?
IN THIS CASTLE? FOREVER?
I MEAN, UNLESS YOU WANT TO RENT, BUT I HARDLY SEE HOW WE'RE GOING TO TOP THIS.
AND I WANT TO SPEND THE REST OF MY LIFE WITH YOU, HERE. AND IT DOESN'T GET ANY BETTER THAN THIS, THIS--THIS CASTLE.
PRINCESSES NEED TO BE PROTECTED.
RAPUNZEL? RAPUNZEL?
I... I, WOW.
I LOVE YOU EUGENE...BUT I CAN'T.

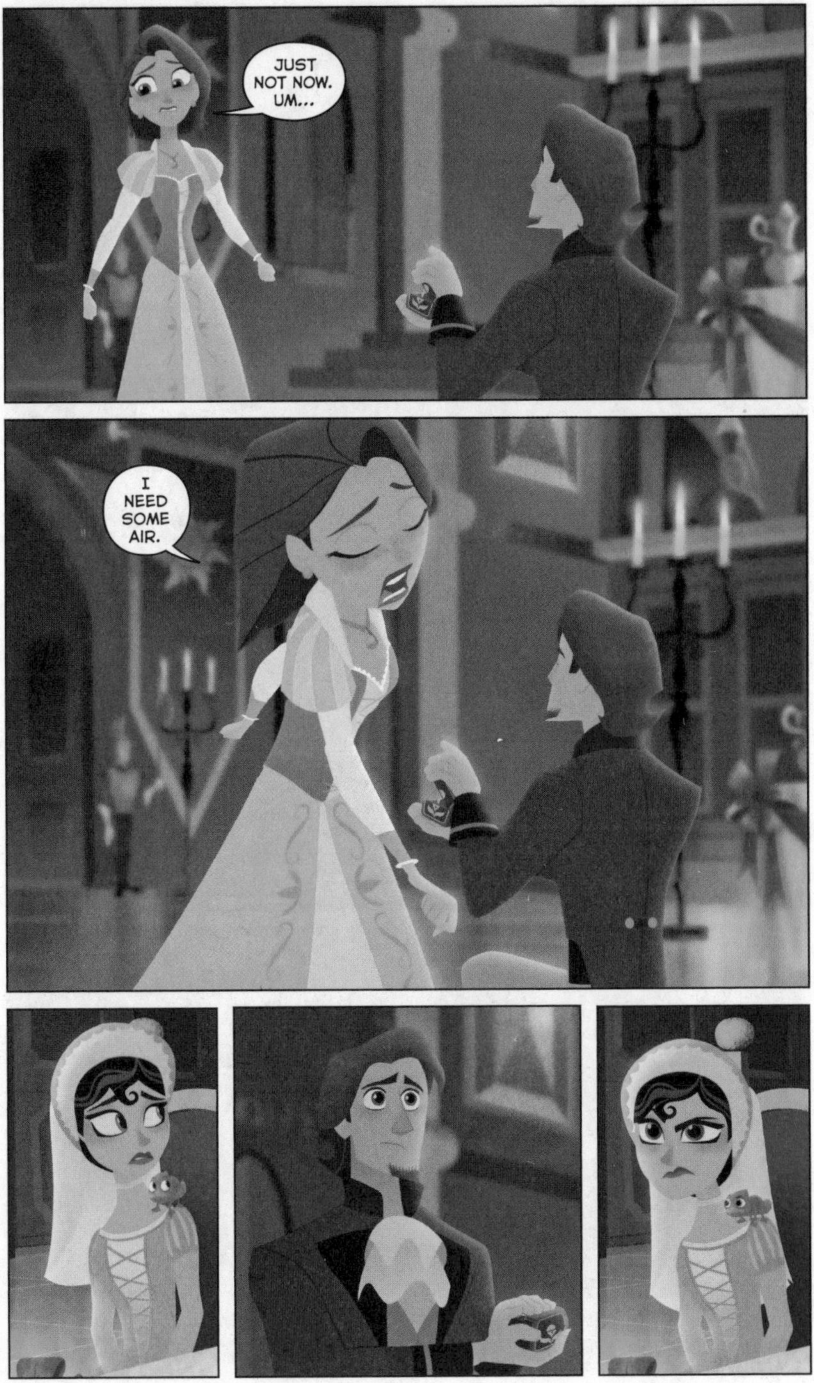
JUST NOT NOW. UM...
I NEED SOME AIR.

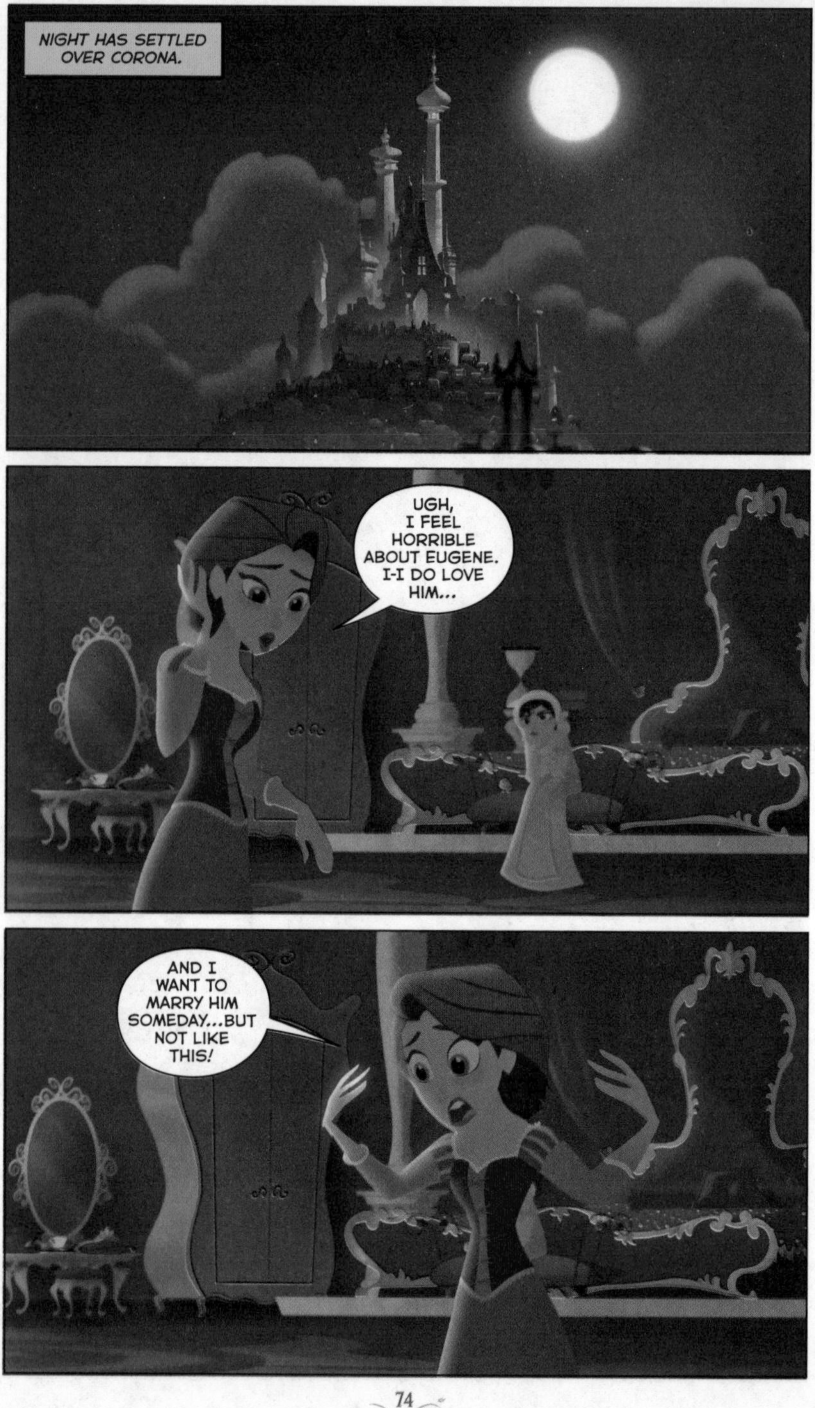
NIGHT HAS SETTLED OVER CORONA.
UGH, I FEEL HORRIBLE ABOUT EUGENE. I-I DO LOVE HIM...
AND I WANT TO MARRY HIM SOMEDAY...BUT NOT LIKE THIS!

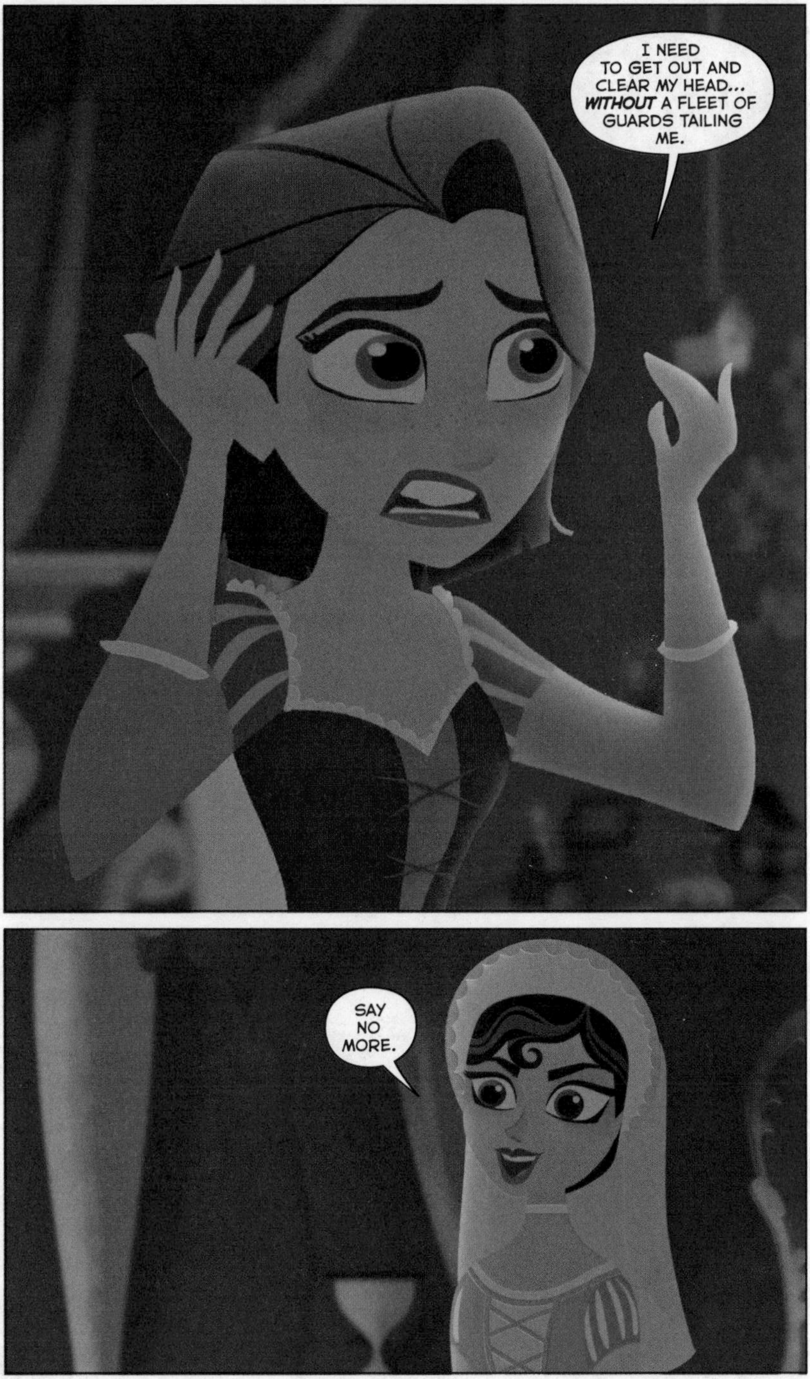
I NEED TO GET OUT AND CLEAR MY HEAD... *WITHOUT* A FLEET OF GUARDS TAILING ME.
SAY NO MORE.

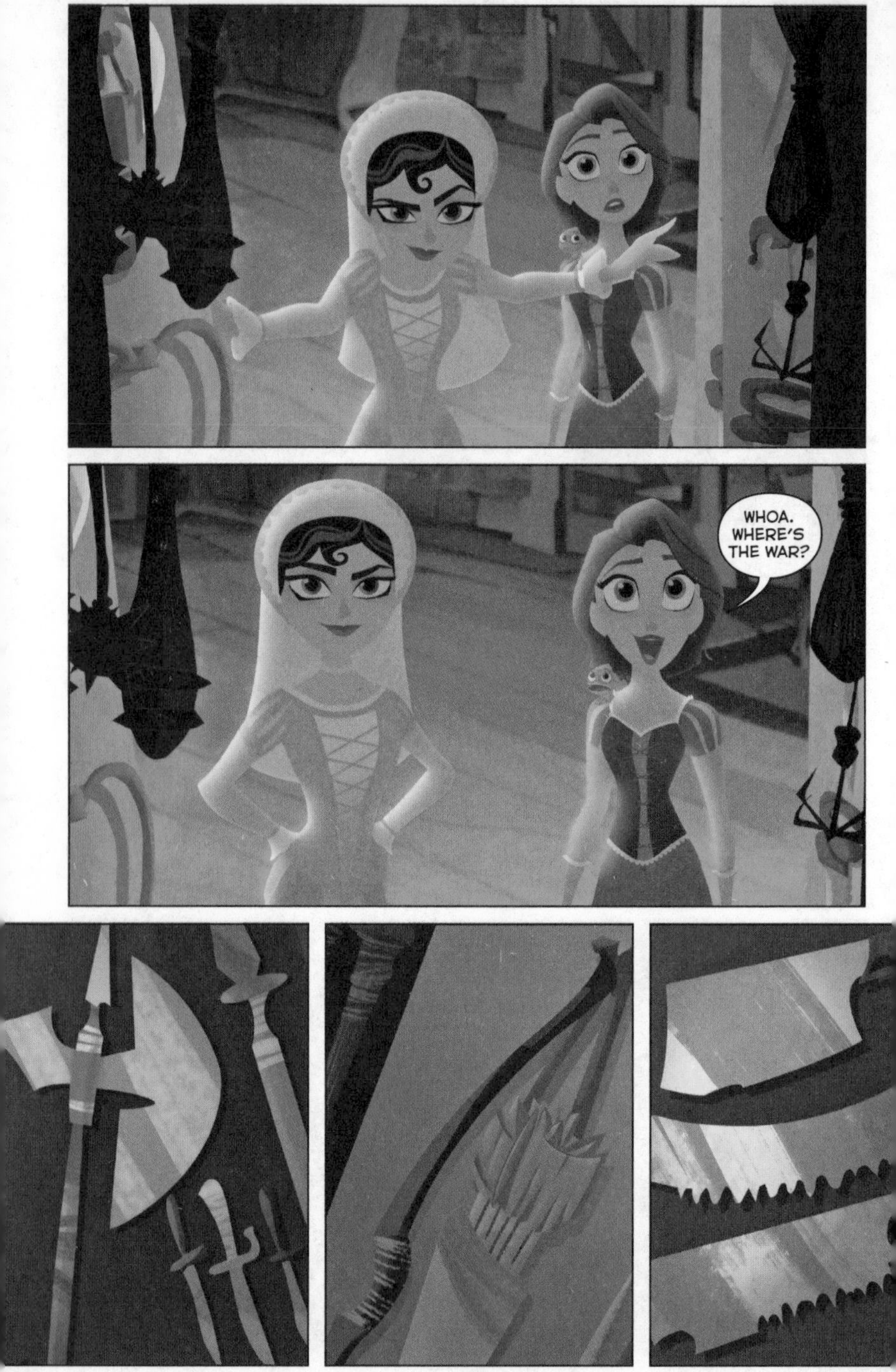
WHOA. WHERE'S THE WAR?

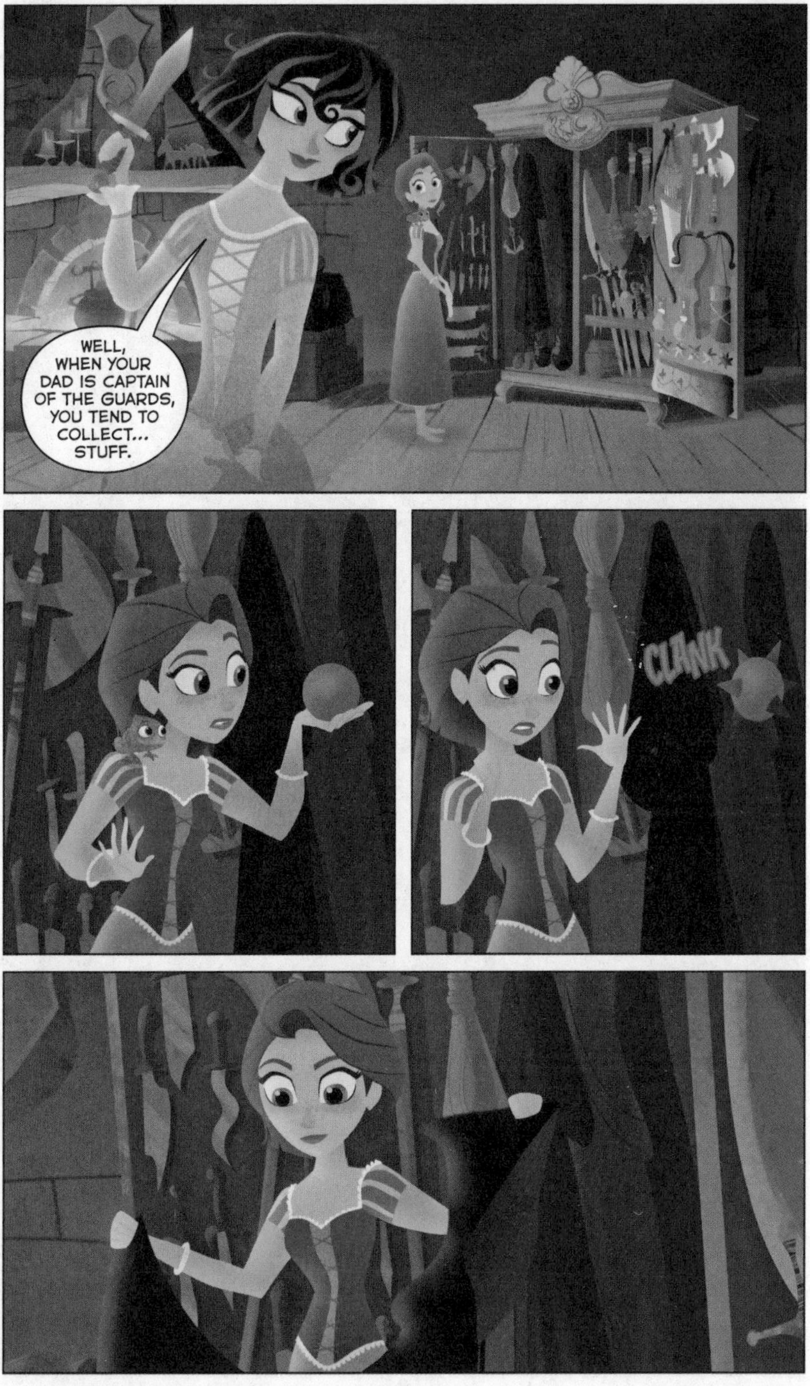
WELL, WHEN YOUR DAD IS CAPTAIN OF THE GUARDS, YOU TEND TO COLLECT... STUFF.
CLANK

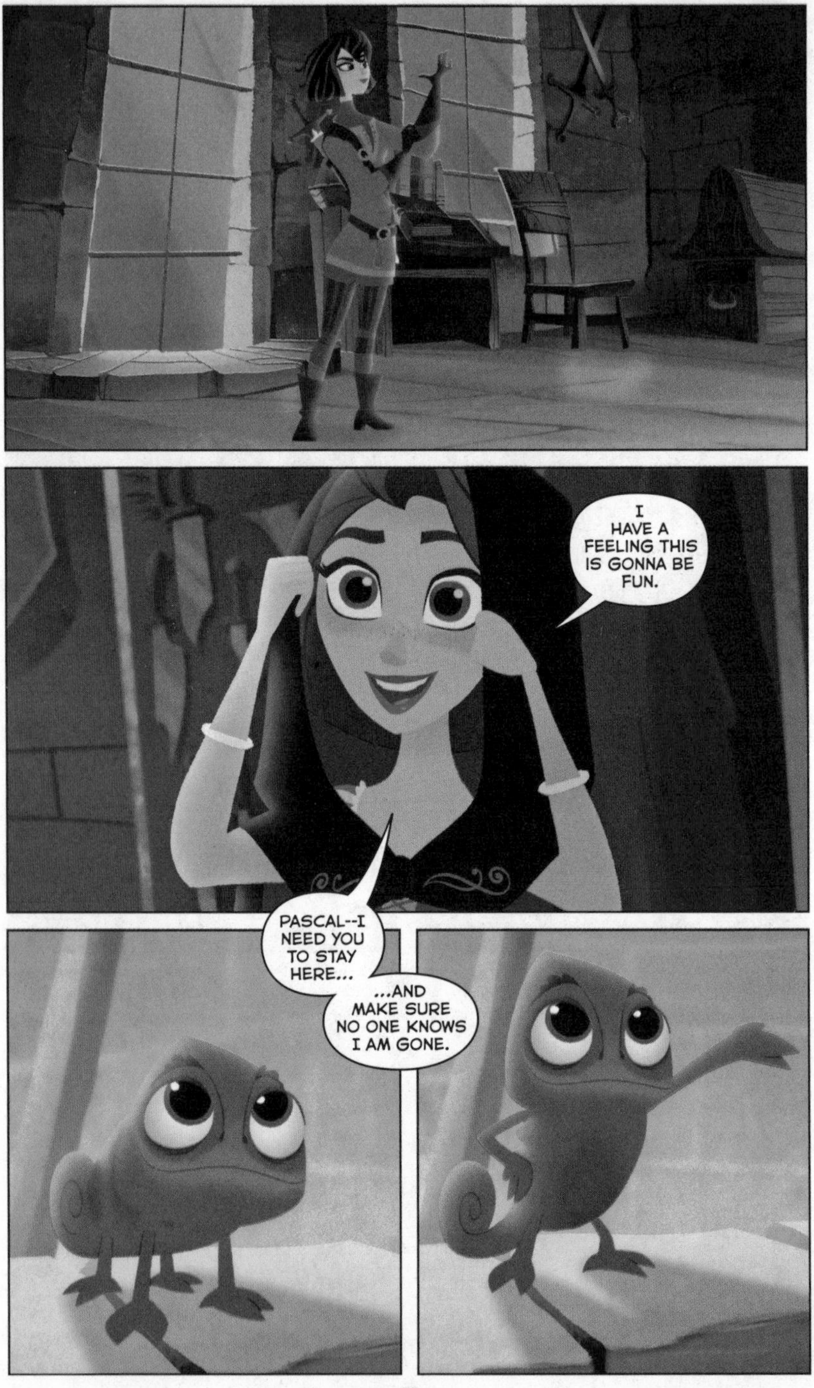
I HAVE A FEELING THIS IS GONNA BE FUN.
PASCAL--I NEED YOU TO STAY HERE...
...AND MAKE SURE NO ONE KNOWS I AM GONE.

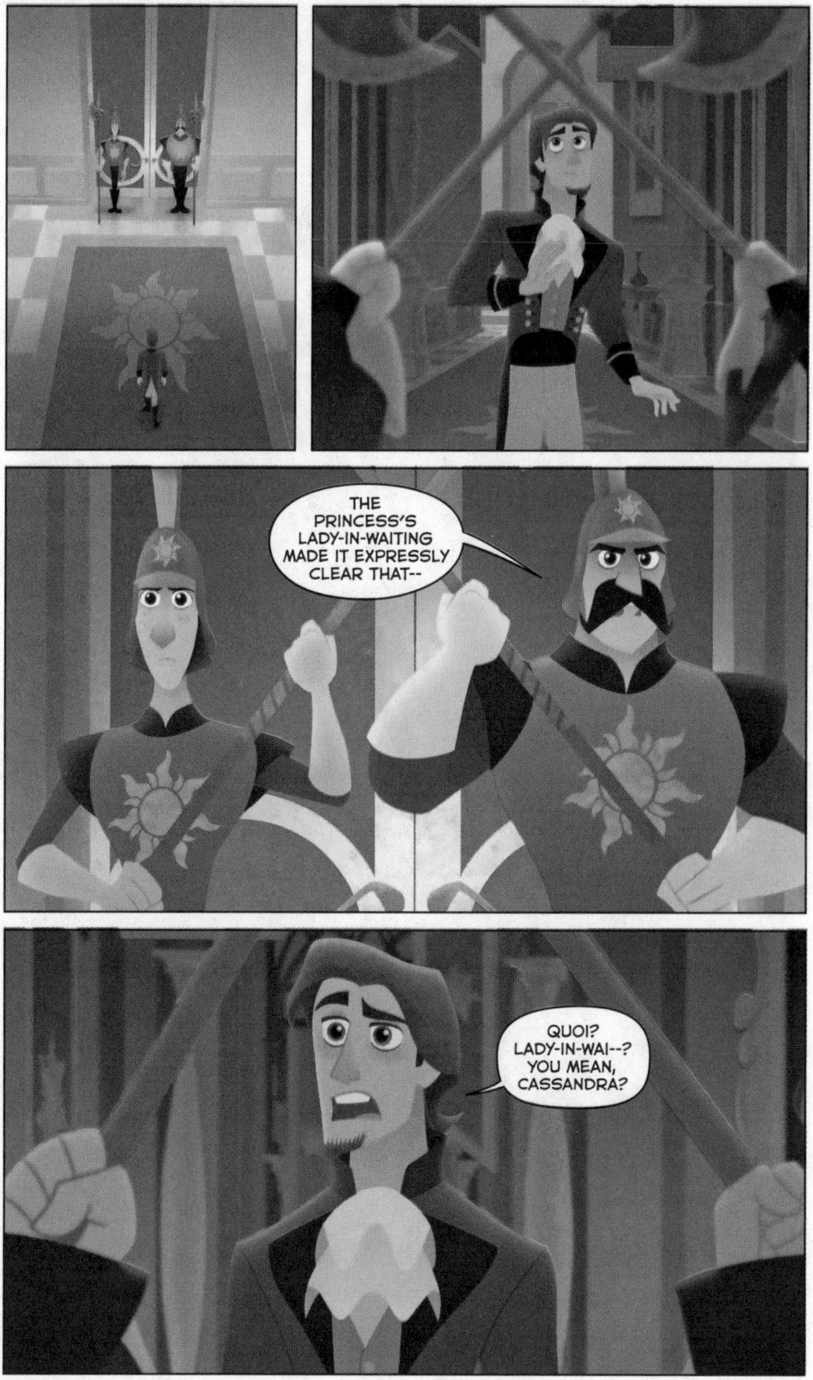
THE PRINCESS'S LADY-IN-WAITING MADE IT EXPRESSLY CLEAR THAT--
QUOI? LADY-IN-WAI--? YOU MEAN, CASSANDRA?

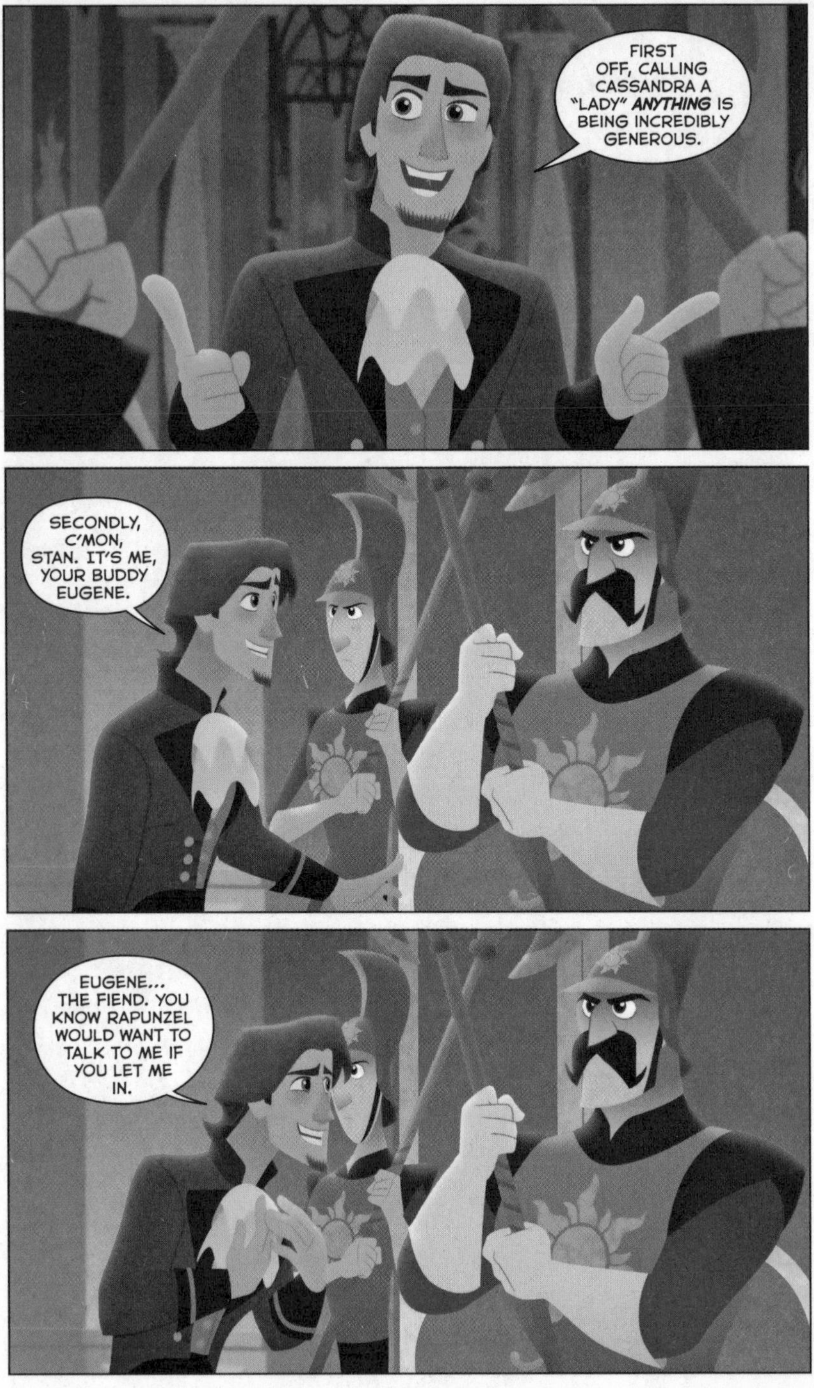
FIRST OFF, CALLING CASSANDRA A "LADY" ANYTHING IS BEING INCREDIBLY GENEROUS.
SECONDLY, C'MON, STAN. IT'S ME, YOUR BUDDY EUGENE.
EUGENE... THE FIEND. YOU KNOW RAPUNZEL WOULD WANT TO TALK TO ME IF YOU LET ME IN.

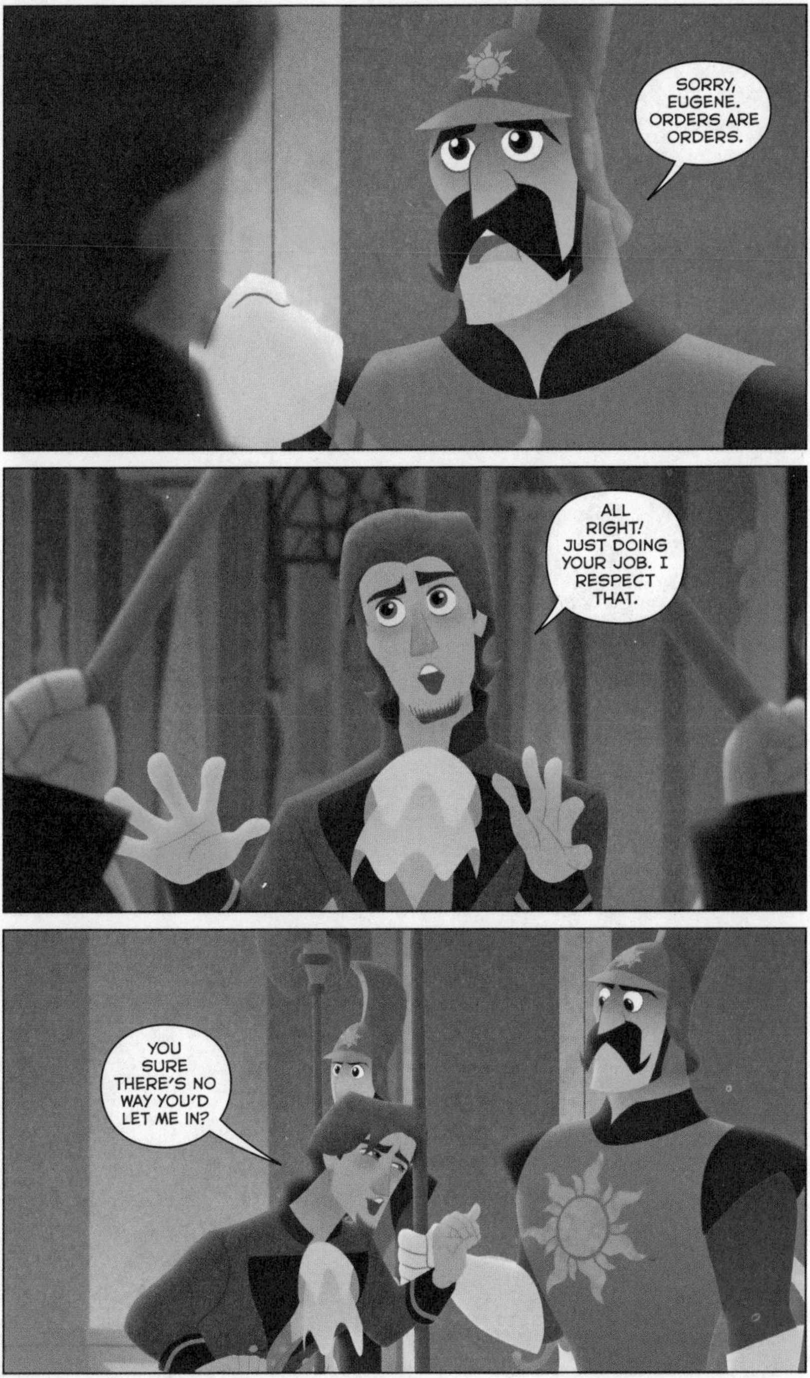
SORRY, EUGENE. ORDERS ARE ORDERS.
ALL RIGHT! JUST DOING YOUR JOB. I RESPECT THAT.
YOU SURE THERE'S NO WAY YOU'D LET ME IN?

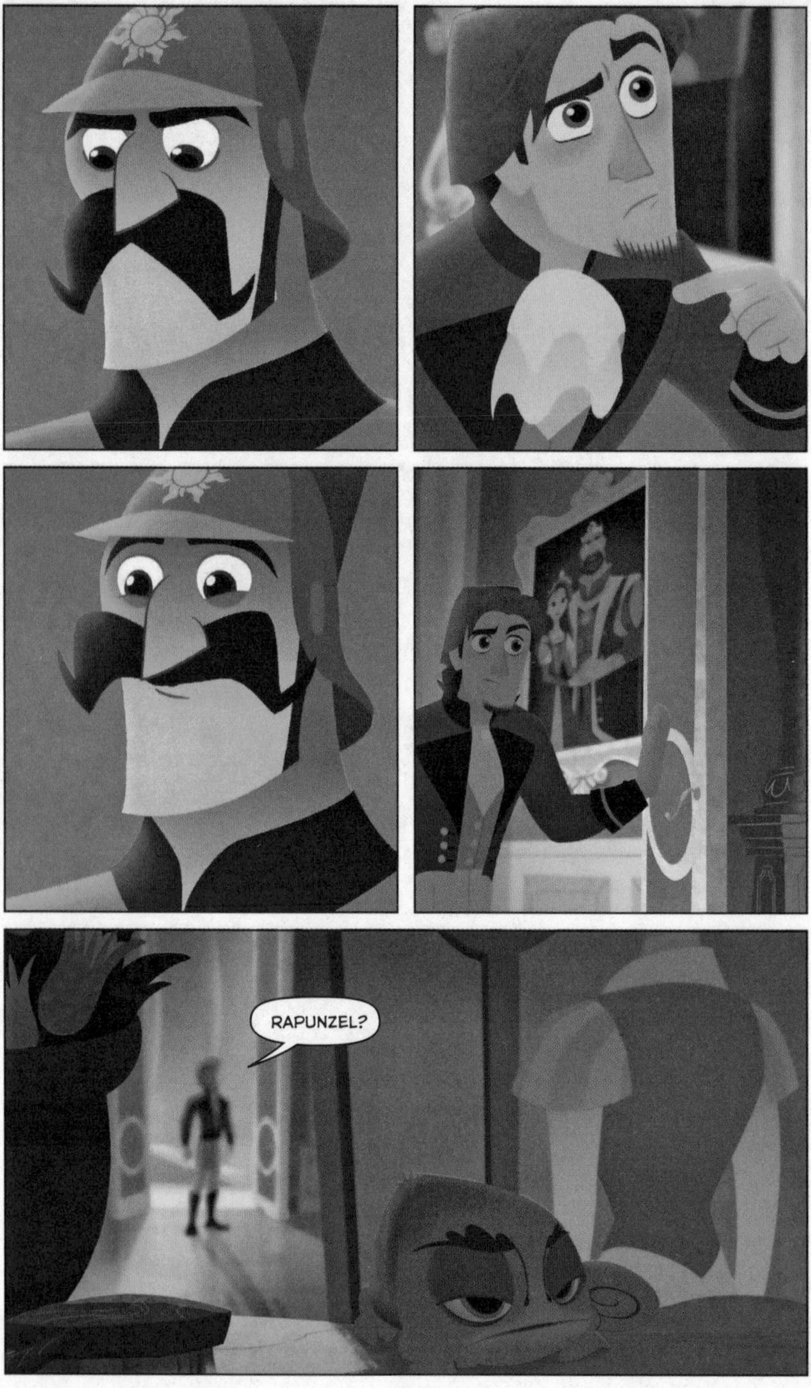
RAPUNZEL?

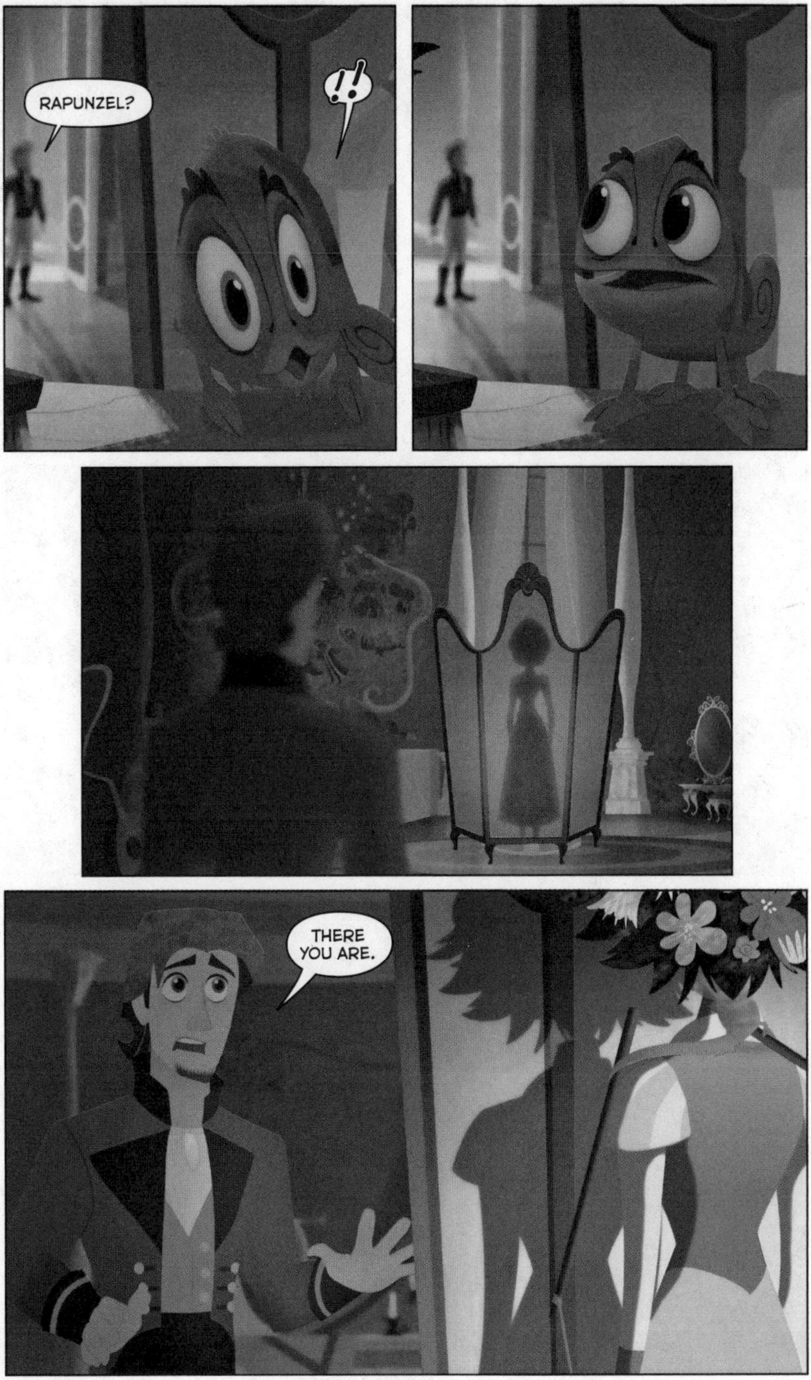
RAPUNZEL?
!!
THERE YOU ARE.

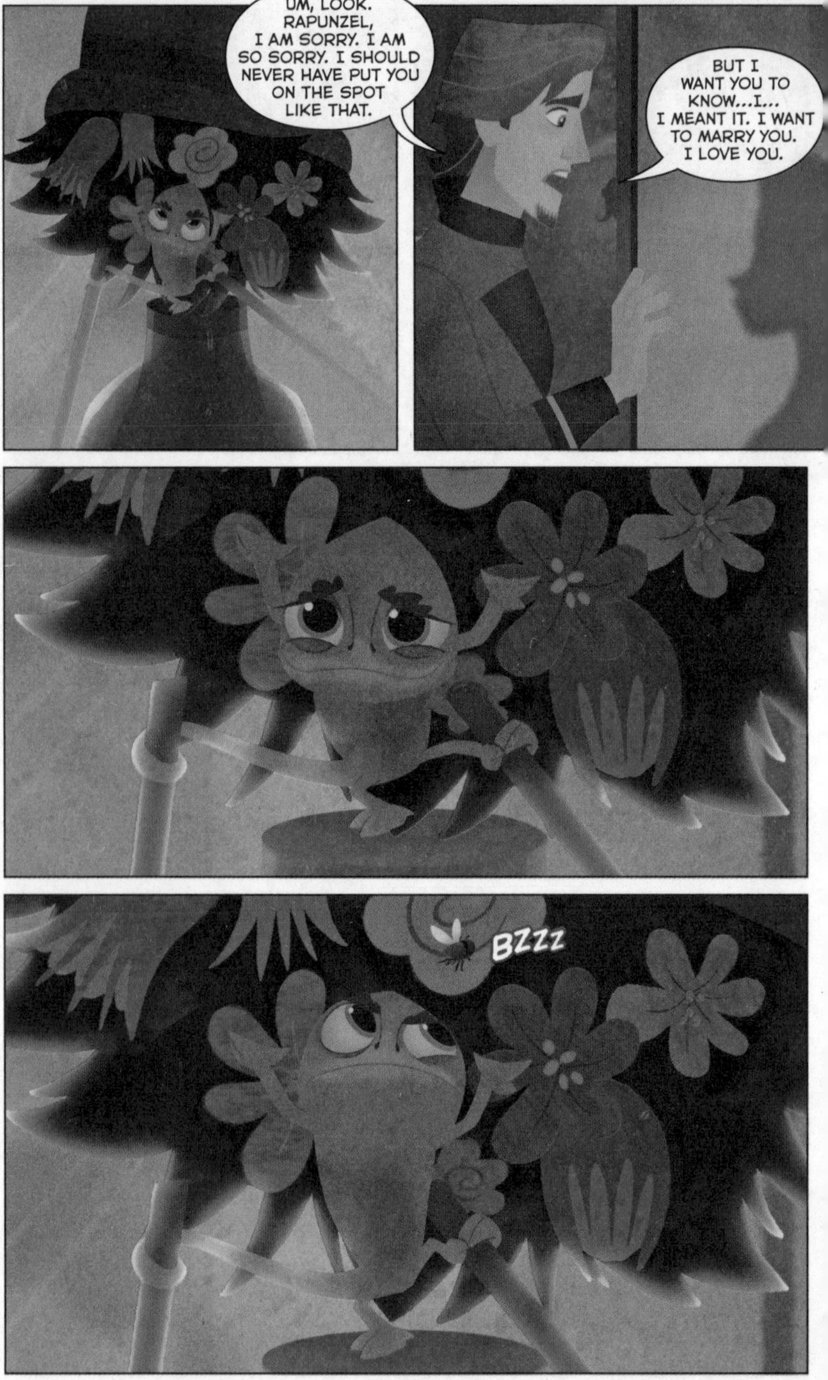
UM, LOOK. RAPUNZEL, I AM SORRY. I AM SO SORRY. I SHOULD NEVER HAVE PUT YOU ON THE SPOT LIKE THAT.
BUT I WANT YOU TO KNOW...I... I MEANT IT. I WANT TO MARRY YOU. I LOVE YOU.
BZZZ

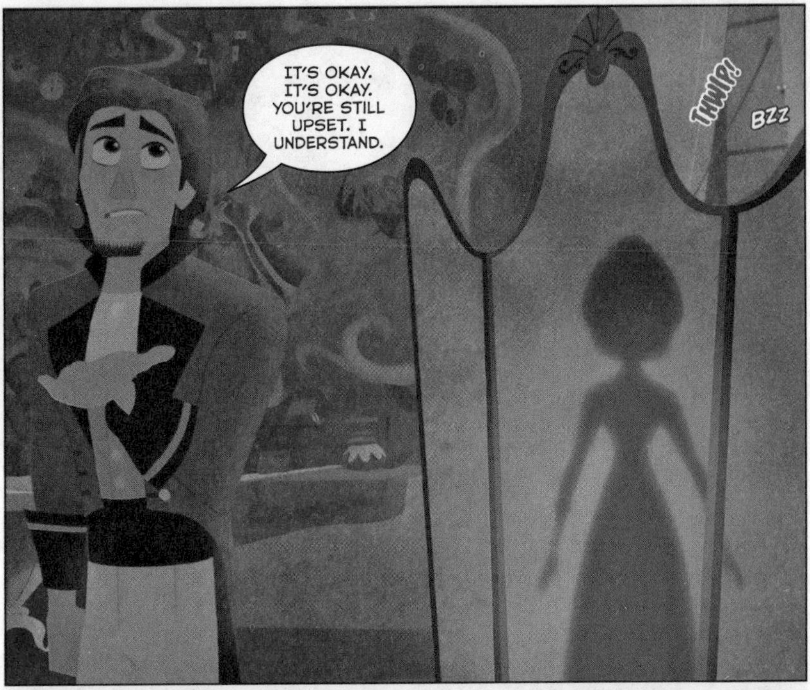
IT'S OKAY. IT'S OKAY. YOU'RE STILL UPSET. I UNDERSTAND.
THWIP!
BZZ

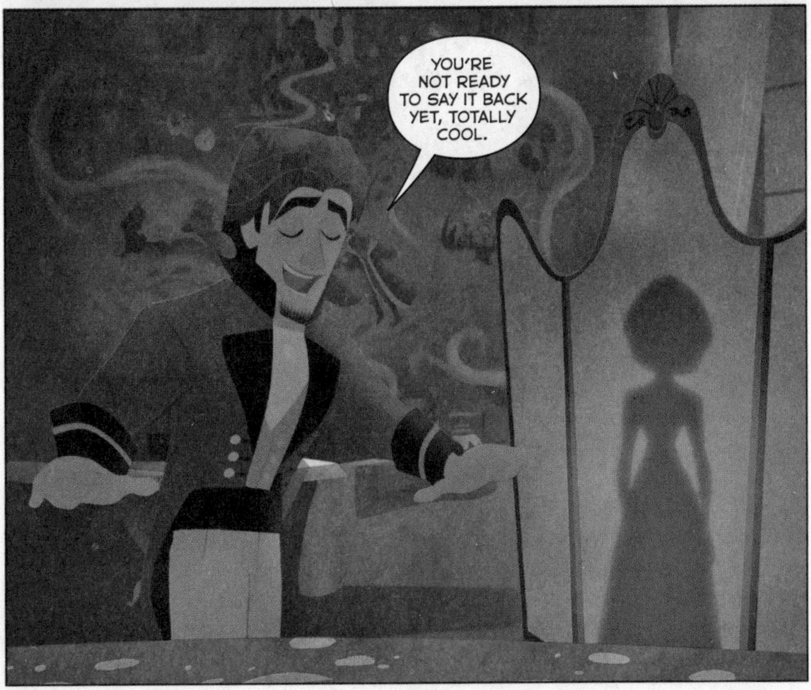
YOU'RE NOT READY TO SAY IT BACK YET, TOTALLY COOL.

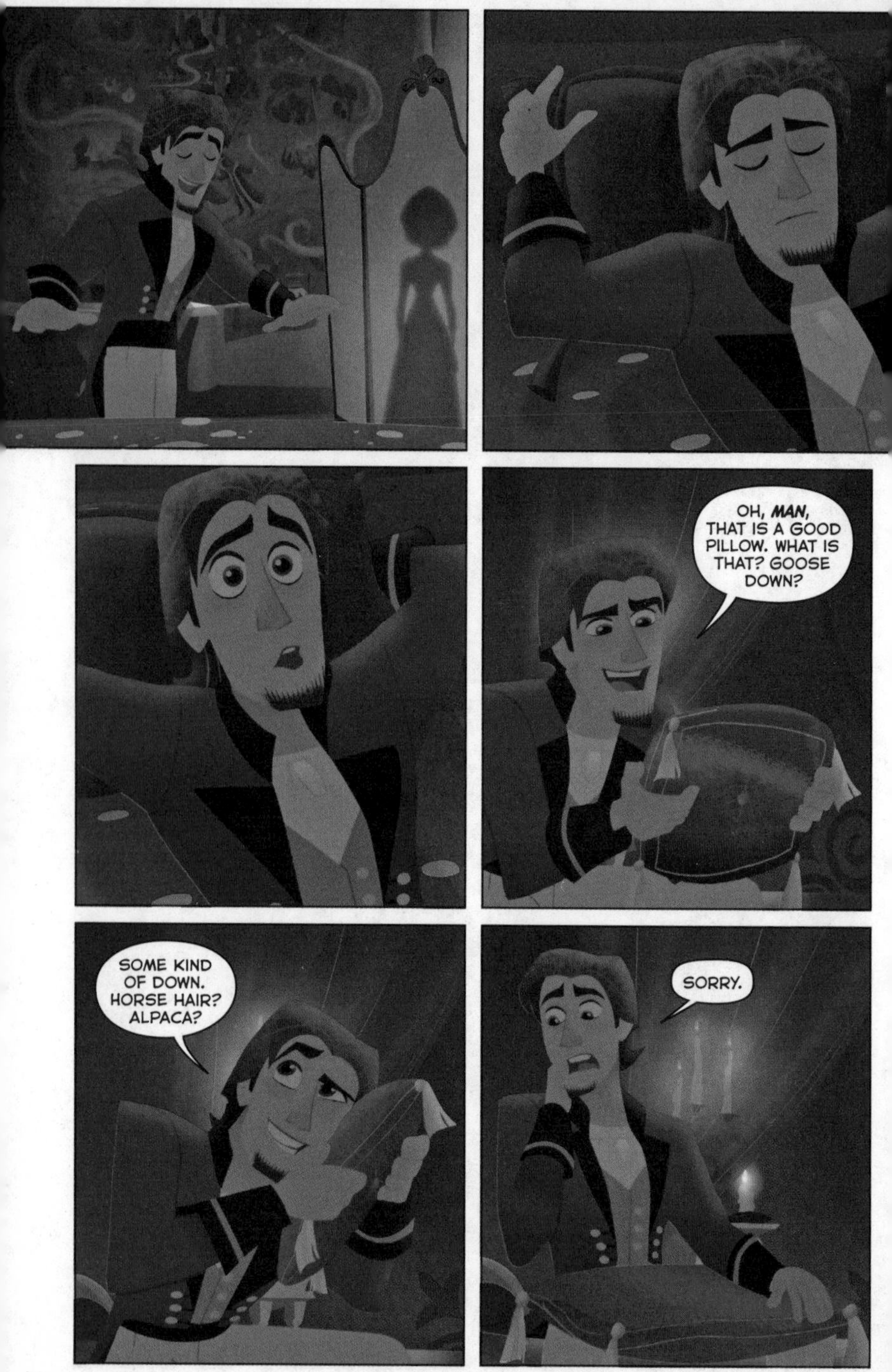
OH, *MAN*, THAT IS A GOOD PILLOW. WHAT IS THAT? GOOSE DOWN?
SOME KIND OF DOWN. HORSE HAIR? ALPACA?
SORRY.

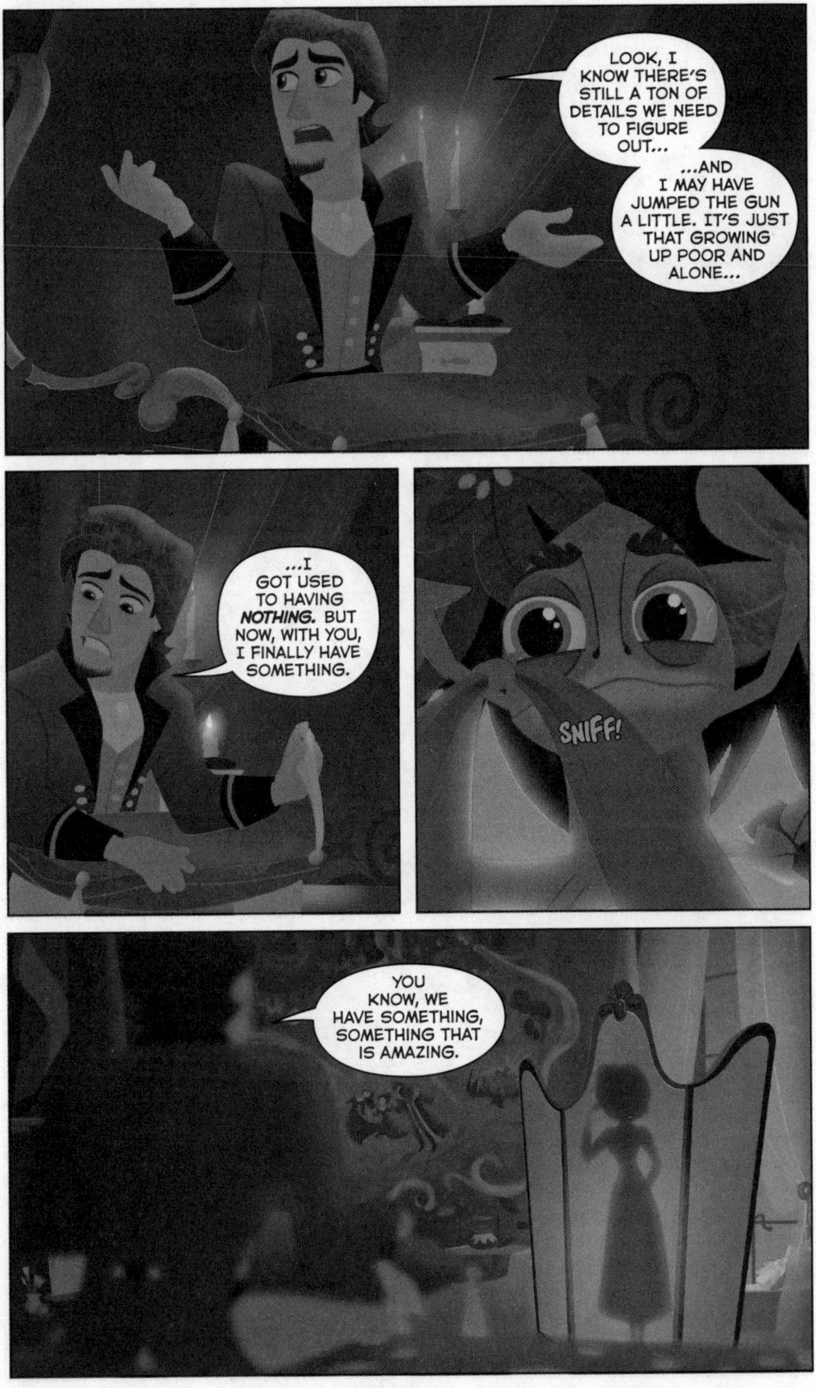
LOOK, I KNOW THERE'S STILL A TON OF DETAILS WE NEED TO FIGURE OUT...
...AND I MAY HAVE JUMPED THE GUN A LITTLE. IT'S JUST THAT GROWING UP POOR AND ALONE...
...I GOT USED TO HAVING *NOTHING.* BUT NOW, WITH YOU, I FINALLY HAVE SOMETHING.
SNIFF!
YOU KNOW, WE HAVE SOMETHING, SOMETHING THAT IS AMAZING.

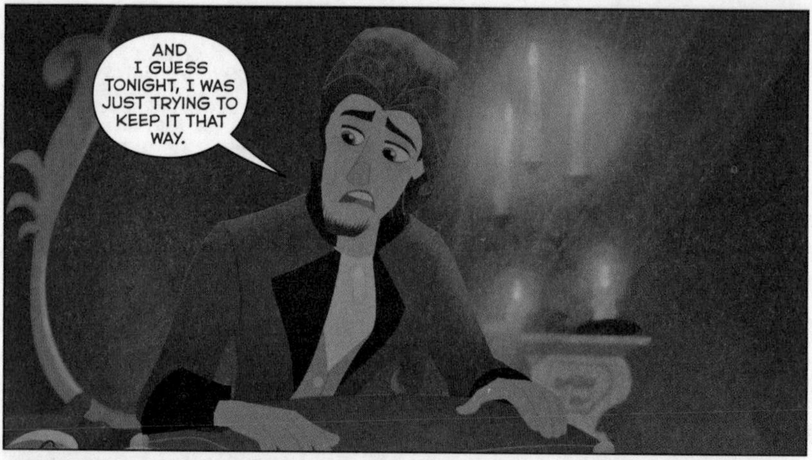

AND I GUESS TONIGHT, I WAS JUST TRYING TO KEEP IT THAT WAY.

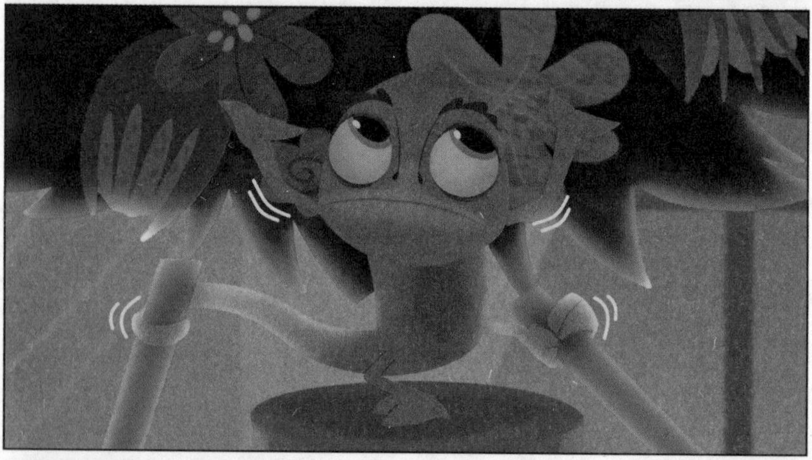

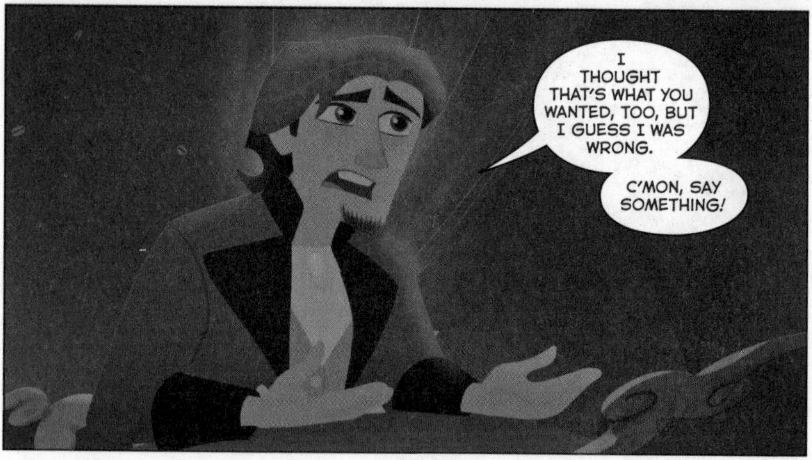

I THOUGHT THAT'S WHAT YOU WANTED, TOO, BUT I GUESS I WAS WRONG.
C'MON, SAY SOMETHING!

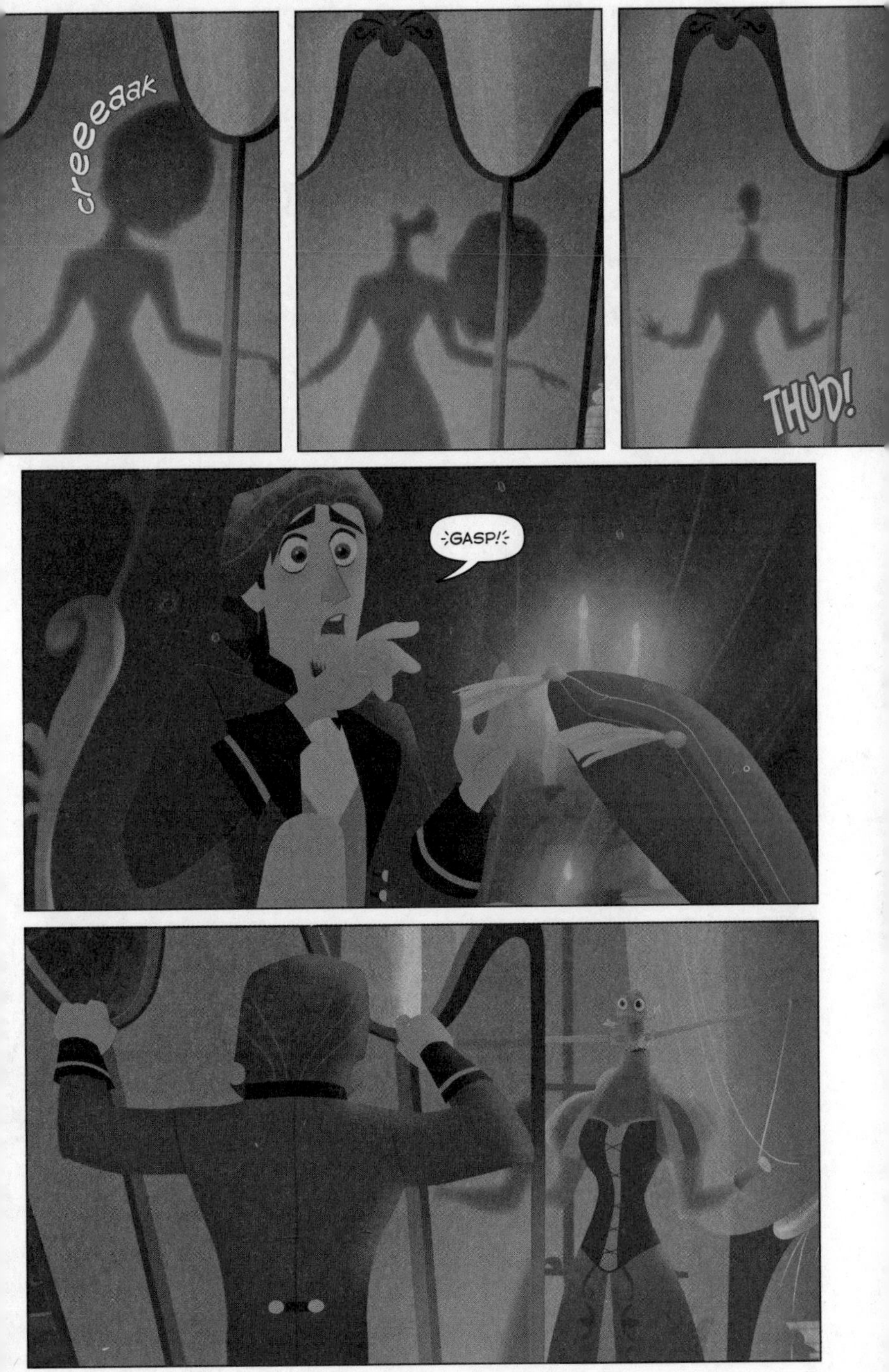
creeeaak
THUD!
GASP!

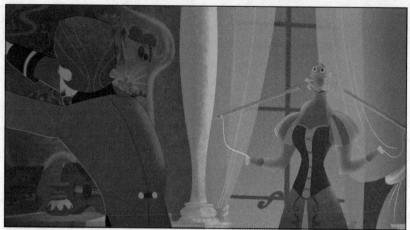

FANTASTIC.

I JUST POURED MY HEART OUT TO A FROG!

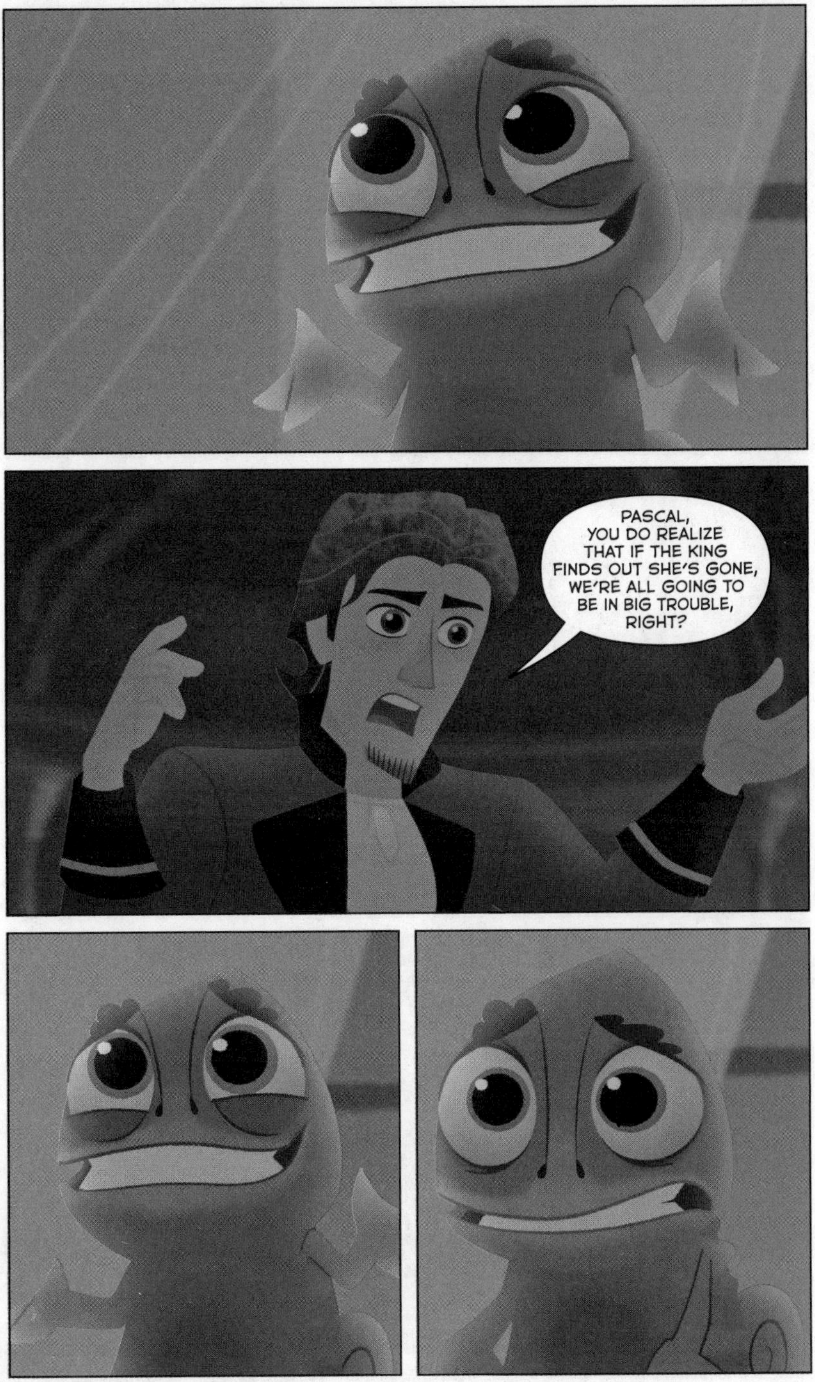
PASCAL, YOU DO REALIZE THAT IF THE KING FINDS OUT SHE'S GONE, WE'RE ALL GOING TO BE IN BIG TROUBLE, RIGHT?

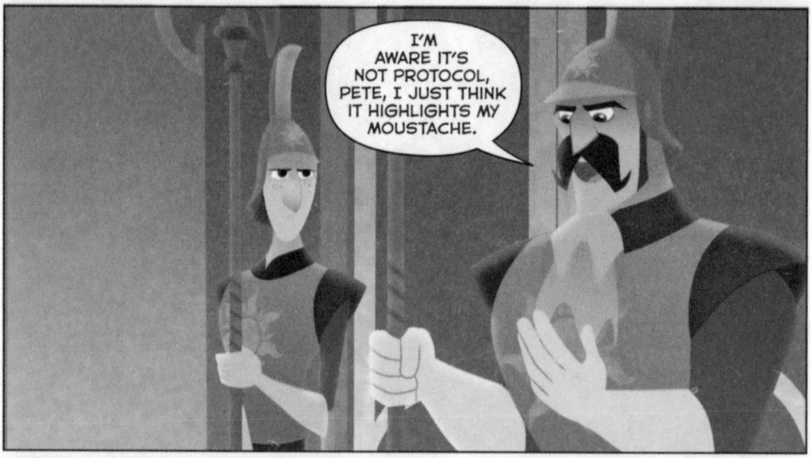
I'M AWARE IT'S NOT PROTOCOL, PETE, I JUST THINK IT HIGHLIGHTS MY MOUSTACHE.

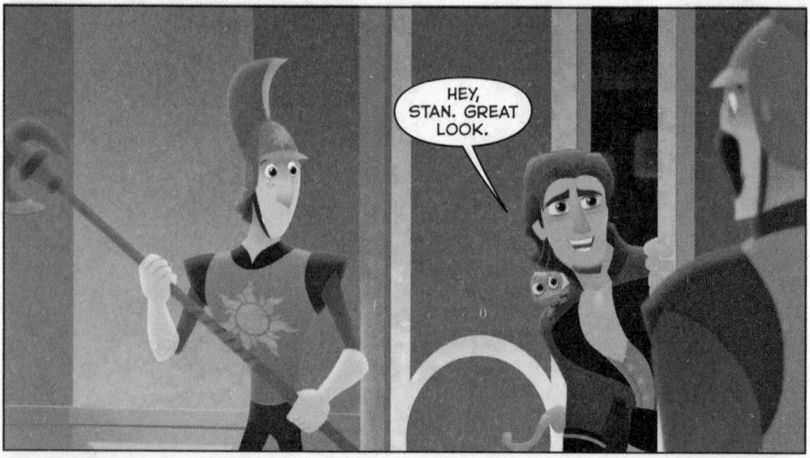
HEY, STAN. GREAT LOOK.

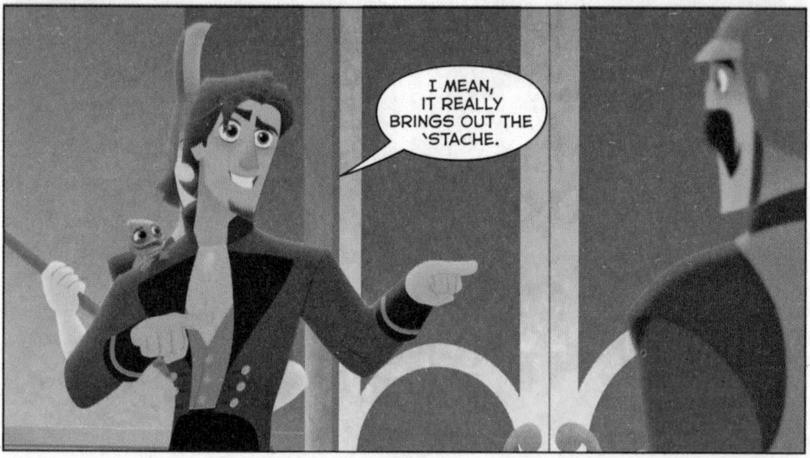
I MEAN, IT REALLY BRINGS OUT THE 'STACHE.

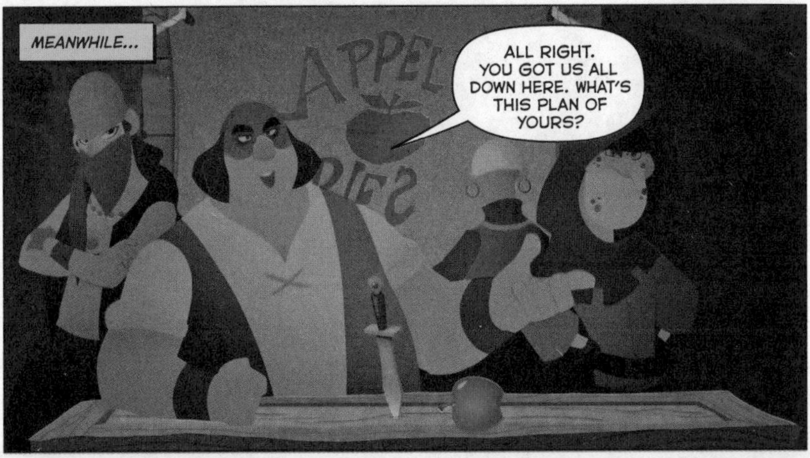
MEANWHILE...
APPEL
ALL RIGHT. YOU GOT US ALL DOWN HERE. WHAT'S THIS PLAN OF YOURS?

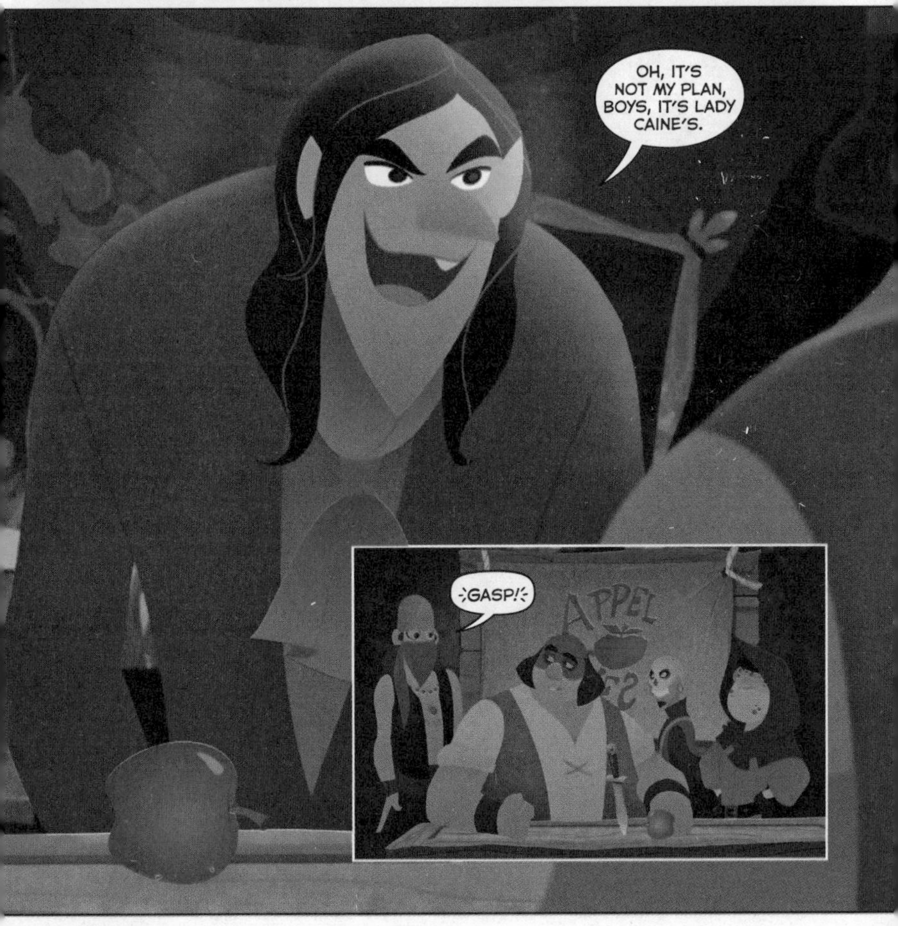
OH, IT'S NOT MY PLAN, BOYS, IT'S LADY CAINE'S.
GASP!
APPEL

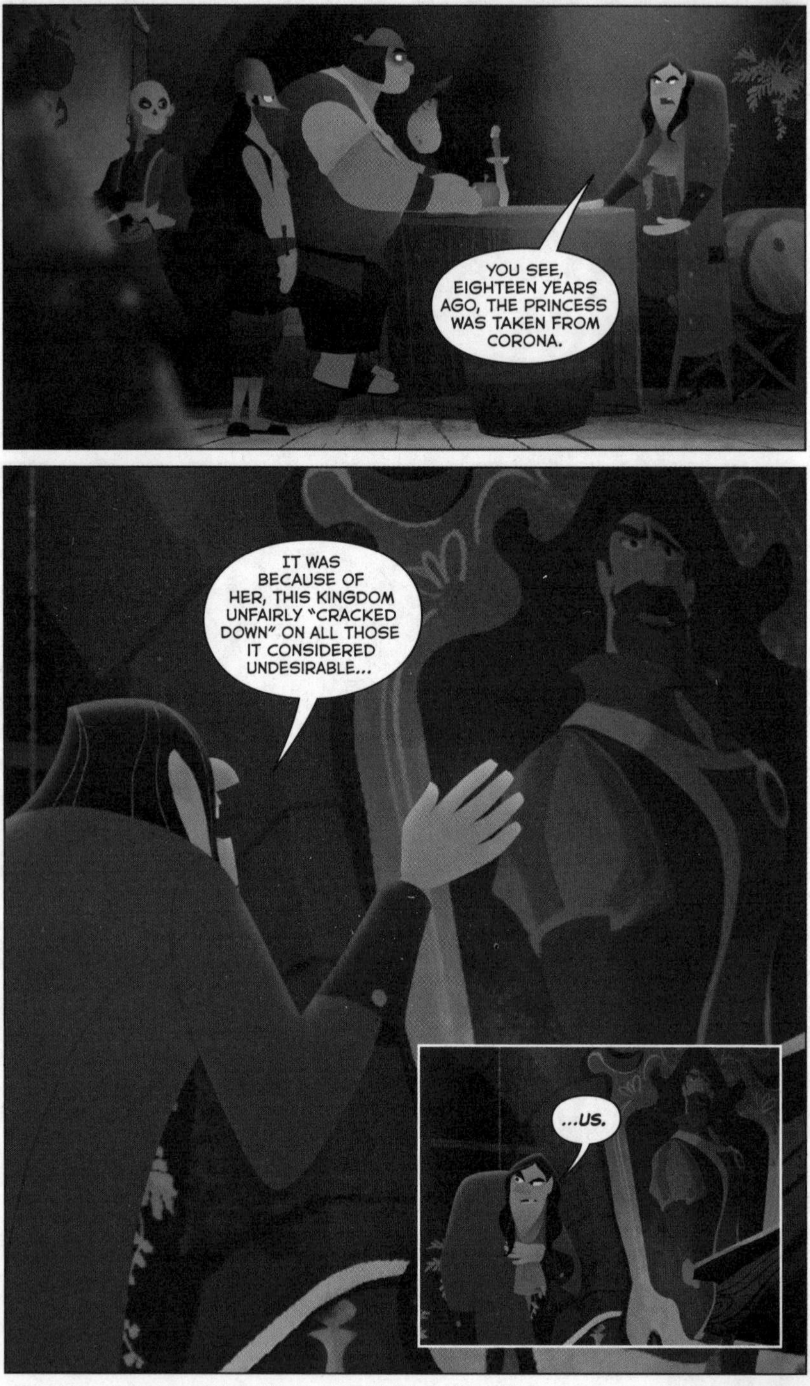
YOU SEE, EIGHTEEN YEARS AGO, THE PRINCESS WAS TAKEN FROM CORONA.
IT WAS BECAUSE OF HER, THIS KINGDOM UNFAIRLY "CRACKED DOWN" ON ALL THOSE IT CONSIDERED UNDESIRABLE...
...US.

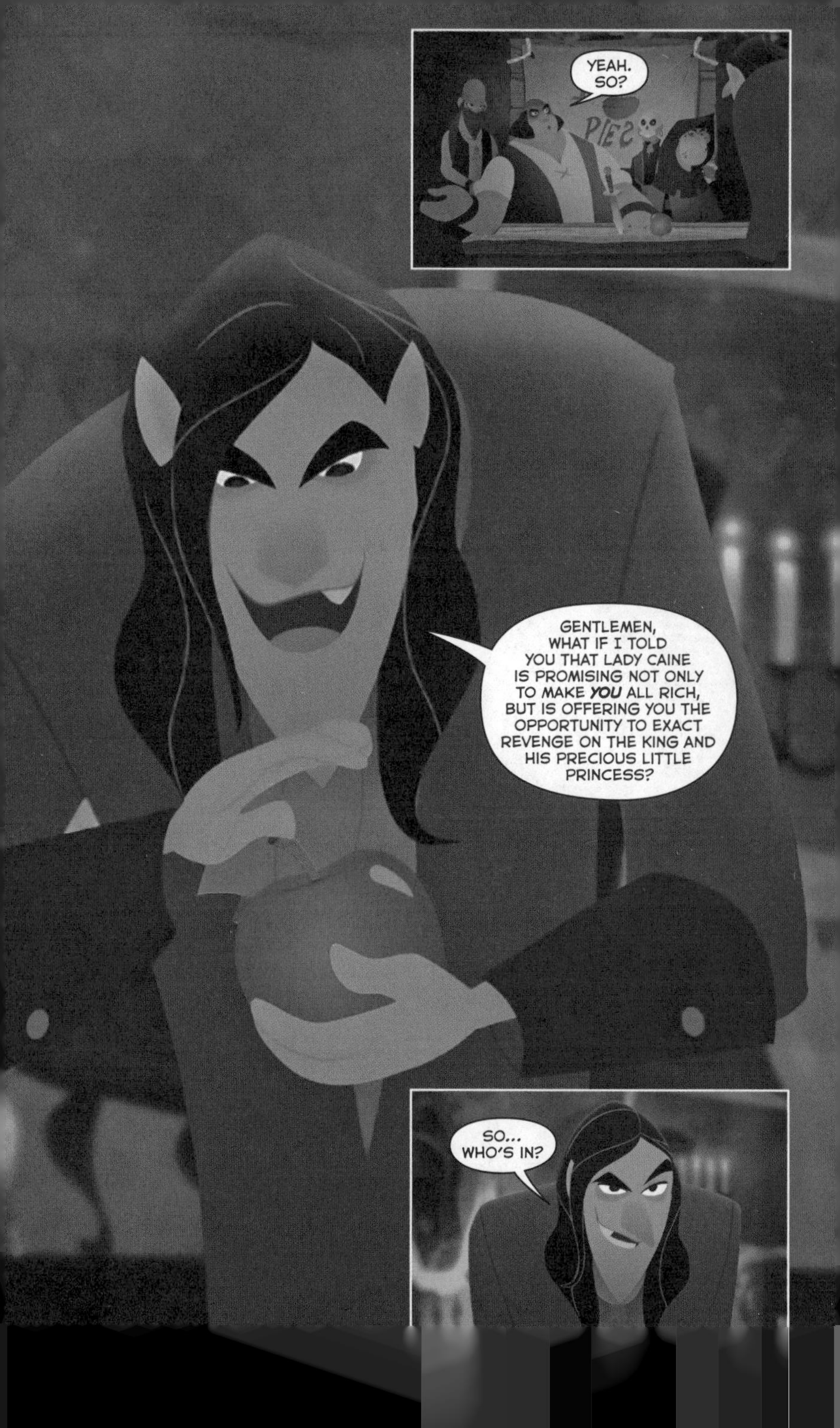
YEAH. SO?
GENTLEMEN, WHAT IF I TOLD YOU THAT LADY CAINE IS PROMISING NOT ONLY TO MAKE *YOU* ALL RICH, BUT IS OFFERING YOU THE OPPORTUNITY TO EXACT REVENGE ON THE KING AND HIS PRECIOUS LITTLE PRINCESS?
SO... WHO'S IN?

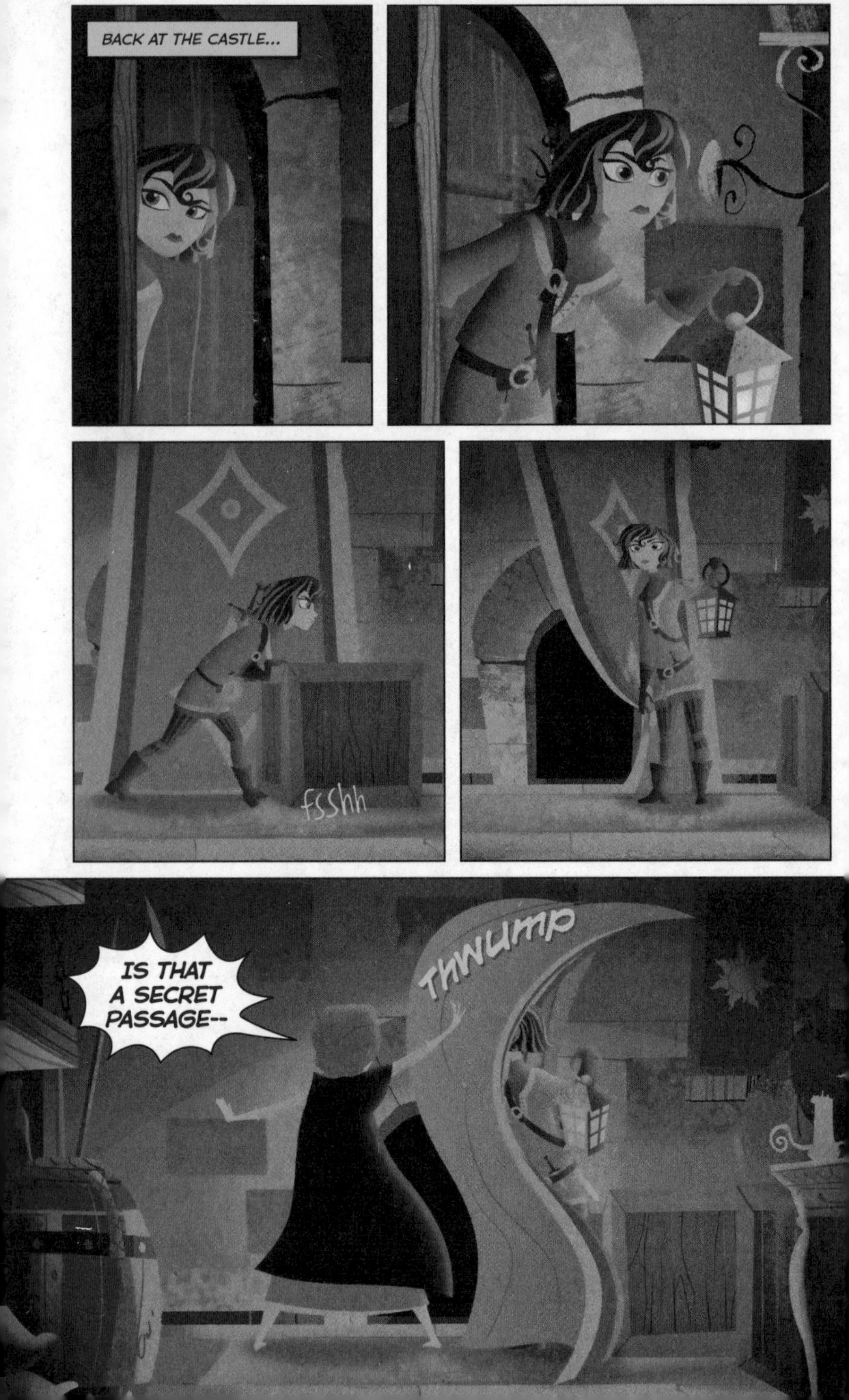

BACK AT THE CASTLE...
fsshh
IS THAT A SECRET PASSAGE--
THWUMP

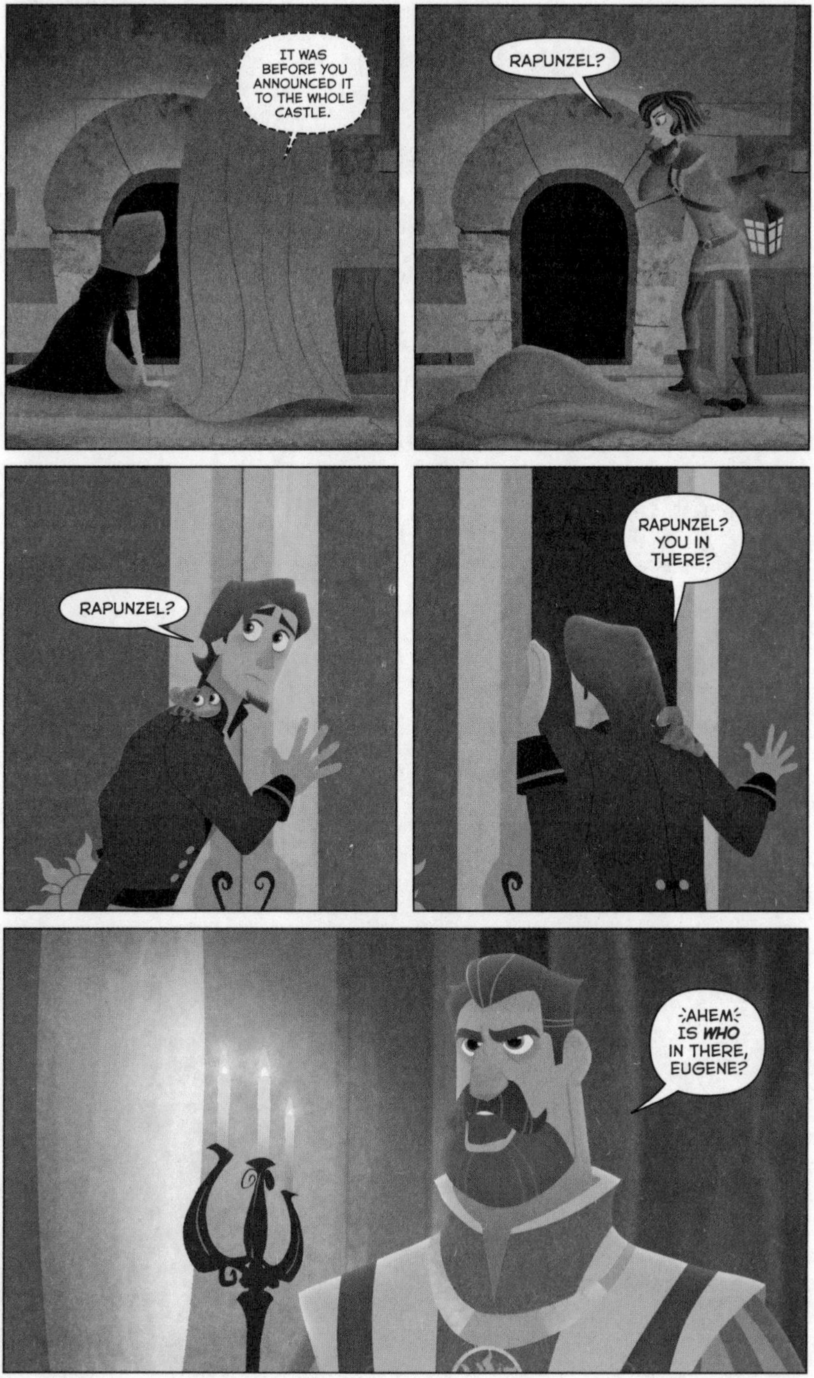
IT WAS BEFORE YOU ANNOUNCED IT TO THE WHOLE CASTLE.
RAPUNZEL?
RAPUNZEL?
RAPUNZEL? YOU IN THERE?
-AHEM- IS WHO IN THERE, EUGENE?

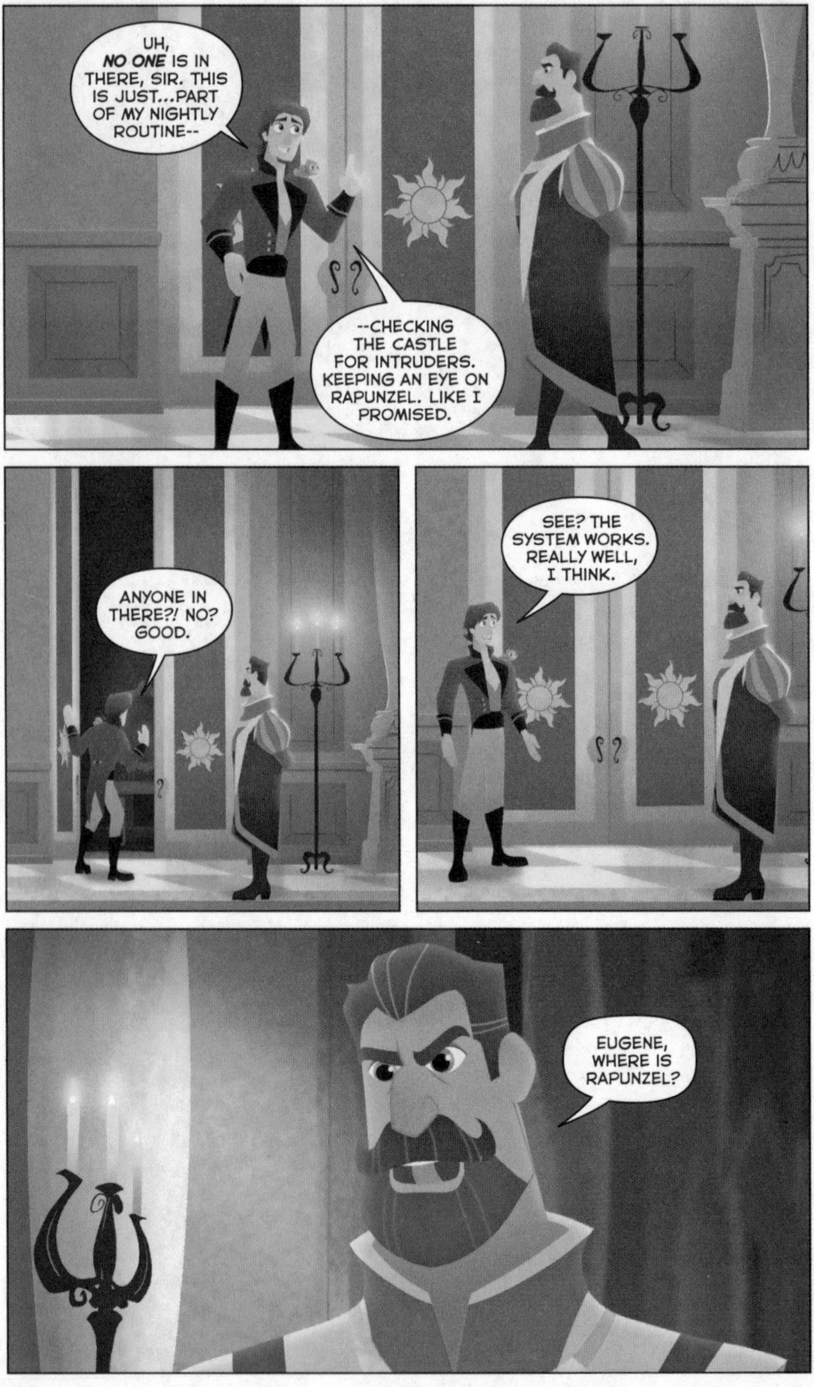
UH, NO ONE IS IN THERE, SIR. THIS IS JUST...PART OF MY NIGHTLY ROUTINE--
--CHECKING THE CASTLE FOR INTRUDERS. KEEPING AN EYE ON RAPUNZEL. LIKE I PROMISED.
ANYONE IN THERE?! NO? GOOD.
SEE? THE SYSTEM WORKS. REALLY WELL, I THINK.
EUGENE, WHERE IS RAPUNZEL?

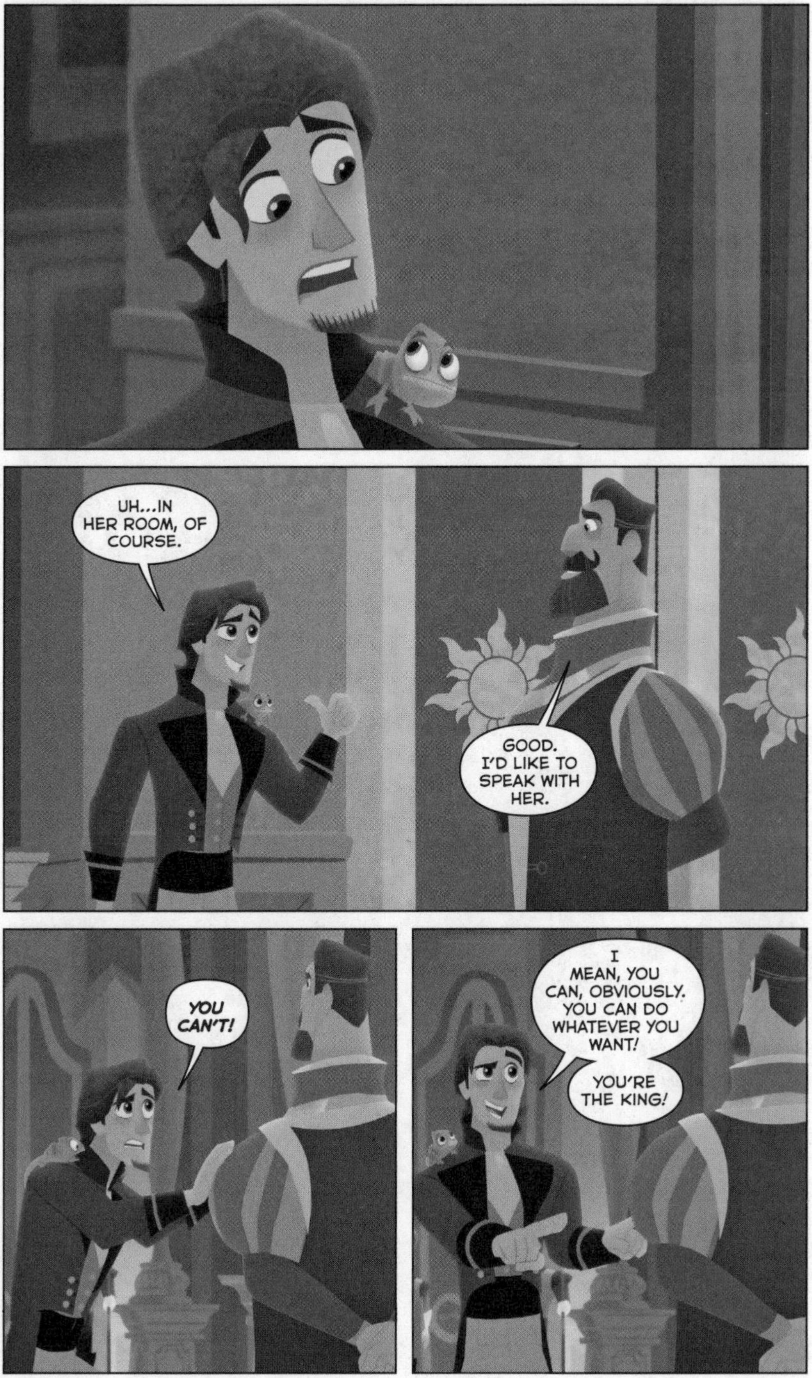
UH...IN HER ROOM, OF COURSE.
GOOD. I'D LIKE TO SPEAK WITH HER.
YOU CAN'T!
I MEAN, YOU CAN, OBVIOUSLY. YOU CAN DO WHATEVER YOU *WANT!*
YOU'RE THE *KING!*

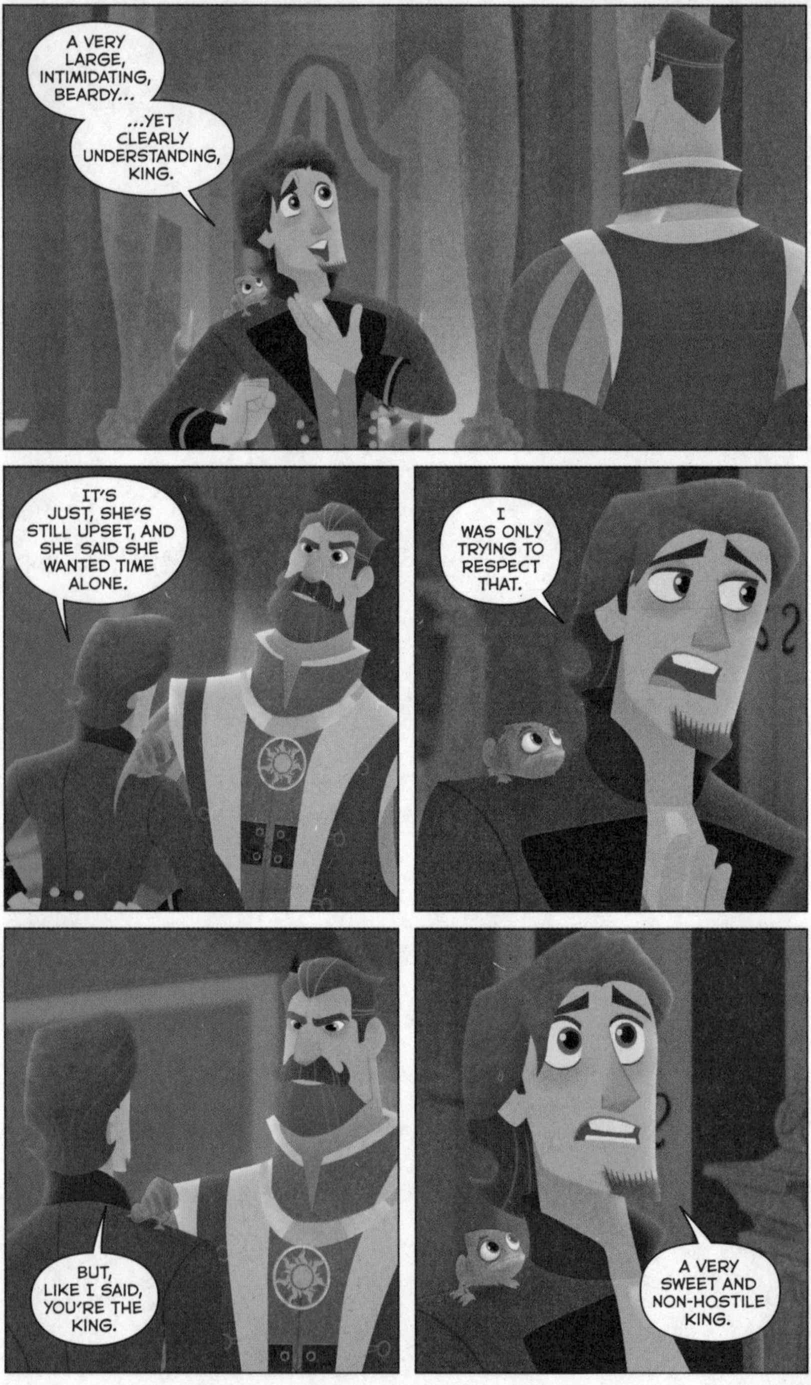
A VERY LARGE, INTIMIDATING, BEARDY...
...YET CLEARLY UNDERSTANDING, KING.
IT'S JUST, SHE'S STILL UPSET, AND SHE SAID SHE WANTED TIME ALONE.
I WAS ONLY TRYING TO RESPECT THAT.
BUT, LIKE I SAID, YOU'RE THE KING.
A VERY SWEET AND NON-HOSTILE KING.

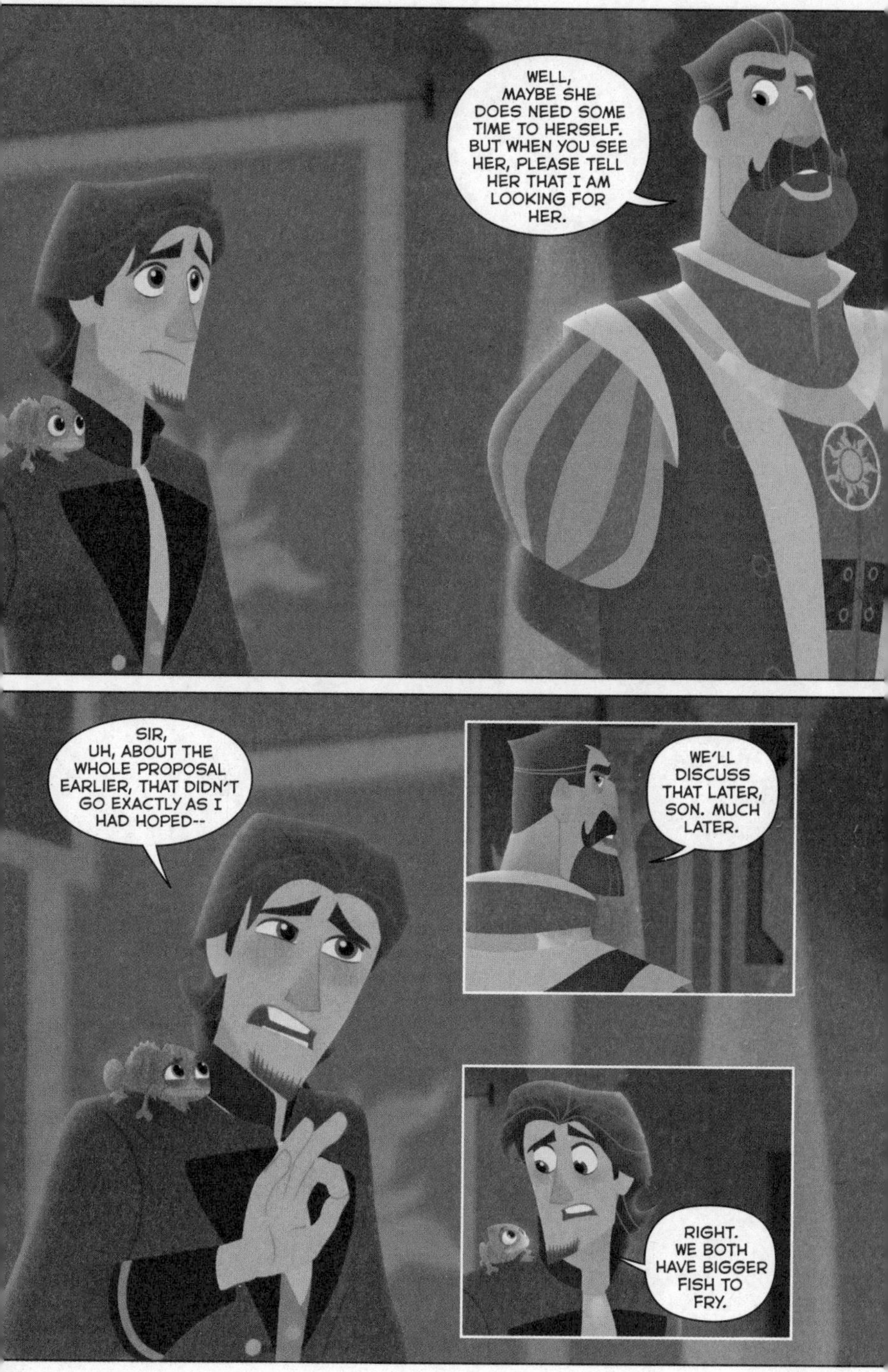
WELL, MAYBE SHE DOES NEED SOME TIME TO HERSELF. BUT WHEN YOU SEE HER, PLEASE TELL HER THAT I AM LOOKING FOR HER.
SIR, UH, ABOUT THE WHOLE PROPOSAL EARLIER, THAT DIDN'T GO EXACTLY AS I HAD HOPED--
WE'LL DISCUSS THAT LATER, SON. MUCH LATER.
RIGHT. WE BOTH HAVE BIGGER FISH TO FRY.

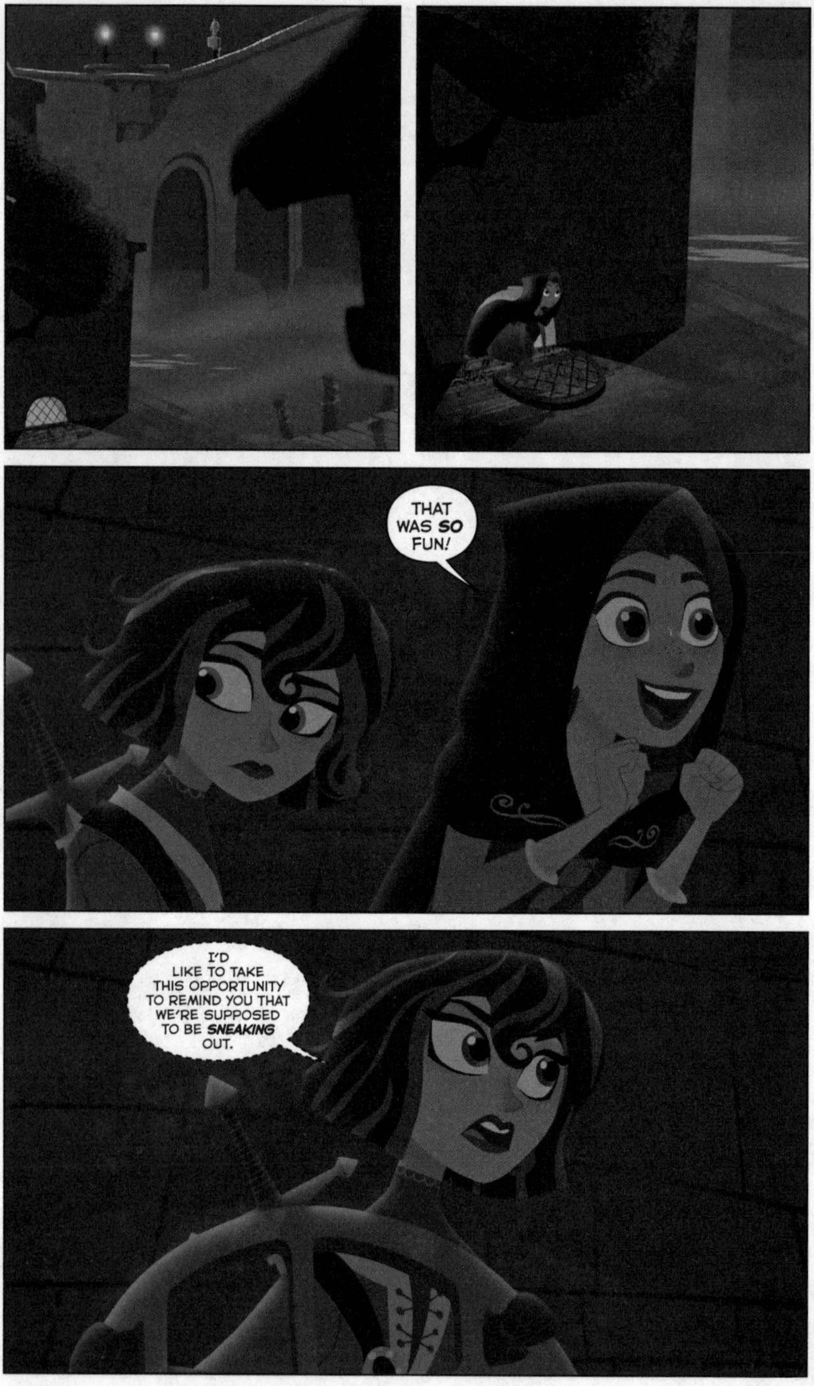
THAT WAS **SO** FUN!
I'D LIKE TO TAKE THIS OPPORTUNITY TO REMIND YOU THAT WE'RE SUPPOSED TO BE ***SNEAKING*** OUT.

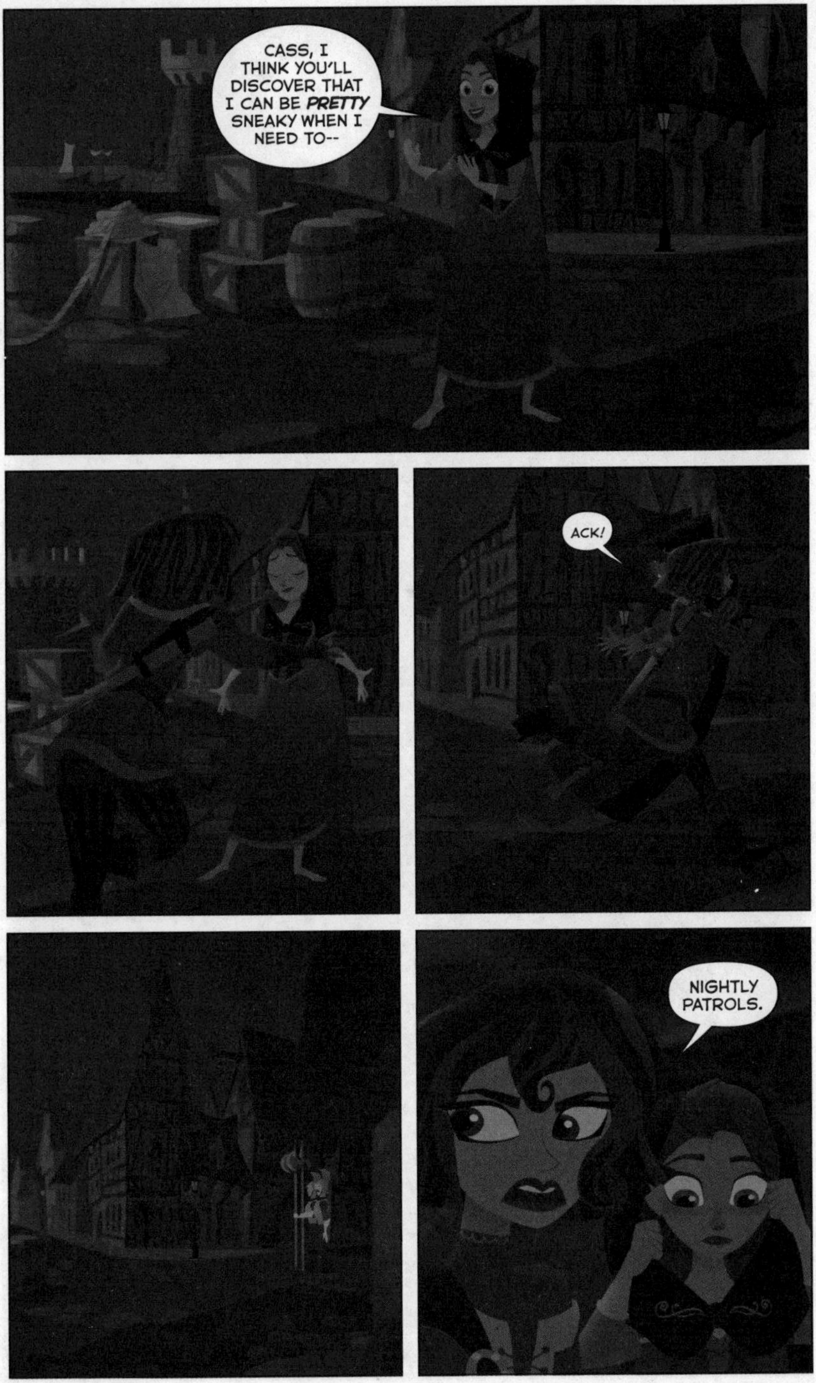
CASS, I THINK YOU'LL DISCOVER THAT I CAN BE *PRETTY* SNEAKY WHEN I NEED TO--
ACK!
NIGHTLY PATROLS.

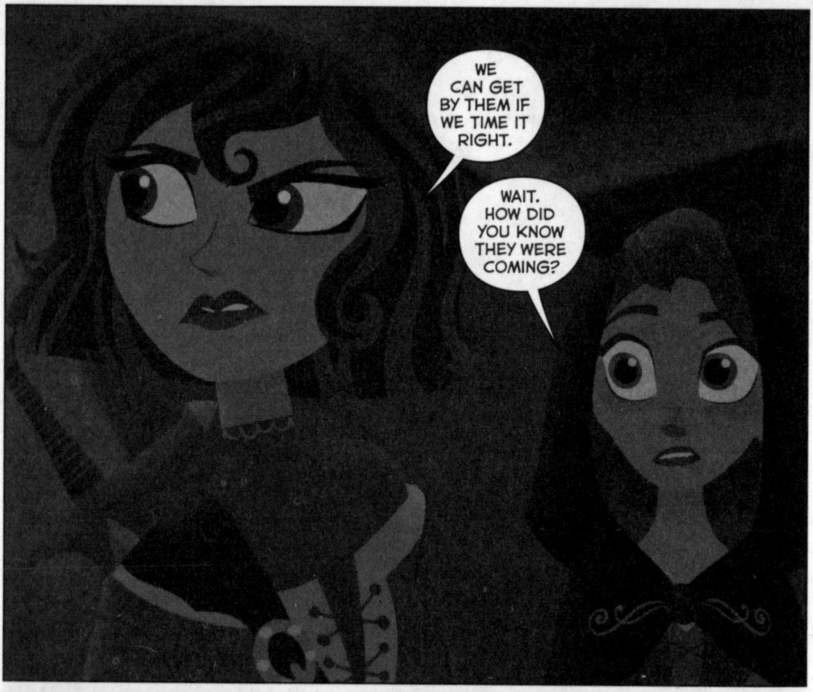
WE CAN GET BY THEM IF WE TIME IT RIGHT.
WAIT. HOW DID YOU KNOW THEY WERE COMING?

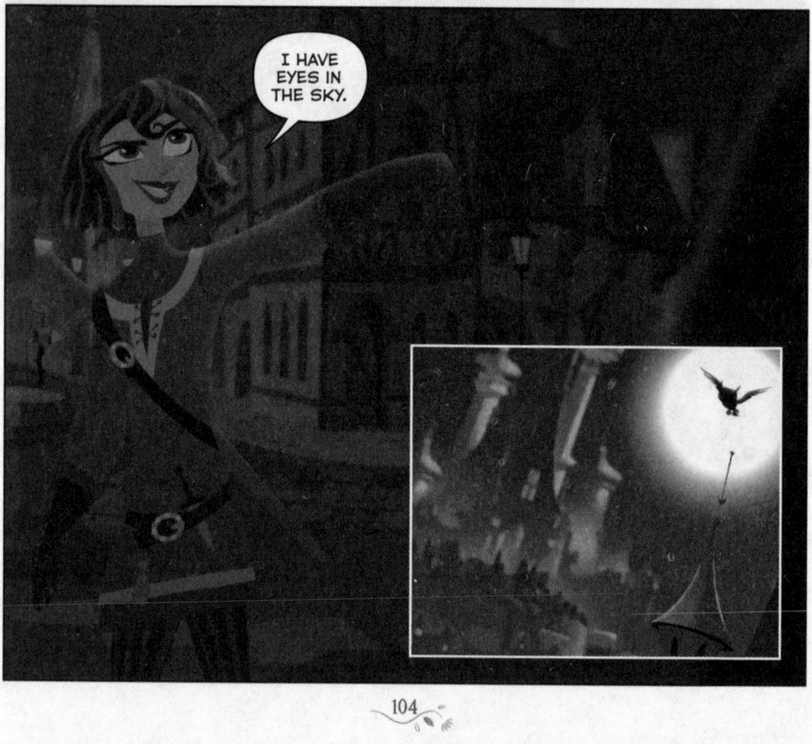
I HAVE EYES IN THE SKY.

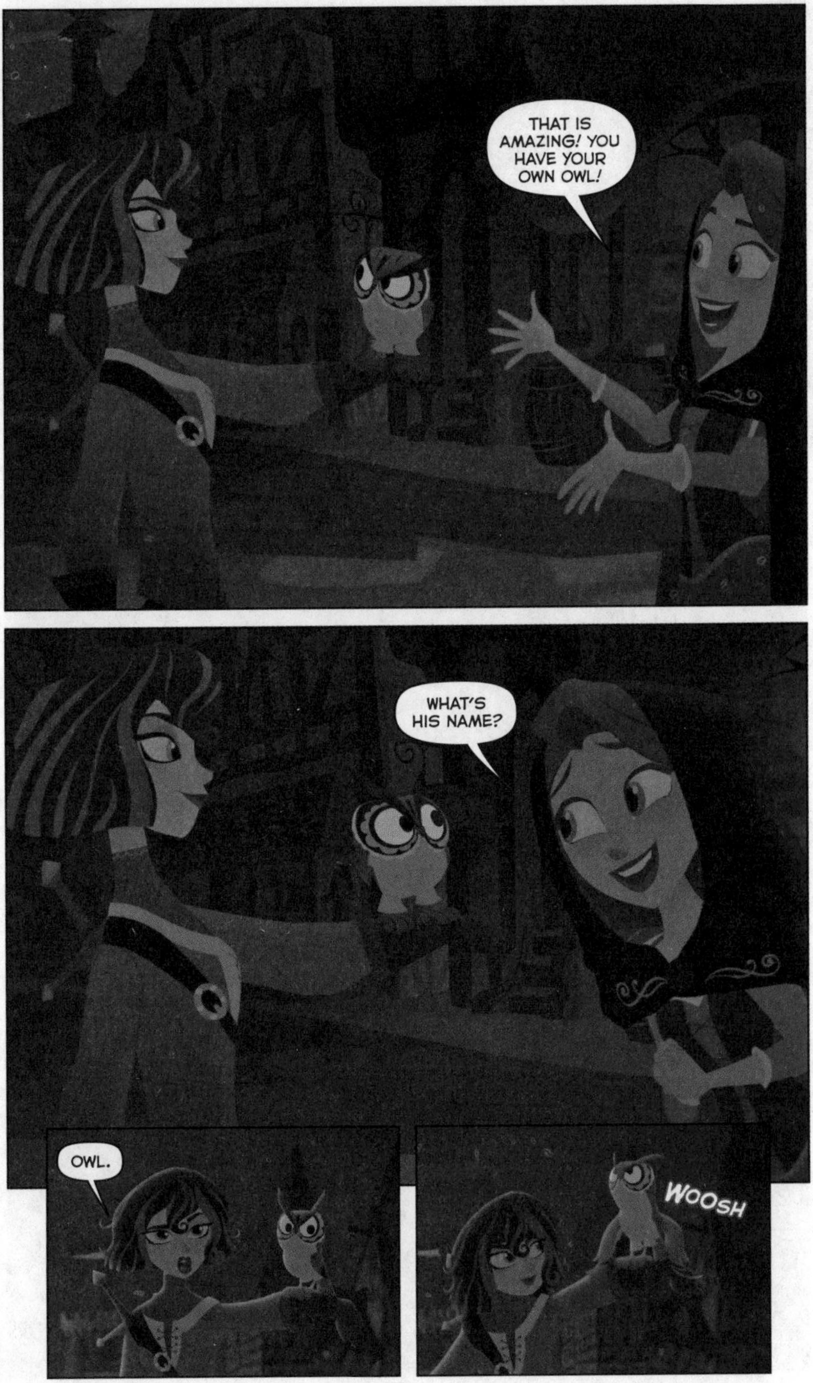
THAT IS AMAZING! YOU HAVE YOUR OWN OWL!
WHAT'S HIS NAME?
OWL.
WOOSH

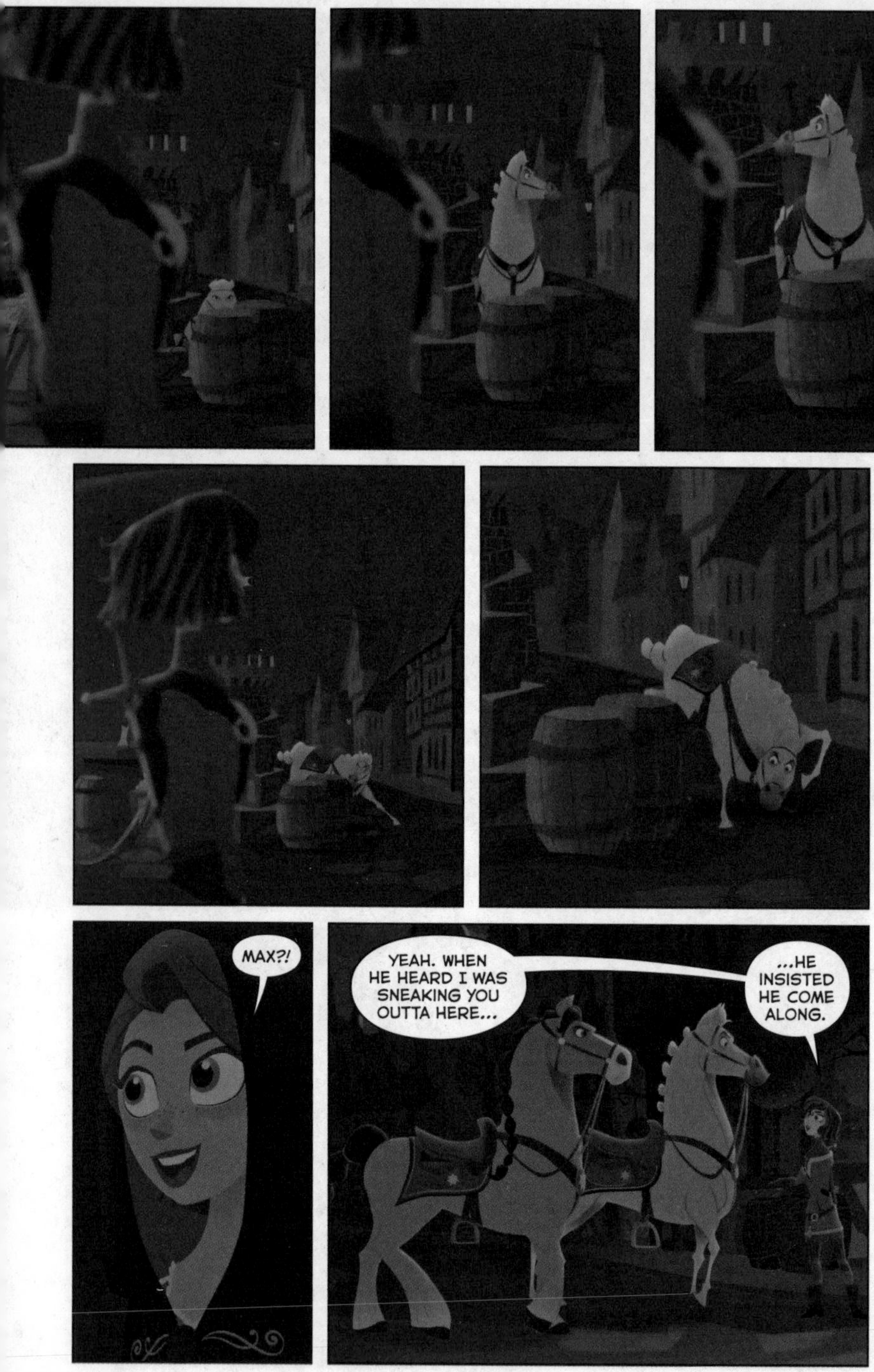
MAX?!
YEAH. WHEN HE HEARD I WAS SNEAKING YOU OUTTA HERE...
...HE INSISTED HE COME ALONG.

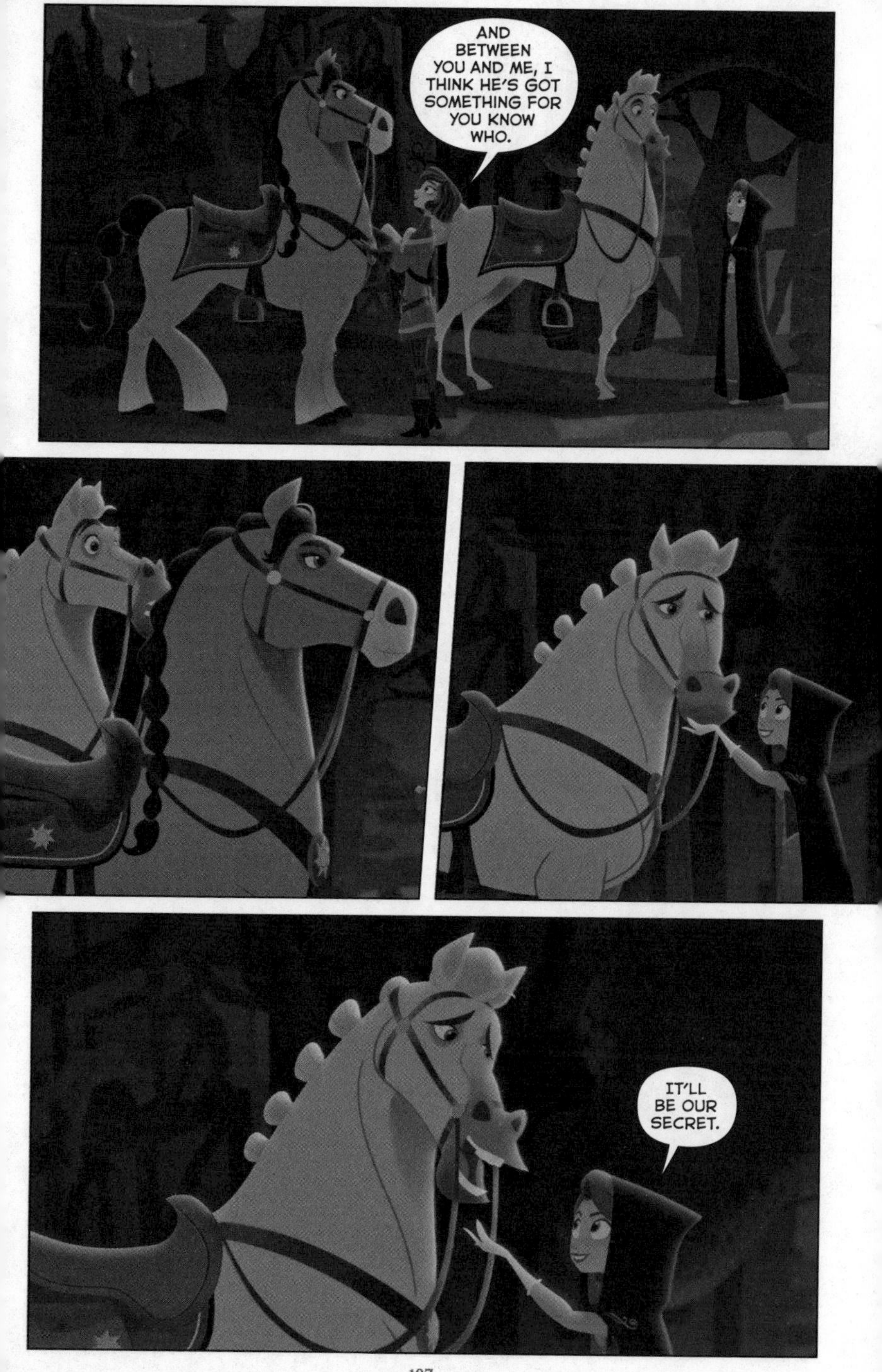
AND BETWEEN YOU AND ME, I THINK HE'S GOT SOMETHING FOR YOU KNOW WHO.
IT'LL BE OUR SECRET.

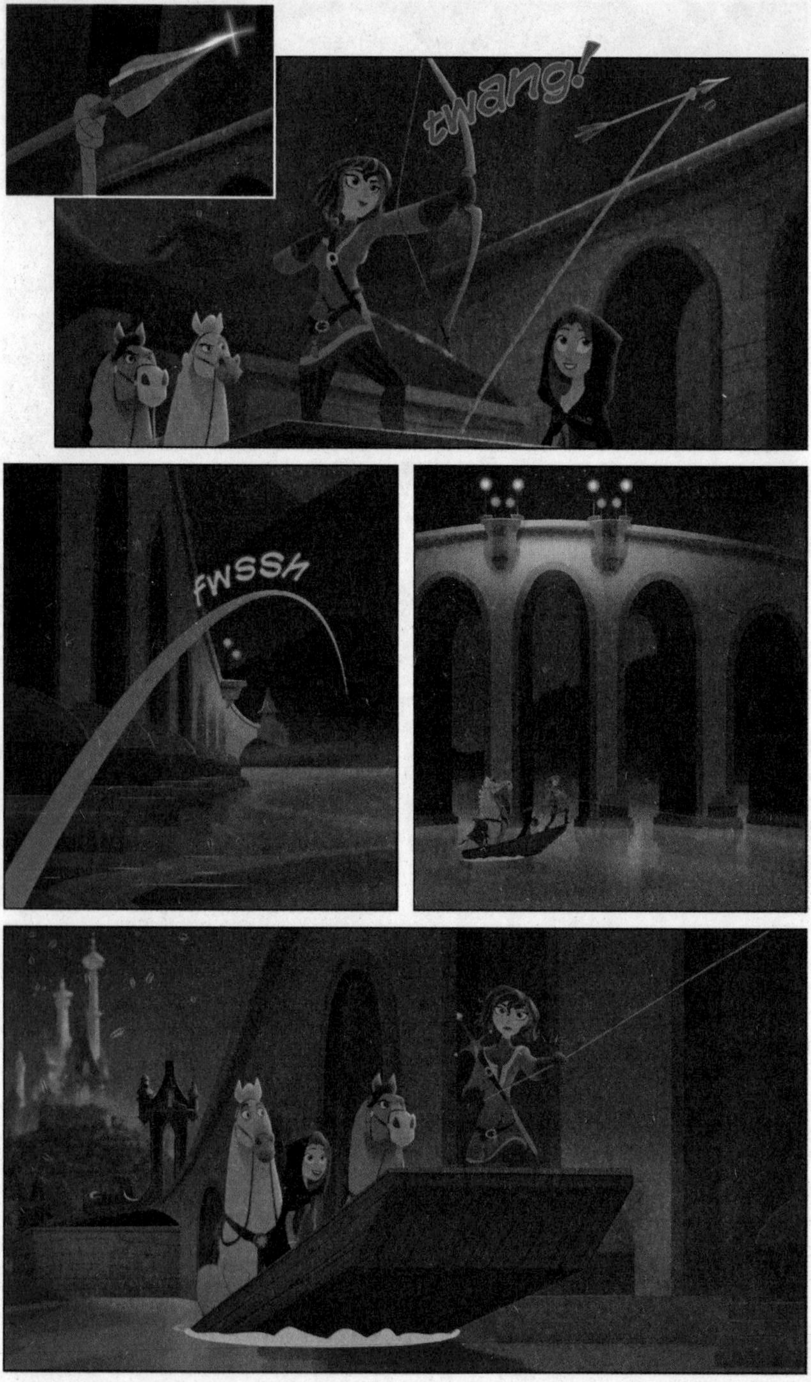
twang!
fwssh

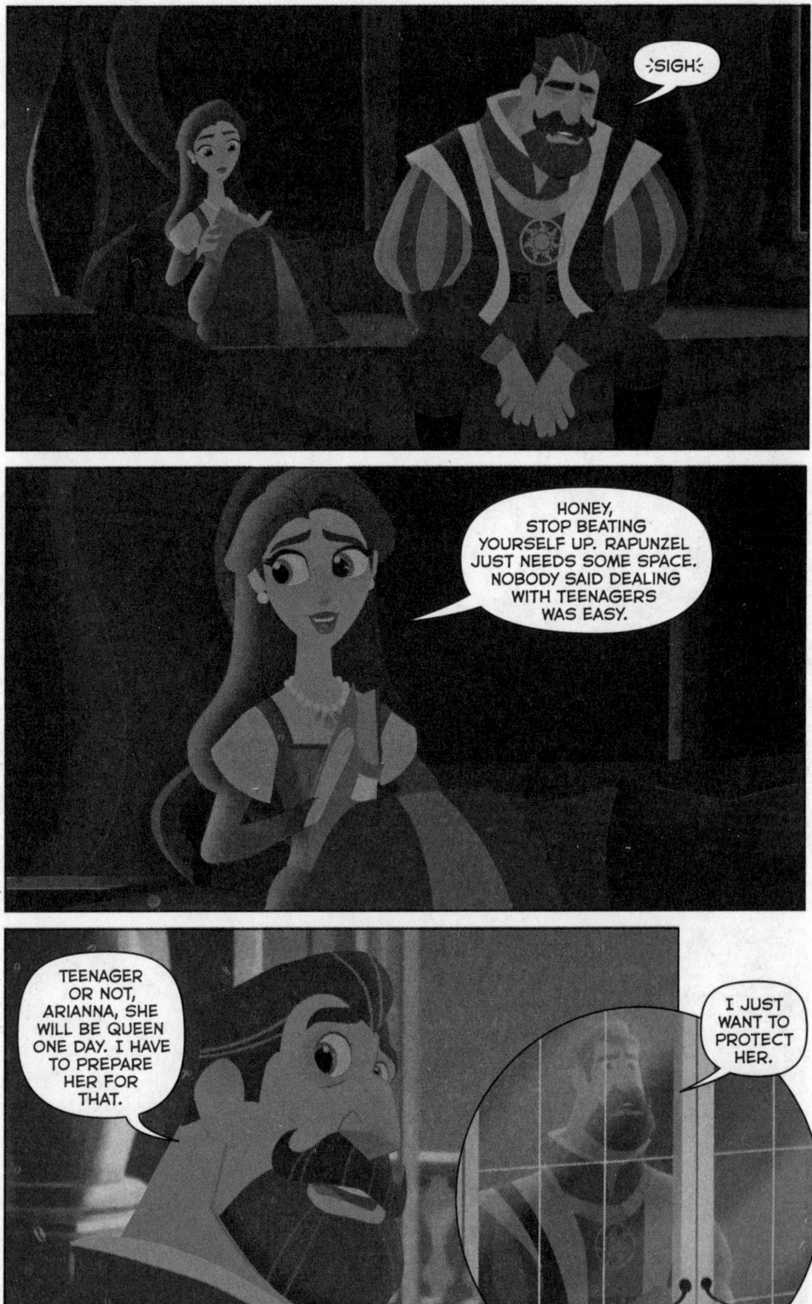
SIGH
HONEY, STOP BEATING YOURSELF UP. RAPUNZEL JUST NEEDS SOME SPACE. NOBODY SAID DEALING WITH TEENAGERS WAS EASY.
TEENAGER OR NOT, ARIANNA, SHE WILL BE QUEEN ONE DAY. I HAVE TO PREPARE HER FOR THAT.
I JUST WANT TO PROTECT HER.

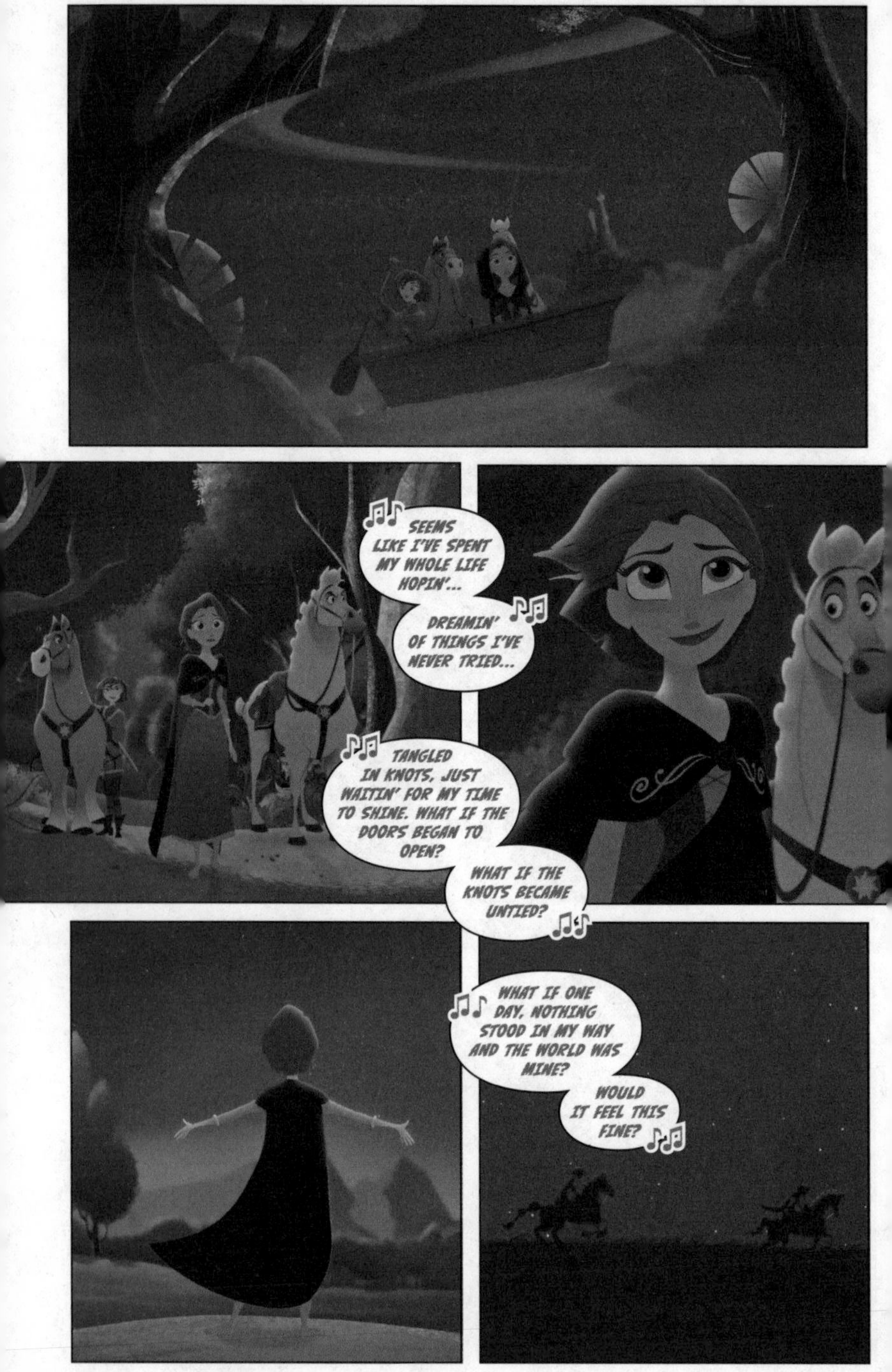
SEEMS LIKE I'VE SPENT MY WHOLE LIFE HOPIN'...
DREAMIN' OF THINGS I'VE NEVER TRIED...
TANGLED IN KNOTS, JUST WAITIN' FOR MY TIME TO SHINE. WHAT IF THE DOORS BEGAN TO OPEN?
WHAT IF THE KNOTS BECAME UNTIED?
WHAT IF ONE DAY, NOTHING STOOD IN MY WAY AND THE WORLD WAS MINE?
WOULD IT FEEL THIS FINE?

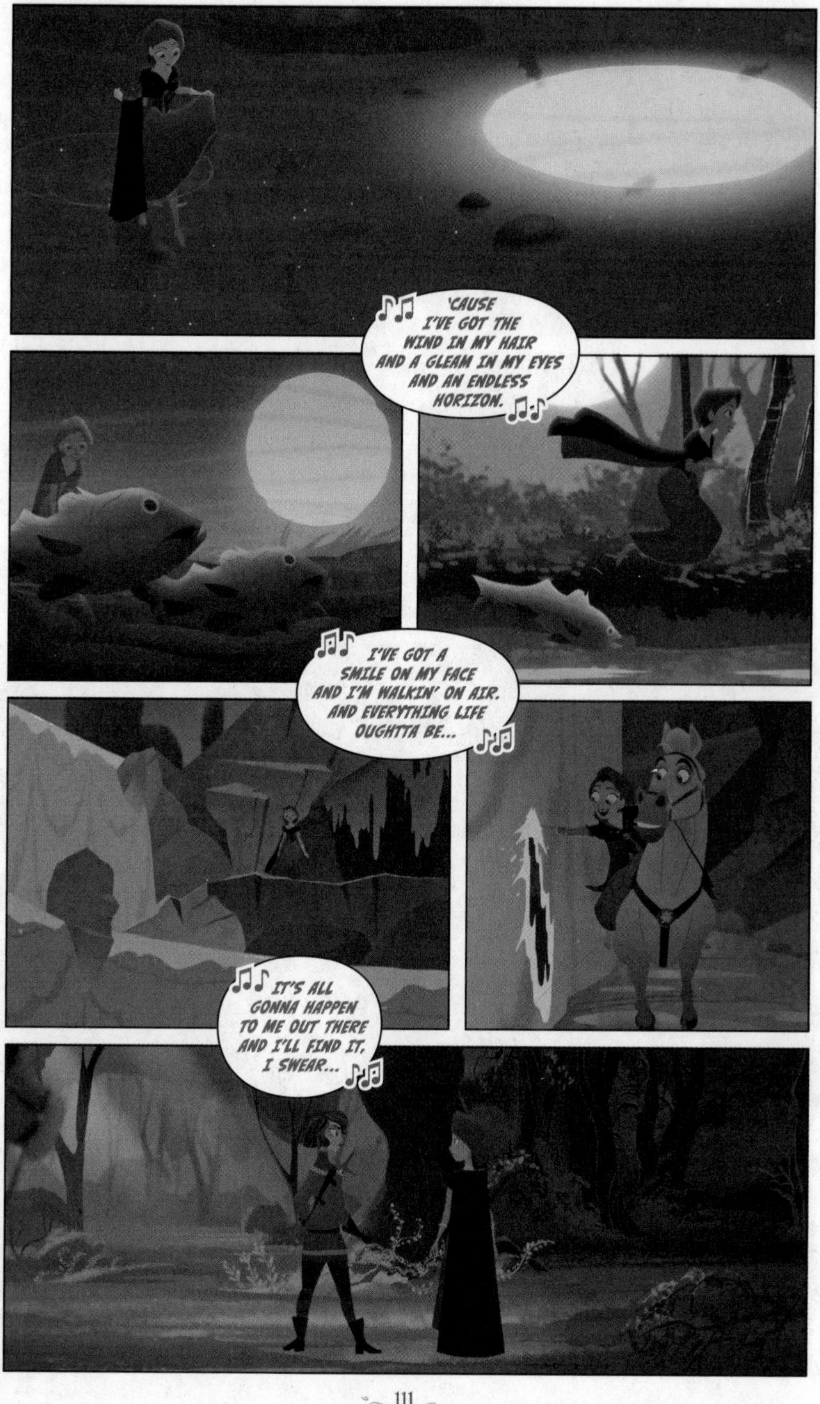
'CAUSE I'VE GOT THE WIND IN MY HAIR AND A GLEAM IN MY EYES AND AN ENDLESS HORIZON.
I'VE GOT A SMILE ON MY FACE AND I'M WALKIN' ON AIR. AND EVERYTHING LIFE OUGHTTA BE...
IT'S ALL GONNA HAPPEN TO ME OUT THERE AND I'LL FIND IT, I SWEAR...

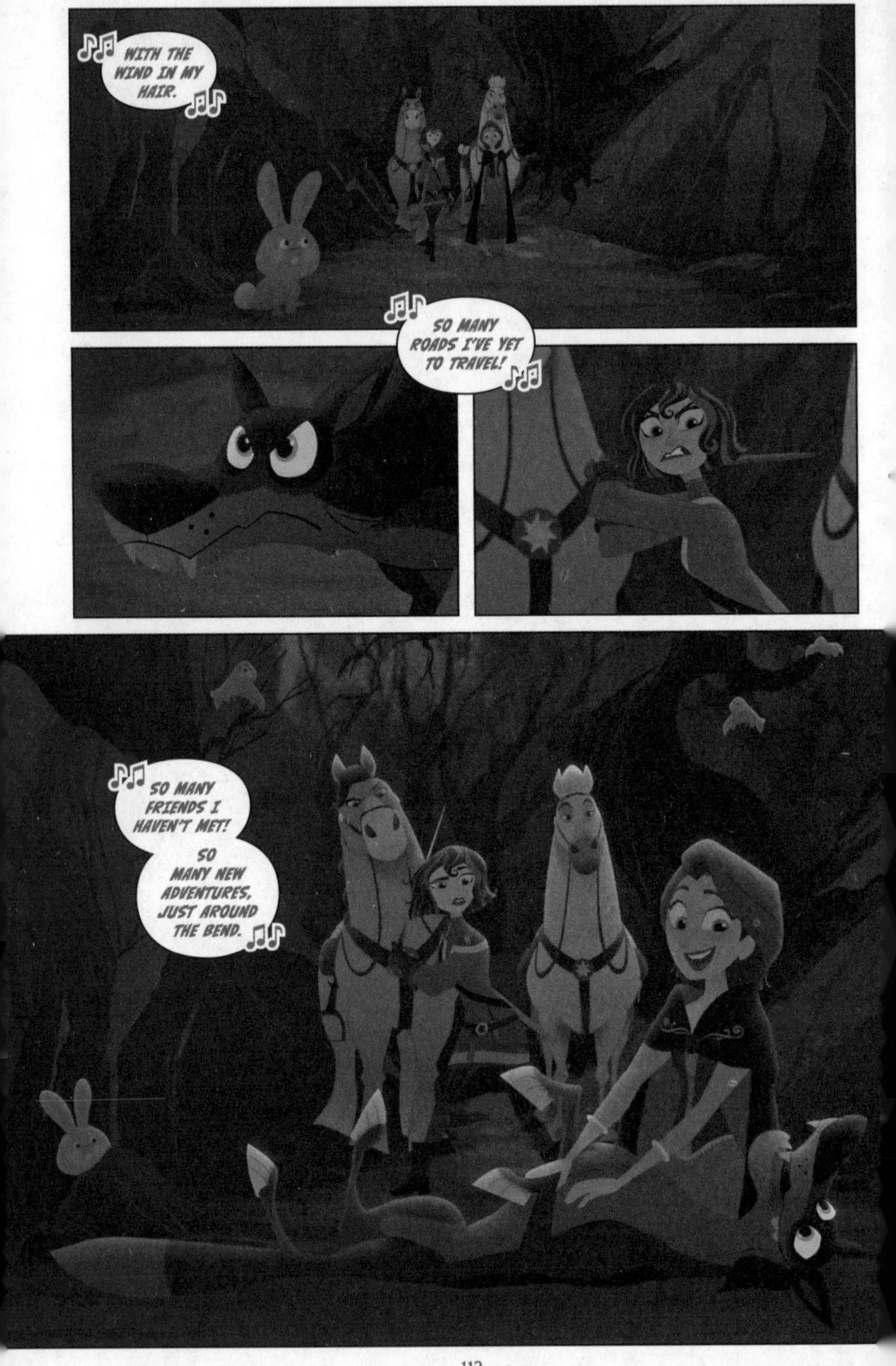
WITH THE WIND IN MY HAIR.
SO MANY ROADS I'VE YET TO TRAVEL!
SO MANY FRIENDS I HAVEN'T MET!
SO MANY NEW ADVENTURES, JUST AROUND THE BEND.

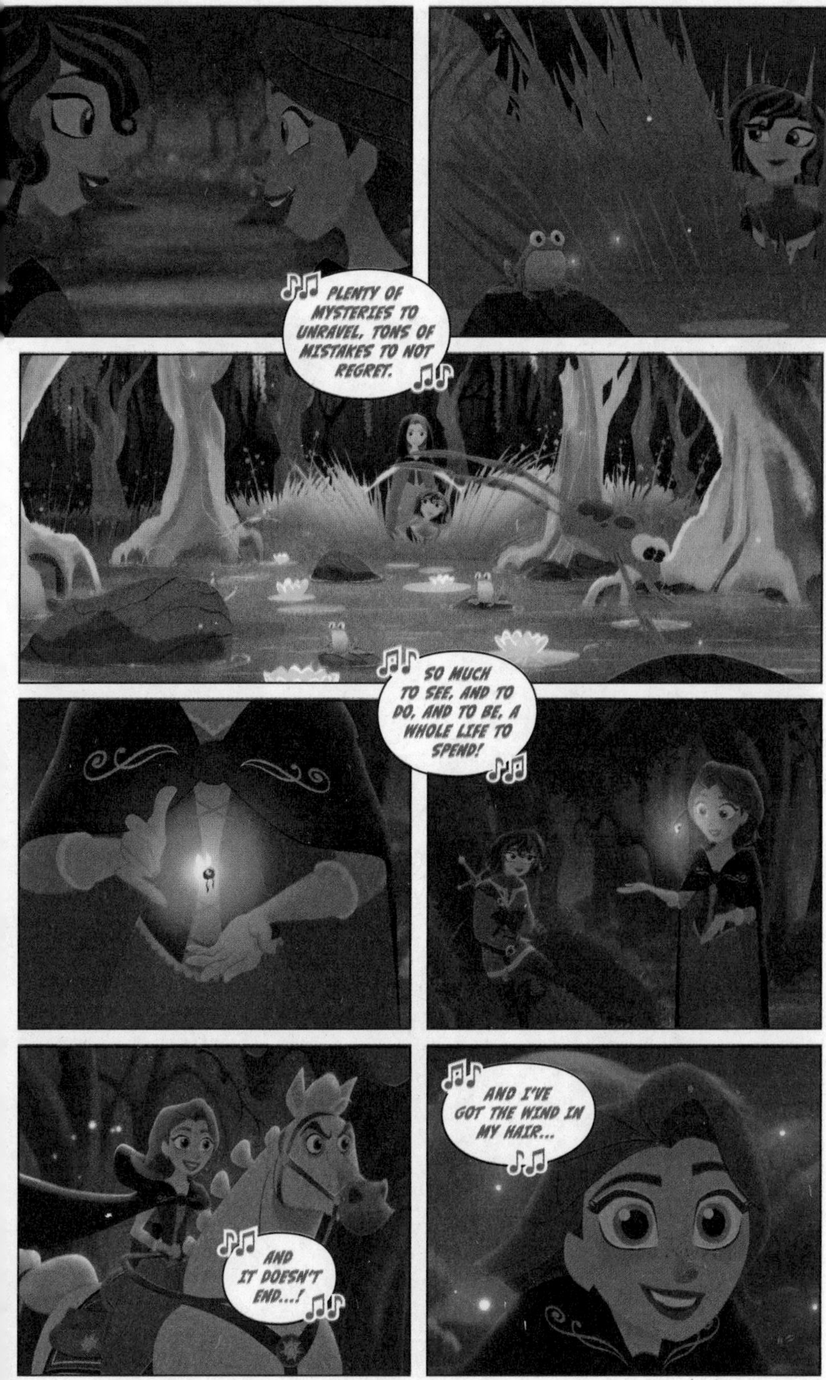
PLENTY OF MYSTERIES TO UNRAVEL, TONS OF MISTAKES TO NOT REGRET.
SO MUCH TO SEE, AND TO DO, AND TO BE, A WHOLE LIFE TO SPEND!
AND IT DOESN'T END...!
AND I'VE GOT THE WIND IN MY HAIR...

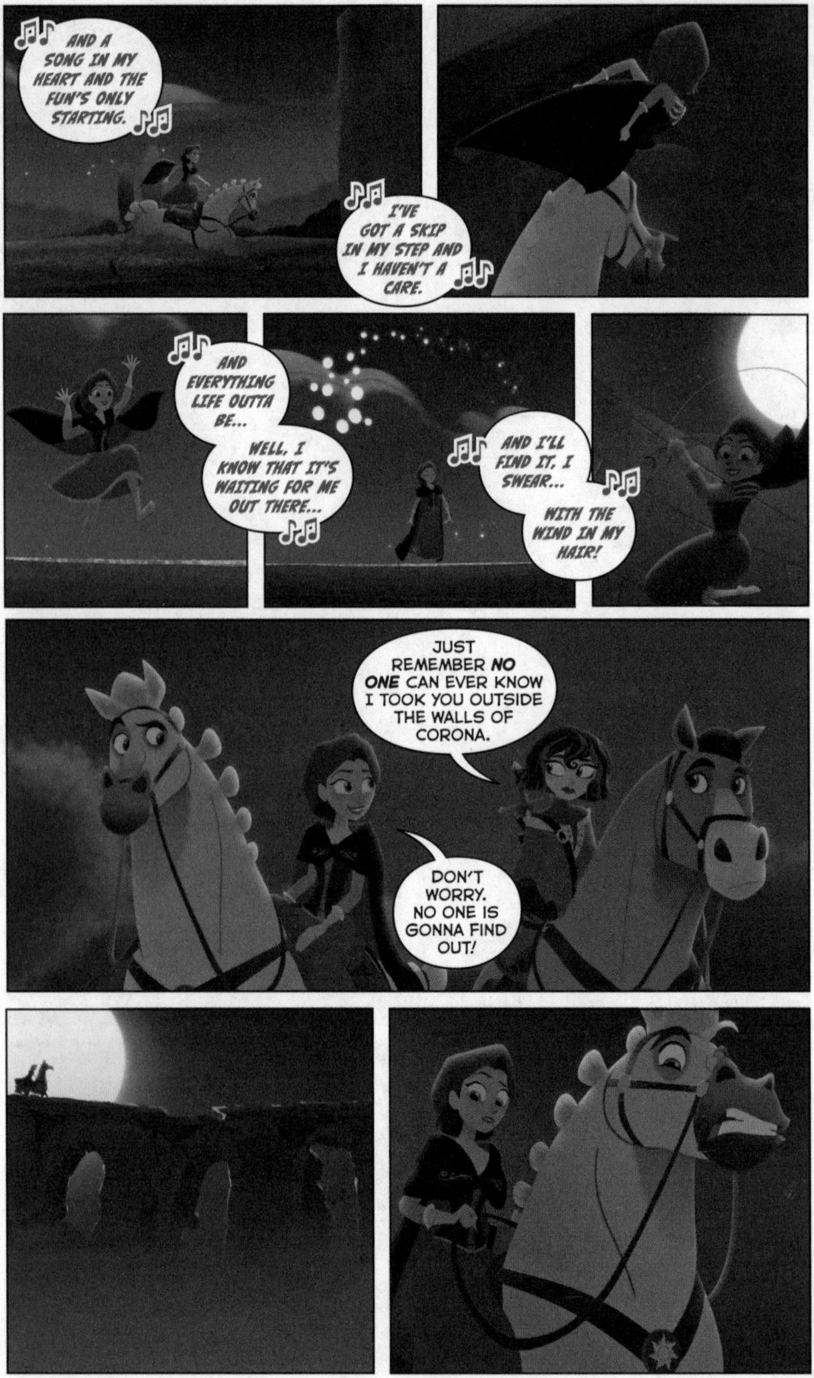
AND A SONG IN MY HEART AND THE FUN'S ONLY STARTING.
I'VE GOT A SKIP IN MY STEP AND I HAVEN'T A CARE.
AND EVERYTHING LIFE OUTTA BE...
WELL, I KNOW THAT IT'S WAITING FOR ME OUT THERE...
AND I'LL FIND IT, I SWEAR...
WITH THE WIND IN MY HAIR!
JUST REMEMBER NO ONE CAN EVER KNOW I TOOK YOU OUTSIDE THE WALLS OF CORONA.
DON'T WORRY. NO ONE IS GONNA FIND OUT!

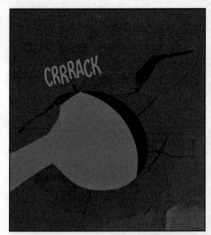

CRRRACK

Neeiigh!

WHOA, WHOA, MAX. THIS LOOKS DANGEROUS. CAN YOU STAY HERE AND WATCH FIDELLA FOR ME?

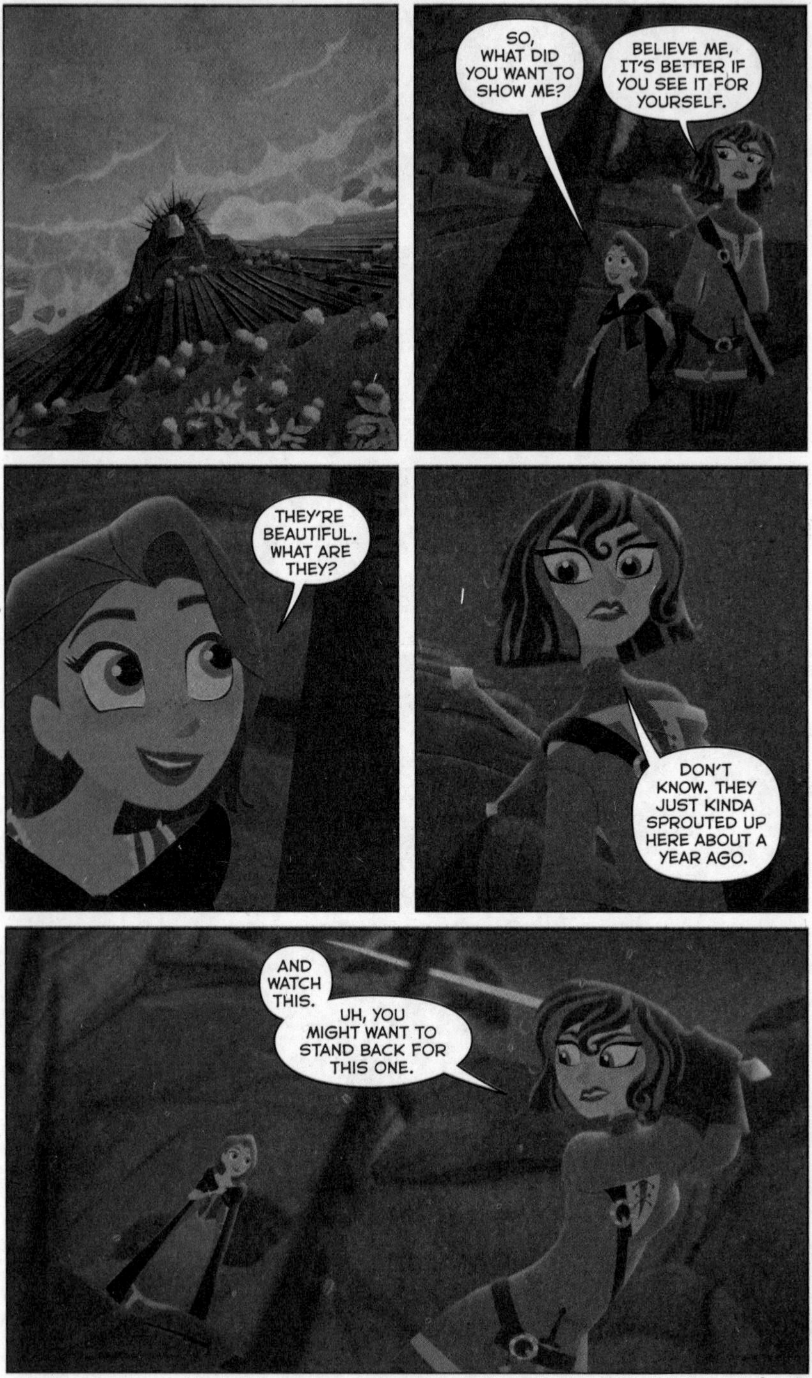
SO, WHAT DID YOU WANT TO SHOW ME?
BELIEVE ME, IT'S BETTER IF YOU SEE IT FOR YOURSELF.
THEY'RE BEAUTIFUL. WHAT ARE THEY?
DON'T KNOW. THEY JUST KINDA SPROUTED UP HERE ABOUT A YEAR AGO.
AND WATCH THIS.
UH, YOU MIGHT WANT TO STAND BACK FOR THIS ONE.

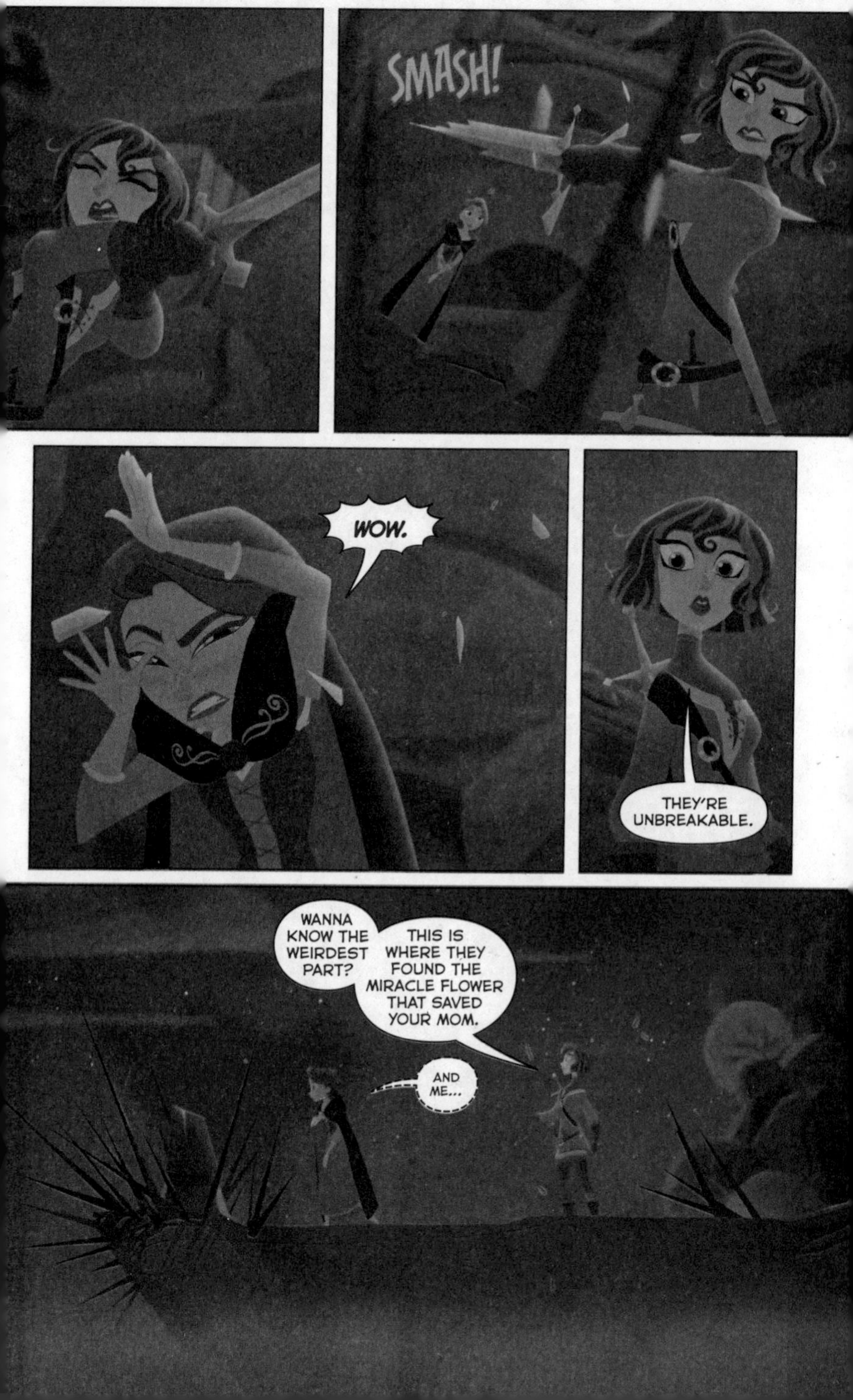
SMASH!
WOW.
THEY'RE UNBREAKABLE.
WANNA KNOW THE WEIRDEST PART?
THIS IS WHERE THEY FOUND THE MIRACLE FLOWER THAT SAVED YOUR MOM.
AND ME...

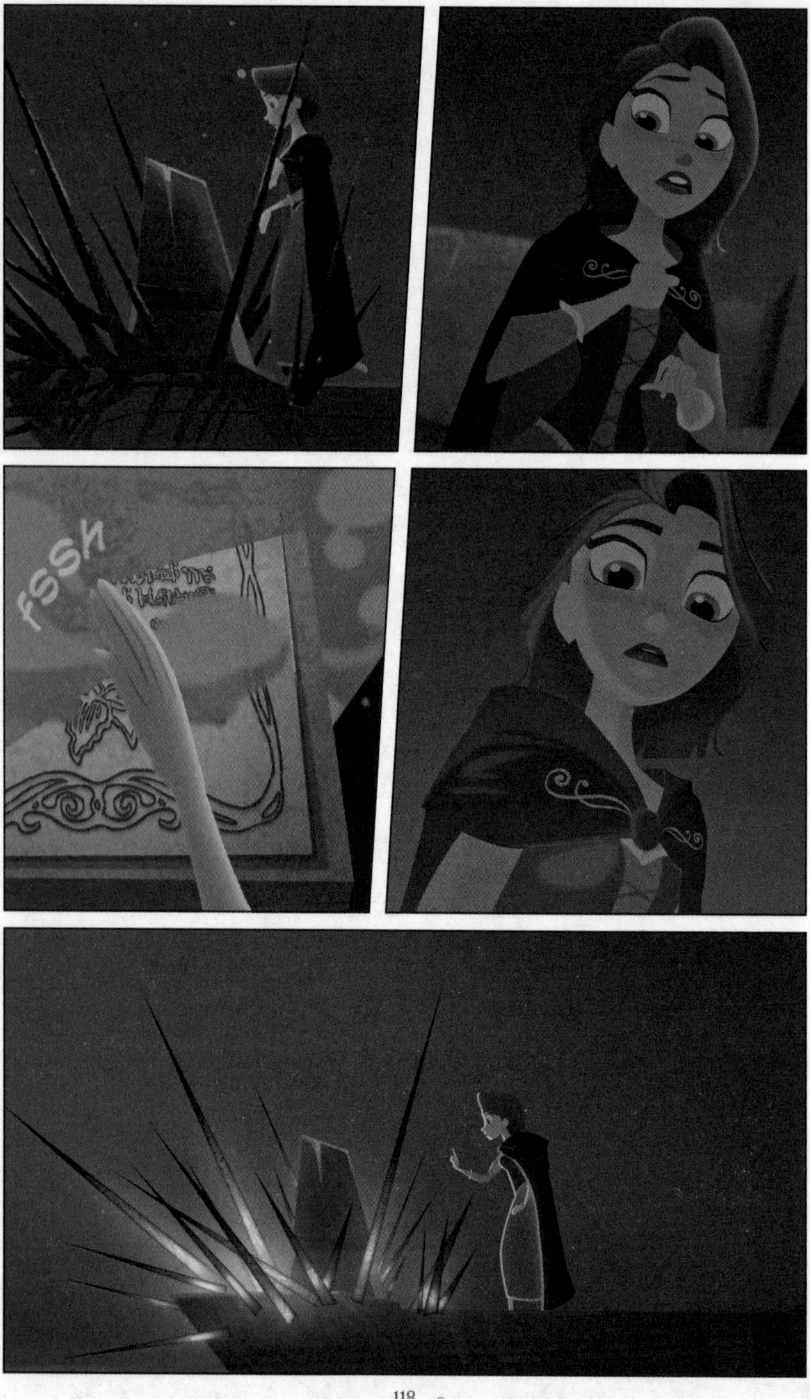
fssh

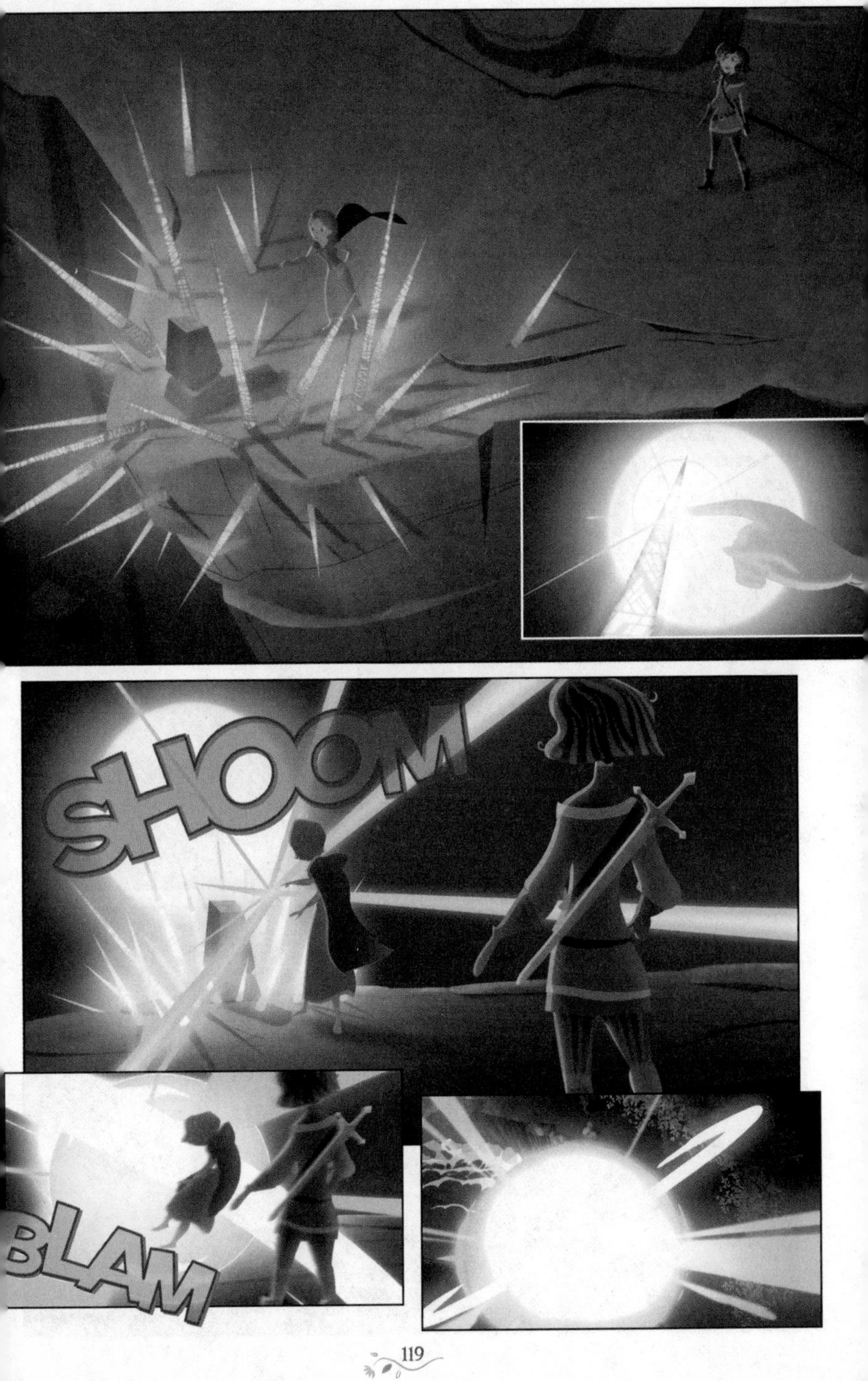
SHOOM
BLAM

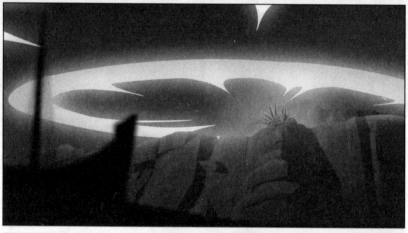

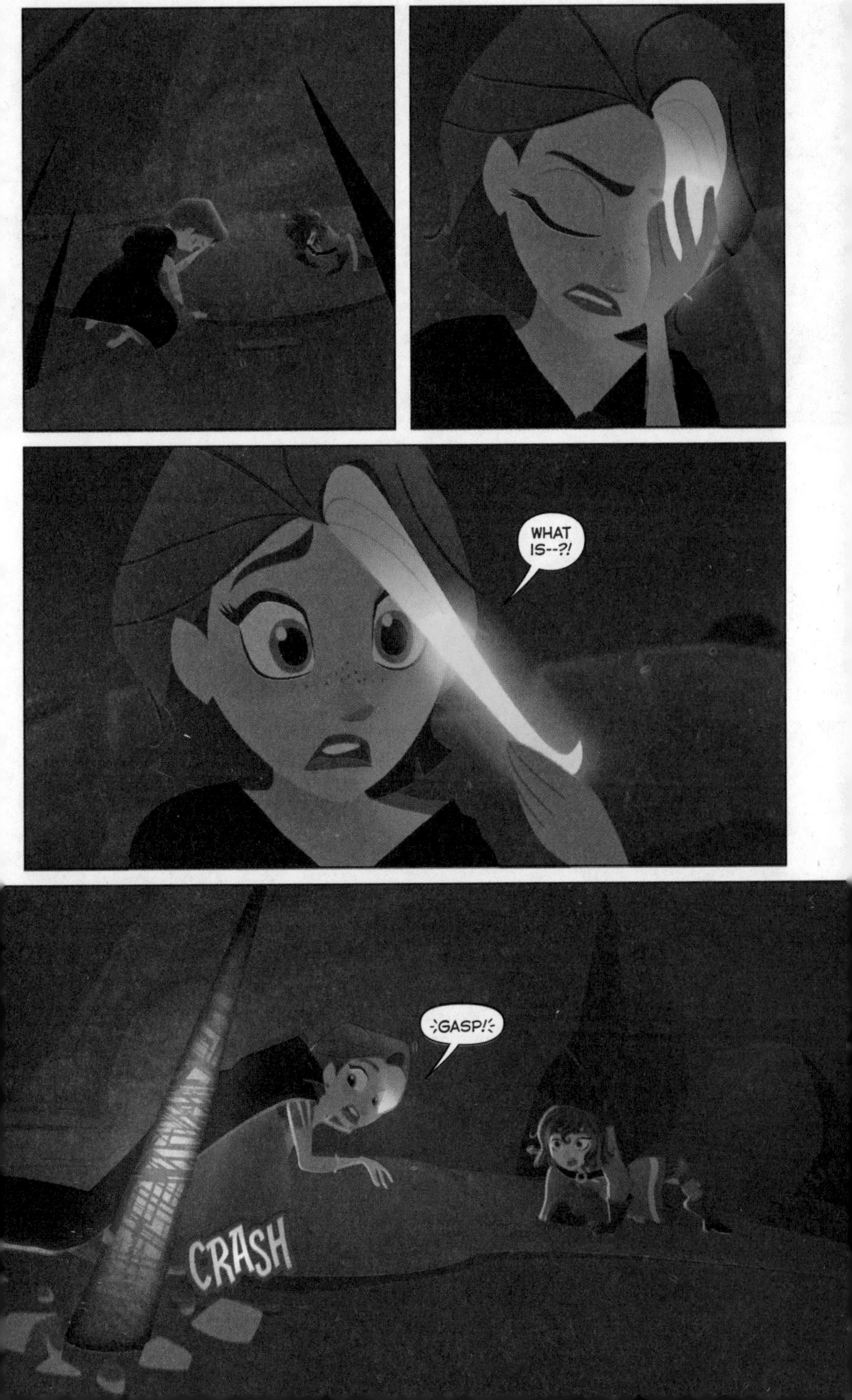
WHAT IS--?!
GASP!
CRASH

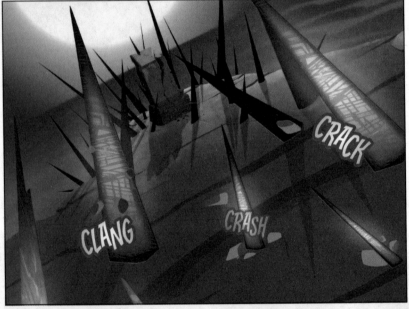

CLANG

CRASH

CRACK

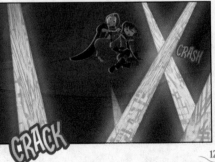

CRASH

CLASH

CRACK

GET TO THE HORSES AS FAST AS YOU CAN...

CRAC

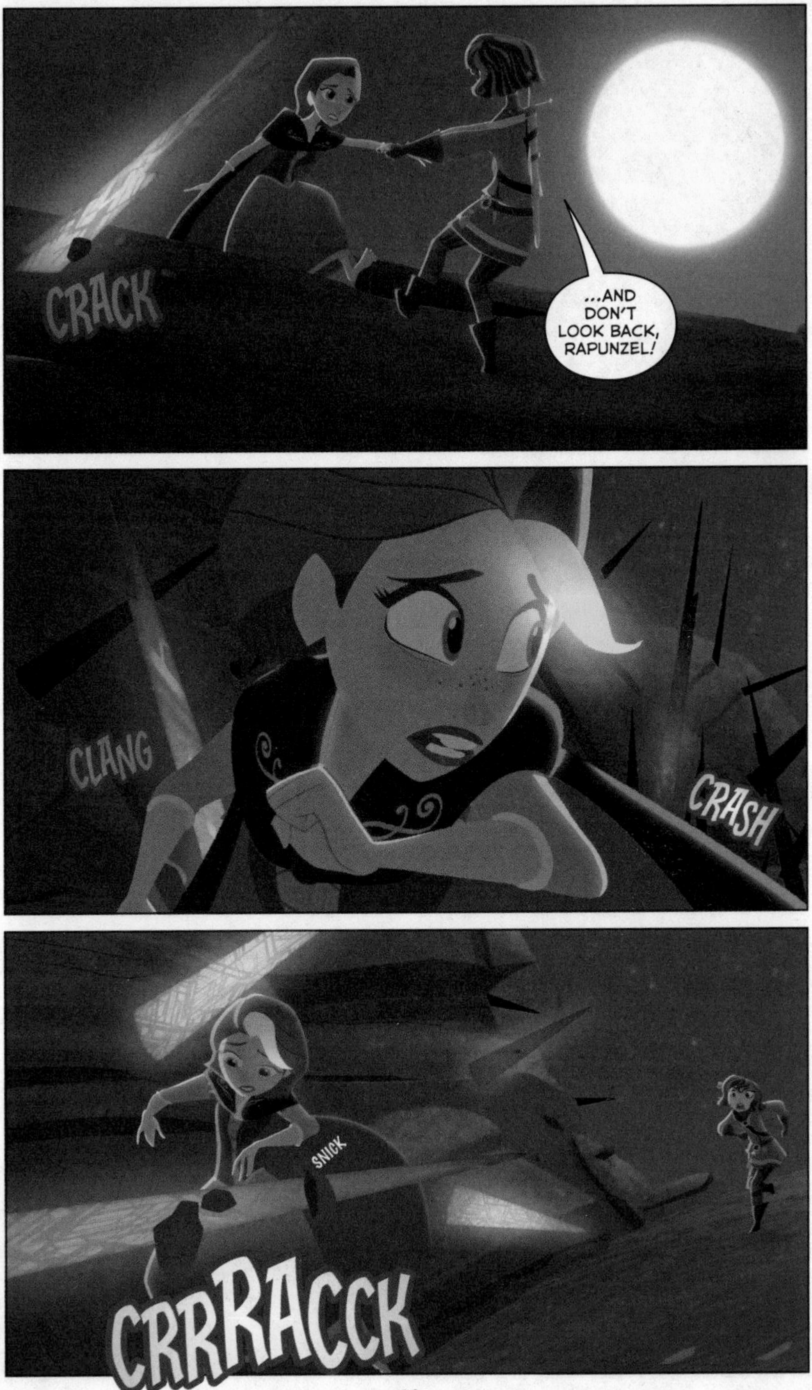
CRACK
...AND DON'T LOOK BACK, RAPUNZEL!
CLANG
CRASH
SNICK
CRRRACCK

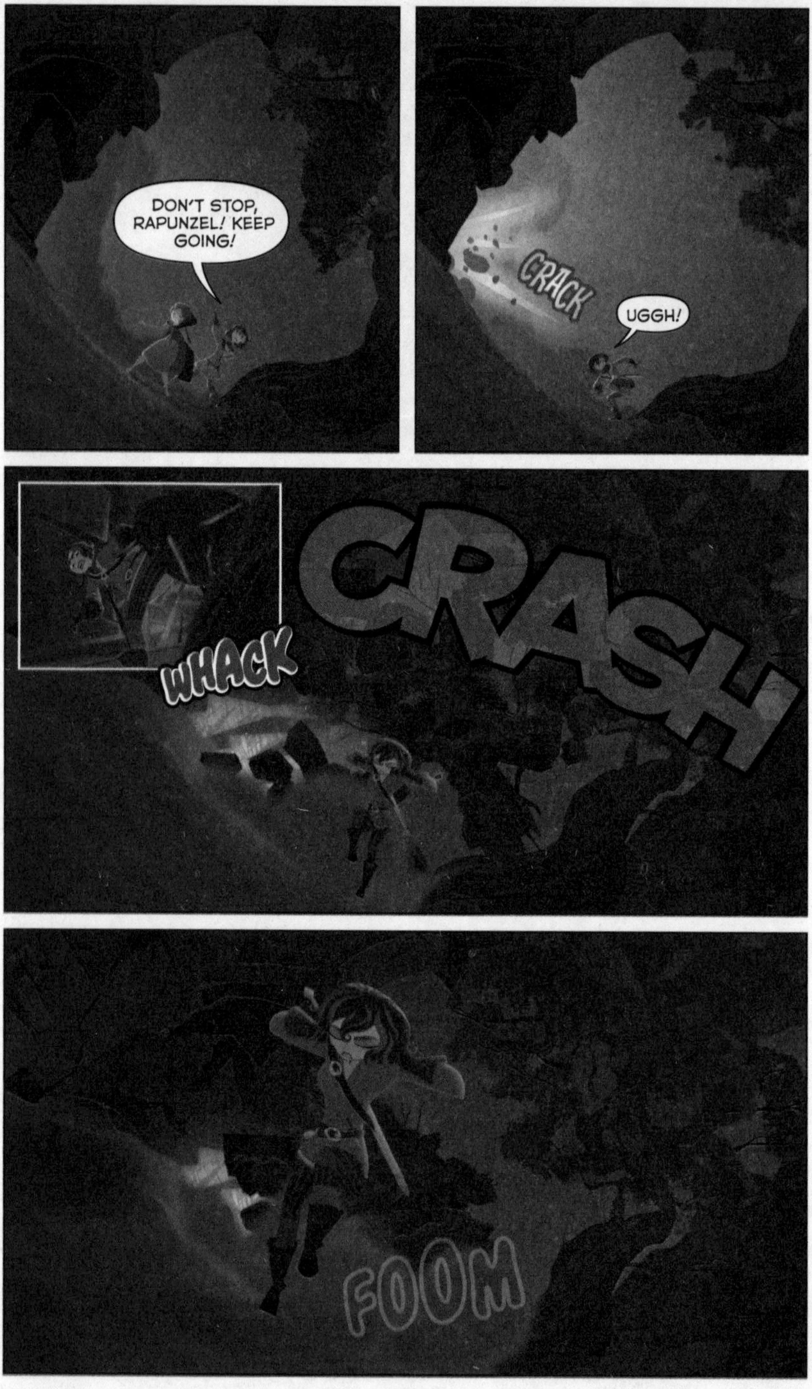
DON'T STOP, RAPUNZEL! KEEP GOING!
CRACK
UGGH!
WHACK
CRASH
FOOM

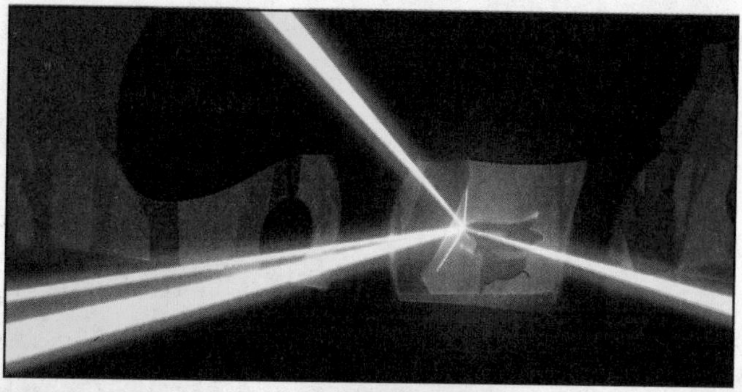

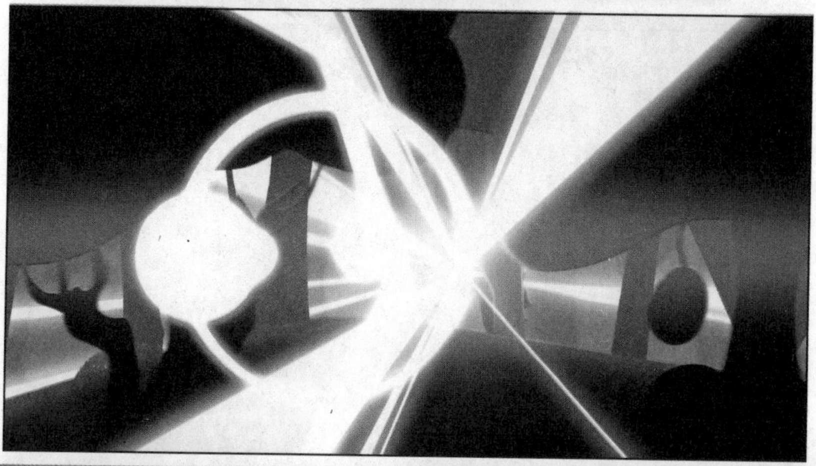

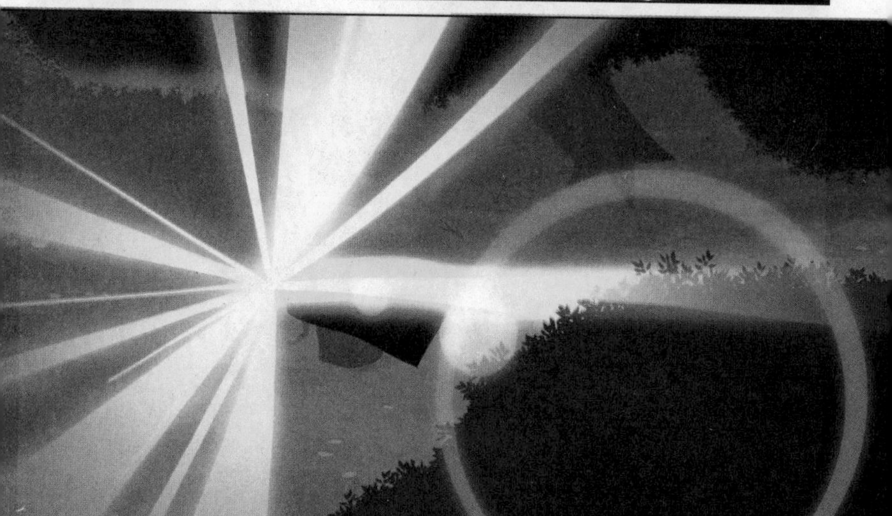

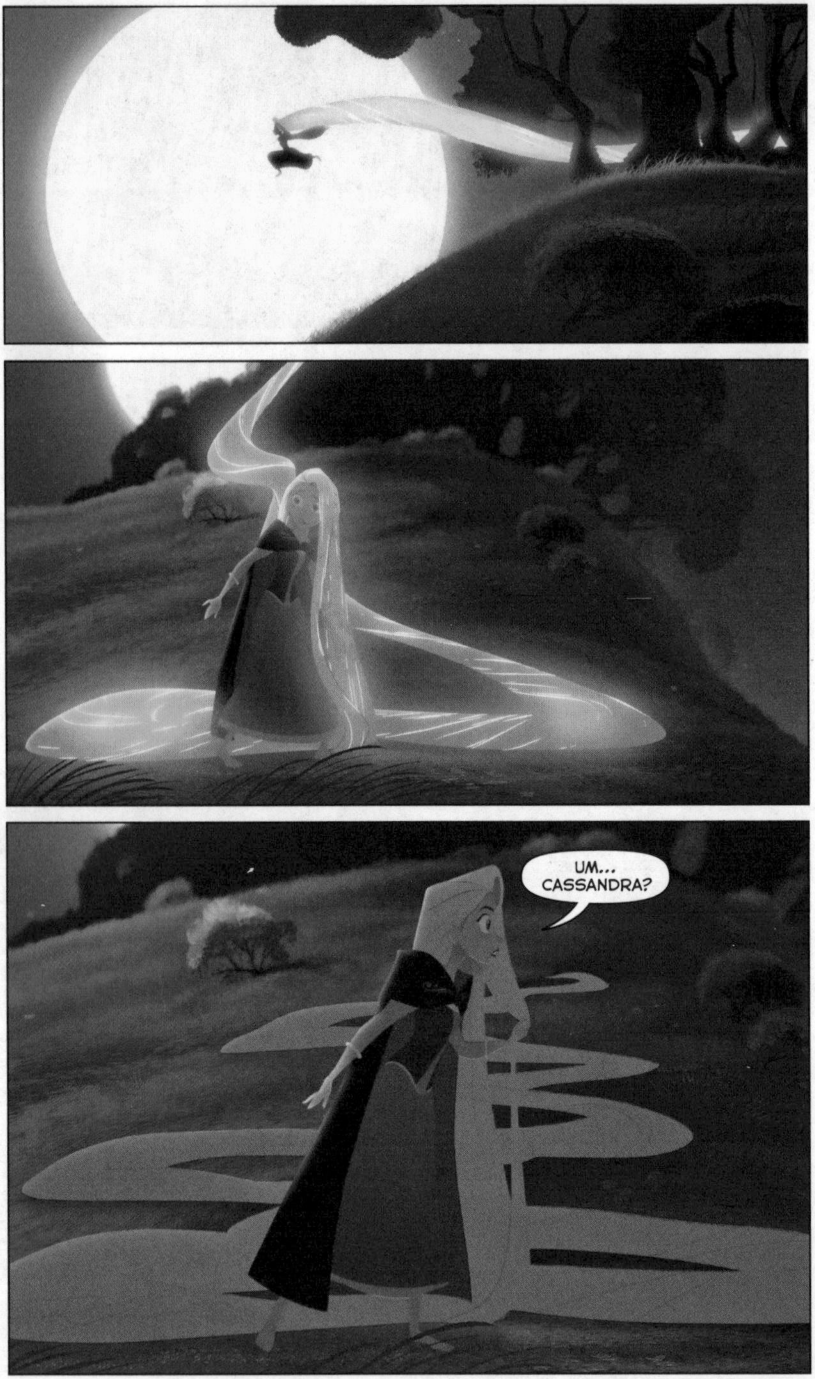
UM...
CASSANDRA?

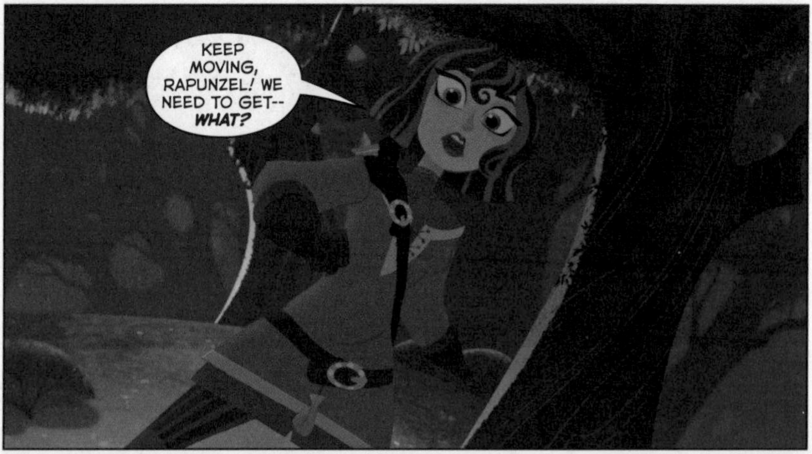
KEEP MOVING, RAPUNZEL! WE NEED TO GET-- *WHAT?*

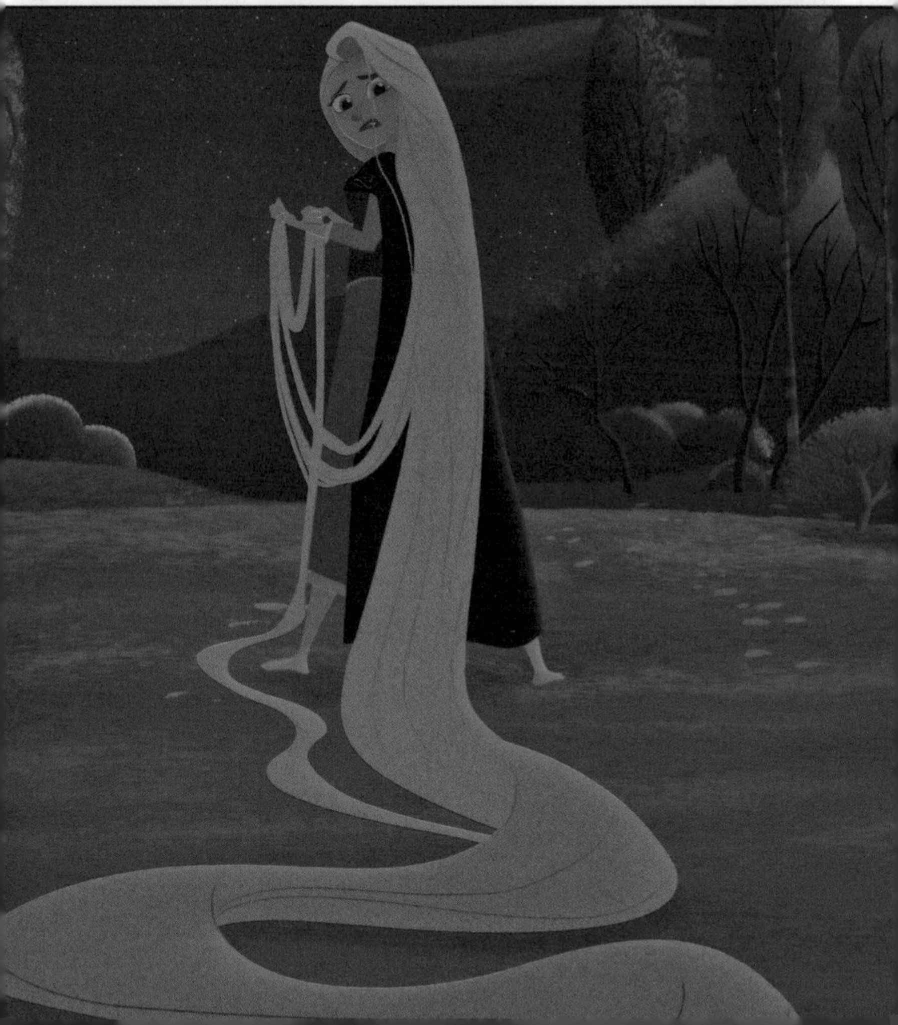

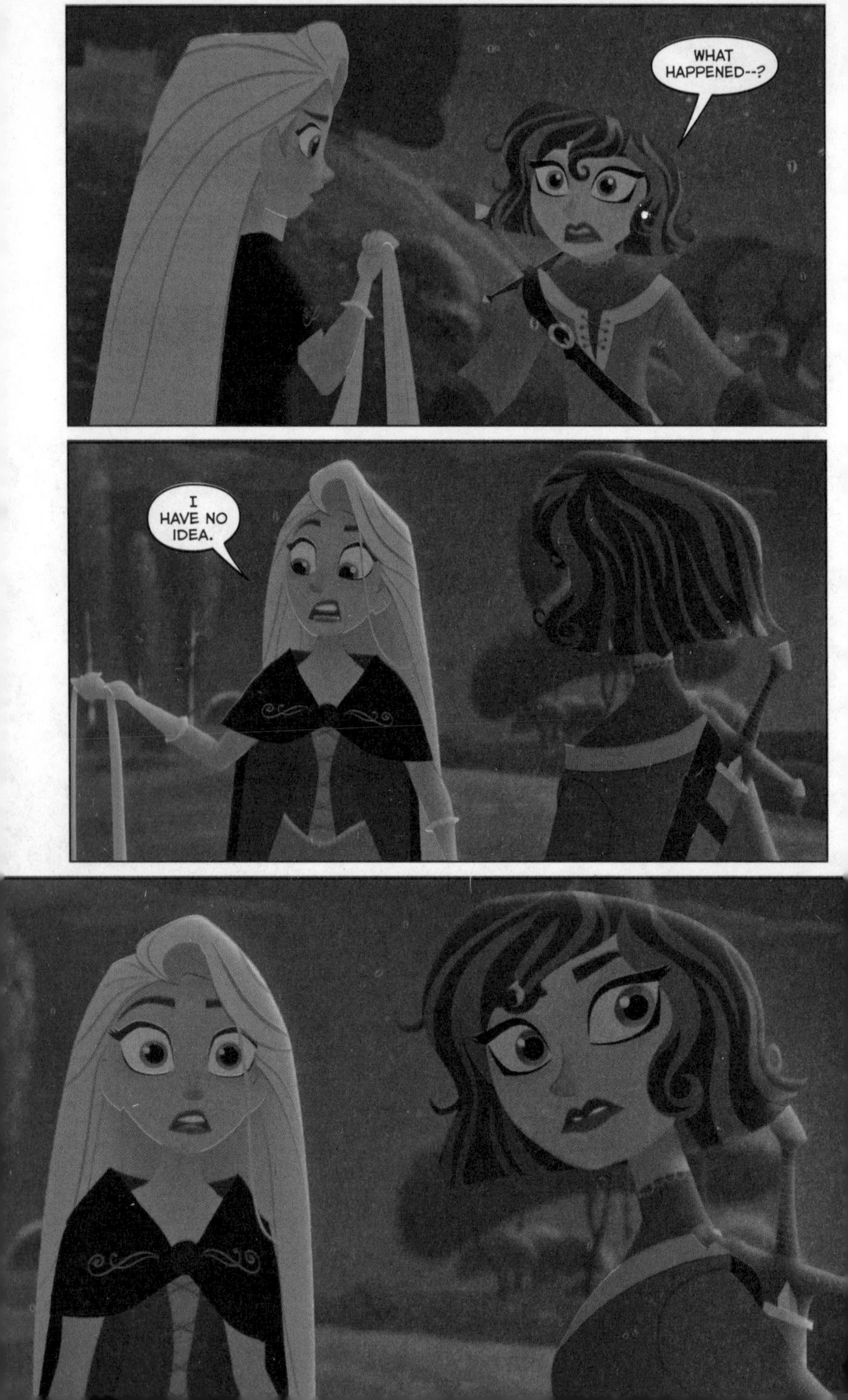
WHAT HAPPENED--?
I HAVE NO IDEA.

CLASH

CLANG

WE'LL HAVE TO DEAL WITH IT LATER. LET'S GO!

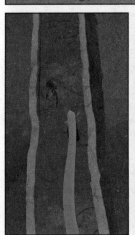

CRRRRK

CRRRACCK

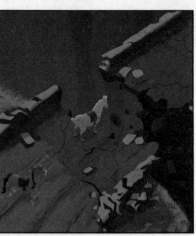

RRRR

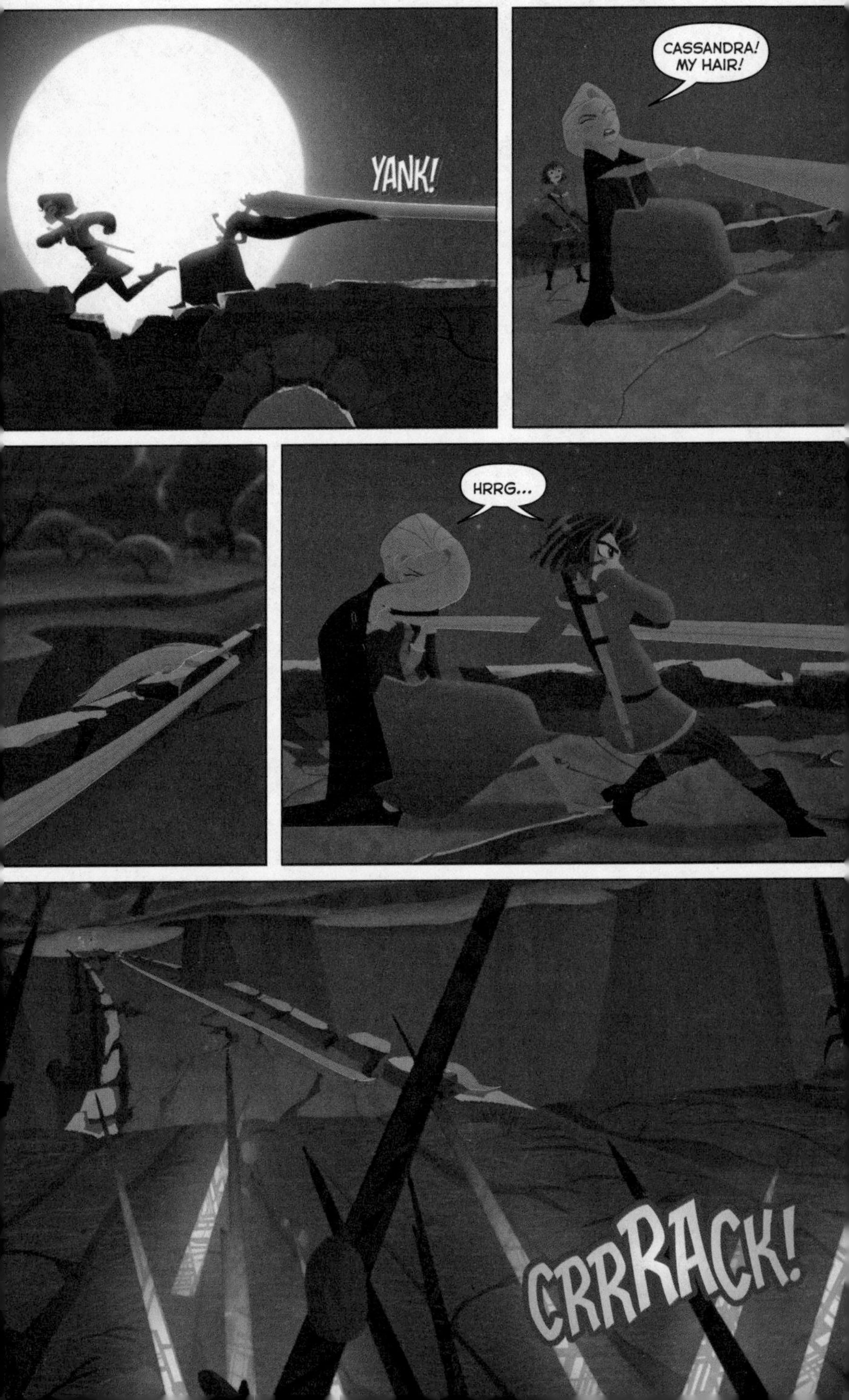
YANK!
CASSANDRA! MY HAIR!
HRRG...
CRRRACK!

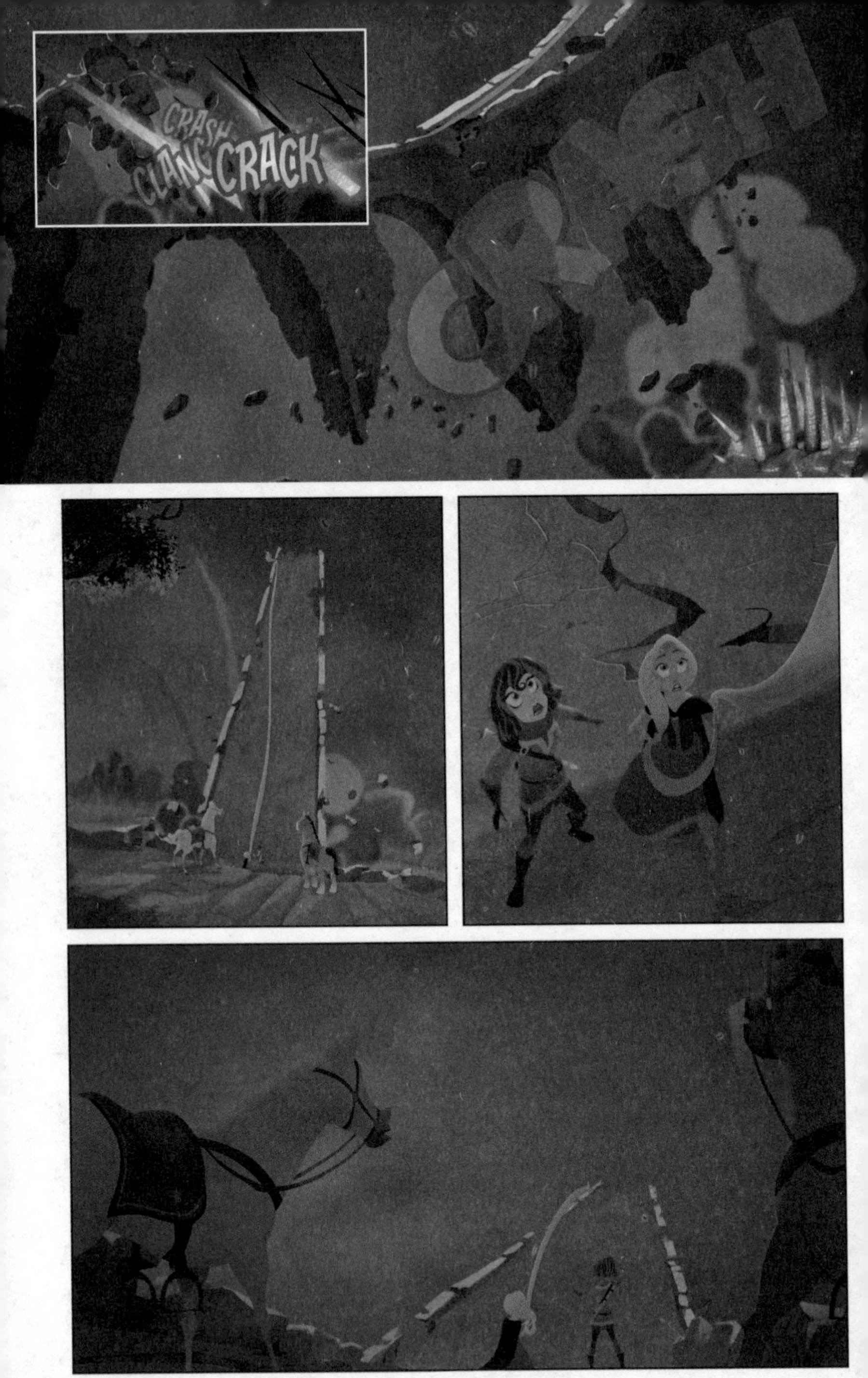
CRASH
CLANG
CRACK
CRASH

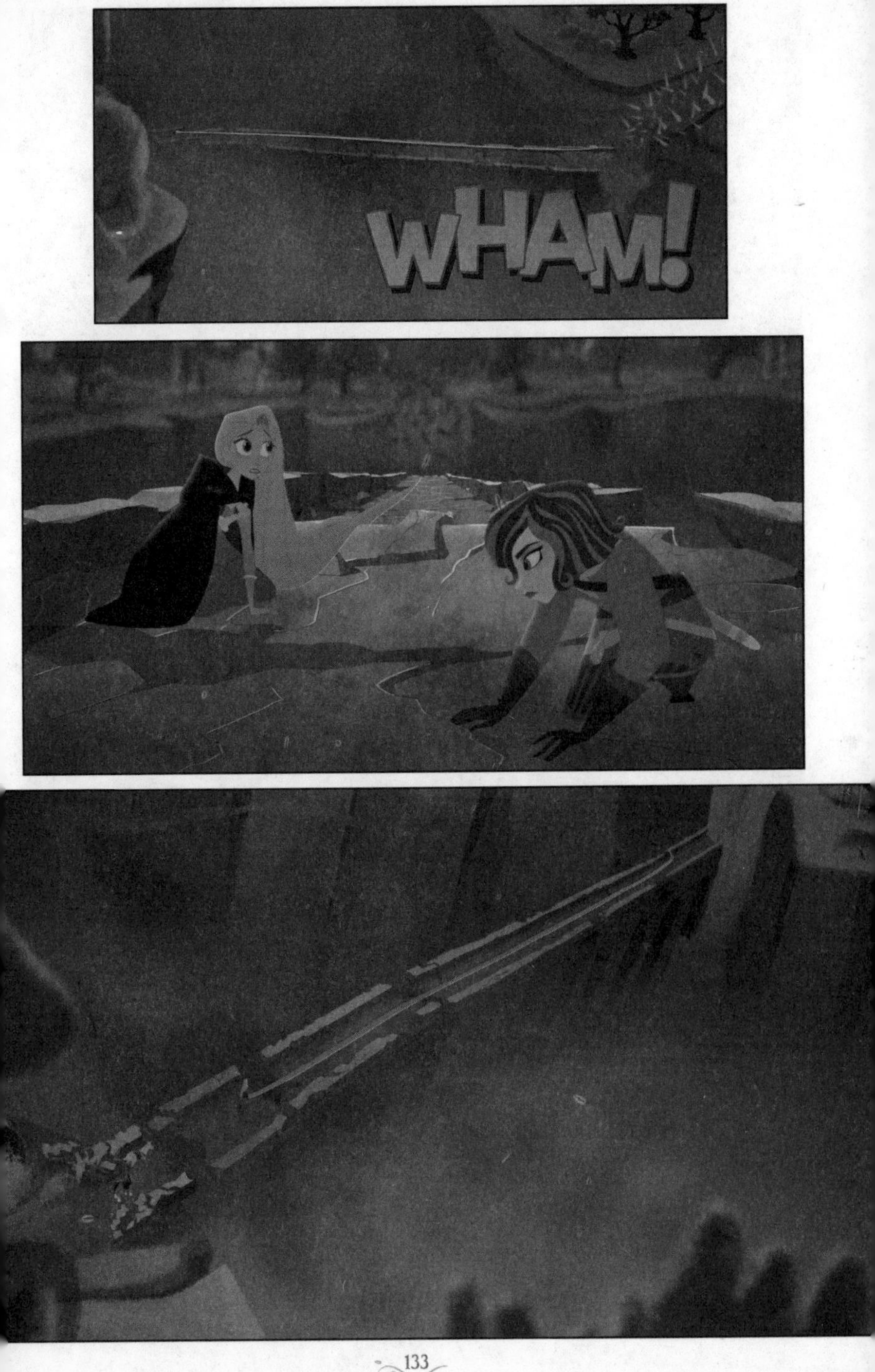
WHAM!

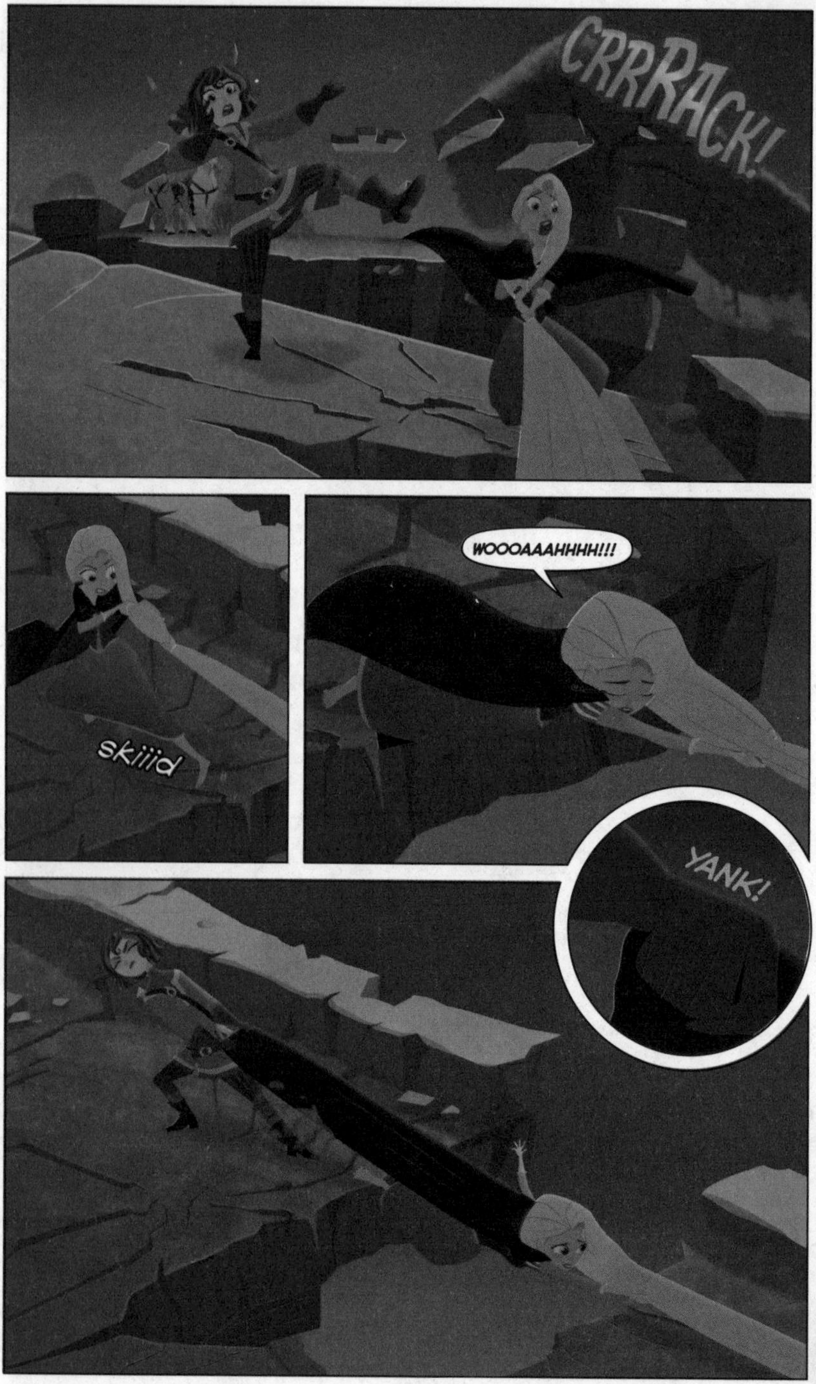
CRRRACK!
skiiid
WOOOAAAHHHH!!!
YANK!

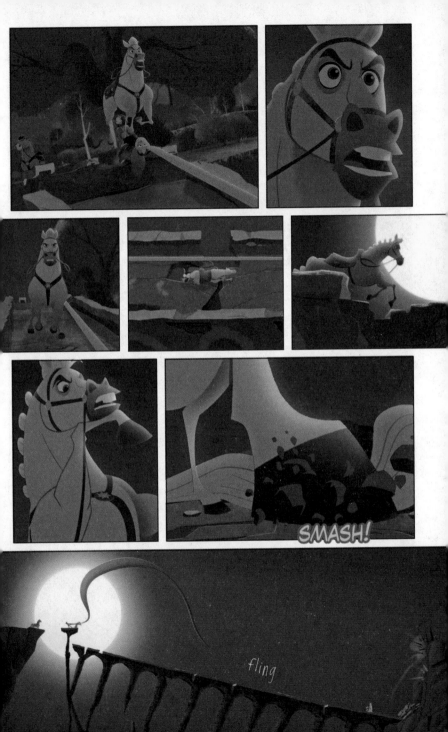

SMASH!

fling

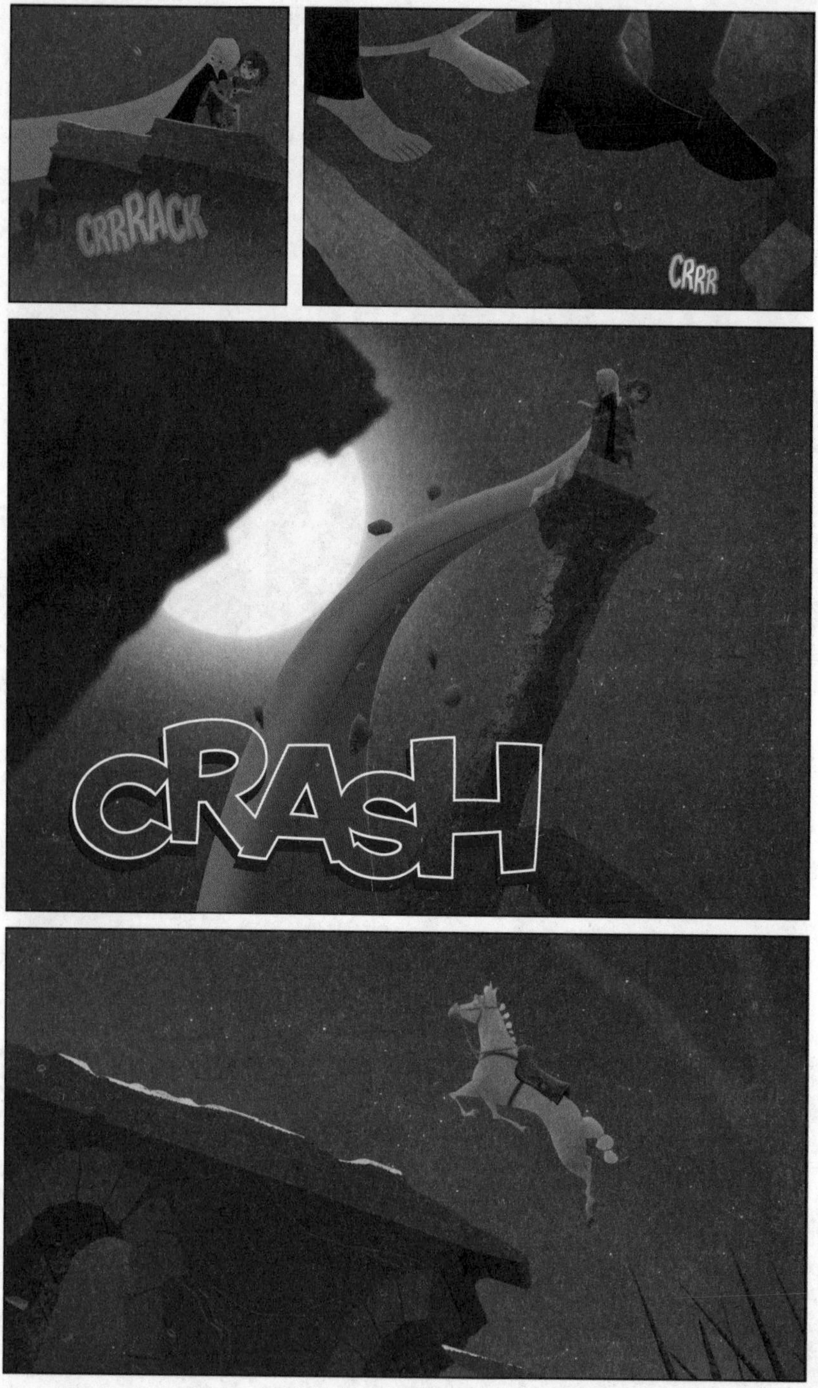
CRRRACK
CRRR
CRASH

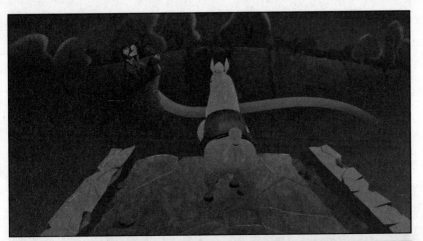

AAAHHHH!!!

SLAM

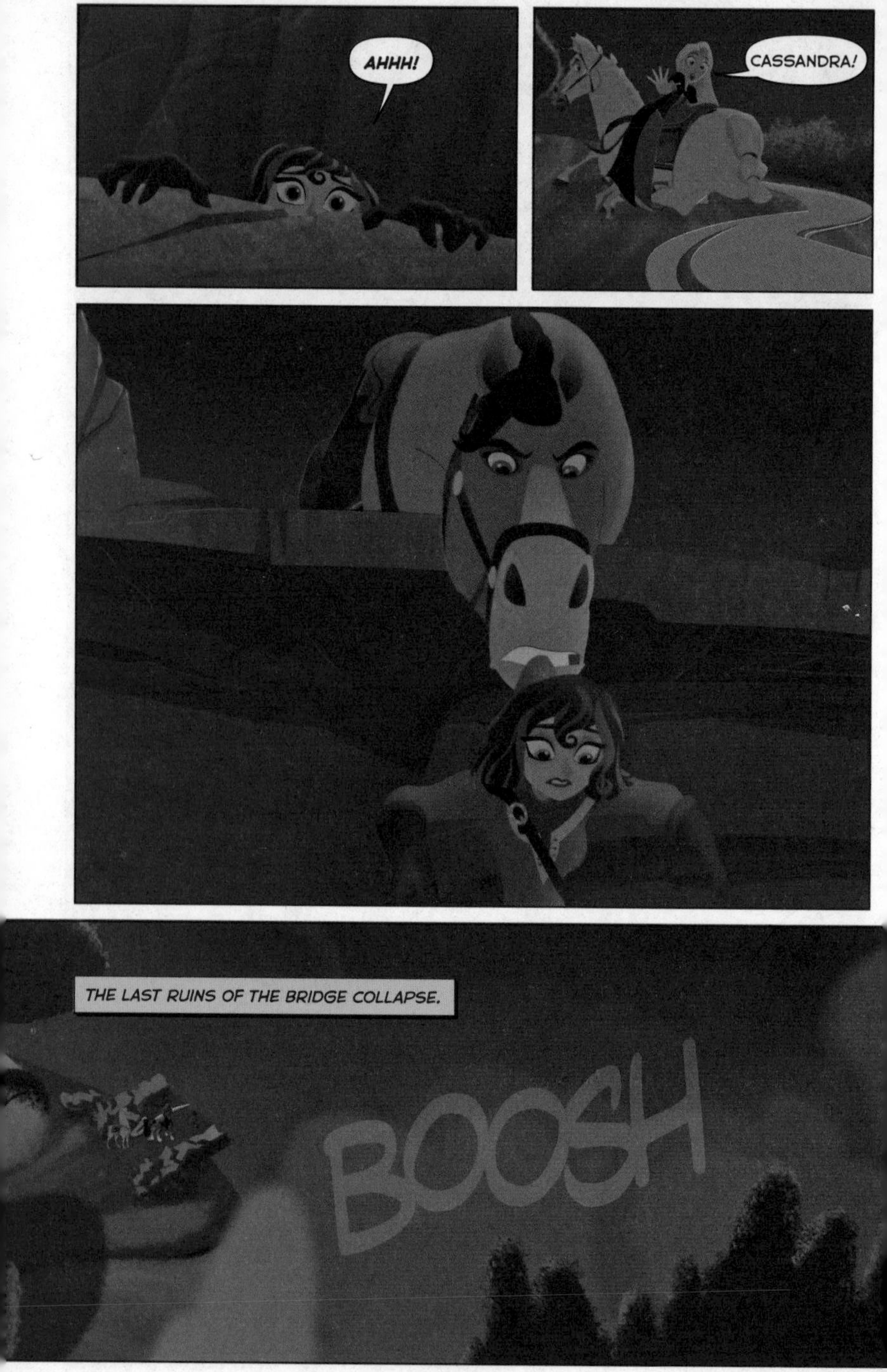
AHHH!
CASSANDRA!
THE LAST RUINS OF THE BRIDGE COLLAPSE.
BOOSH

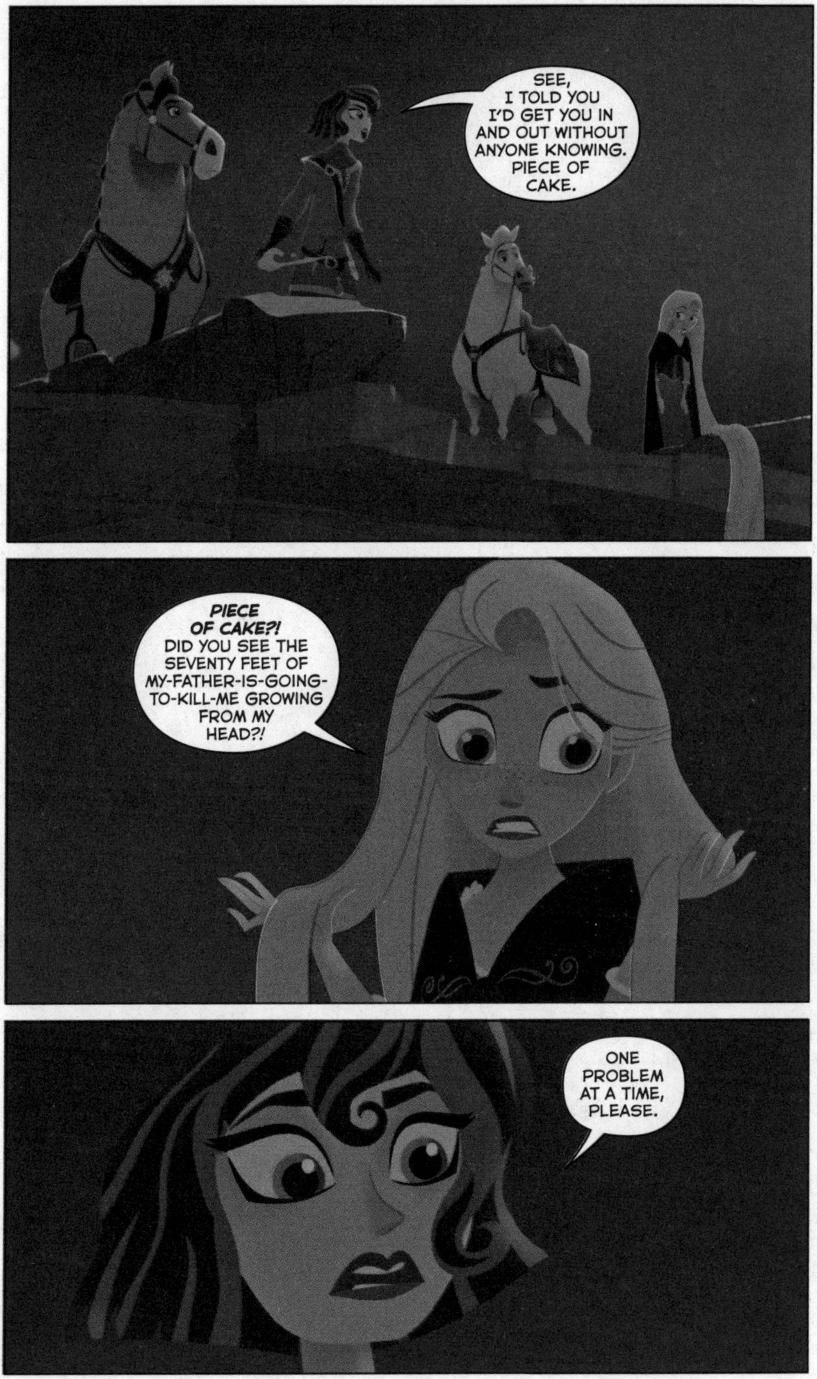
SEE, I TOLD YOU I'D GET YOU IN AND OUT WITHOUT ANYONE KNOWING. PIECE OF CAKE.
PIECE OF CAKE?! DID YOU SEE THE SEVENTY FEET OF MY-FATHER-IS-GOING-TO-KILL-ME GROWING FROM MY HEAD?!
ONE PROBLEM AT A TIME, PLEASE.

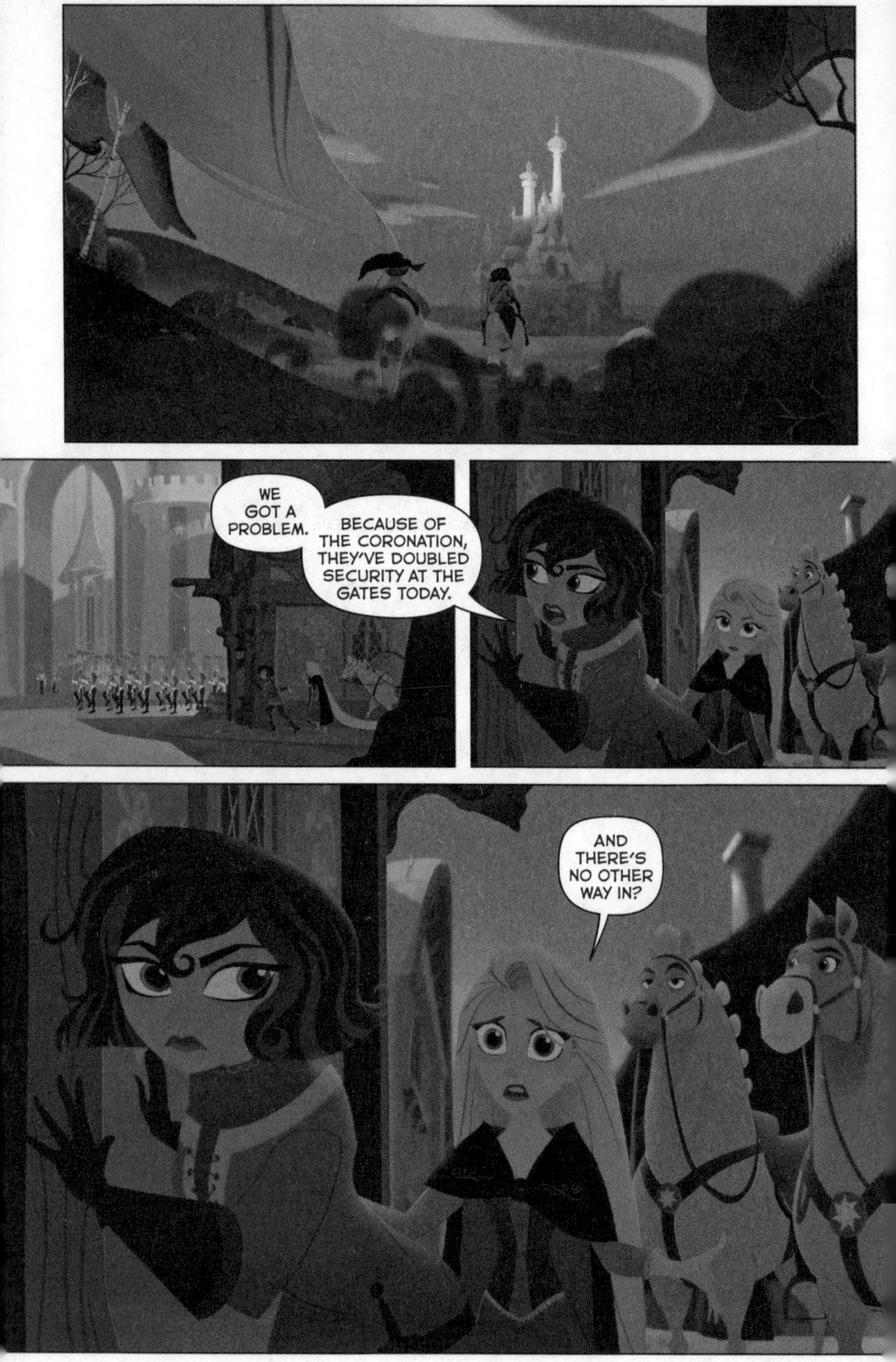
WE GOT A PROBLEM.
BECAUSE OF THE CORONATION, THEY'VE DOUBLED SECURITY AT THE GATES TODAY.
AND THERE'S NO OTHER WAY IN?

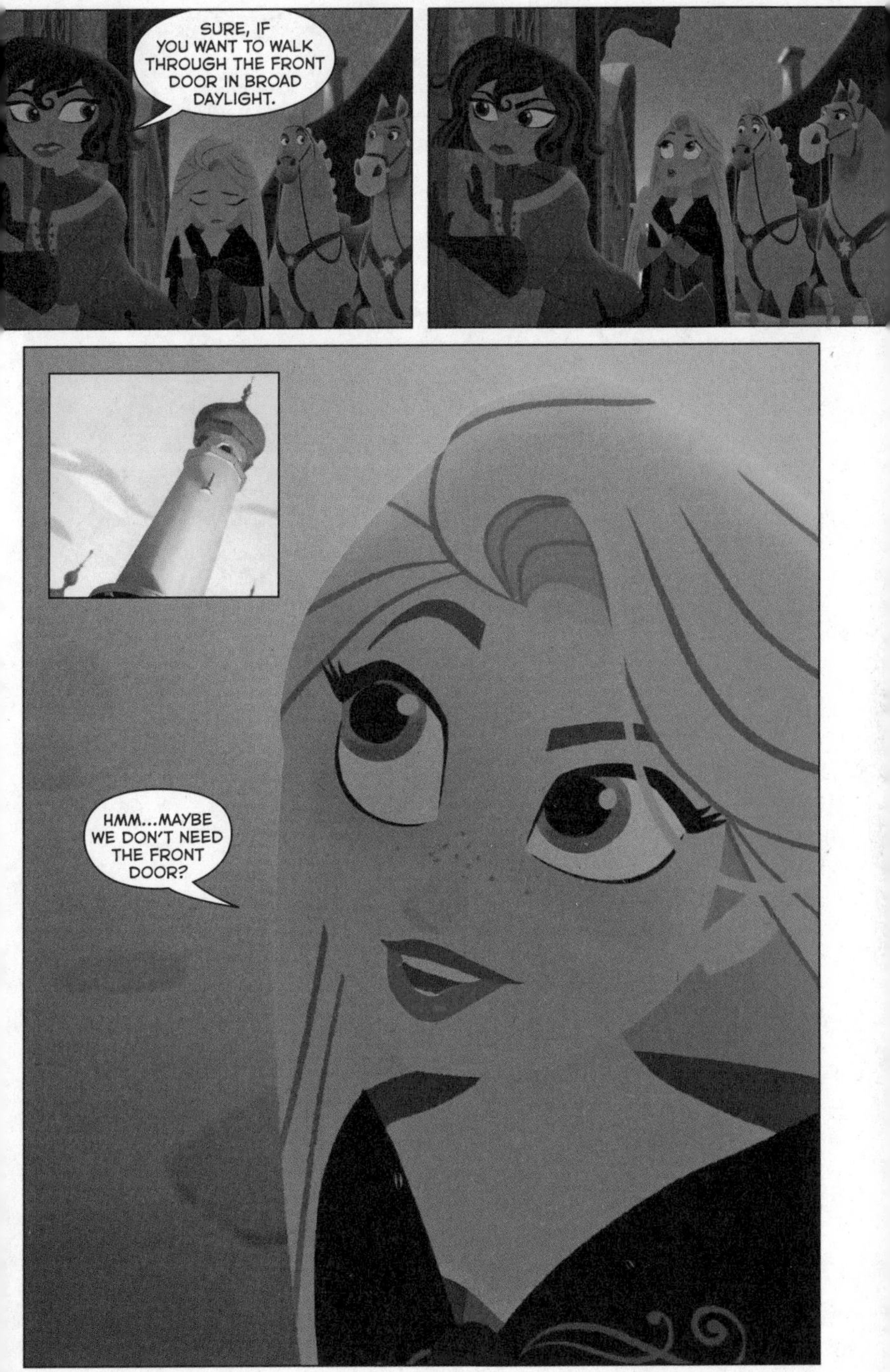
SURE, IF YOU WANT TO WALK THROUGH THE FRONT DOOR IN BROAD DAYLIGHT.
HMM...MAYBE WE DON'T NEED THE FRONT DOOR?

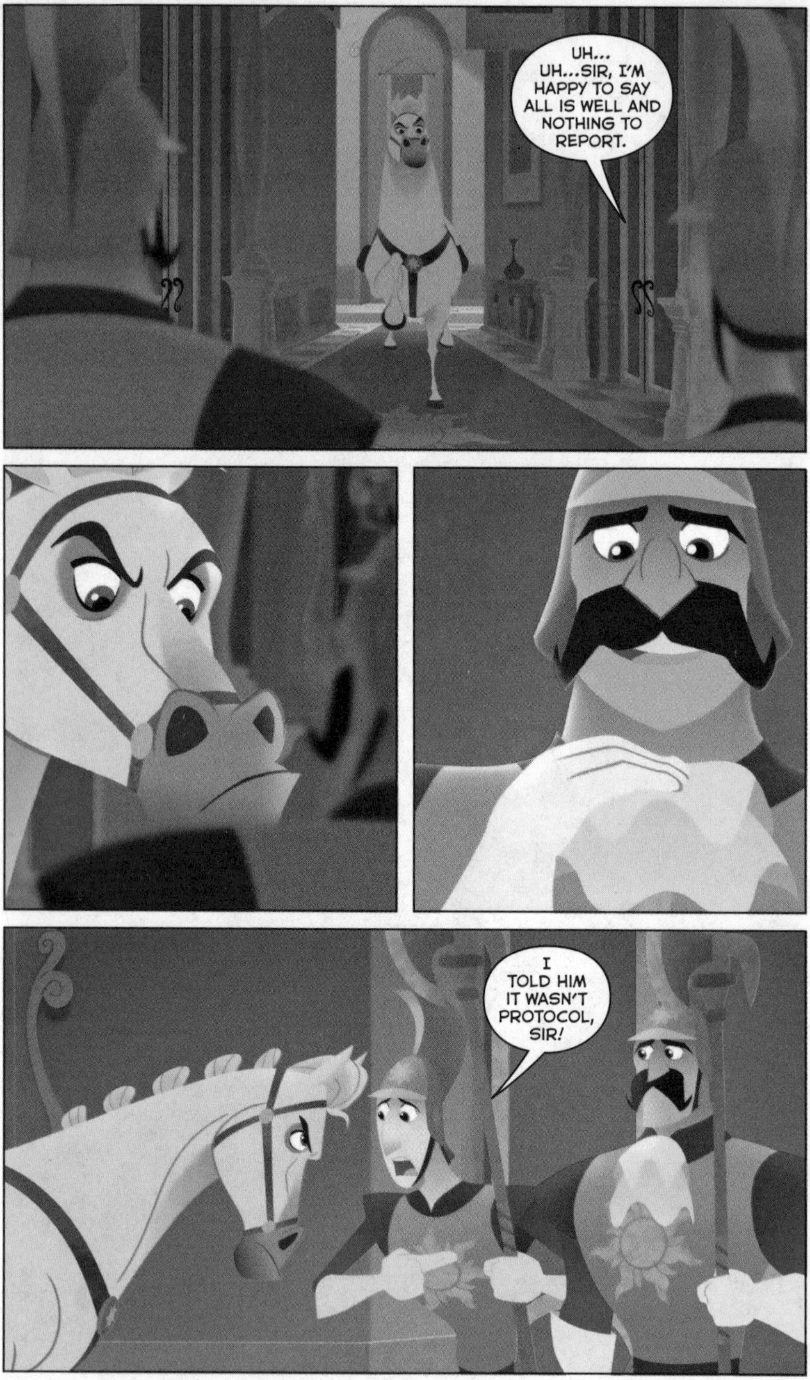
UH...
UH...SIR, I'M HAPPY TO SAY ALL IS WELL AND NOTHING TO REPORT.
I TOLD HIM IT WASN'T PROTOCOL, SIR!

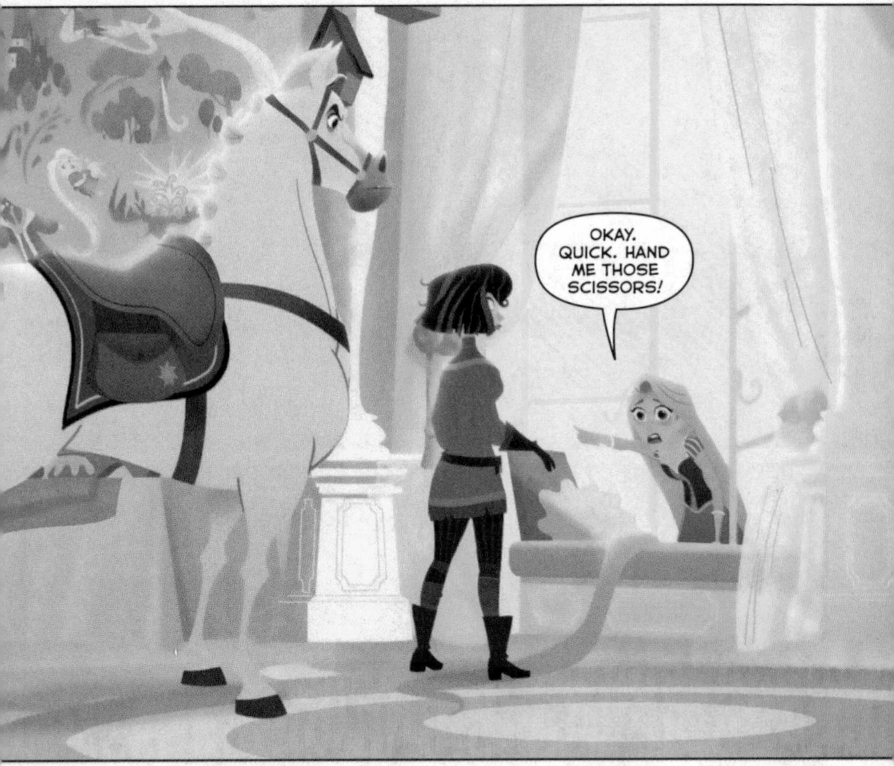
OKAY. QUICK. HAND ME THOSE SCISSORS!

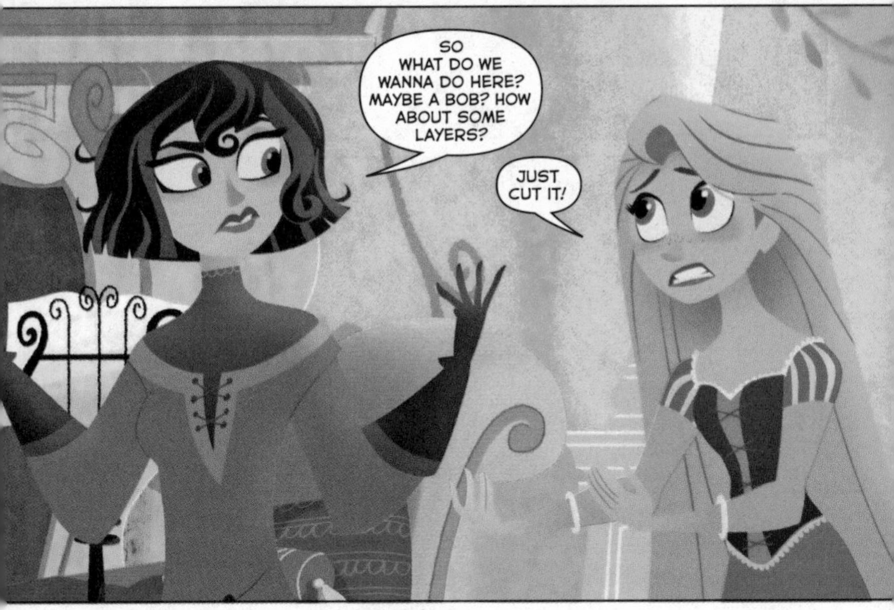
SO WHAT DO WE WANNA DO HERE? MAYBE A BOB? HOW ABOUT SOME LAYERS?
JUST CUT IT!

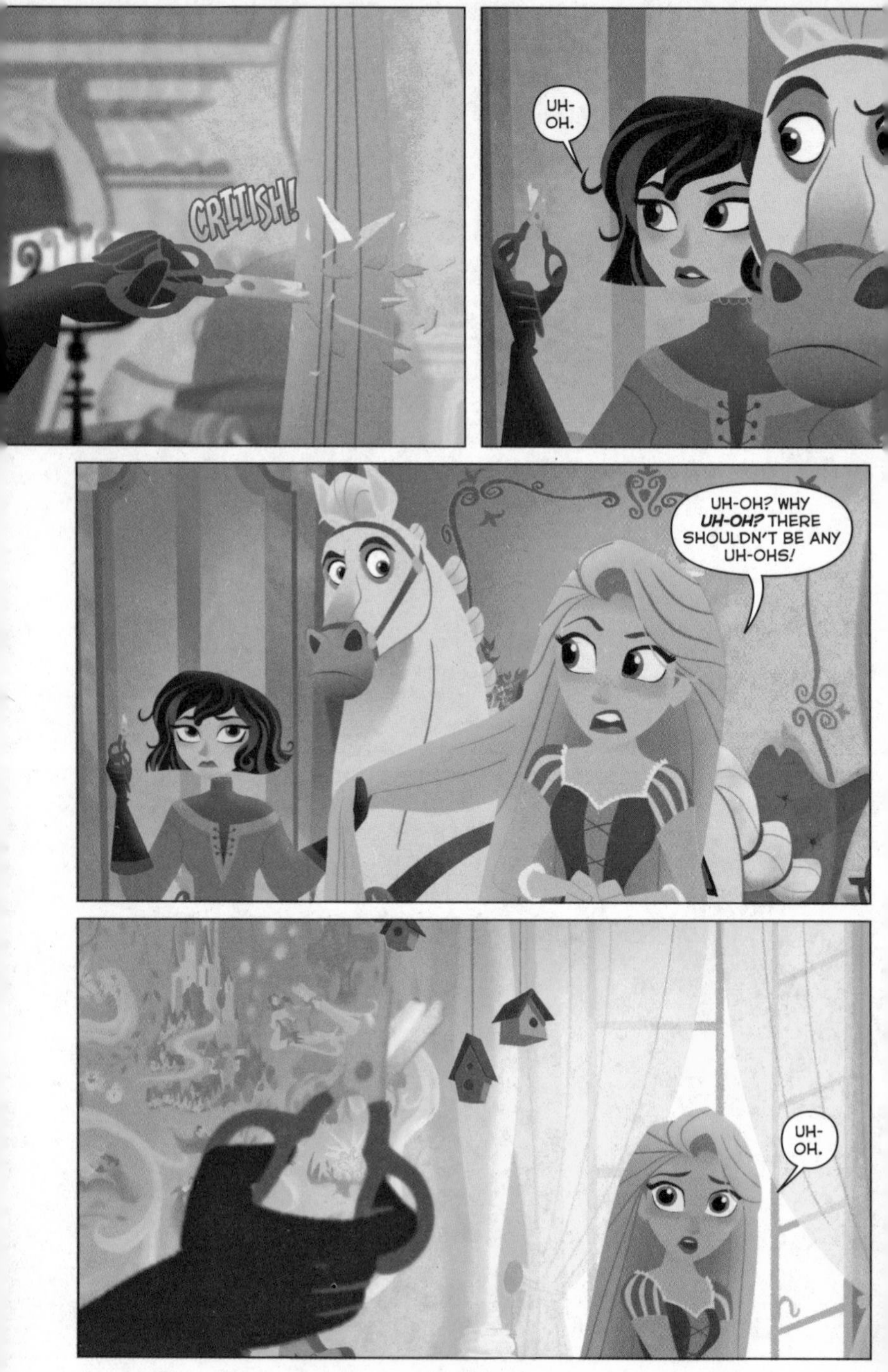
CRIIISH!
UH-OH.
UH-OH? WHY *UH-OH?* THERE SHOULDN'T BE ANY UH-OHS!
UH-OH.

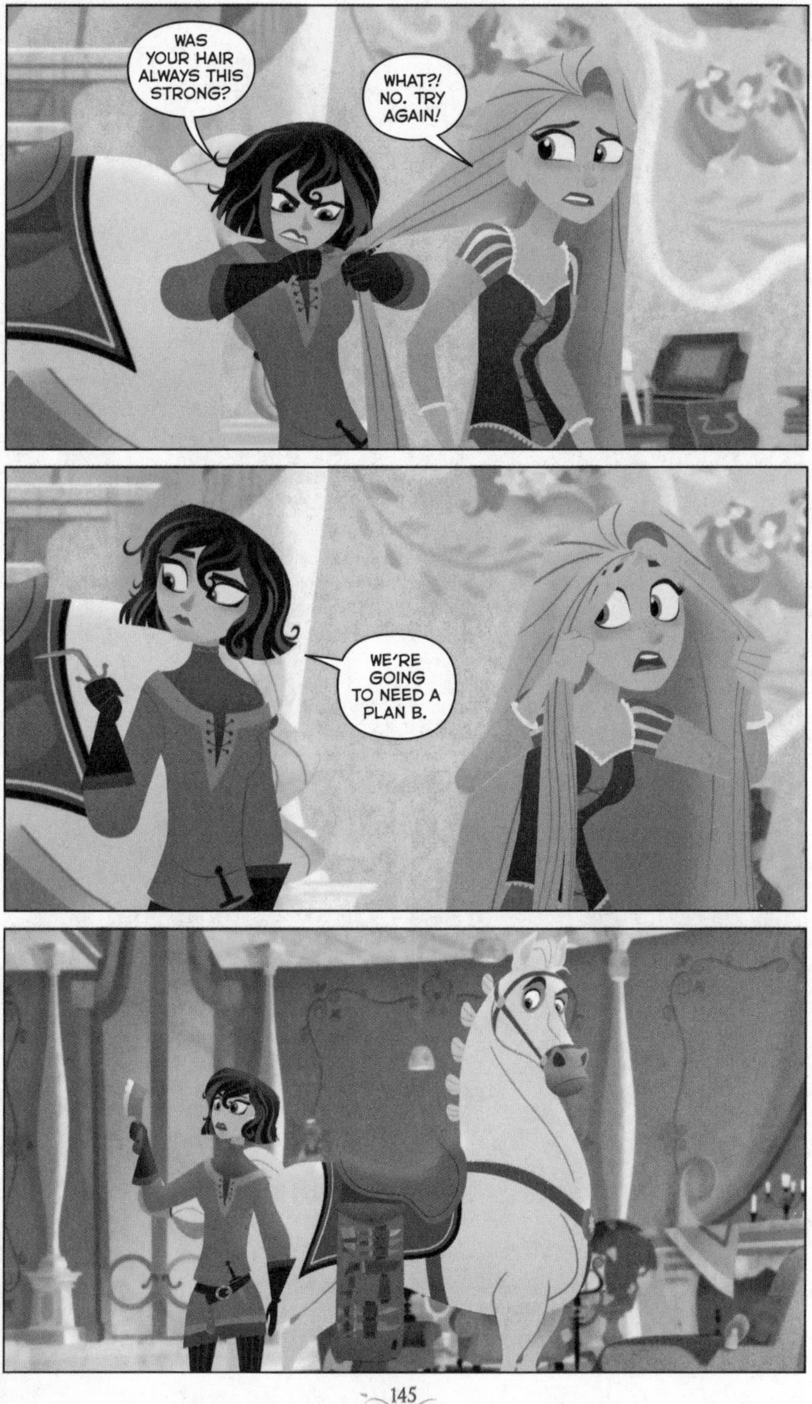
WAS YOUR HAIR ALWAYS THIS STRONG?
WHAT?! NO. TRY AGAIN!
WE'RE GOING TO NEED A PLAN B.

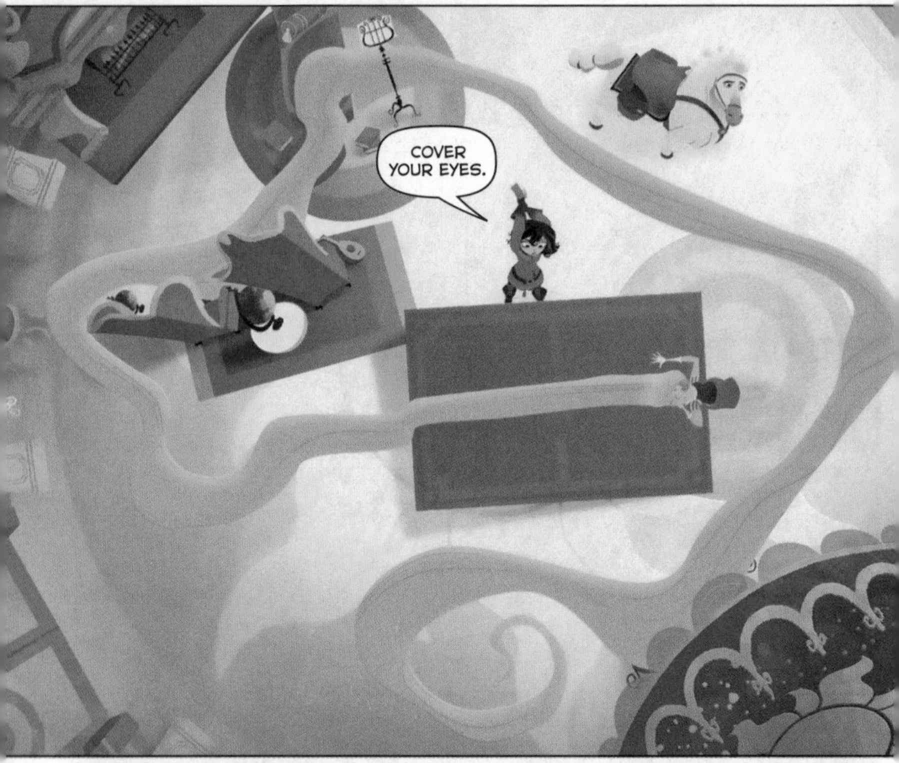
COVER YOUR EYES.

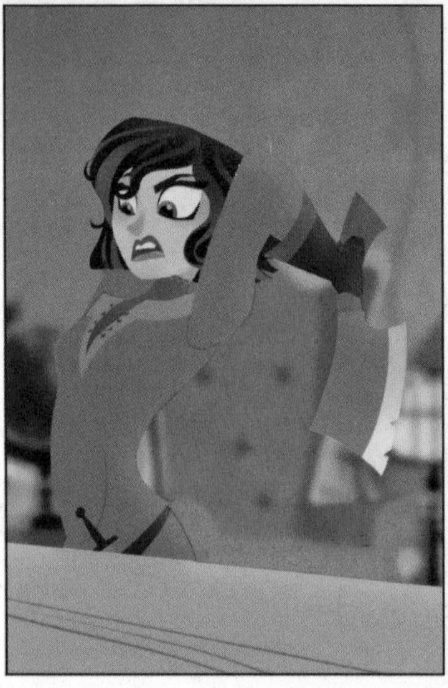

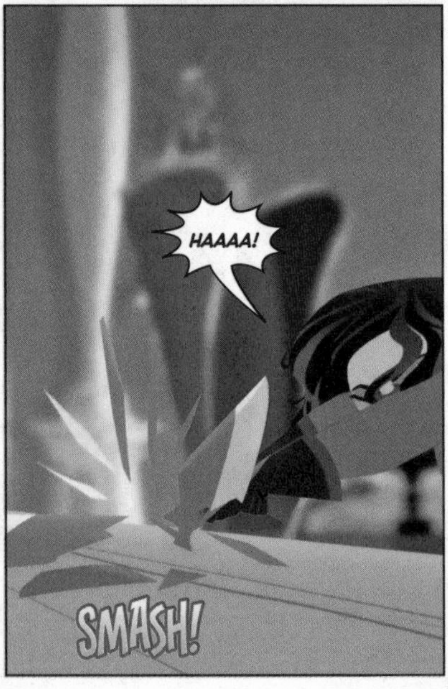
HAAAA!
SMASH!

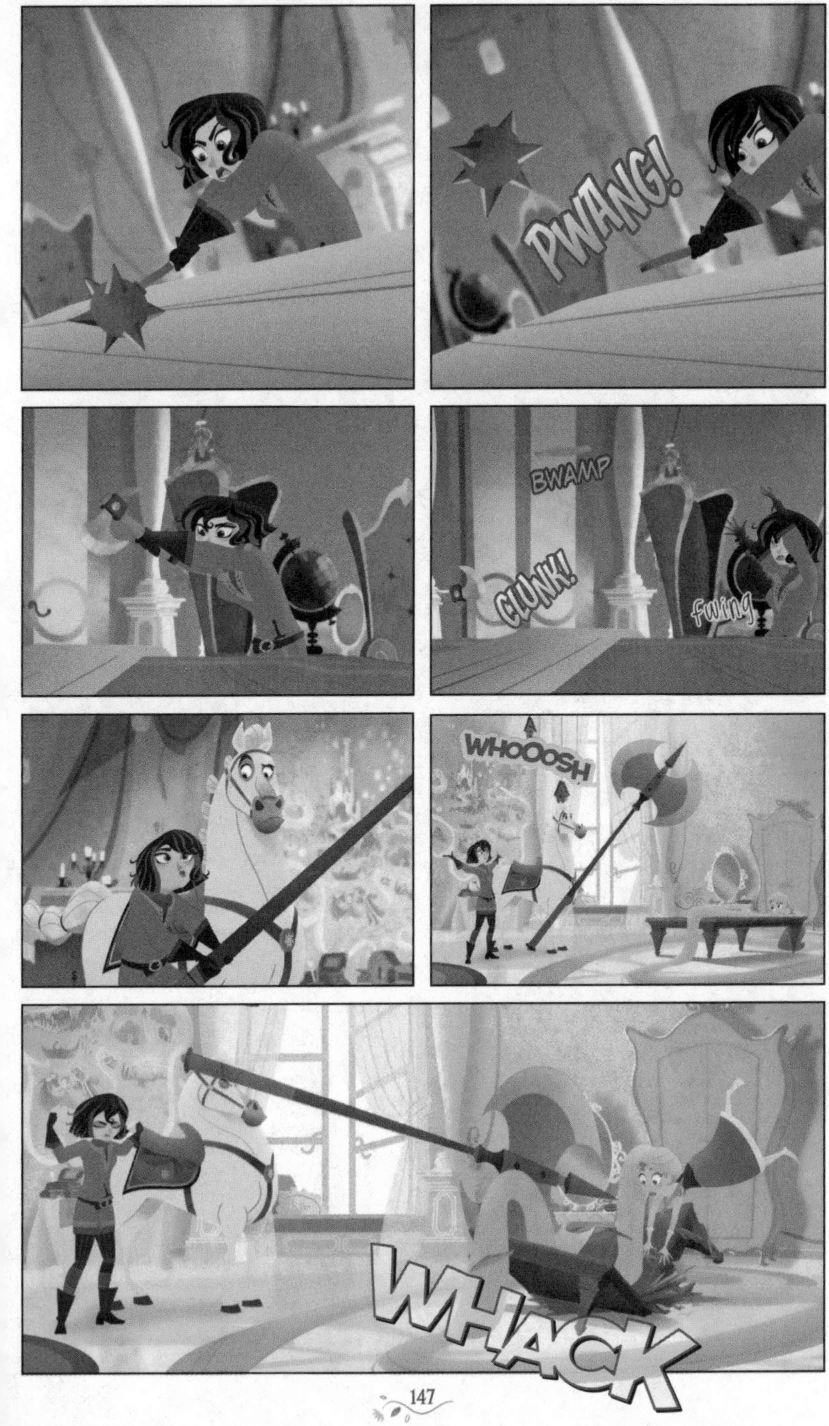
PWANG!
BWAMP
CLUNK!
fwing
WHOOOSH
WHACK

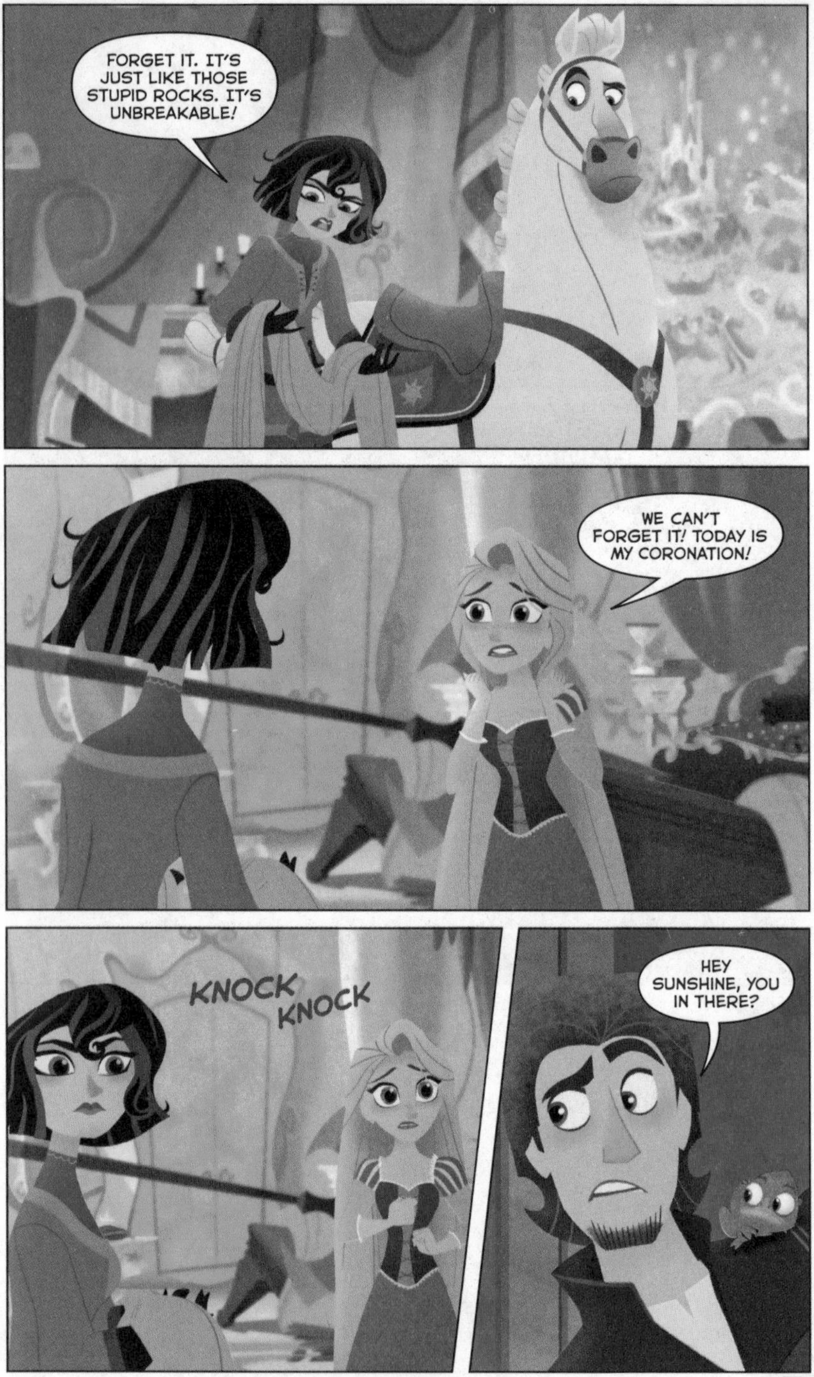
FORGET IT. IT'S JUST LIKE THOSE STUPID ROCKS. IT'S UNBREAKABLE!
WE CAN'T FORGET IT! TODAY IS MY CORONATION!
KNOCK KNOCK
HEY SUNSHINE, YOU IN THERE?

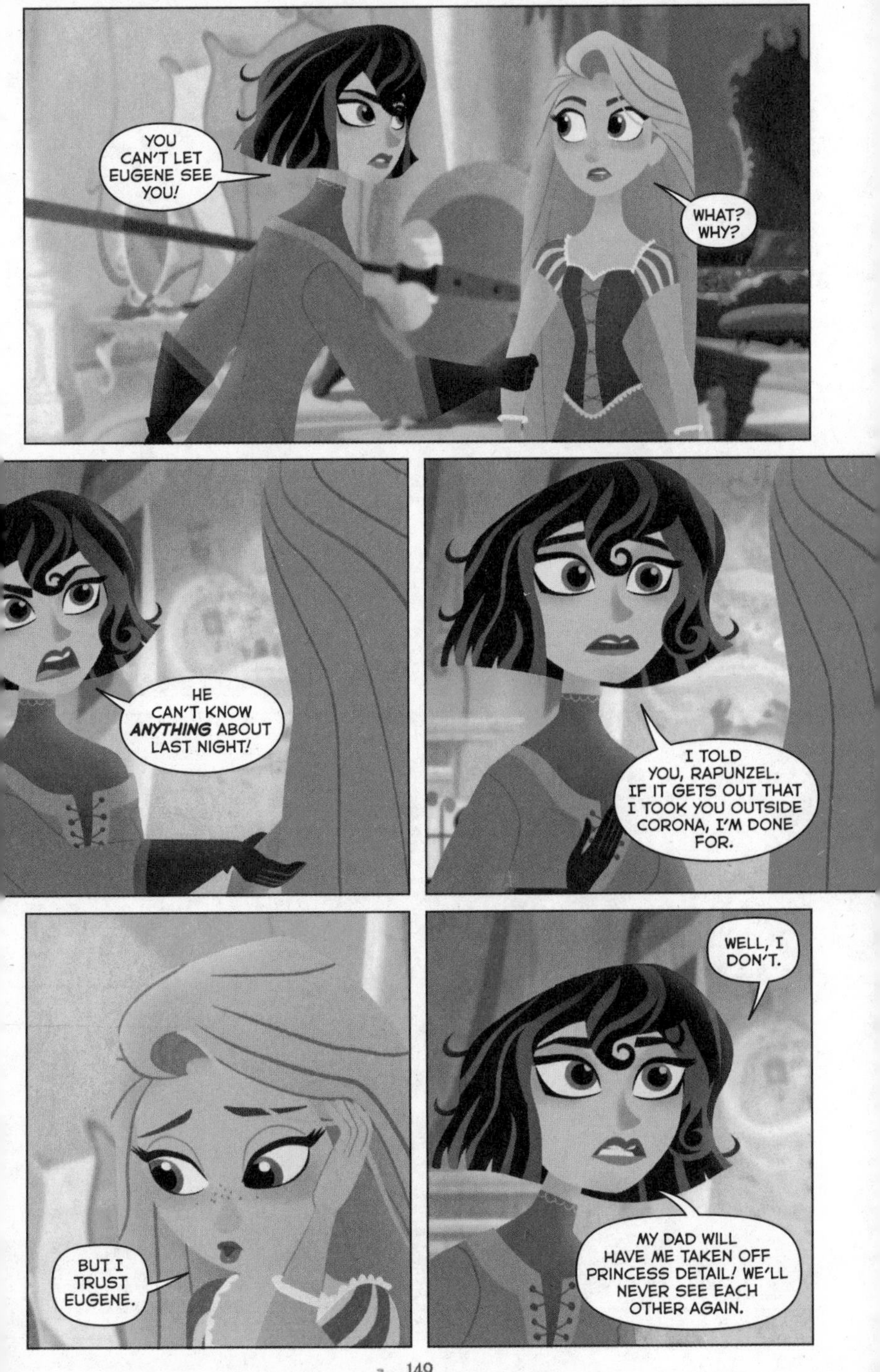
YOU CAN'T LET EUGENE SEE YOU!
WHAT? WHY?
HE CAN'T KNOW ***ANYTHING*** ABOUT LAST NIGHT!
I TOLD YOU, RAPUNZEL. IF IT GETS OUT THAT I TOOK YOU OUTSIDE CORONA, I'M DONE FOR.
BUT I TRUST EUGENE.
WELL, I DON'T.
MY DAD WILL HAVE ME TAKEN OFF PRINCESS DETAIL! WE'LL NEVER SEE EACH OTHER AGAIN.

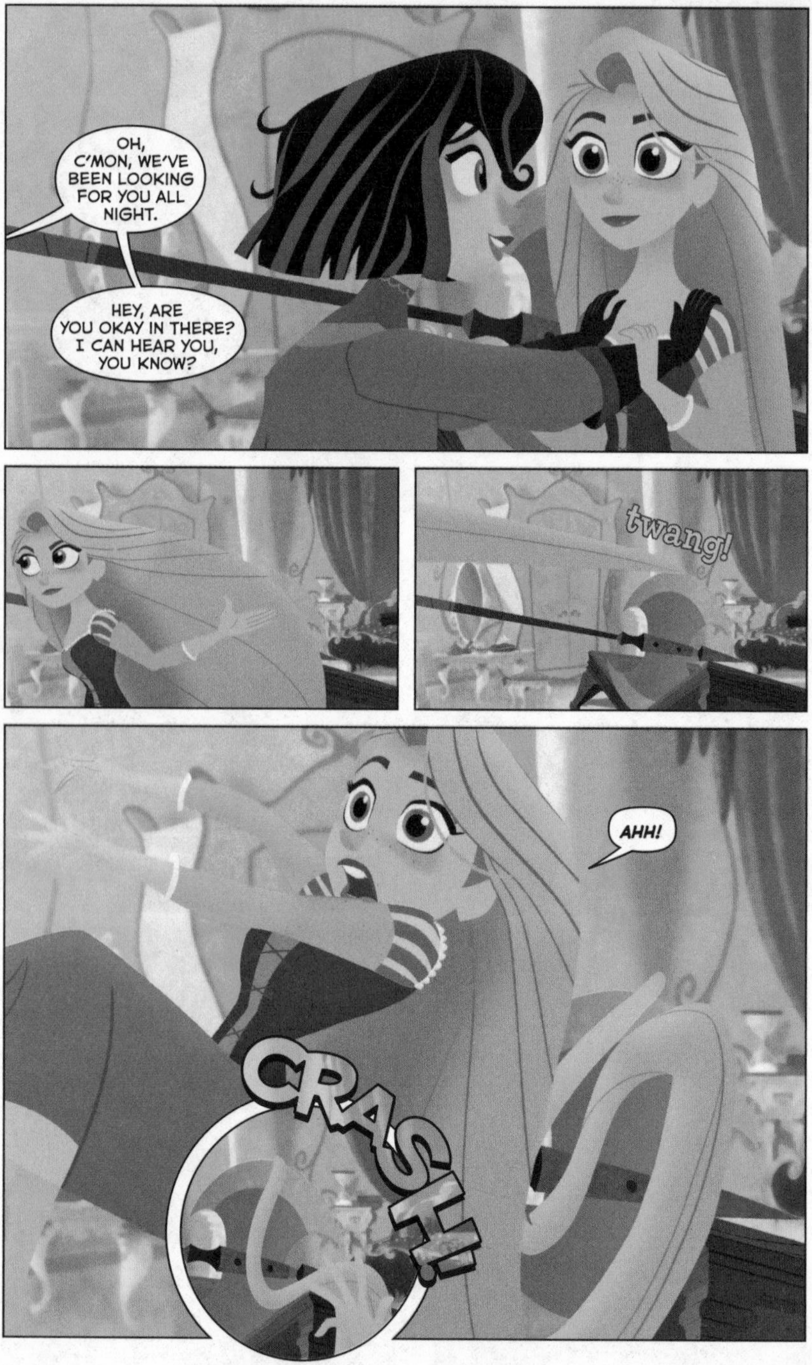
OH, C'MON, WE'VE BEEN LOOKING FOR YOU ALL NIGHT.
HEY, ARE YOU OKAY IN THERE? I CAN HEAR YOU, YOU KNOW?
twang!
AHH!
CRASH!

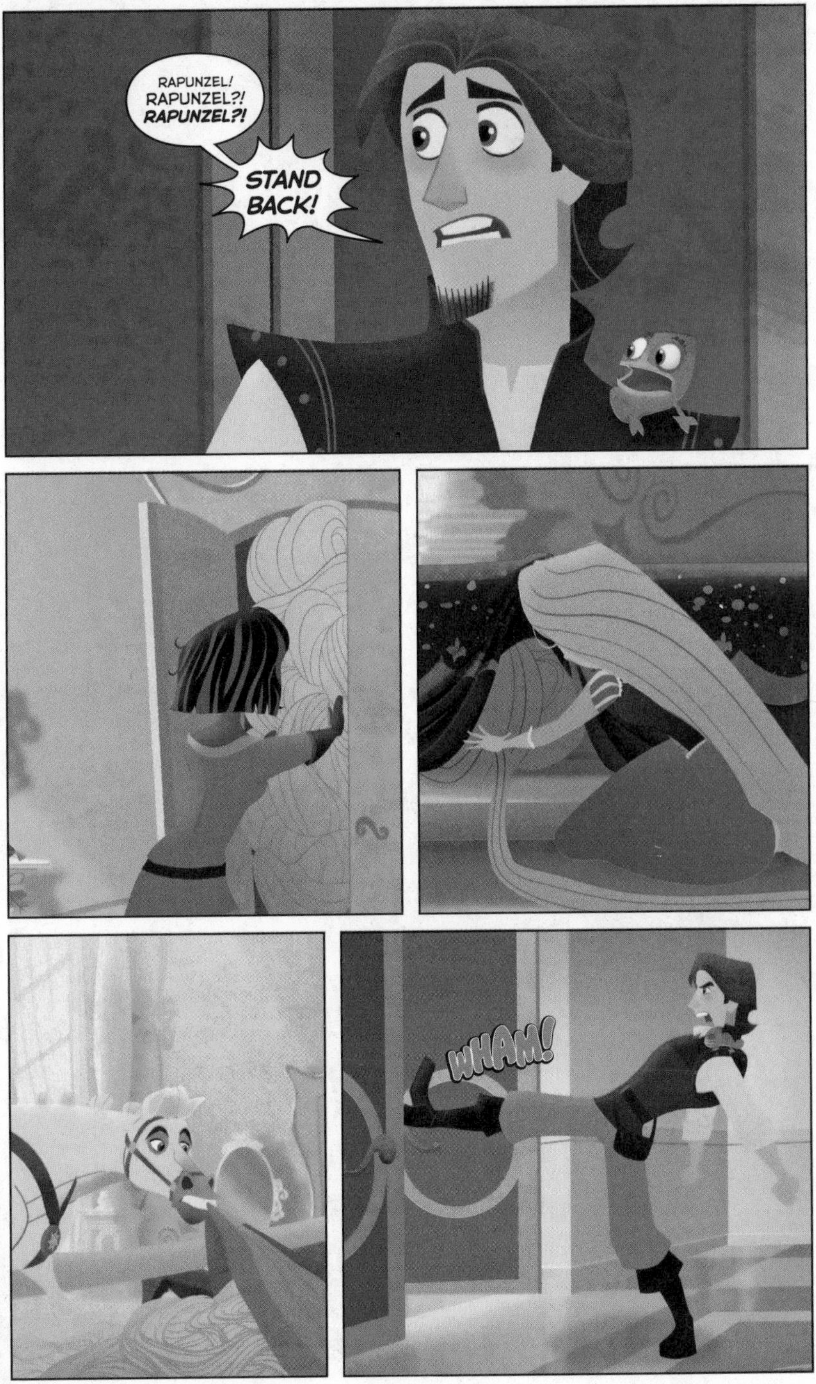
RAPUNZEL!
RAPUNZEL?!
RAPUNZEL?!
STAND BACK!
WHAM!

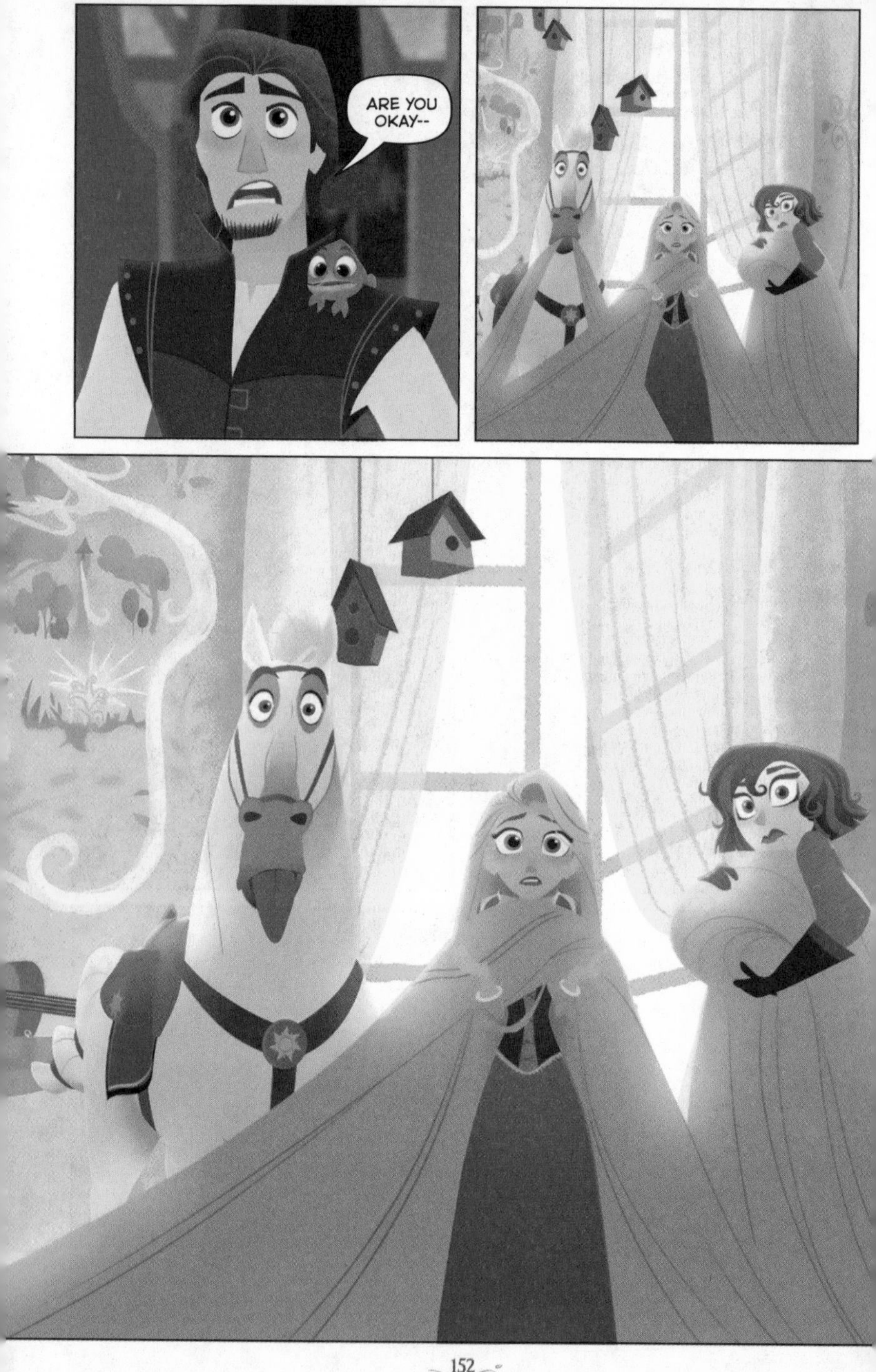
ARE YOU
OKAY--

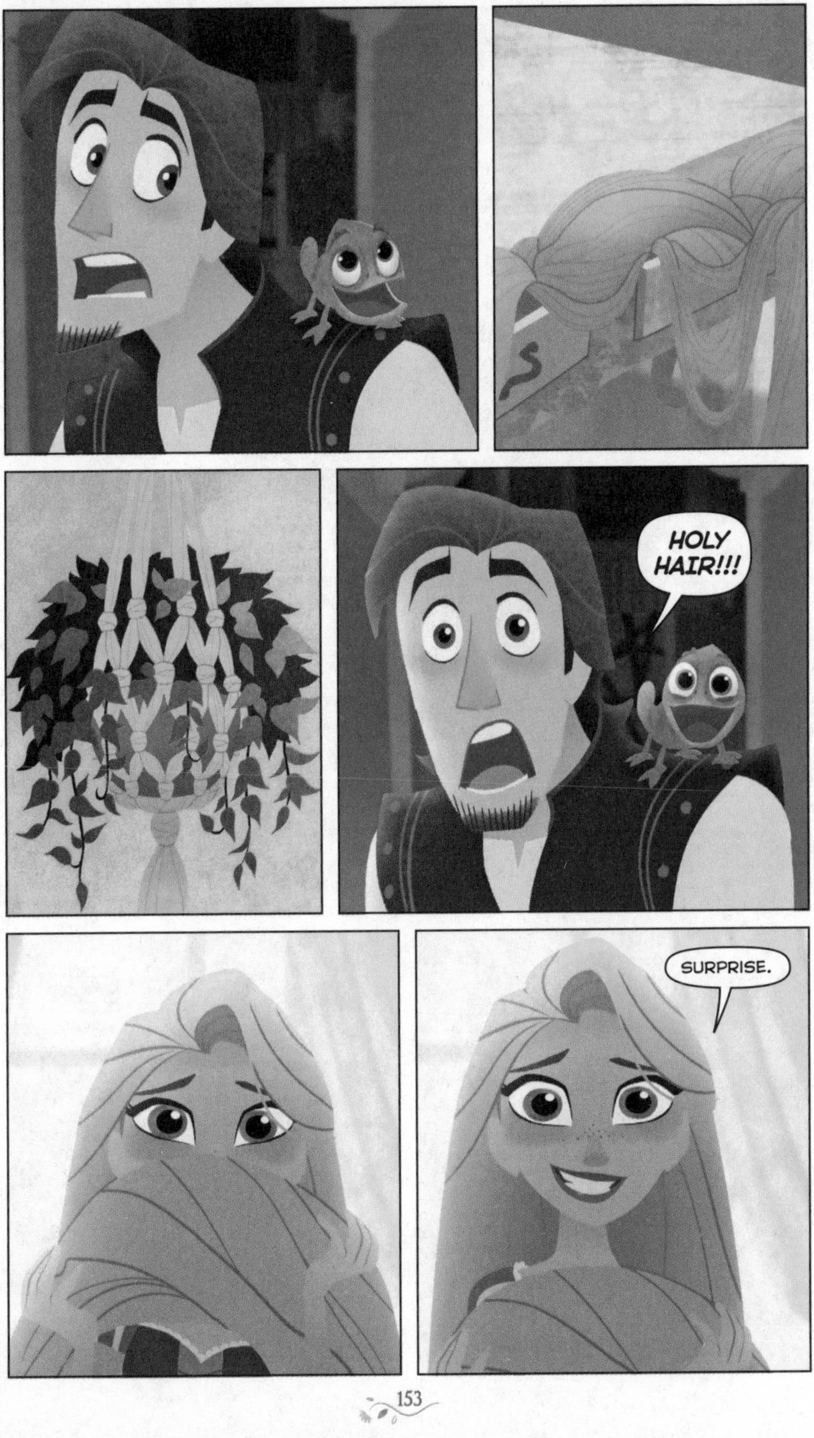
HOLY HAIR!!!
SURPRISE.

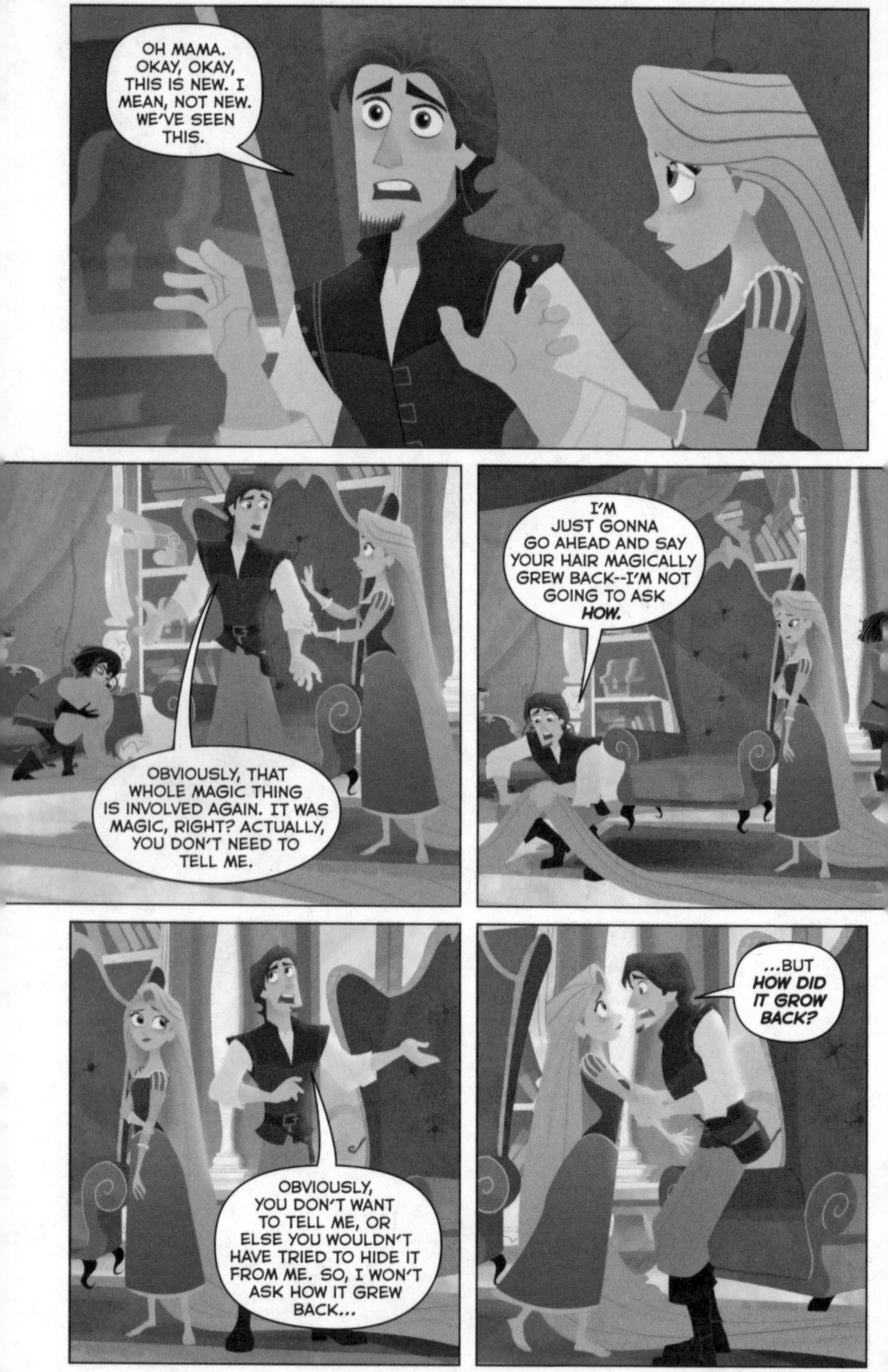
OH MAMA. OKAY, OKAY, THIS IS NEW. I MEAN, NOT NEW. WE'VE SEEN THIS.
OBVIOUSLY, THAT WHOLE MAGIC THING IS INVOLVED AGAIN. IT WAS MAGIC, RIGHT? ACTUALLY, YOU DON'T NEED TO TELL ME.
I'M JUST GONNA GO AHEAD AND SAY YOUR HAIR MAGICALLY GREW BACK--I'M NOT GOING TO ASK ***HOW.***
OBVIOUSLY, YOU DON'T WANT TO TELL ME, OR ELSE YOU WOULDN'T HAVE TRIED TO HIDE IT FROM ME. SO, I WON'T ASK HOW IT GREW BACK...
...BUT ***HOW DID IT GROW BACK?***

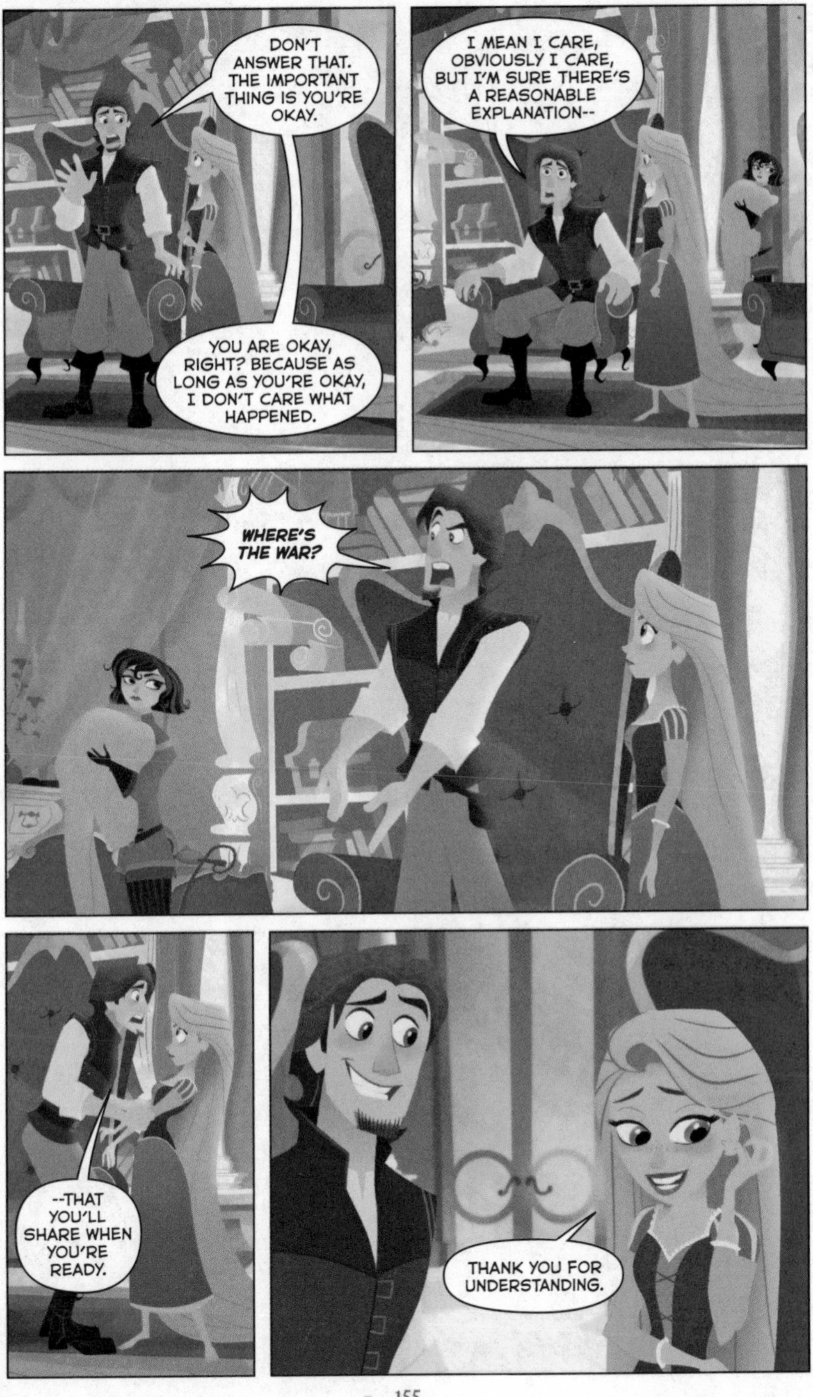
DON'T ANSWER THAT. THE IMPORTANT THING IS YOU'RE OKAY.
YOU ARE OKAY, RIGHT? BECAUSE AS LONG AS YOU'RE OKAY, I DON'T CARE WHAT HAPPENED.
I MEAN I CARE, OBVIOUSLY I CARE, BUT I'M SURE THERE'S A REASONABLE EXPLANATION--
WHERE'S THE WAR?
--THAT YOU'LL SHARE WHEN YOU'RE READY.
THANK YOU FOR UNDERSTANDING.

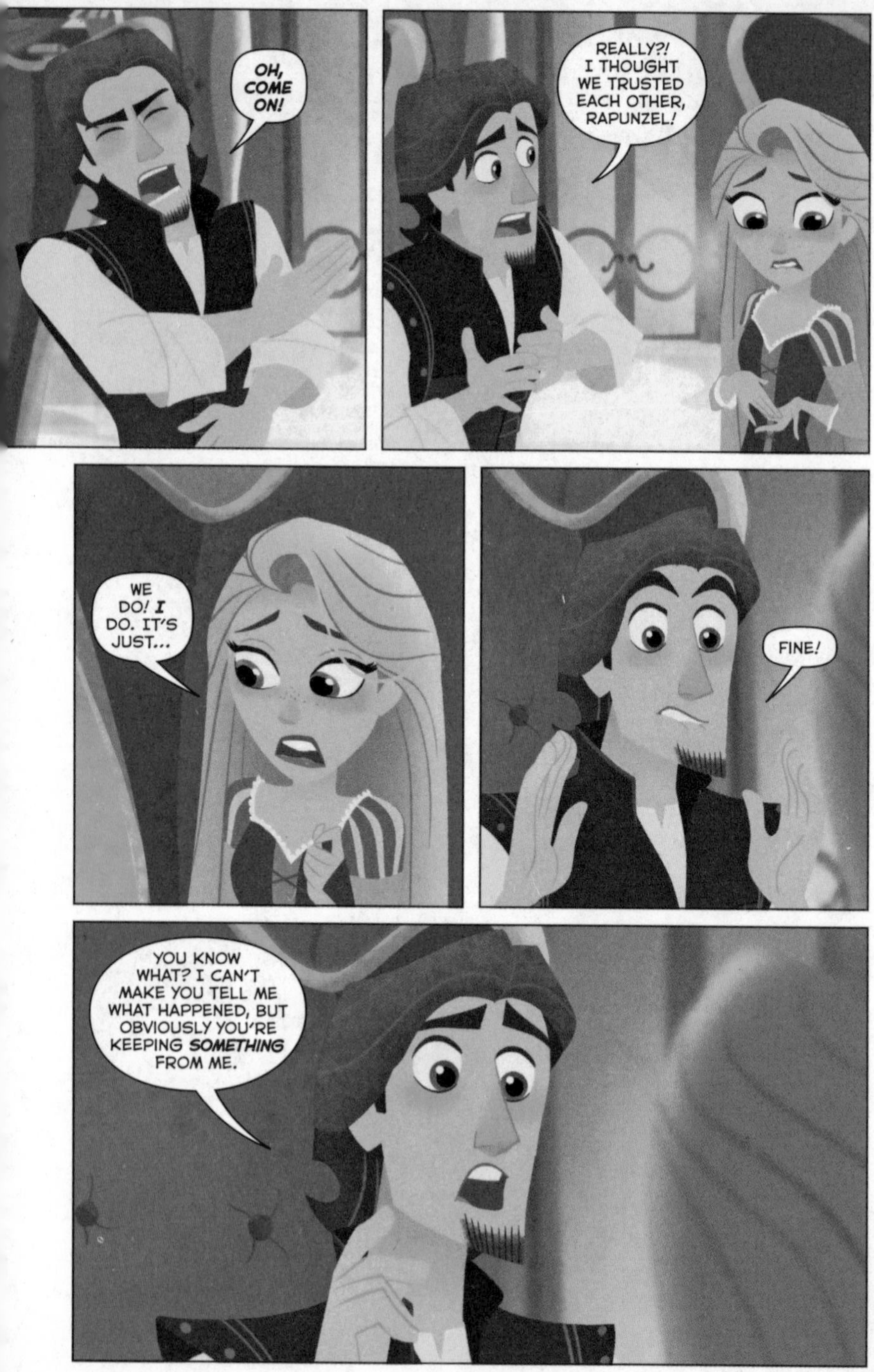
OH, COME ON!
REALLY?! I THOUGHT WE TRUSTED EACH OTHER, RAPUNZEL!
WE DO! I DO. IT'S JUST...
FINE!
YOU KNOW WHAT? I CAN'T MAKE YOU TELL ME WHAT HAPPENED, BUT OBVIOUSLY YOU'RE KEEPING SOMETHING FROM ME.

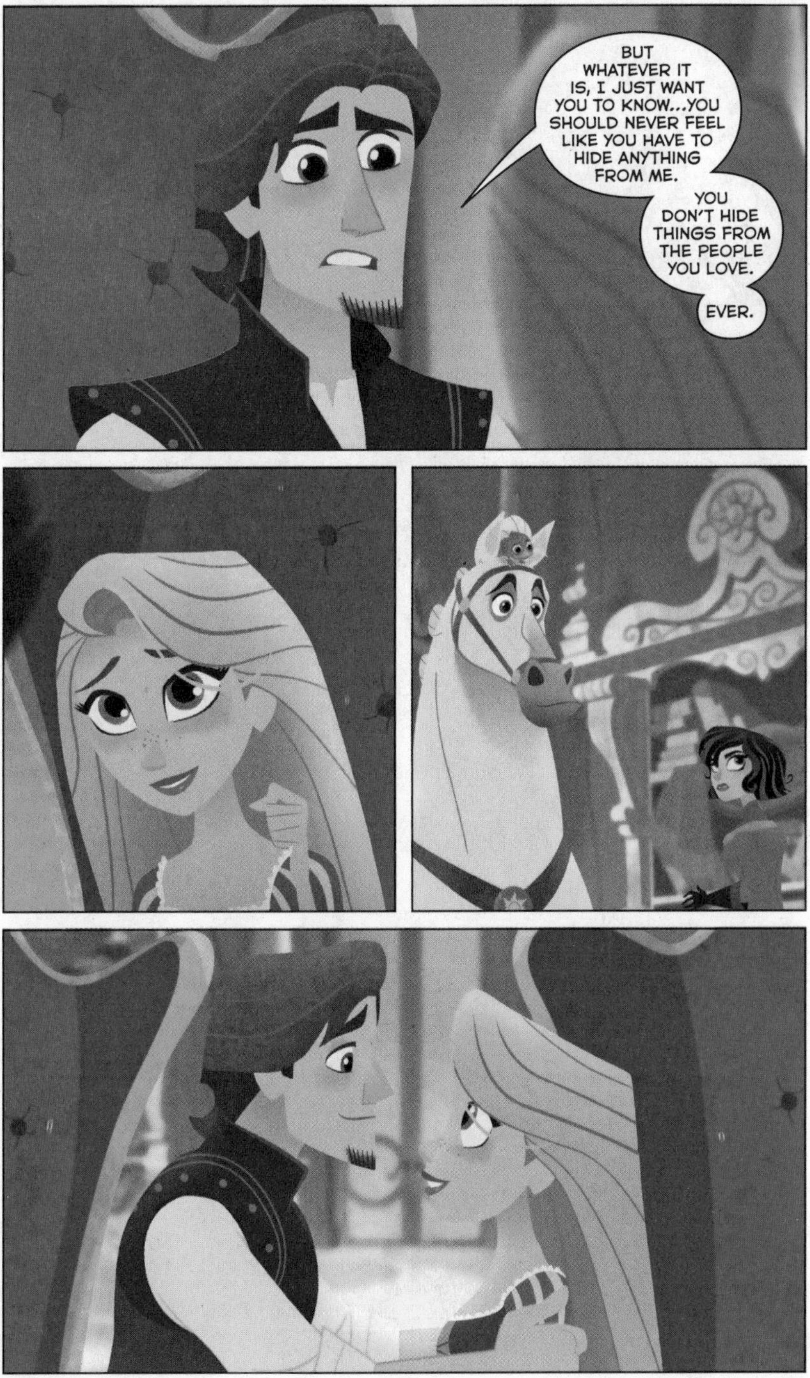
BUT WHATEVER IT IS, I JUST WANT YOU TO KNOW...YOU SHOULD NEVER FEEL LIKE YOU HAVE TO HIDE ANYTHING FROM ME.
YOU DON'T HIDE THINGS FROM THE PEOPLE YOU LOVE.
EVER.

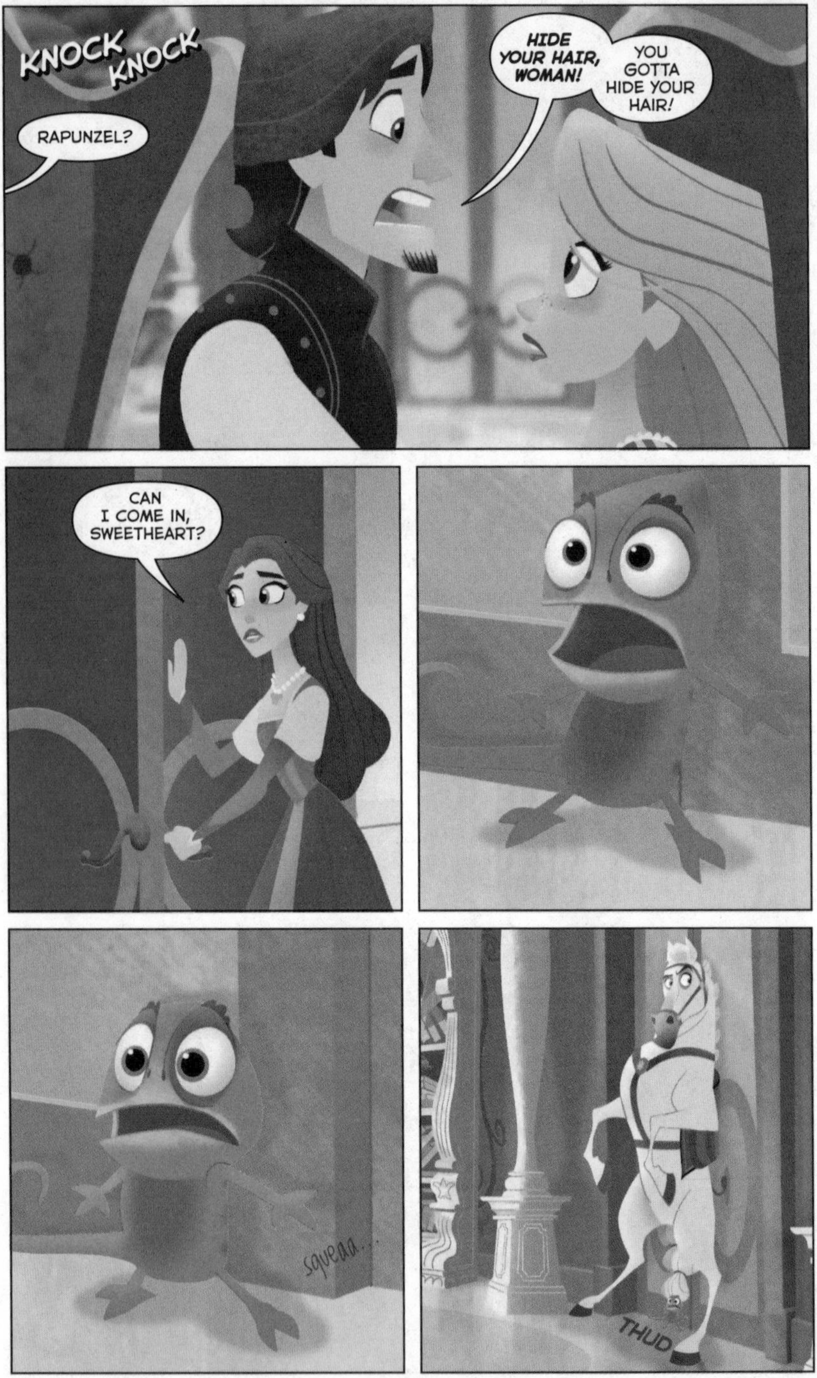

KNOCK KNOCK
RAPUNZEL?
HIDE YOUR HAIR, WOMAN!
YOU GOTTA HIDE YOUR HAIR!
CAN I COME IN, SWEETHEART?
squeaa...
THUD

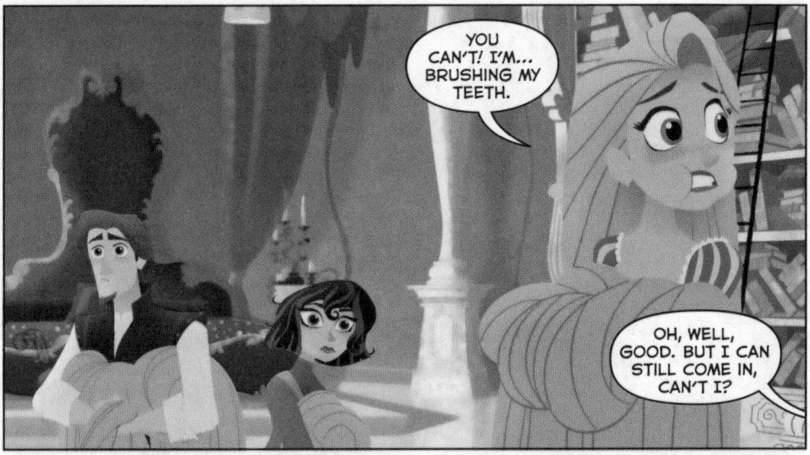
YOU CAN'T! I'M... BRUSHING MY TEETH.
OH, WELL, GOOD. BUT I CAN STILL COME IN, CAN'T I?

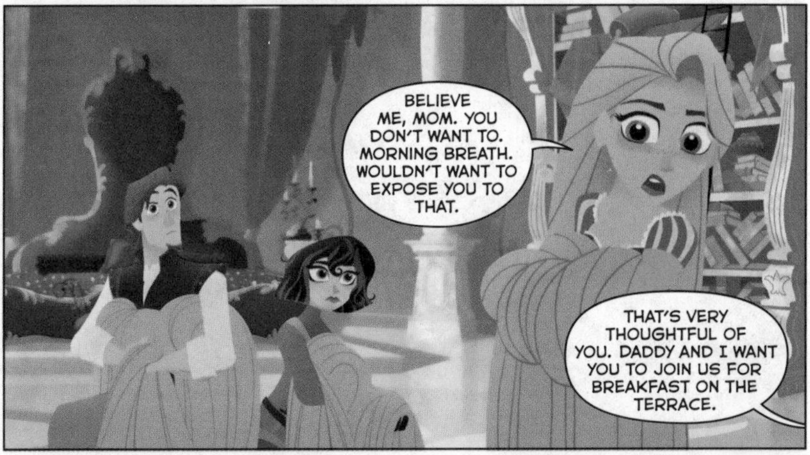
BELIEVE ME, MOM. YOU DON'T WANT TO. MORNING BREATH. WOULDN'T WANT TO EXPOSE YOU TO THAT.
THAT'S VERY THOUGHTFUL OF YOU. DADDY AND I WANT YOU TO JOIN US FOR BREAKFAST ON THE TERRACE.

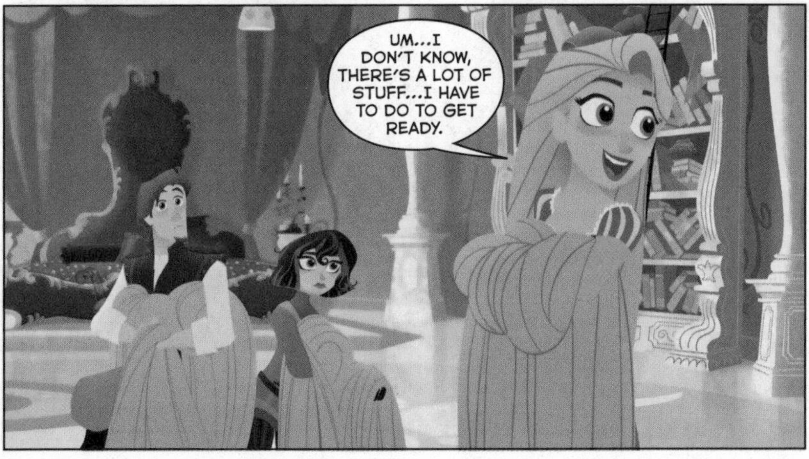
UM...I DON'T KNOW, THERE'S A LOT OF STUFF...I HAVE TO DO TO GET READY.

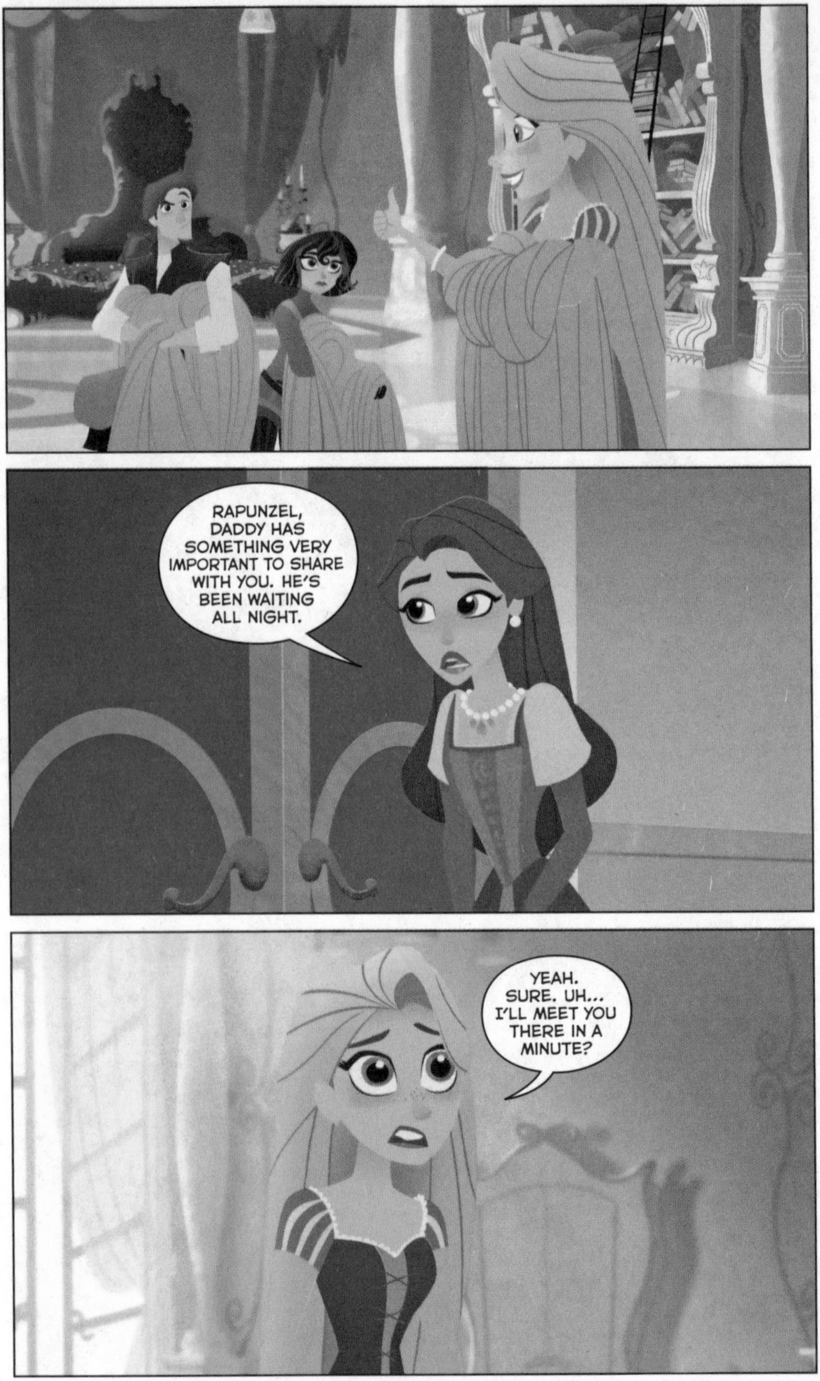
RAPUNZEL, DADDY HAS SOMETHING VERY IMPORTANT TO SHARE WITH YOU. HE'S BEEN WAITING ALL NIGHT.
YEAH. SURE. UH... I'LL MEET YOU THERE IN A MINUTE?

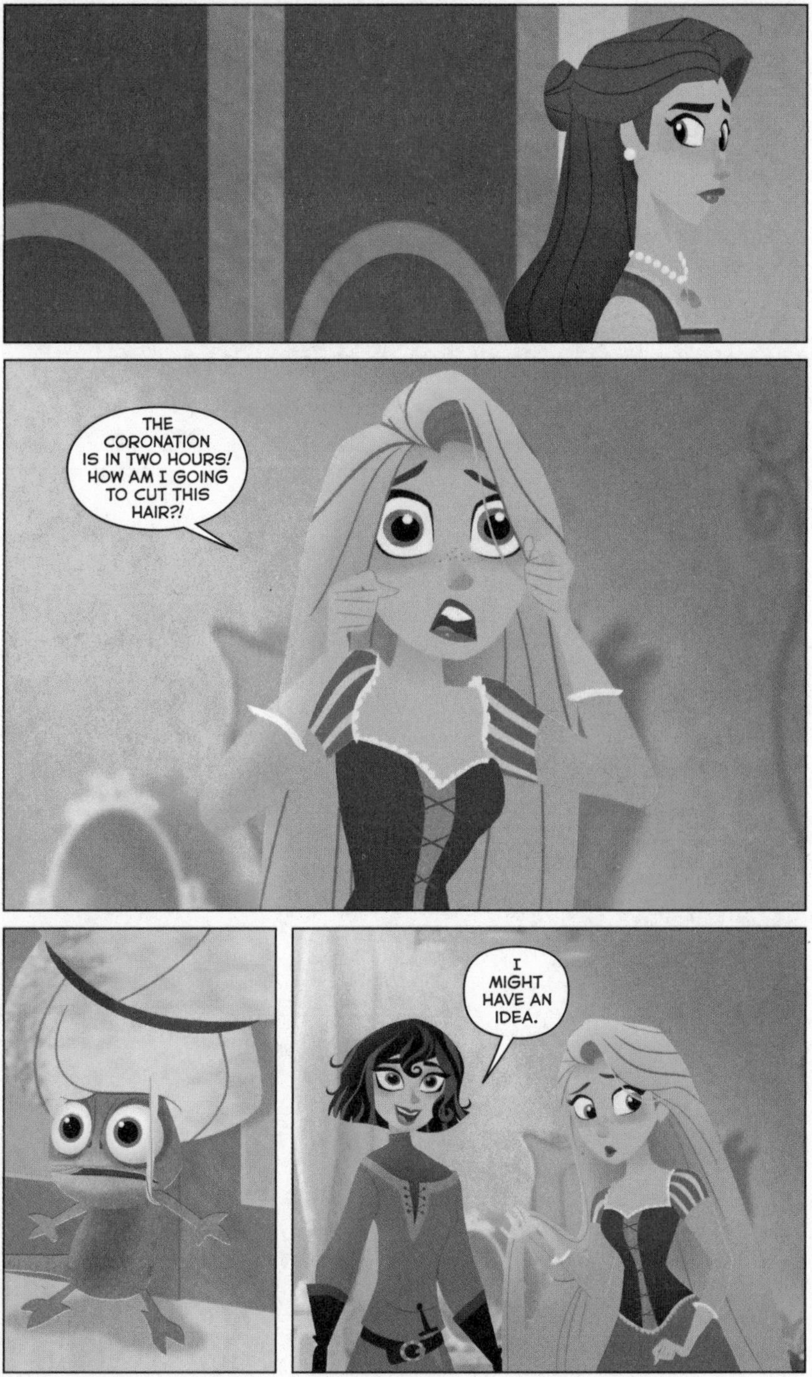
THE CORONATION IS IN TWO HOURS! HOW AM I GOING TO CUT THIS HAIR?!
I MIGHT HAVE AN IDEA.

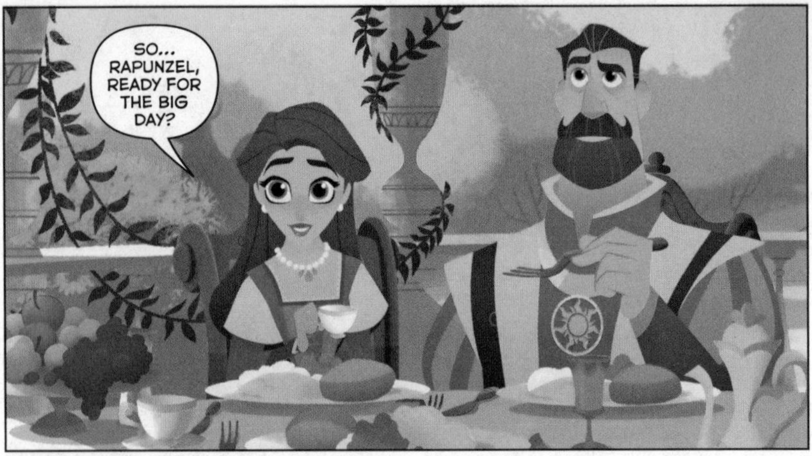
SO... RAPUNZEL, READY FOR THE BIG DAY?

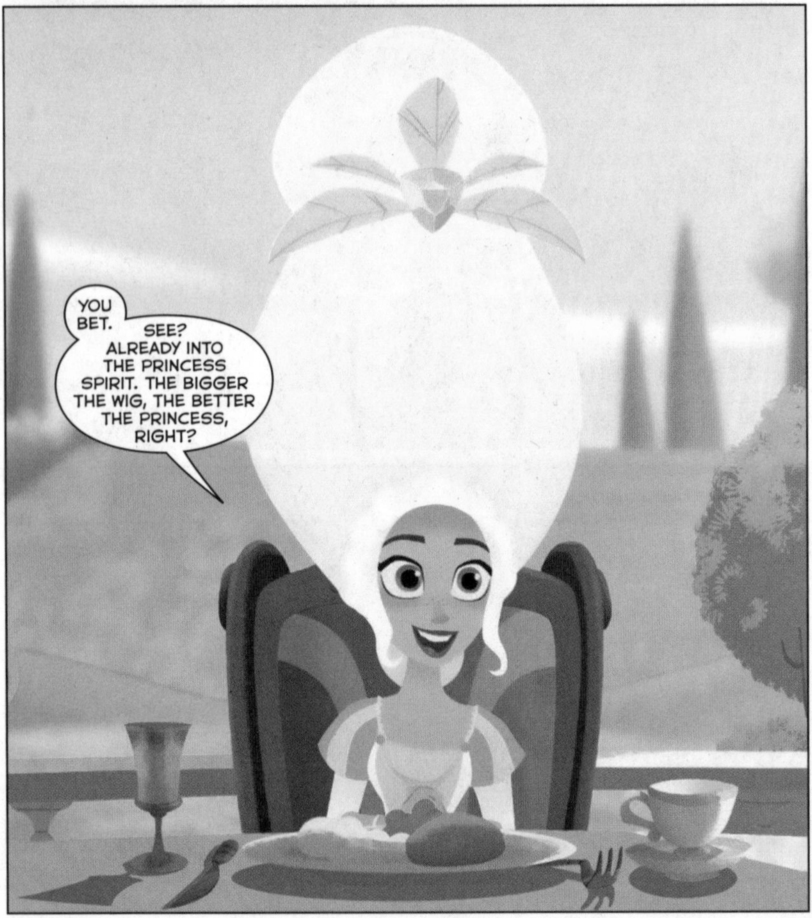
YOU BET.
SEE? ALREADY INTO THE PRINCESS SPIRIT. THE BIGGER THE WIG, THE BETTER THE PRINCESS, RIGHT?

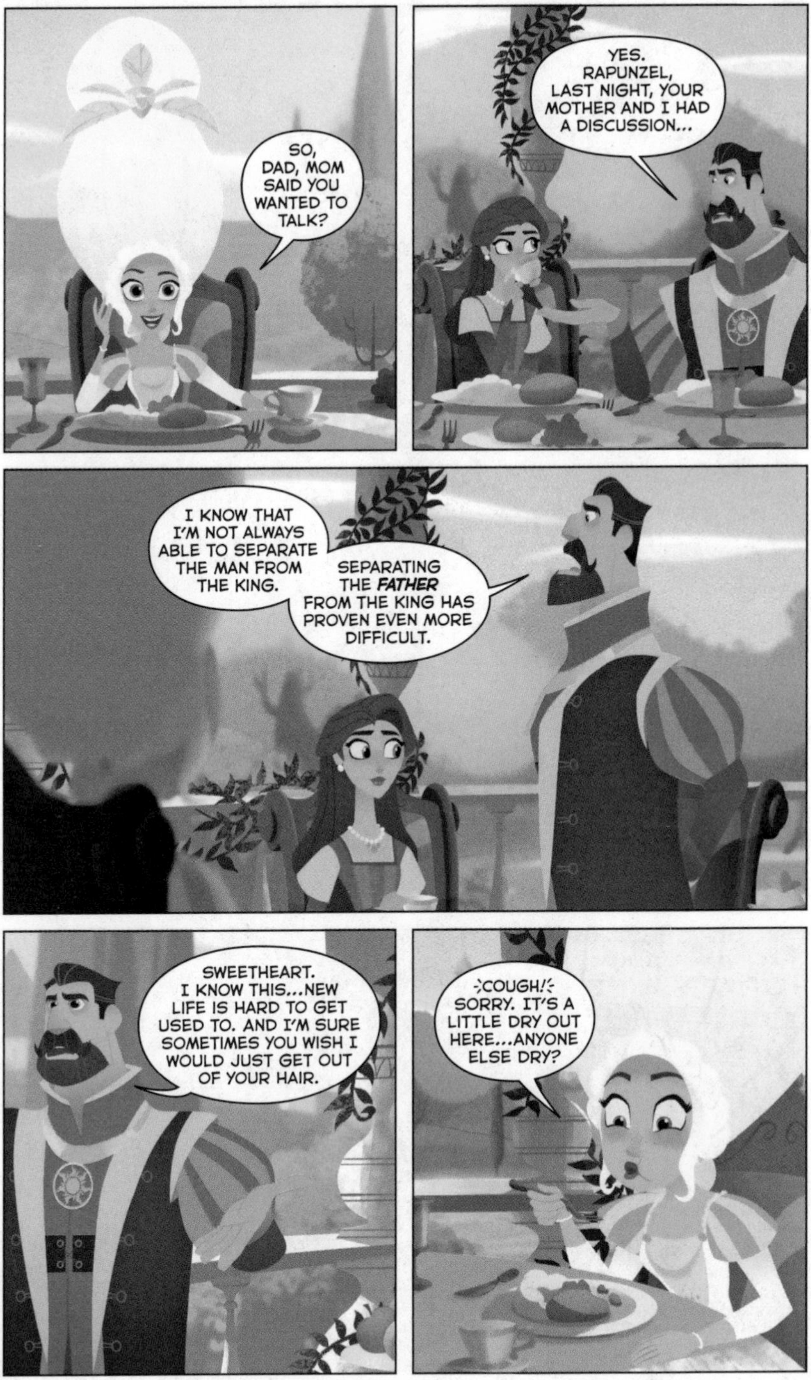
SO, DAD, MOM SAID YOU WANTED TO TALK?
YES. RAPUNZEL, LAST NIGHT, YOUR MOTHER AND I HAD A DISCUSSION...
I KNOW THAT I'M NOT ALWAYS ABLE TO SEPARATE THE MAN FROM THE KING.
SEPARATING THE *FATHER* FROM THE KING HAS PROVEN EVEN MORE DIFFICULT.
SWEETHEART. I KNOW THIS...NEW LIFE IS HARD TO GET USED TO. AND I'M SURE SOMETIMES YOU WISH I WOULD JUST GET OUT OF YOUR HAIR.
COUGH! SORRY. IT'S A LITTLE DRY OUT HERE...ANYONE ELSE DRY?

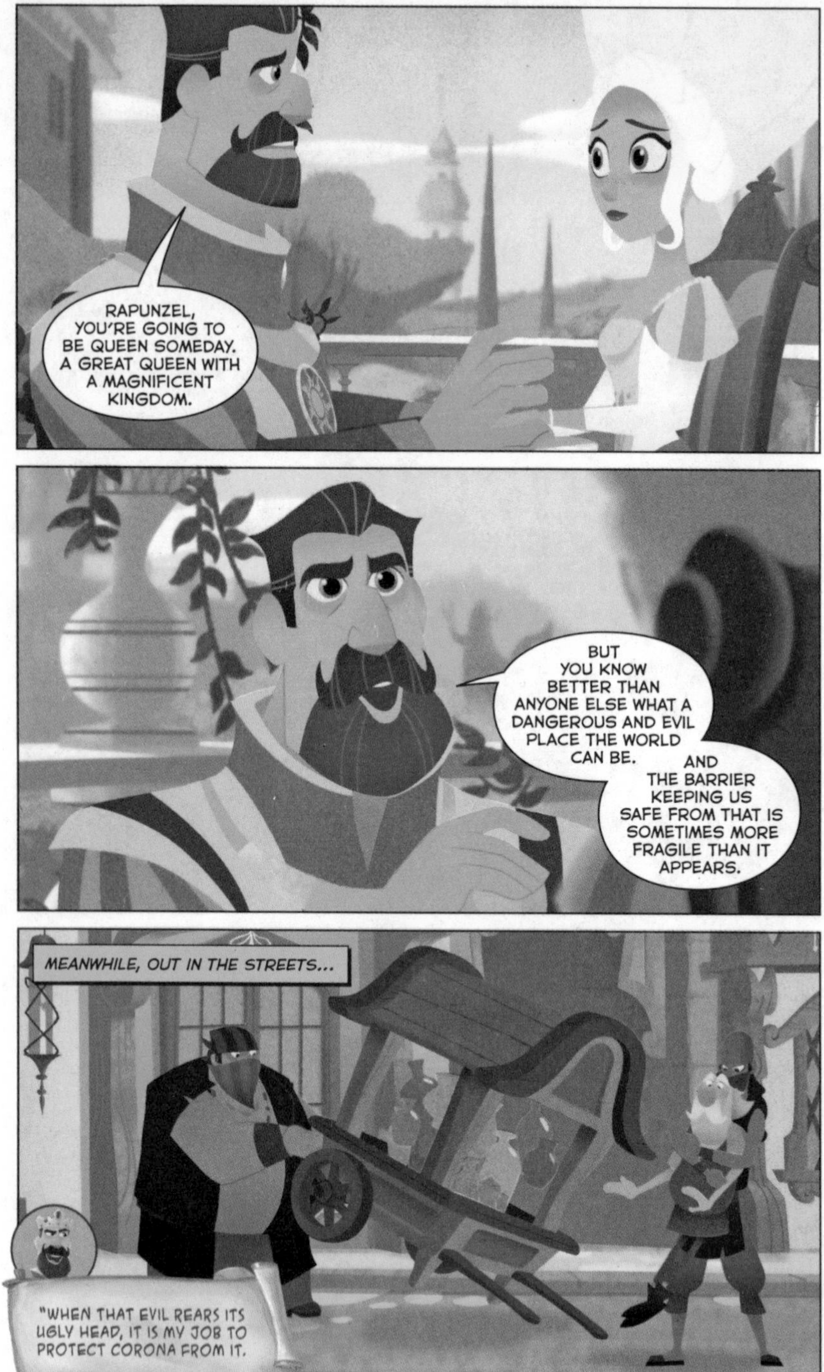
RAPUNZEL, YOU'RE GOING TO BE QUEEN SOMEDAY. A GREAT QUEEN WITH A MAGNIFICENT KINGDOM.
BUT YOU KNOW BETTER THAN ANYONE ELSE WHAT A DANGEROUS AND EVIL PLACE THE WORLD CAN BE.
AND THE BARRIER KEEPING US SAFE FROM THAT IS SOMETIMES MORE FRAGILE THAN IT APPEARS.
MEANWHILE, OUT IN THE STREETS...
"WHEN THAT EVIL REARS ITS UGLY HEAD, IT IS MY JOB TO PROTECT CORONA FROM IT.

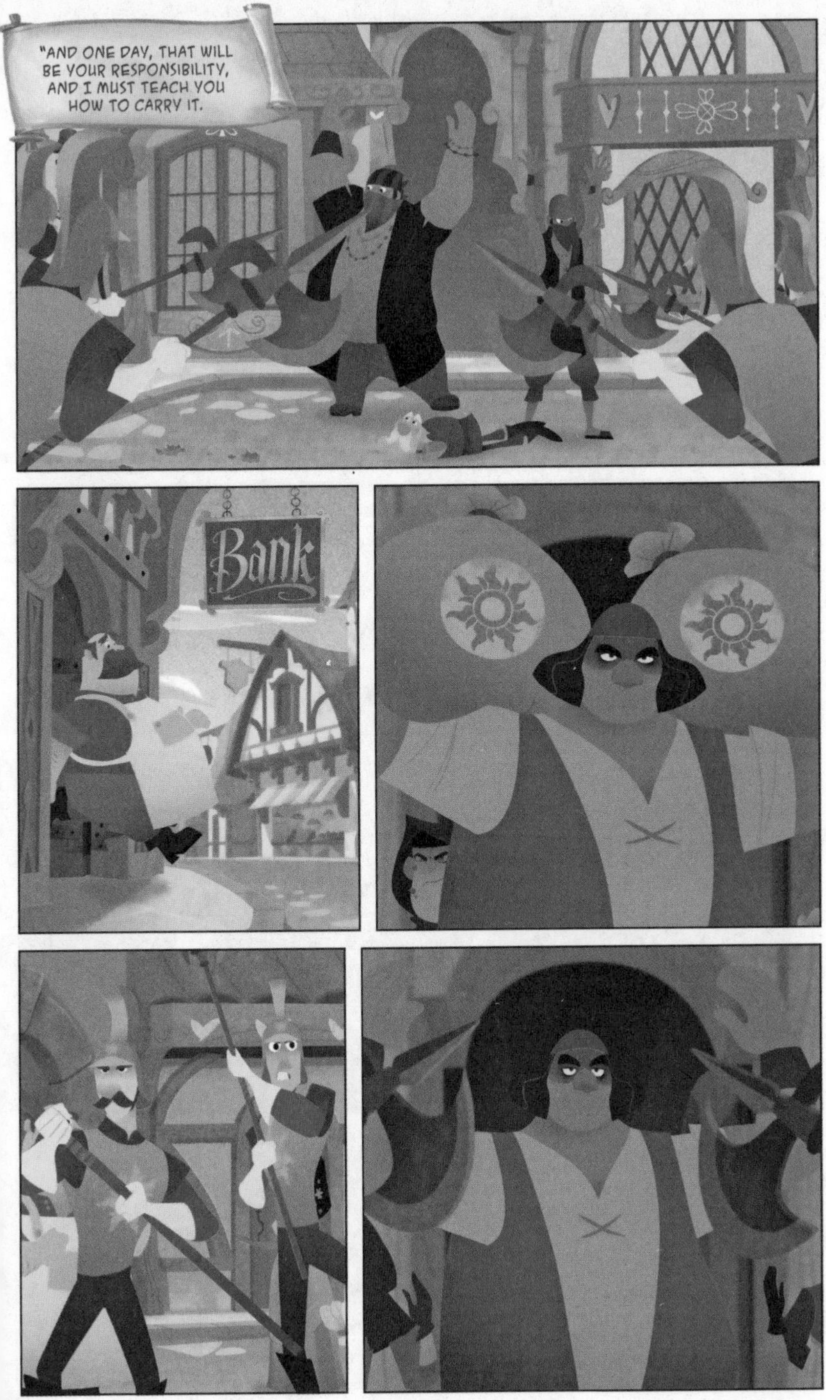
"AND ONE DAY, THAT WILL BE YOUR RESPONSIBILITY, AND I MUST TEACH YOU HOW TO CARRY IT.
Bank

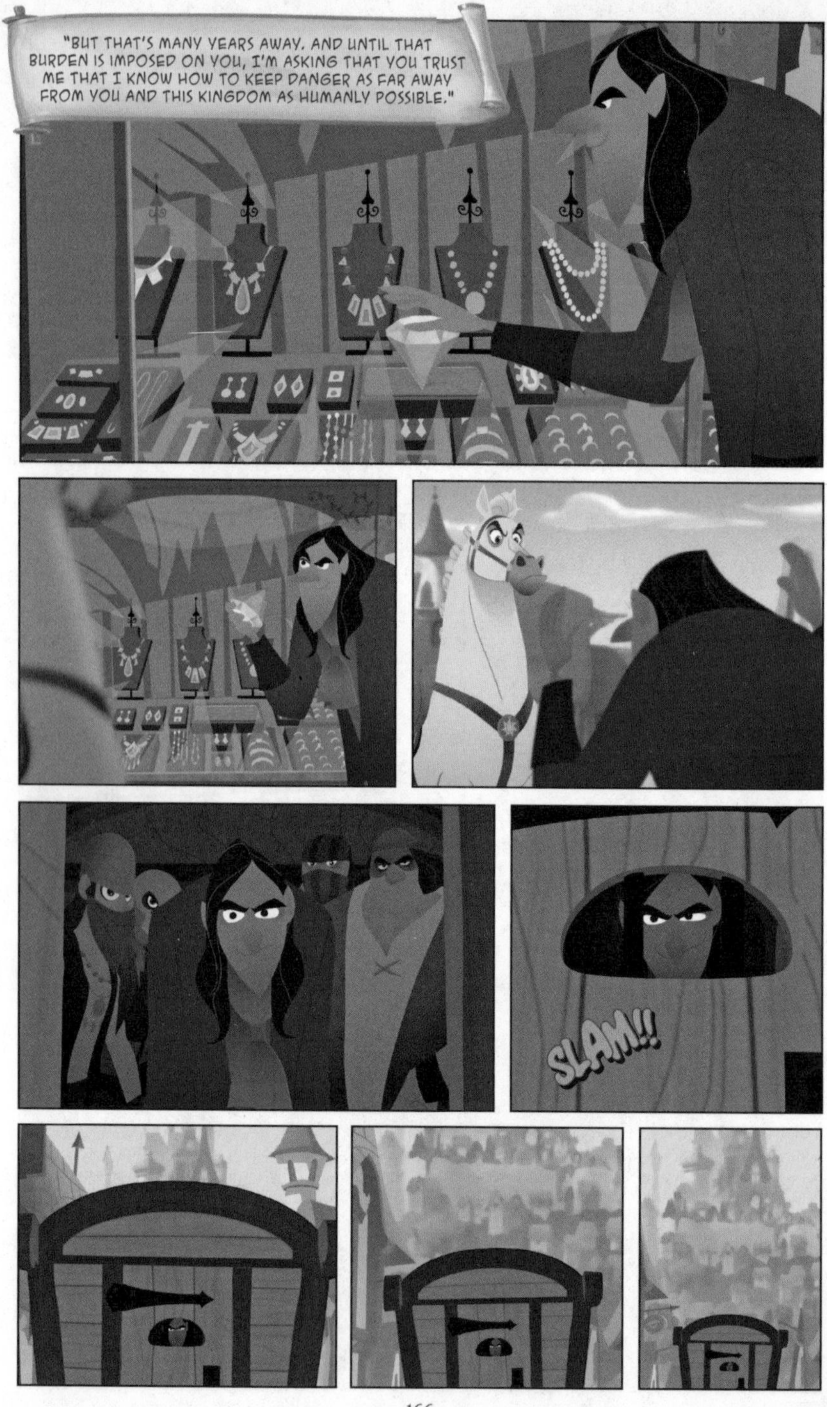
"BUT THAT'S MANY YEARS AWAY. AND UNTIL THAT BURDEN IS IMPOSED ON YOU, I'M ASKING THAT YOU TRUST ME THAT I KNOW HOW TO KEEP DANGER AS FAR AWAY FROM YOU AND THIS KINGDOM AS HUMANLY POSSIBLE."
SLAM!!

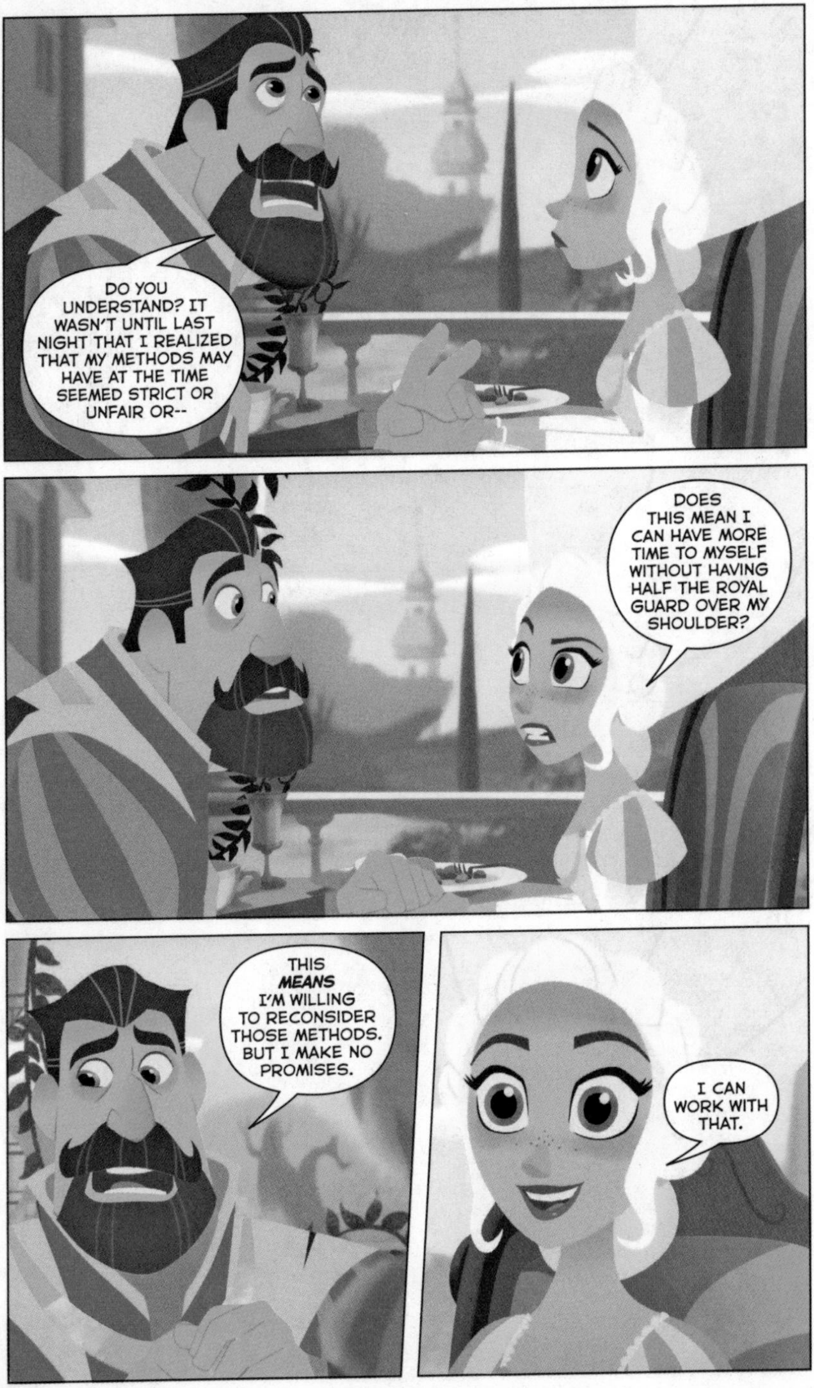
DO YOU UNDERSTAND? IT WASN'T UNTIL LAST NIGHT THAT I REALIZED THAT MY METHODS MAY HAVE AT THE TIME SEEMED STRICT OR UNFAIR OR--
DOES THIS MEAN I CAN HAVE MORE TIME TO MYSELF WITHOUT HAVING HALF THE ROYAL GUARD OVER MY SHOULDER?
THIS ***MEANS*** I'M WILLING TO RECONSIDER THOSE METHODS. BUT I MAKE NO PROMISES.
I CAN WORK WITH THAT.

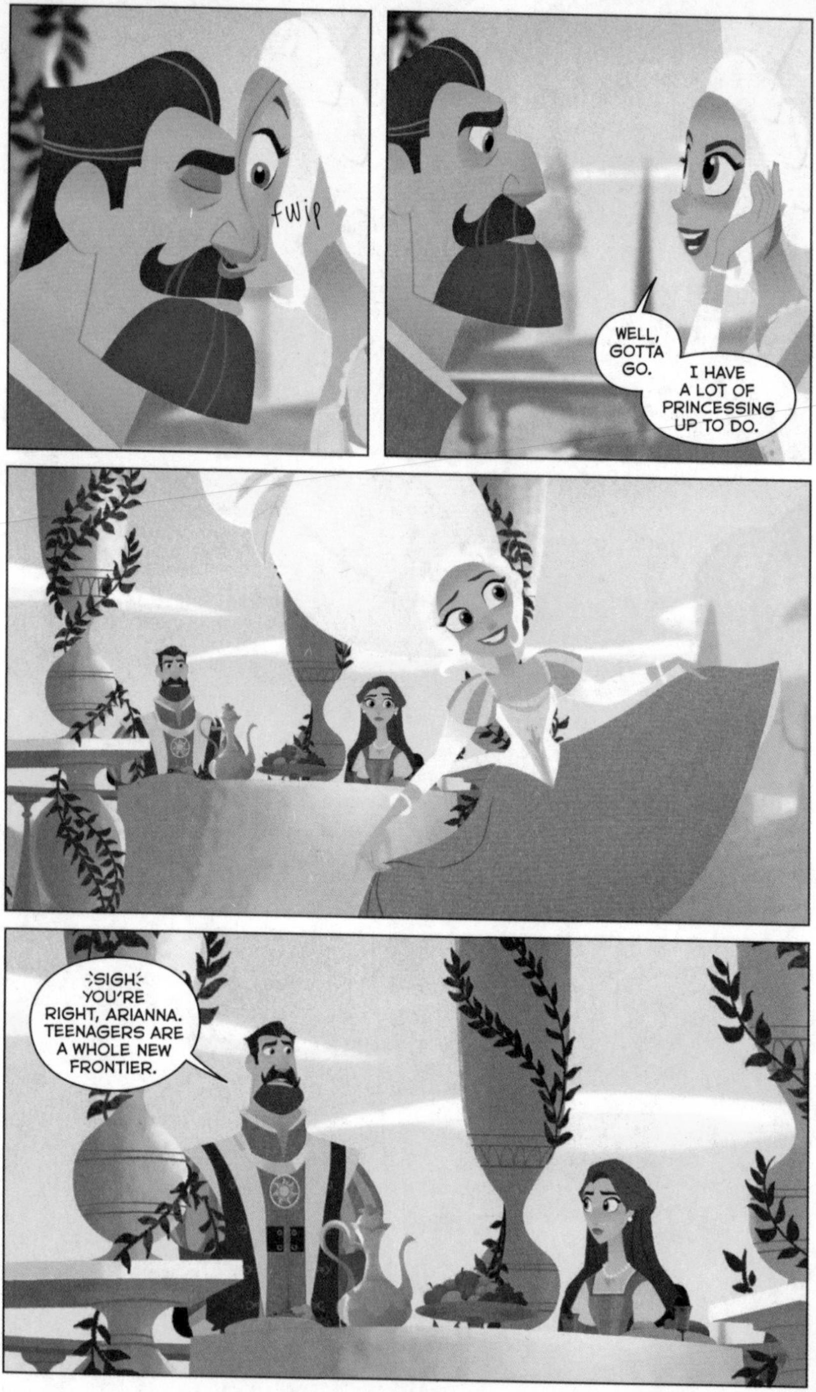
FWIP
WELL, GOTTA GO.
I HAVE A LOT OF PRINCESSING UP TO DO.
-SIGH- YOU'RE RIGHT, ARIANNA. TEENAGERS ARE A WHOLE NEW FRONTIER.

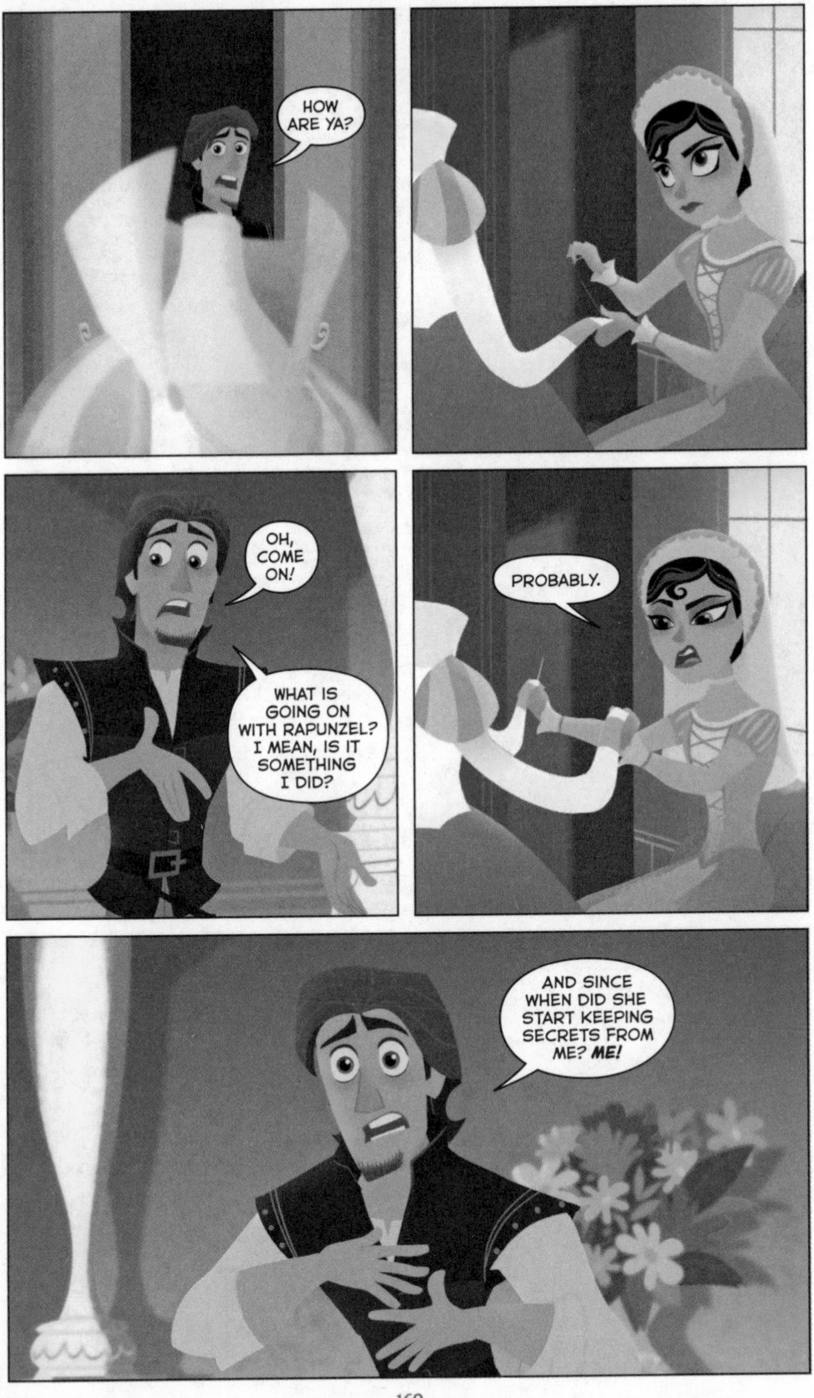
HOW ARE YA?
OH, COME ON!
WHAT IS GOING ON WITH RAPUNZEL? I MEAN, IS IT SOMETHING I DID?
PROBABLY.
AND SINCE WHEN DID SHE START KEEPING SECRETS FROM ME? *ME!*

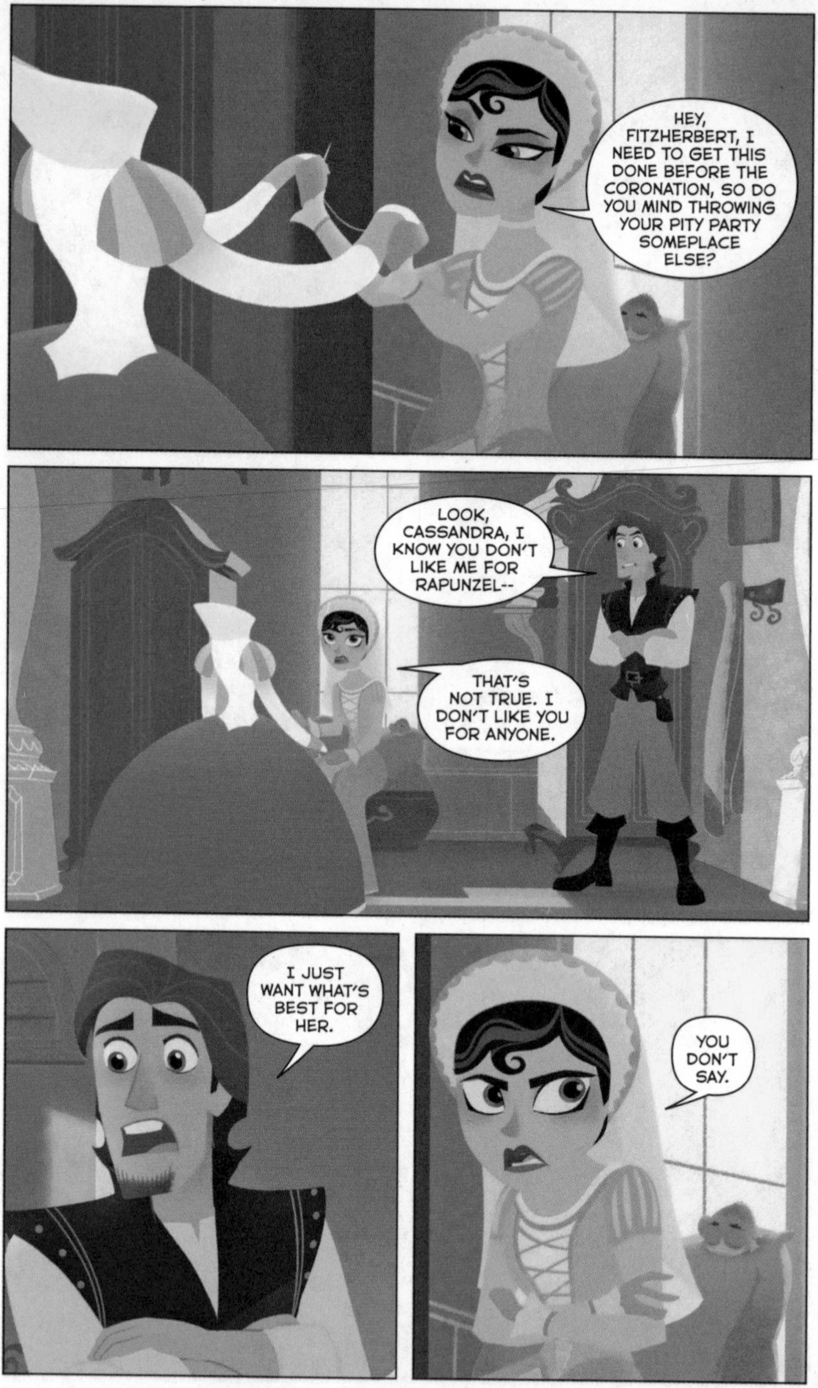
HEY, FITZHERBERT, I NEED TO GET THIS DONE BEFORE THE CORONATION, SO DO YOU MIND THROWING YOUR PITY PARTY SOMEPLACE ELSE?
LOOK, CASSANDRA, I KNOW YOU DON'T LIKE ME FOR RAPUNZEL--
THAT'S NOT TRUE. I DON'T LIKE YOU FOR ANYONE.
I JUST WANT WHAT'S BEST FOR HER.
YOU DON'T SAY.

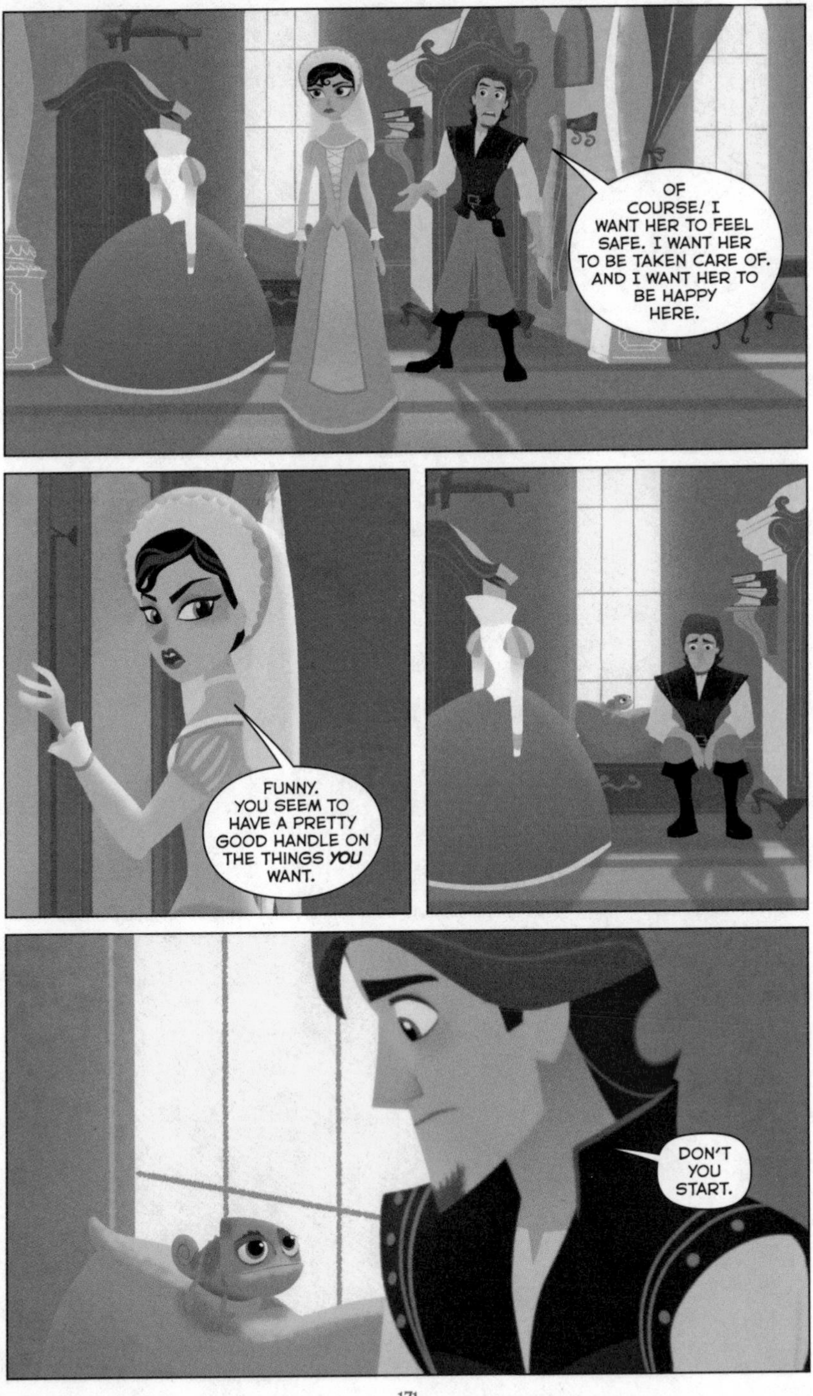
OF COURSE! I WANT HER TO FEEL SAFE. I WANT HER TO BE TAKEN CARE OF. AND I WANT HER TO BE HAPPY HERE.
FUNNY. YOU SEEM TO HAVE A PRETTY GOOD HANDLE ON THE THINGS *YOU* WANT.
DON'T YOU START.

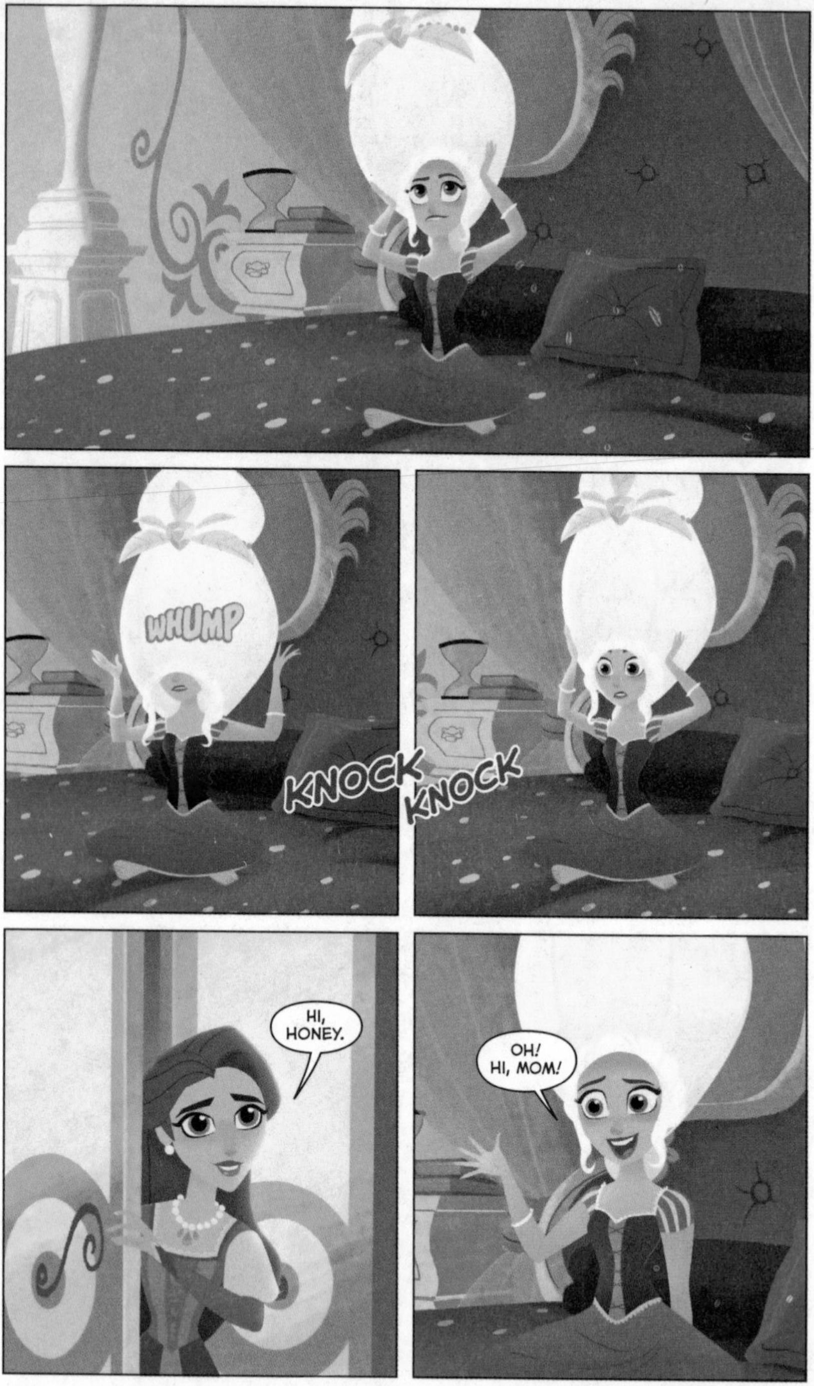
WHUMP
KNOCK
KNOCK
HI, HONEY.
OH! HI, MOM!

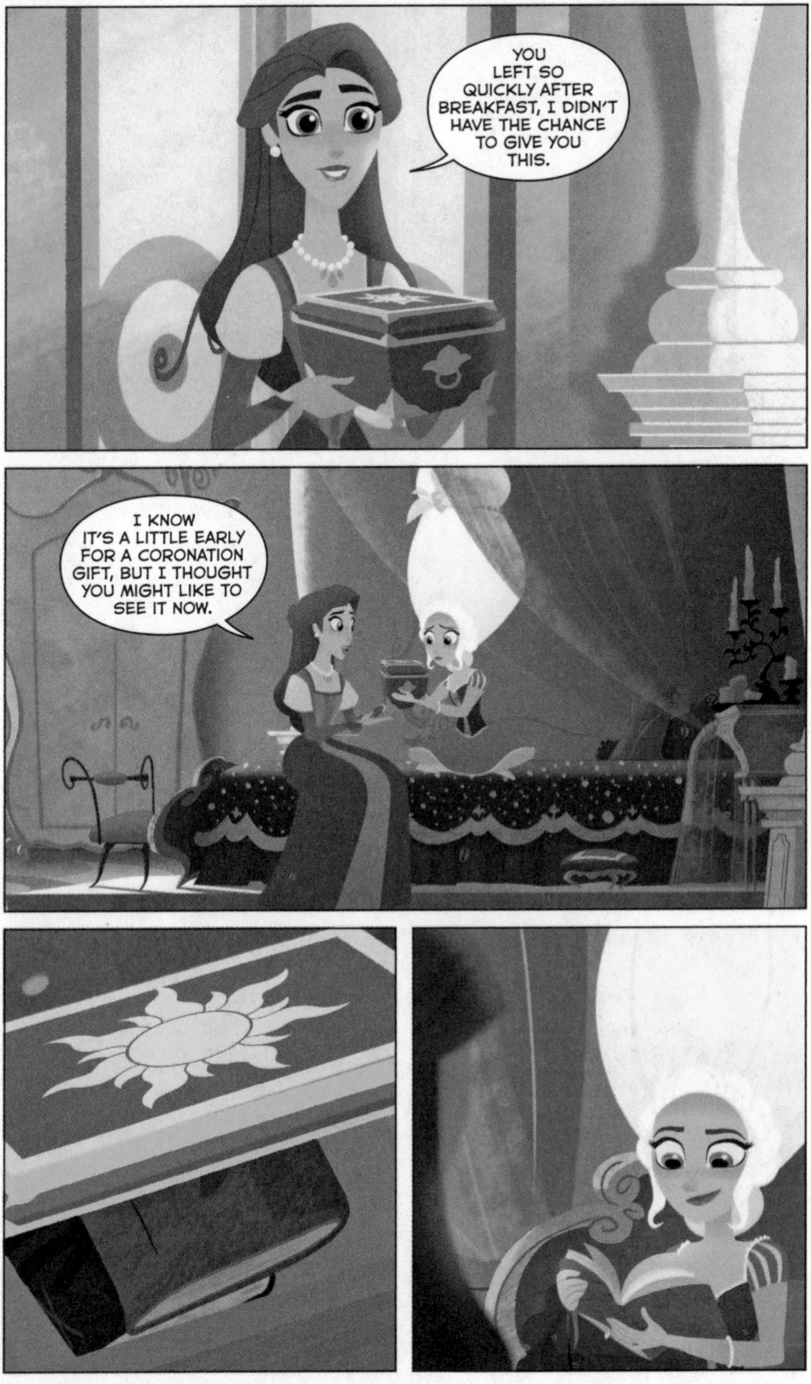
YOU LEFT SO QUICKLY AFTER BREAKFAST, I DIDN'T HAVE THE CHANCE TO GIVE YOU THIS.
I KNOW IT'S A LITTLE EARLY FOR A CORONATION GIFT, BUT I THOUGHT YOU MIGHT LIKE TO SEE IT NOW.

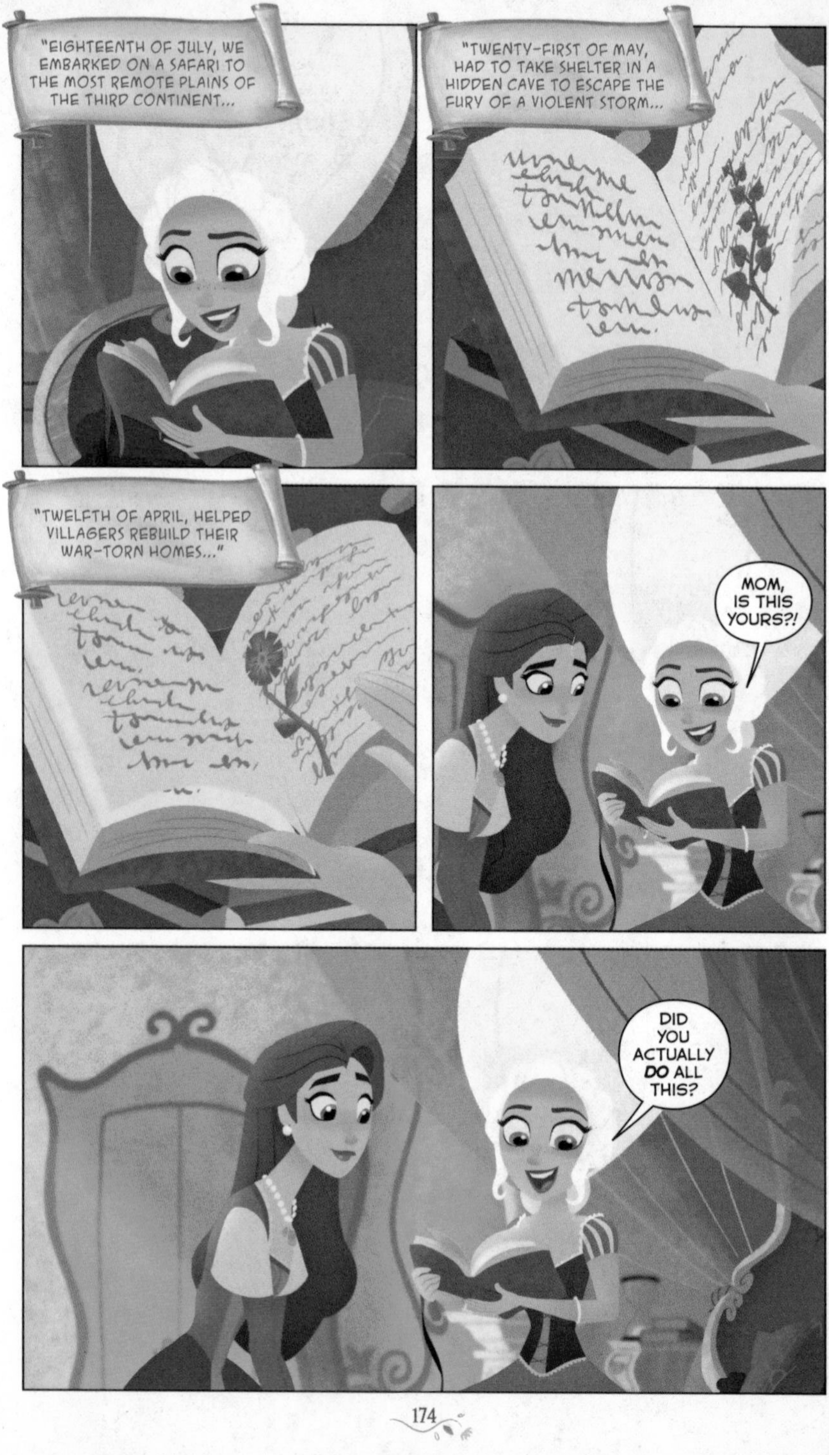
"EIGHTEENTH OF JULY, WE EMBARKED ON A SAFARI TO THE MOST REMOTE PLAINS OF THE THIRD CONTINENT...
"TWENTY-FIRST OF MAY, HAD TO TAKE SHELTER IN A HIDDEN CAVE TO ESCAPE THE FURY OF A VIOLENT STORM...
"TWELFTH OF APRIL, HELPED VILLAGERS REBUILD THEIR WAR-TORN HOMES..."
MOM, IS THIS YOURS?!
DID YOU ACTUALLY DO ALL THIS?

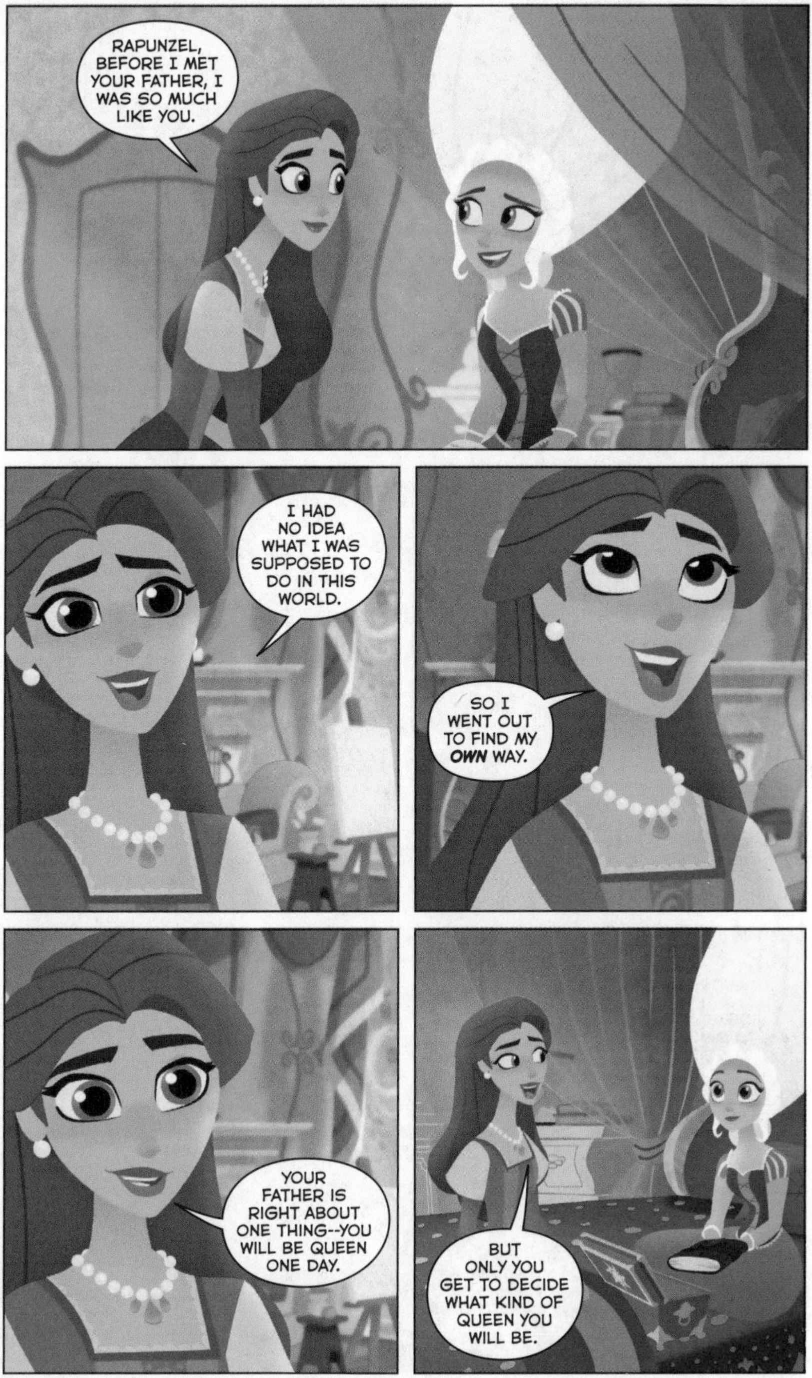
RAPUNZEL, BEFORE I MET YOUR FATHER, I WAS SO MUCH LIKE YOU.
I HAD NO IDEA WHAT I WAS SUPPOSED TO DO IN THIS WORLD.
SO I WENT OUT TO FIND MY ***OWN*** WAY.
YOUR FATHER IS RIGHT ABOUT ONE THING--YOU WILL BE QUEEN ONE DAY.
BUT ONLY YOU GET TO DECIDE WHAT KIND OF QUEEN YOU WILL BE.

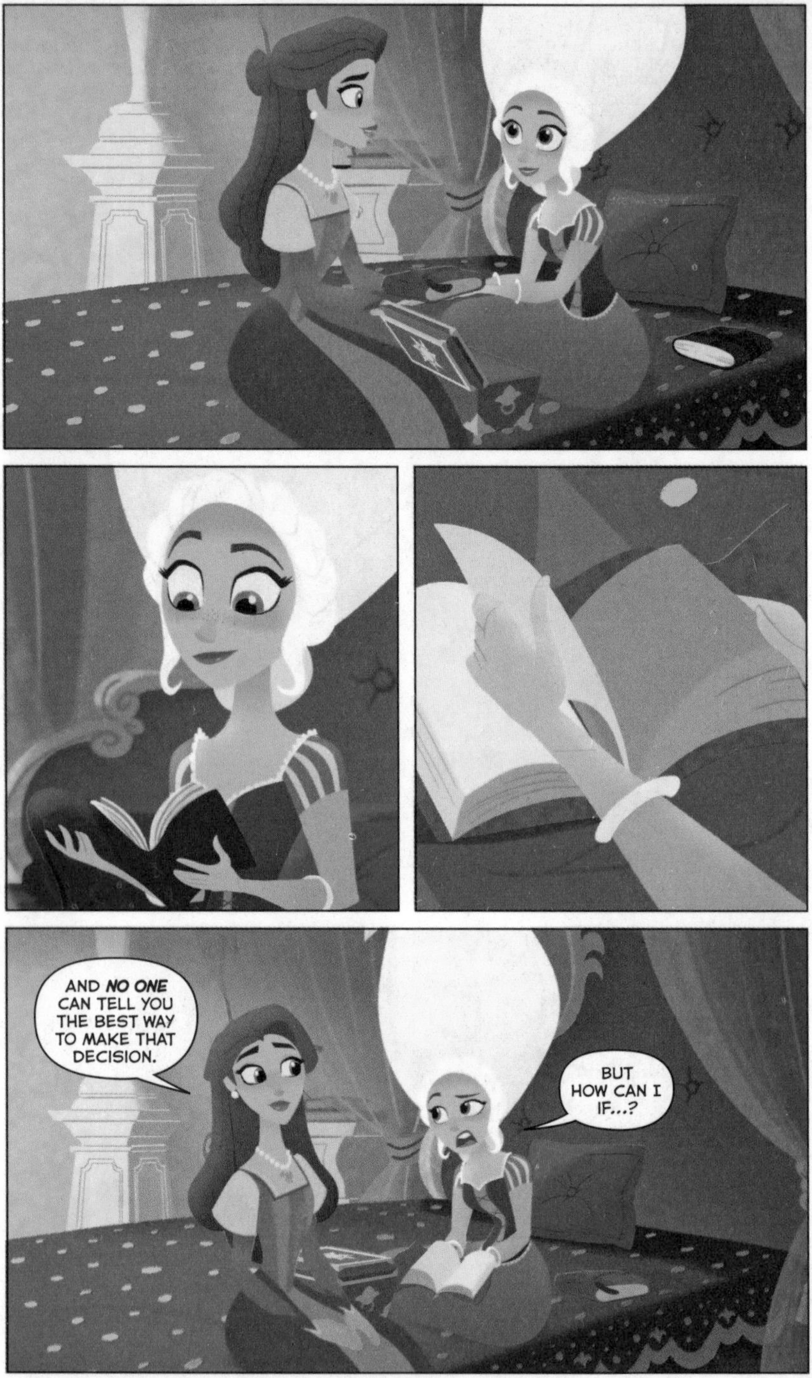
AND *NO ONE* CAN TELL YOU THE BEST WAY TO MAKE THAT DECISION.
BUT HOW CAN I IF...?

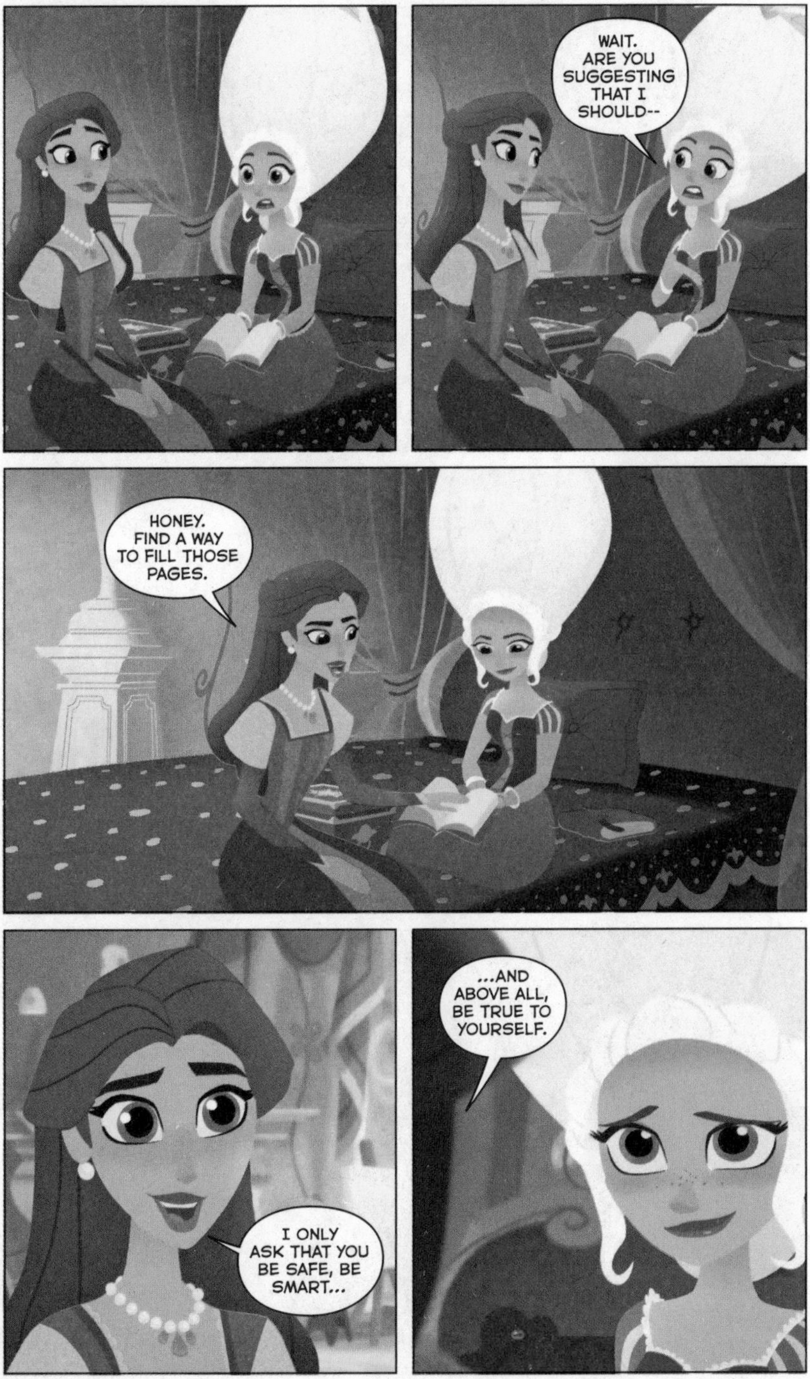
WAIT. ARE YOU SUGGESTING THAT I SHOULD--
HONEY. FIND A WAY TO FILL THOSE PAGES.
I ONLY ASK THAT YOU BE SAFE, BE SMART...
...AND ABOVE ALL, BE TRUE TO YOURSELF.

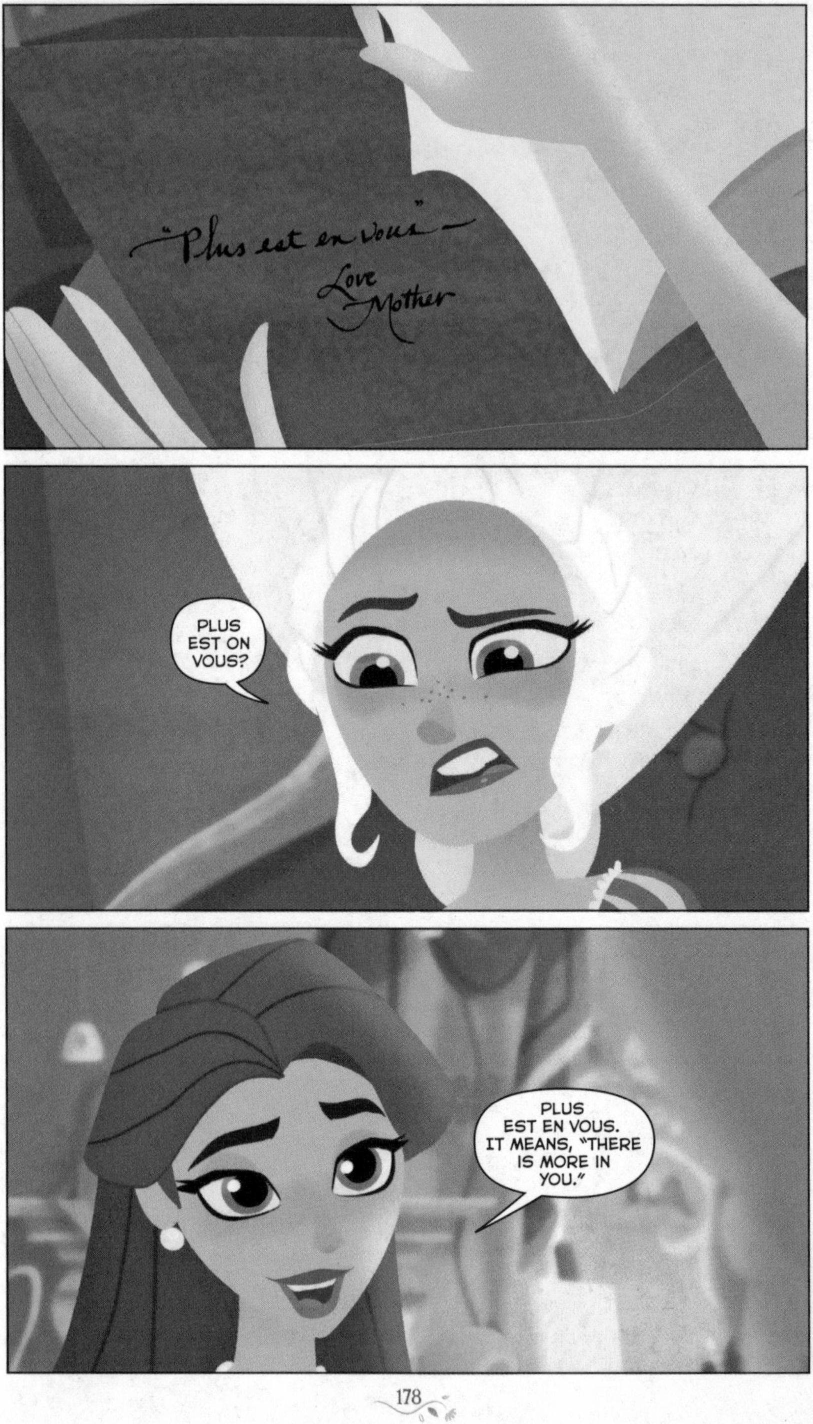
"Plus est en vous" — Love Mother
PLUS EST ON VOUS?
PLUS EST EN VOUS. IT MEANS, "THERE IS MORE IN YOU."

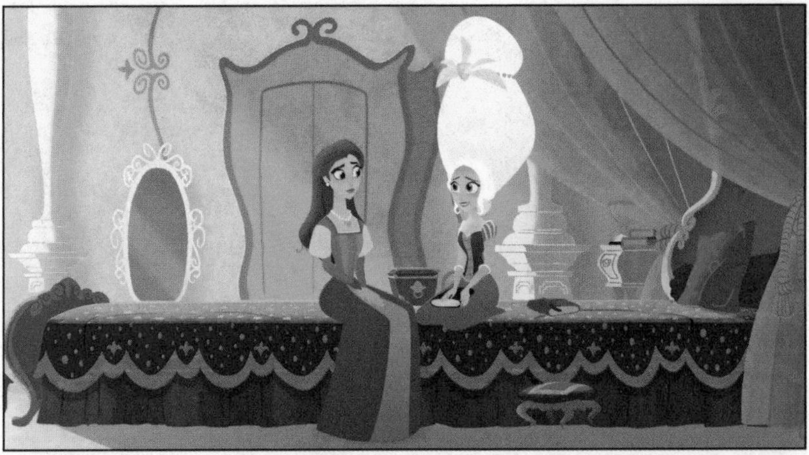

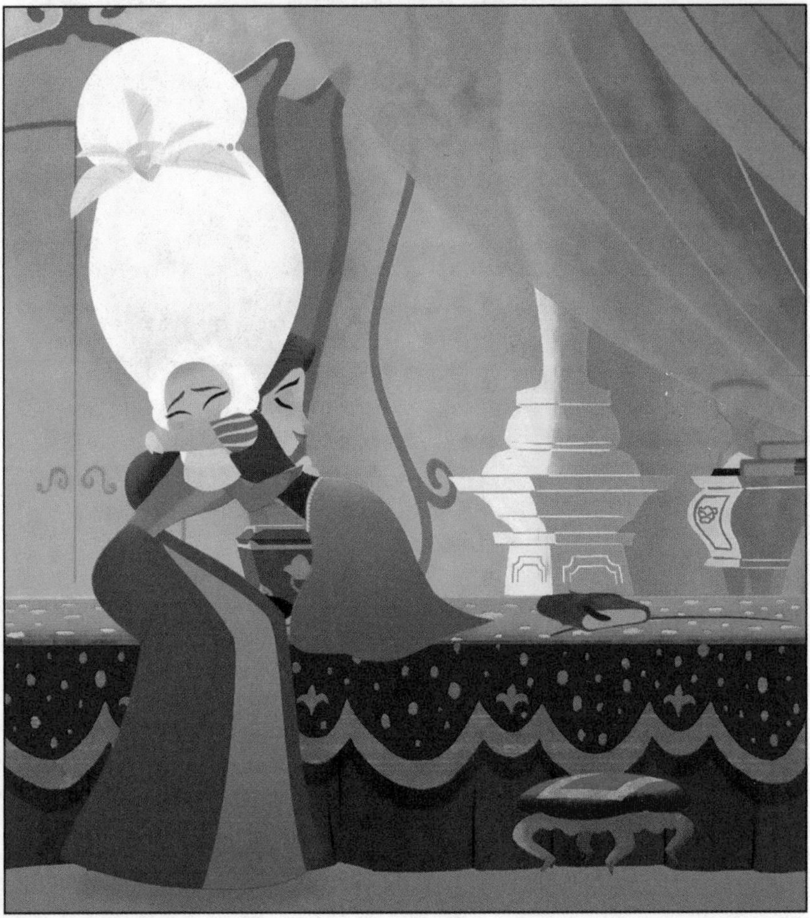

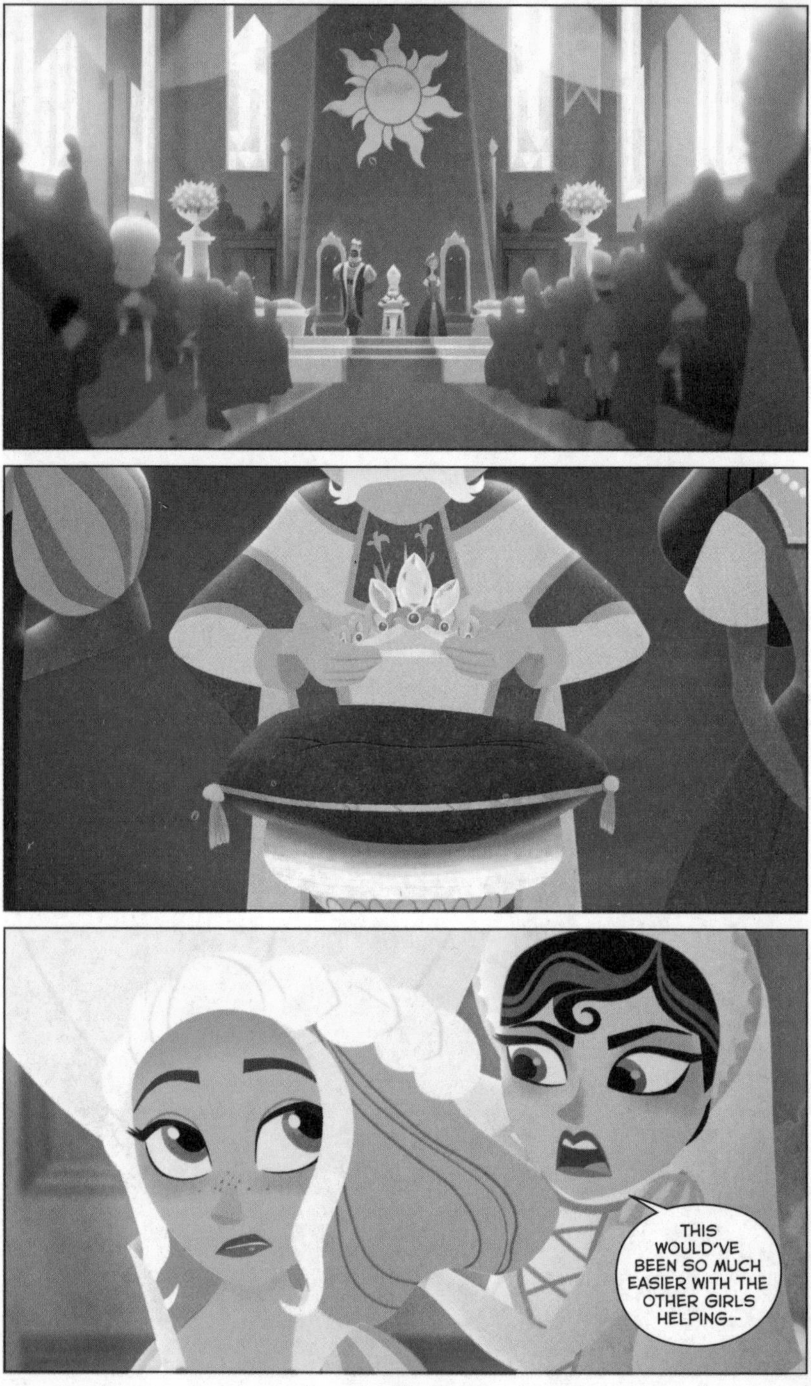
THIS WOULD'VE BEEN SO MUCH EASIER WITH THE OTHER GIRLS HELPING--

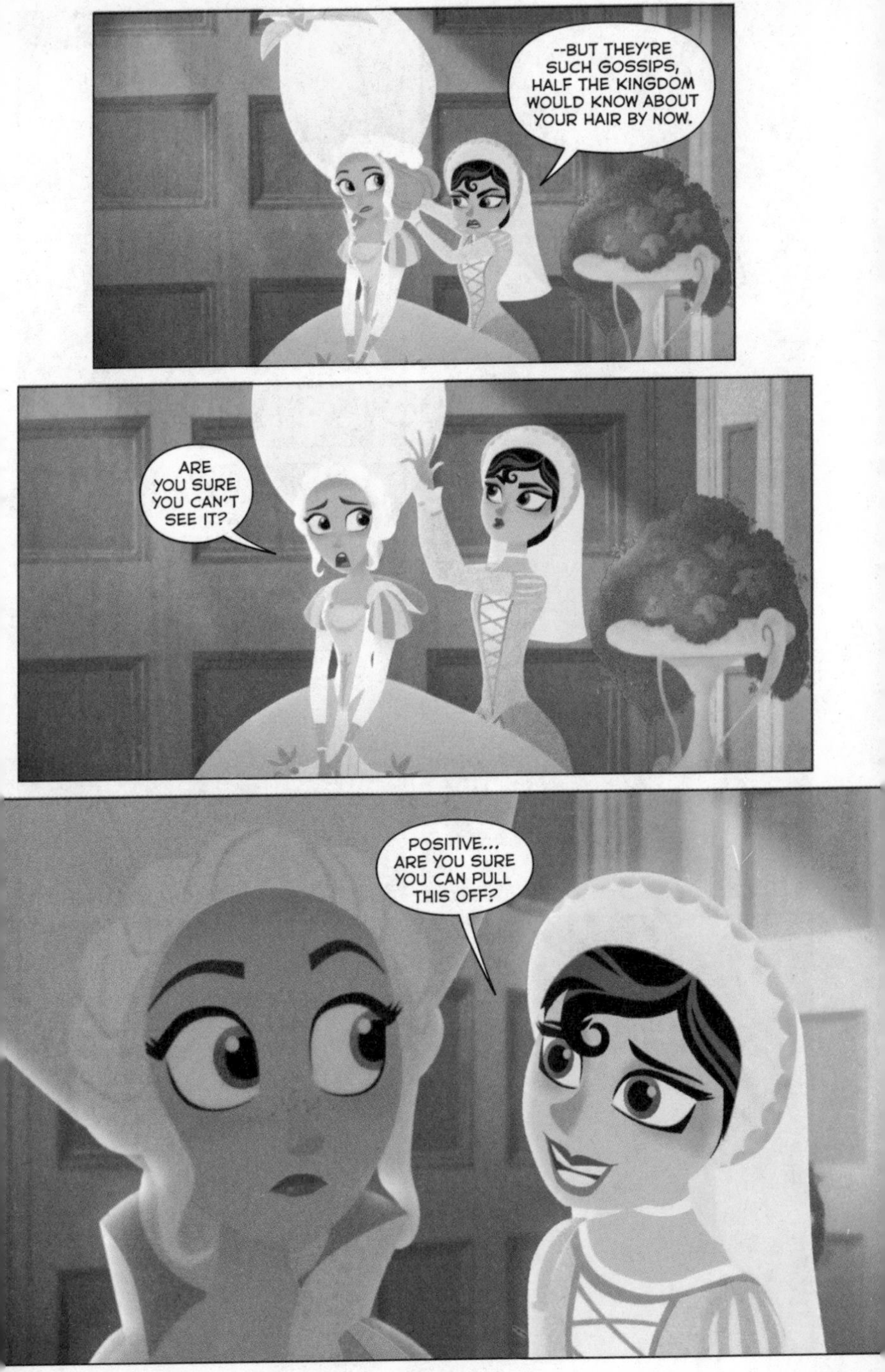
--BUT THEY'RE SUCH GOSSIPS, HALF THE KINGDOM WOULD KNOW ABOUT YOUR HAIR BY NOW.
ARE YOU SURE YOU CAN'T SEE IT?
POSITIVE... ARE YOU SURE YOU CAN PULL THIS OFF?

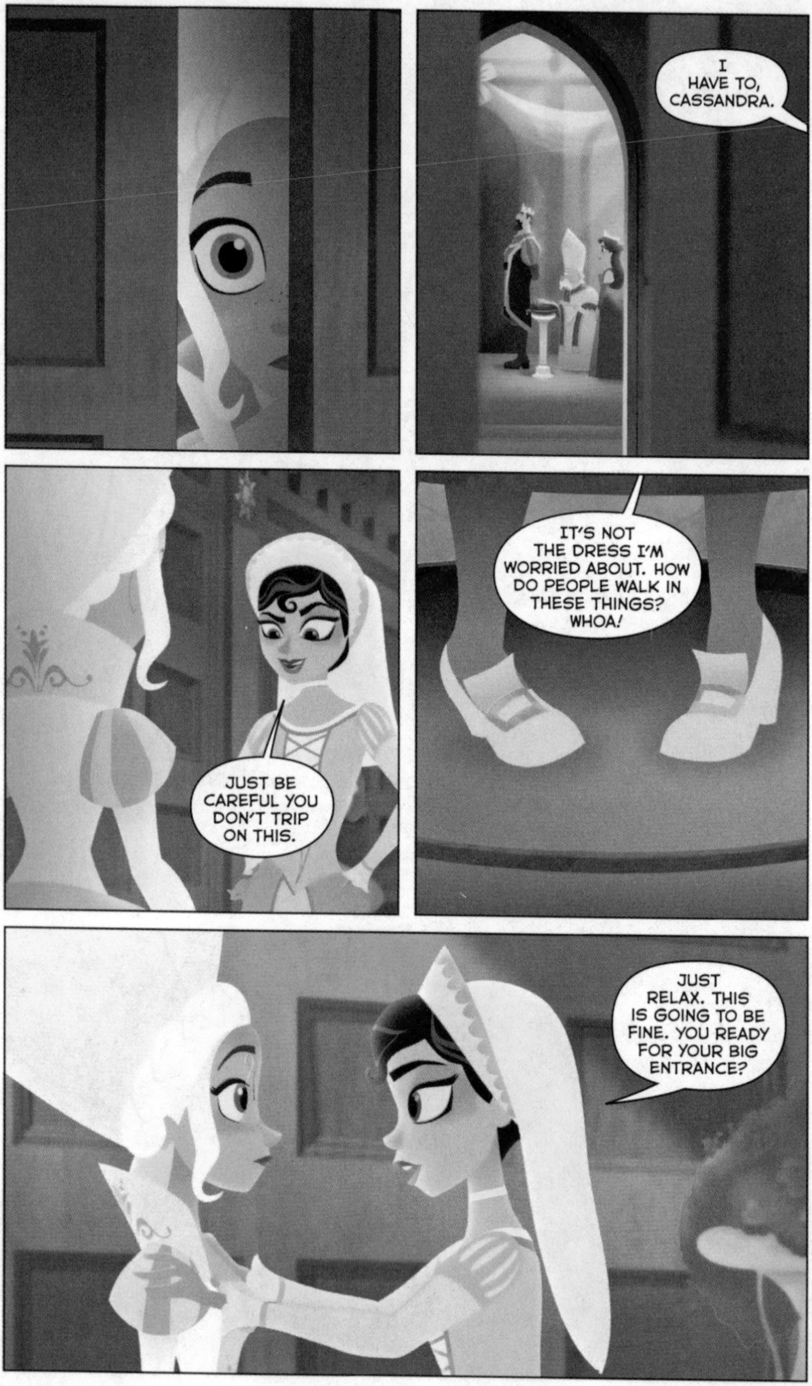
I HAVE TO, CASSANDRA.
IT'S NOT THE DRESS I'M WORRIED ABOUT. HOW DO PEOPLE WALK IN THESE THINGS? WHOA!
JUST BE CAREFUL YOU DON'T TRIP ON THIS.
JUST RELAX. THIS IS GOING TO BE FINE. YOU READY FOR YOUR BIG ENTRANCE?

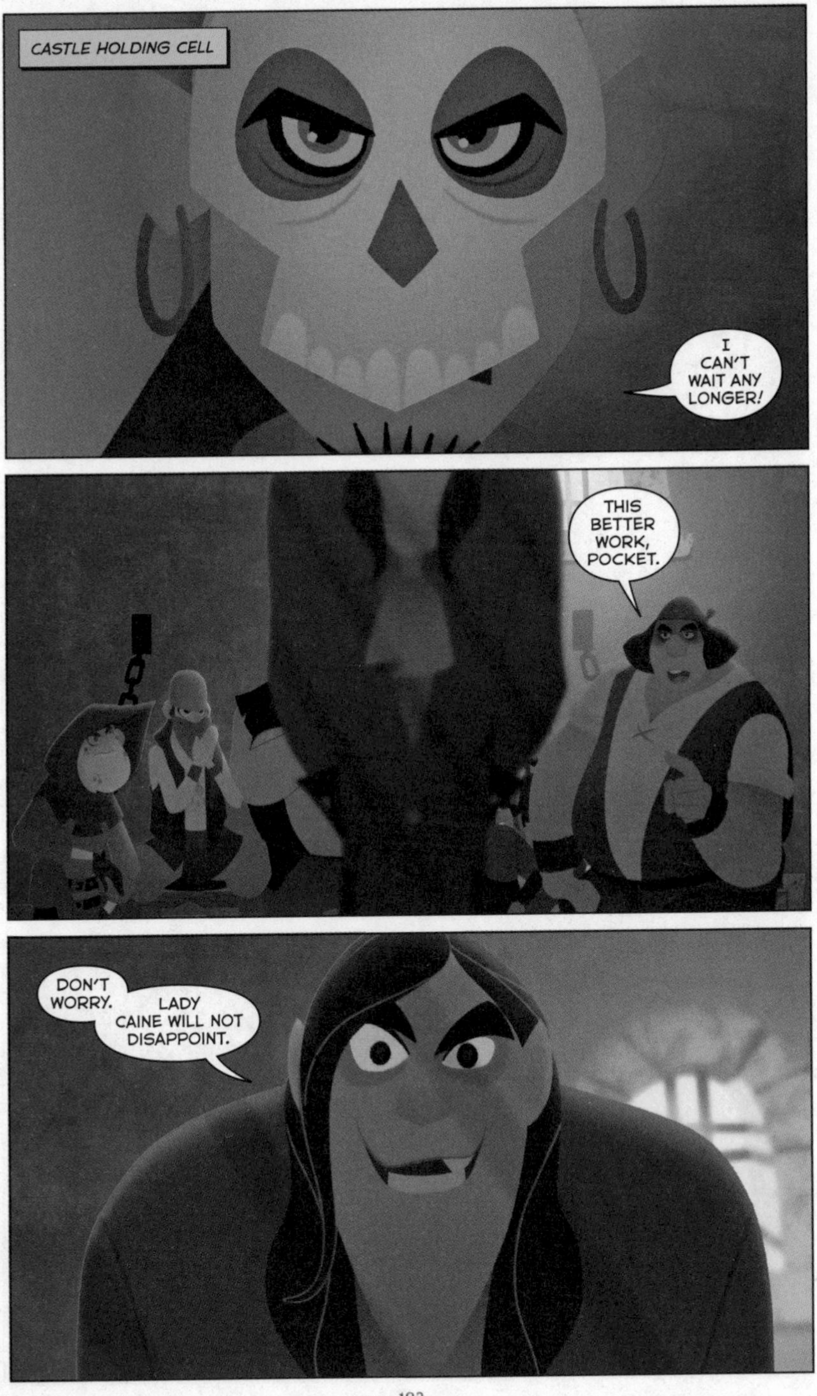
CASTLE HOLDING CELL
I CAN'T WAIT ANY LONGER!
THIS BETTER WORK, POCKET.
DON'T WORRY.
LADY CAINE WILL NOT DISAPPOINT.

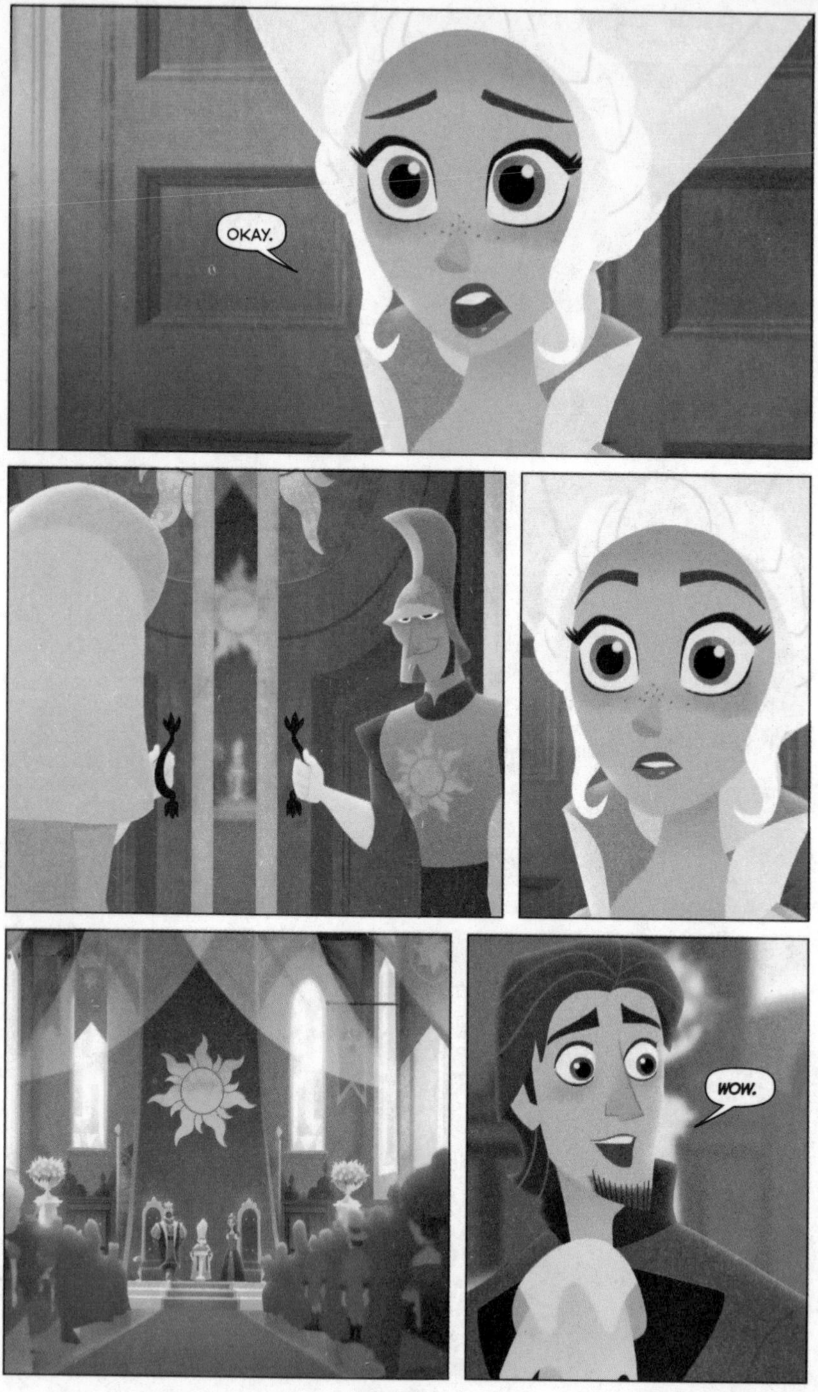
OKAY.
WOW.

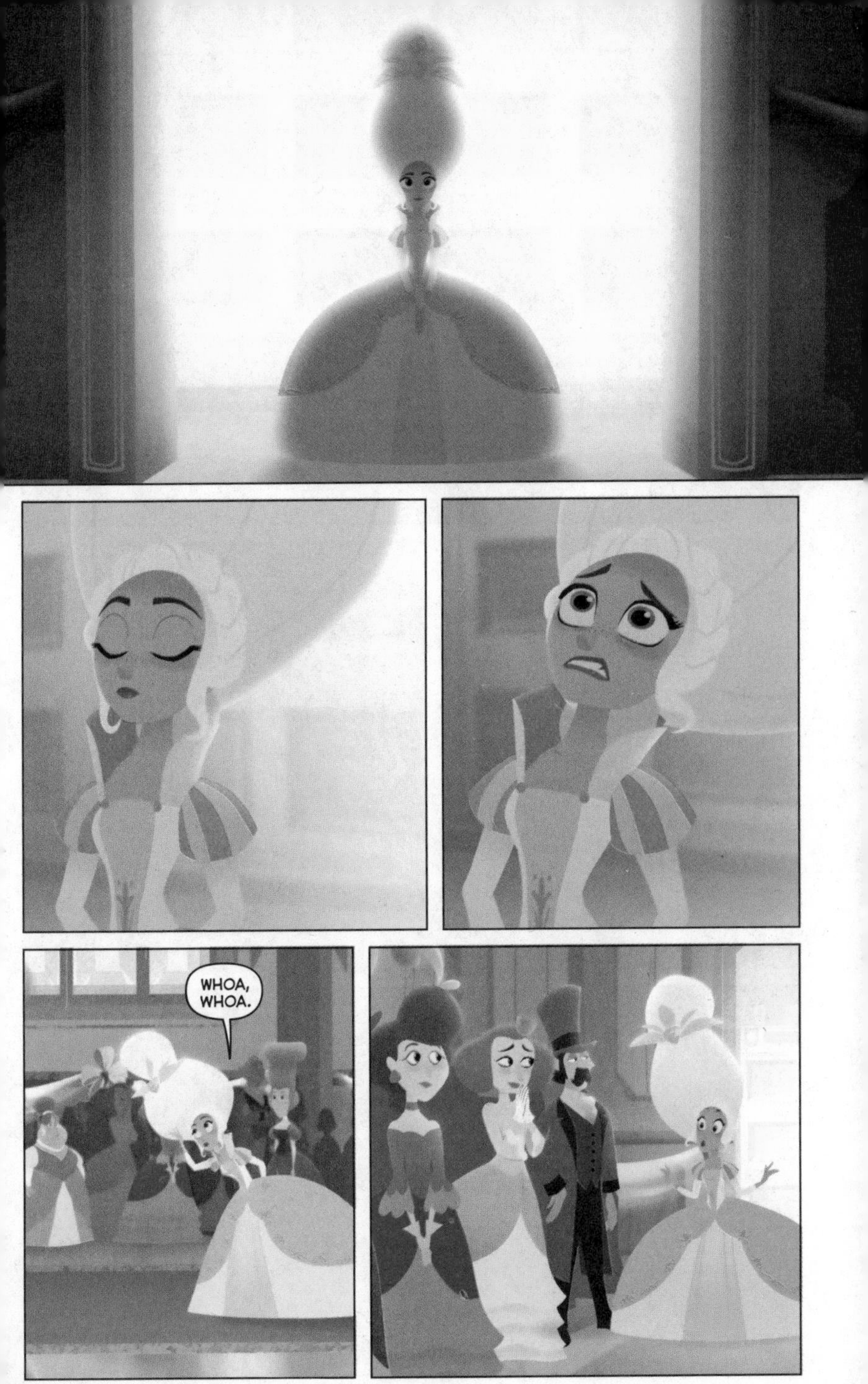
WHOA,
WHOA.

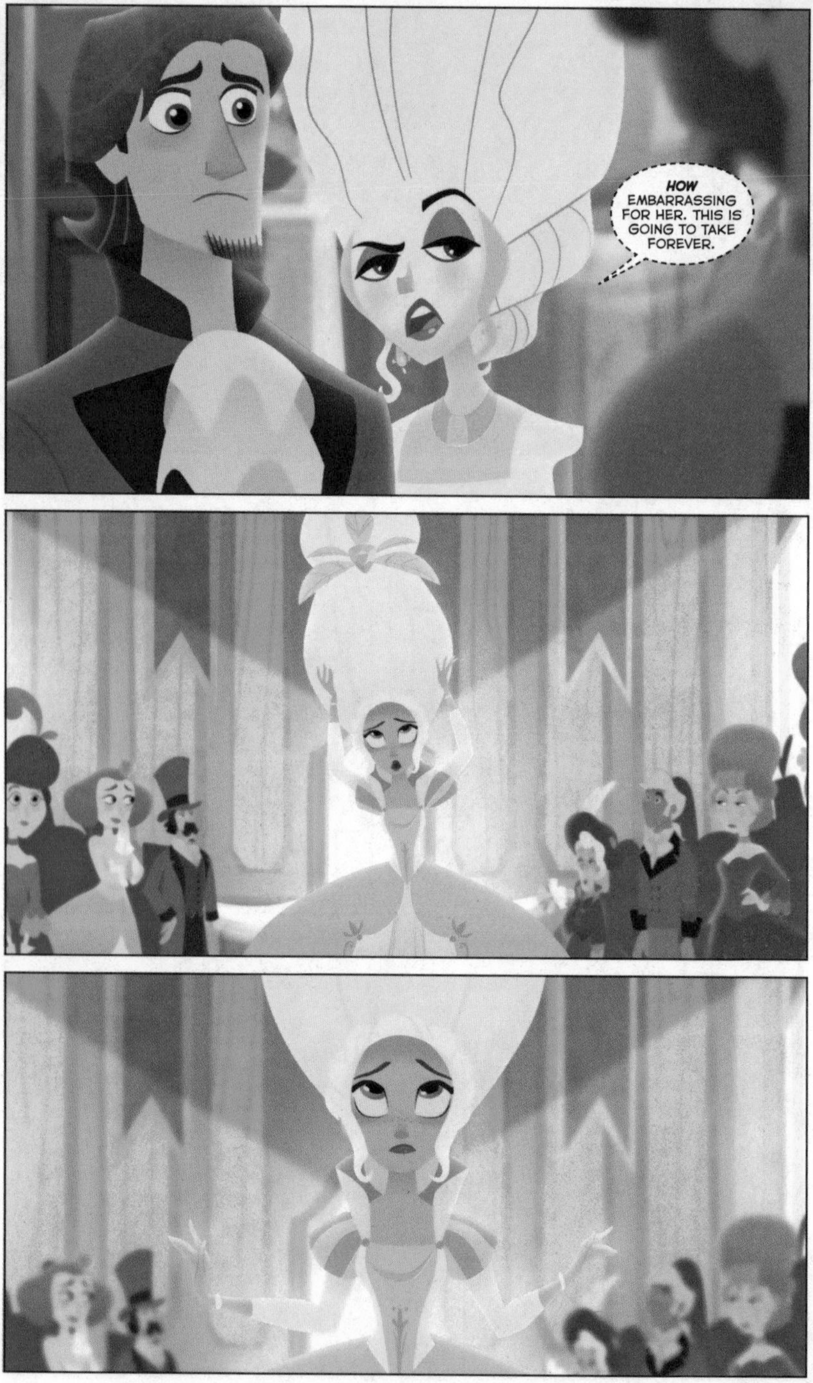
HOW EMBARRASSING FOR HER. THIS IS GOING TO TAKE FOREVER.

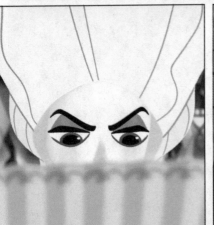

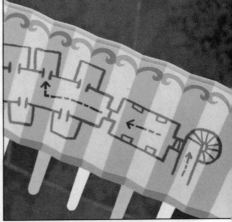

HELLO,
CAN ANYONE
HELP ME? I...I
MUST HAVE TAKEN
A WRONG TURN
SOMEWHERE.

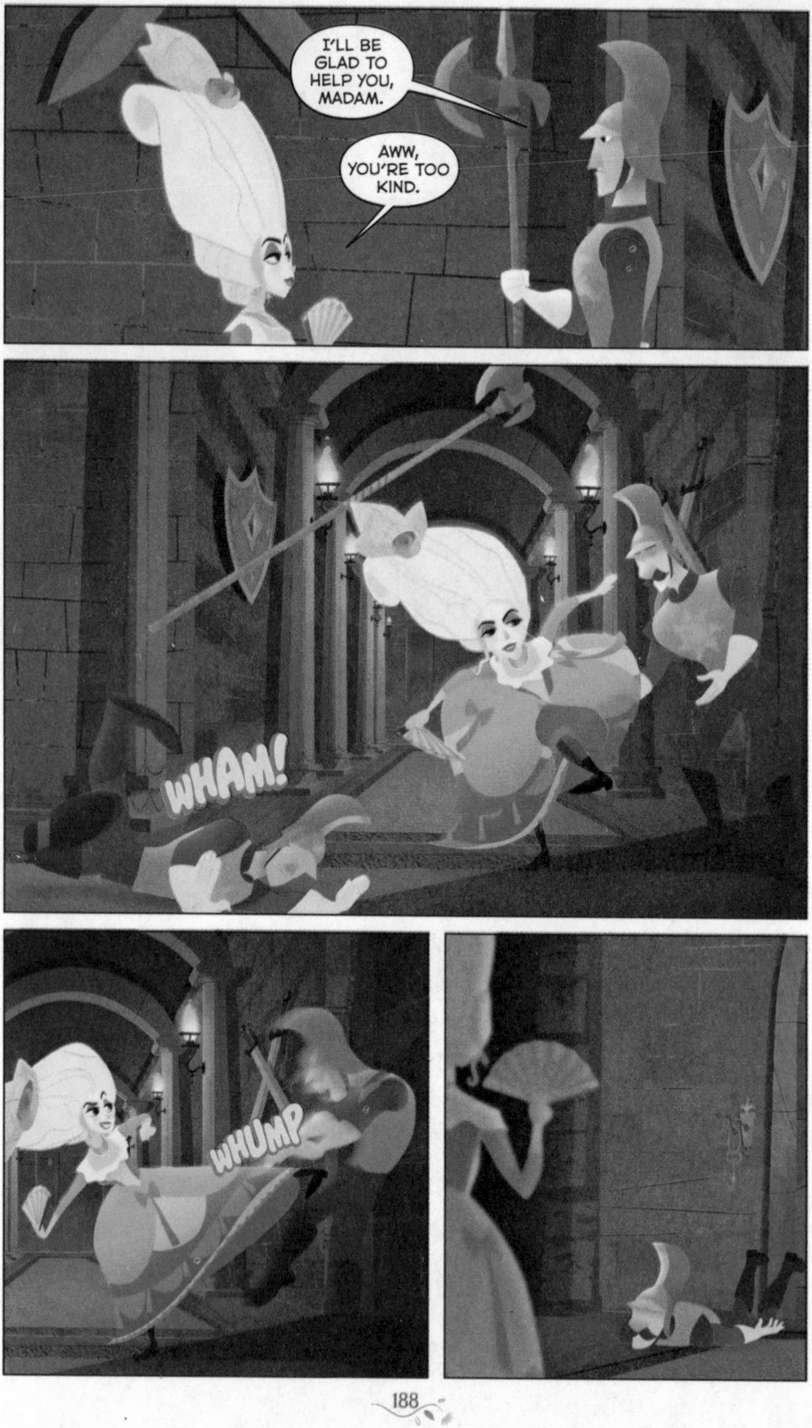
I'LL BE GLAD TO HELP YOU, MADAM.
AWW, YOU'RE TOO KIND.
WHAM!
WHUMP

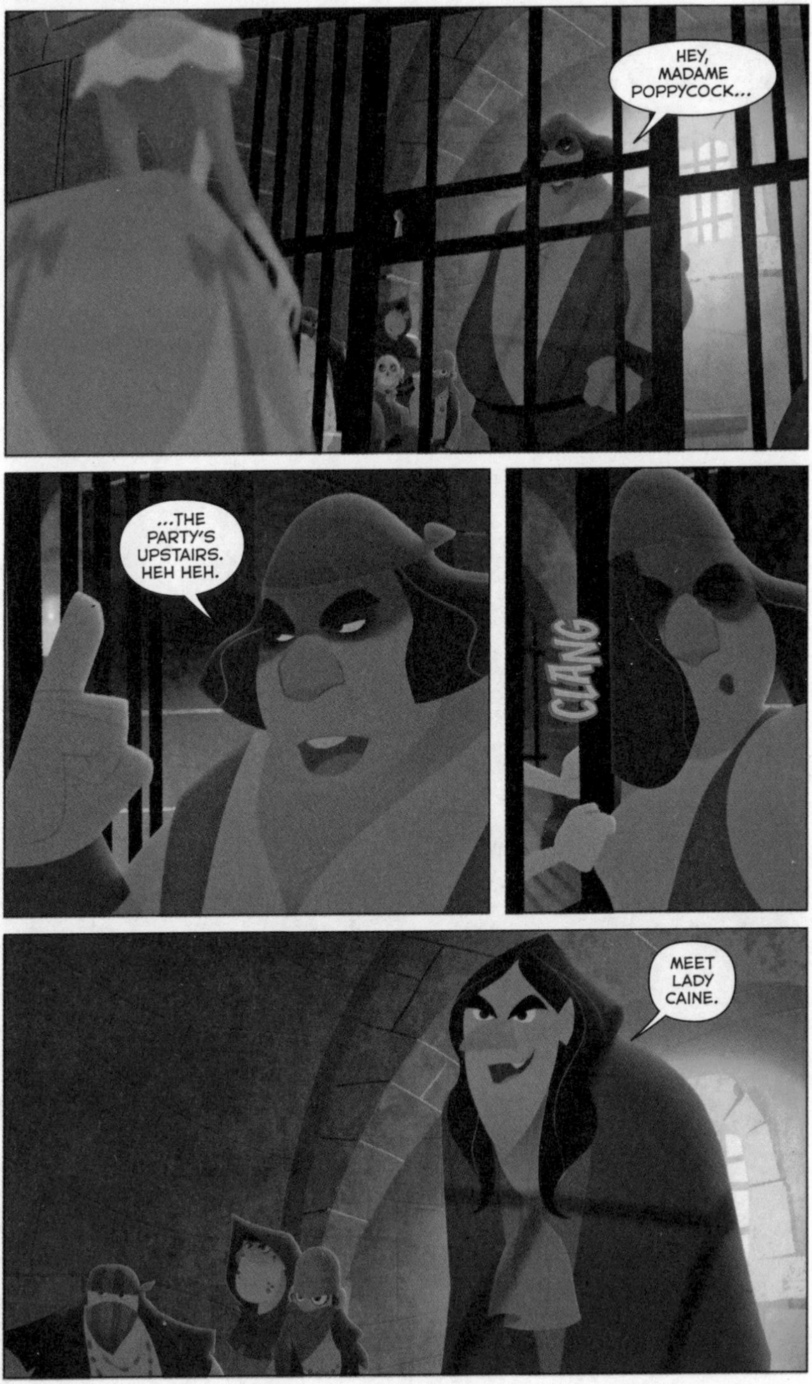
HEY, MADAME POPPYCOCK...
...THE PARTY'S UPSTAIRS. HEH HEH.
CLANG
MEET LADY CAINE.

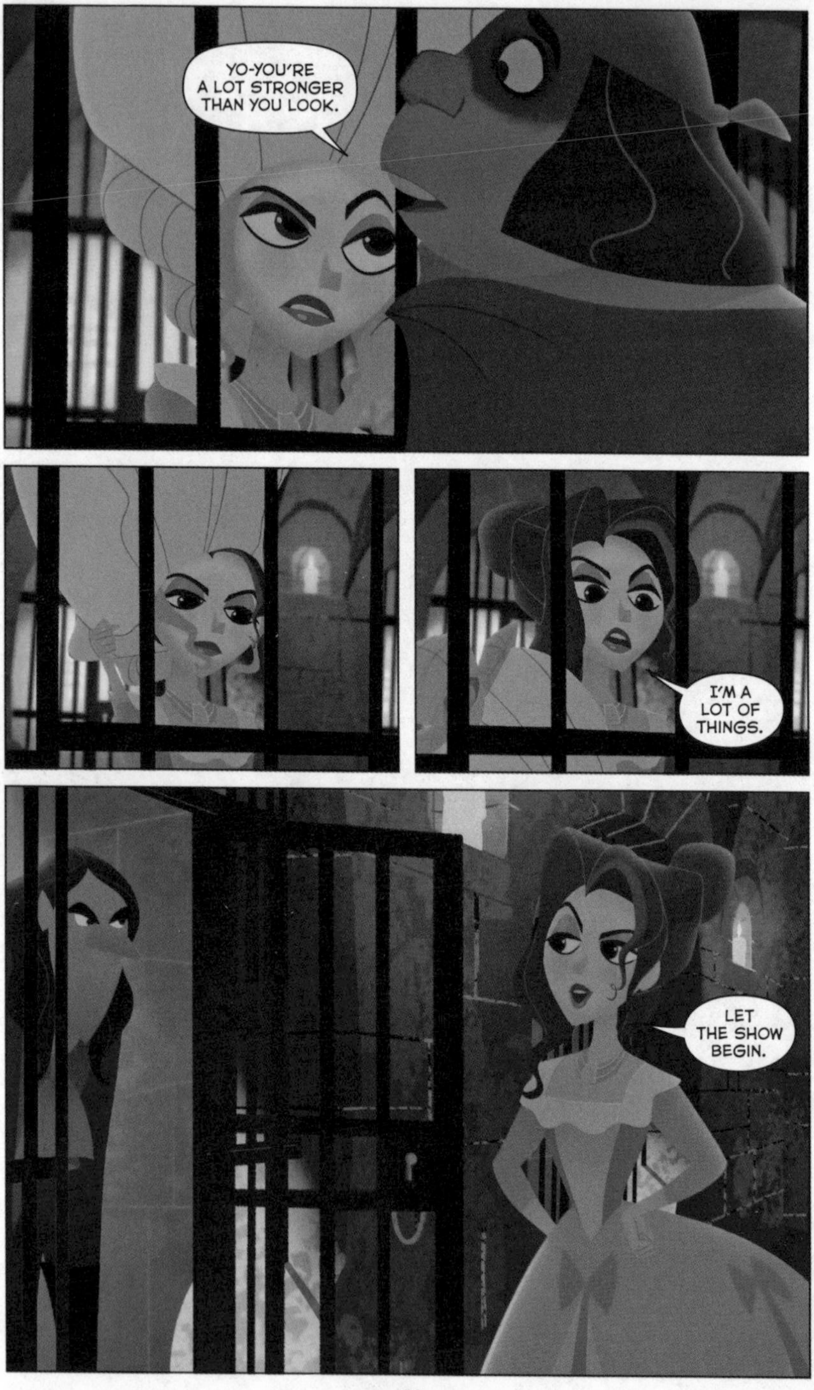
YO-YOU'RE A LOT STRONGER THAN YOU LOOK.
I'M A LOT OF THINGS.
LET THE SHOW BEGIN.

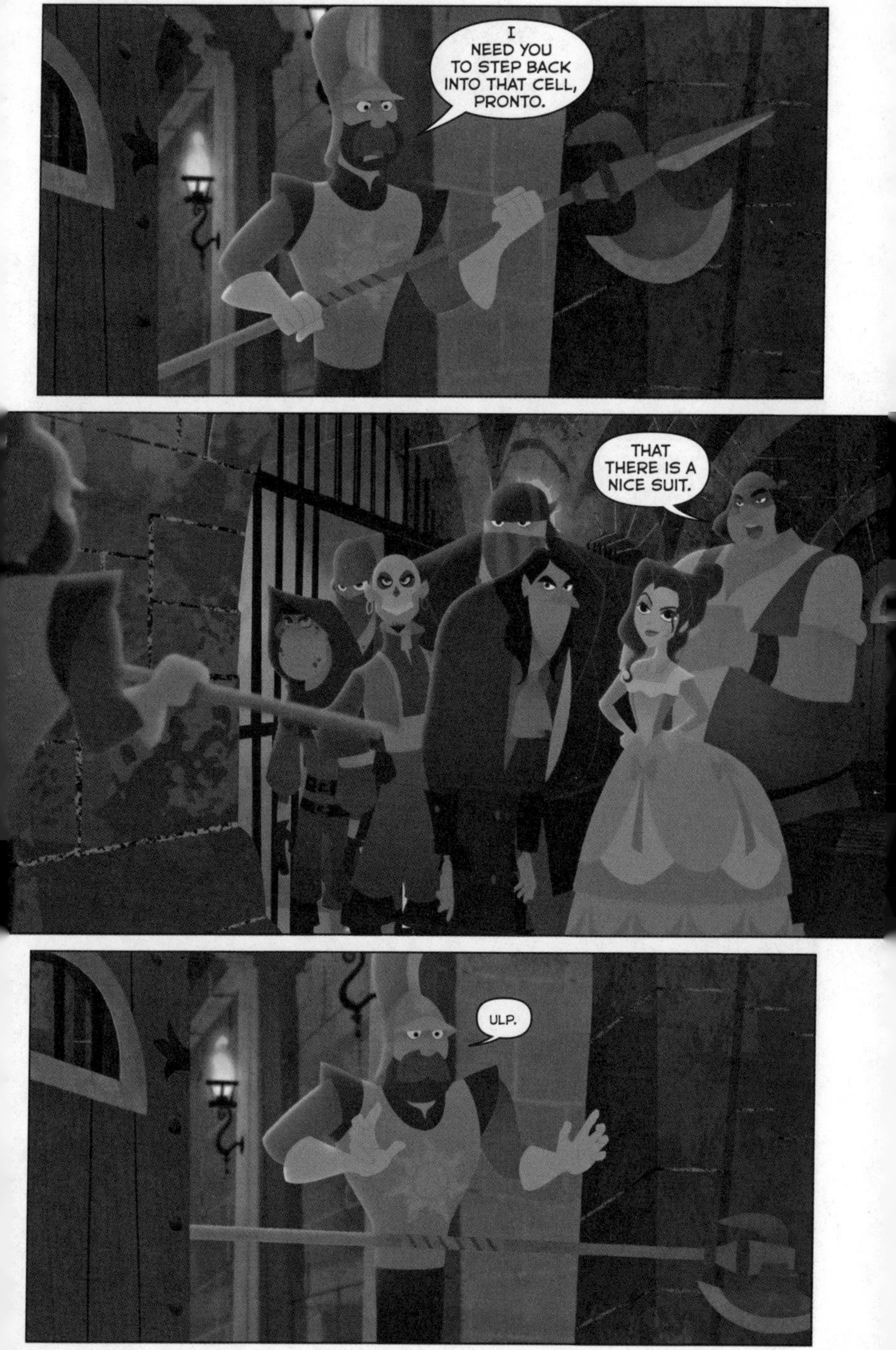
I NEED YOU TO STEP BACK INTO THAT CELL, PRONTO.
THAT THERE IS A NICE SUIT.
ULP.

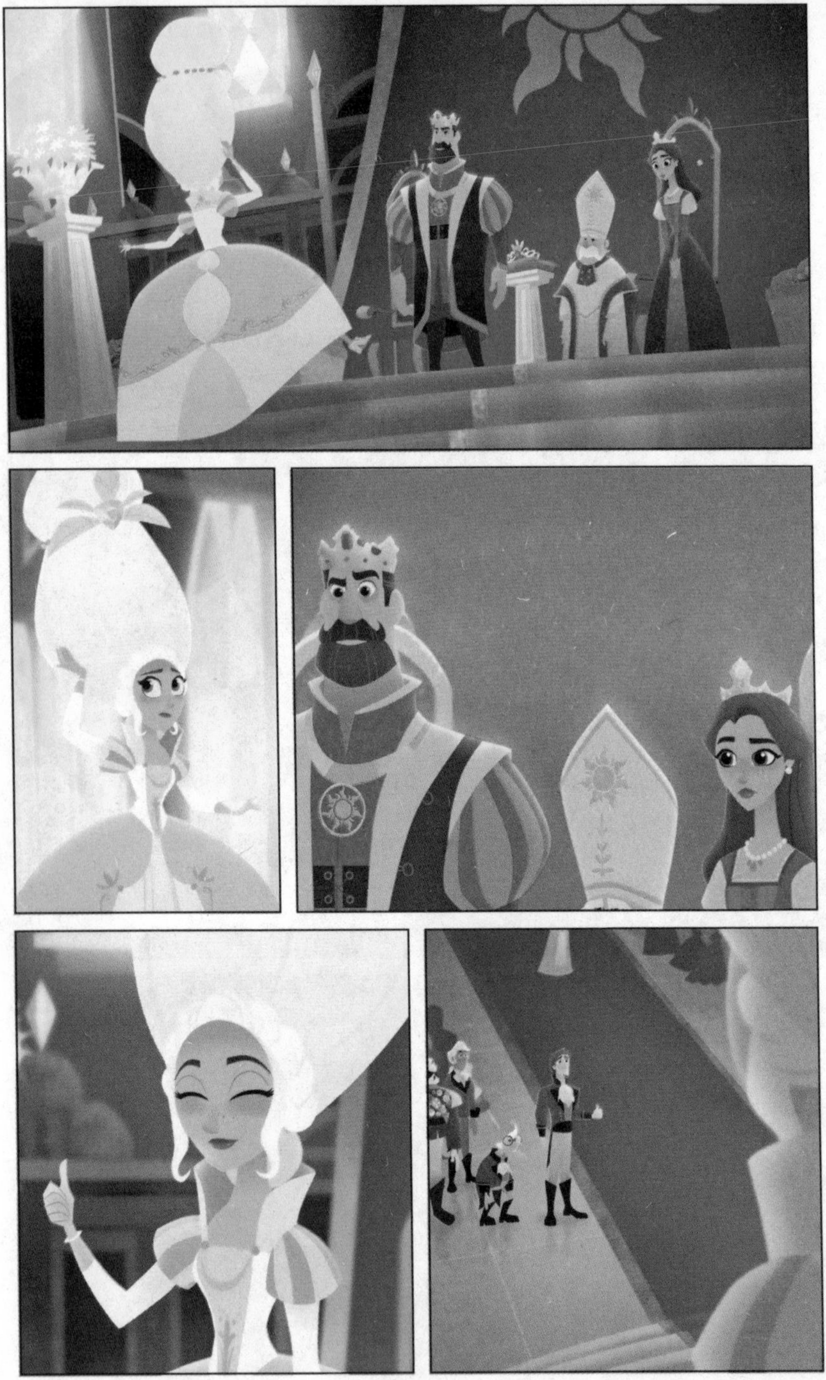

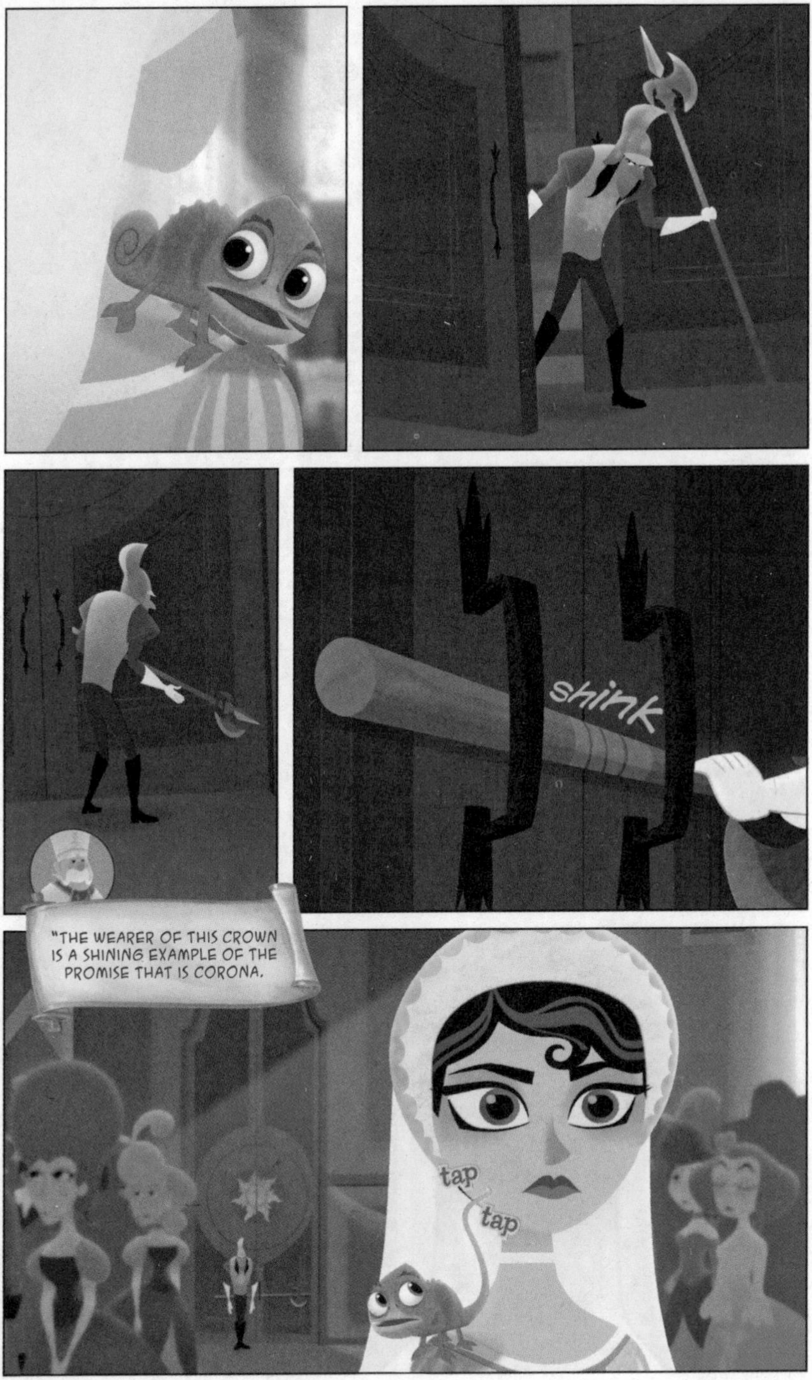
shink
"THE WEARER OF THIS CROWN IS A SHINING EXAMPLE OF THE PROMISE THAT IS CORONA.
tap
tap

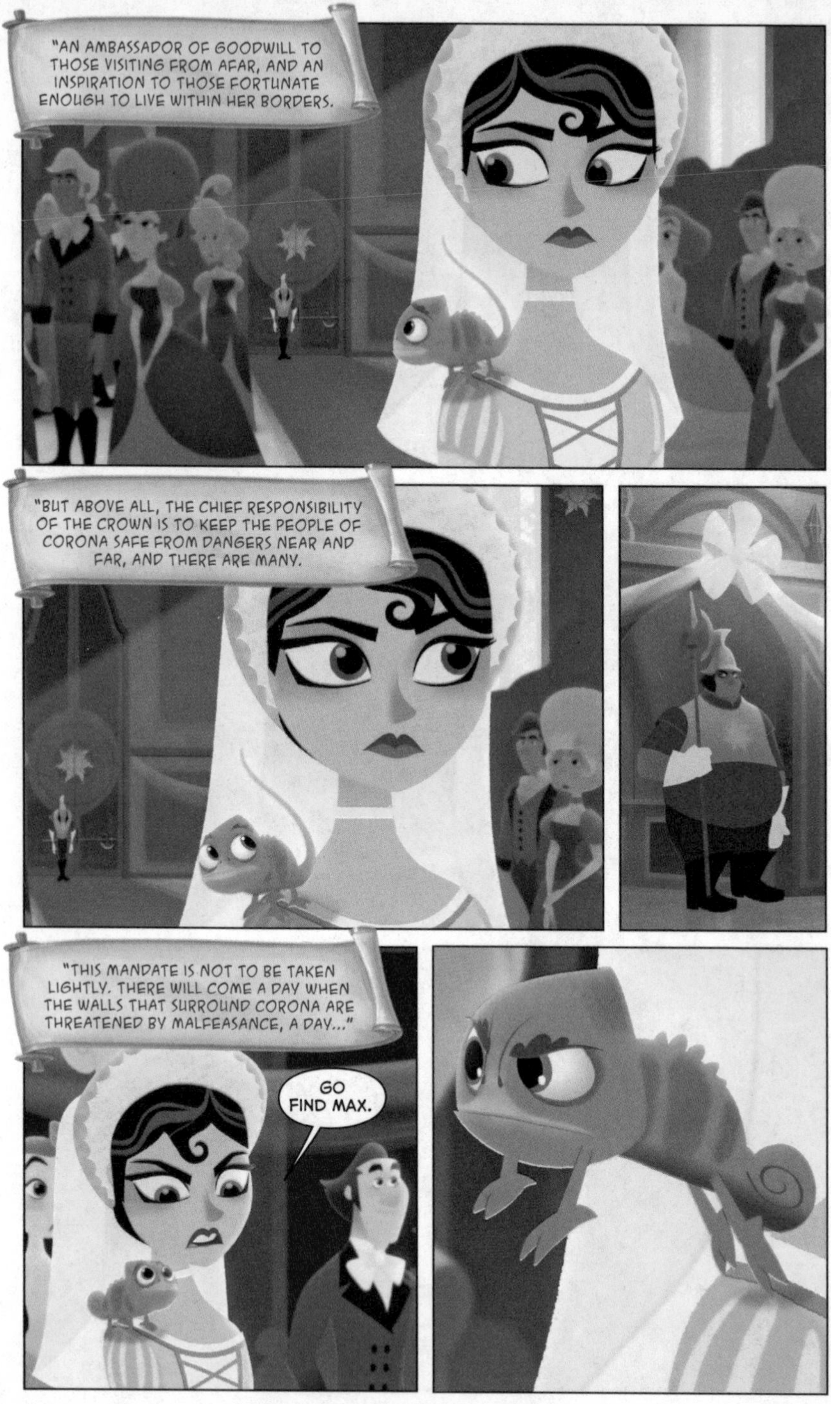
"AN AMBASSADOR OF GOODWILL TO THOSE VISITING FROM AFAR, AND AN INSPIRATION TO THOSE FORTUNATE ENOUGH TO LIVE WITHIN HER BORDERS.
"BUT ABOVE ALL, THE CHIEF RESPONSIBILITY OF THE CROWN IS TO KEEP THE PEOPLE OF CORONA SAFE FROM DANGERS NEAR AND FAR, AND THERE ARE MANY.
"THIS MANDATE IS NOT TO BE TAKEN LIGHTLY. THERE WILL COME A DAY WHEN THE WALLS THAT SURROUND CORONA ARE THREATENED BY MALFEASANCE, A DAY..."
GO FIND MAX.

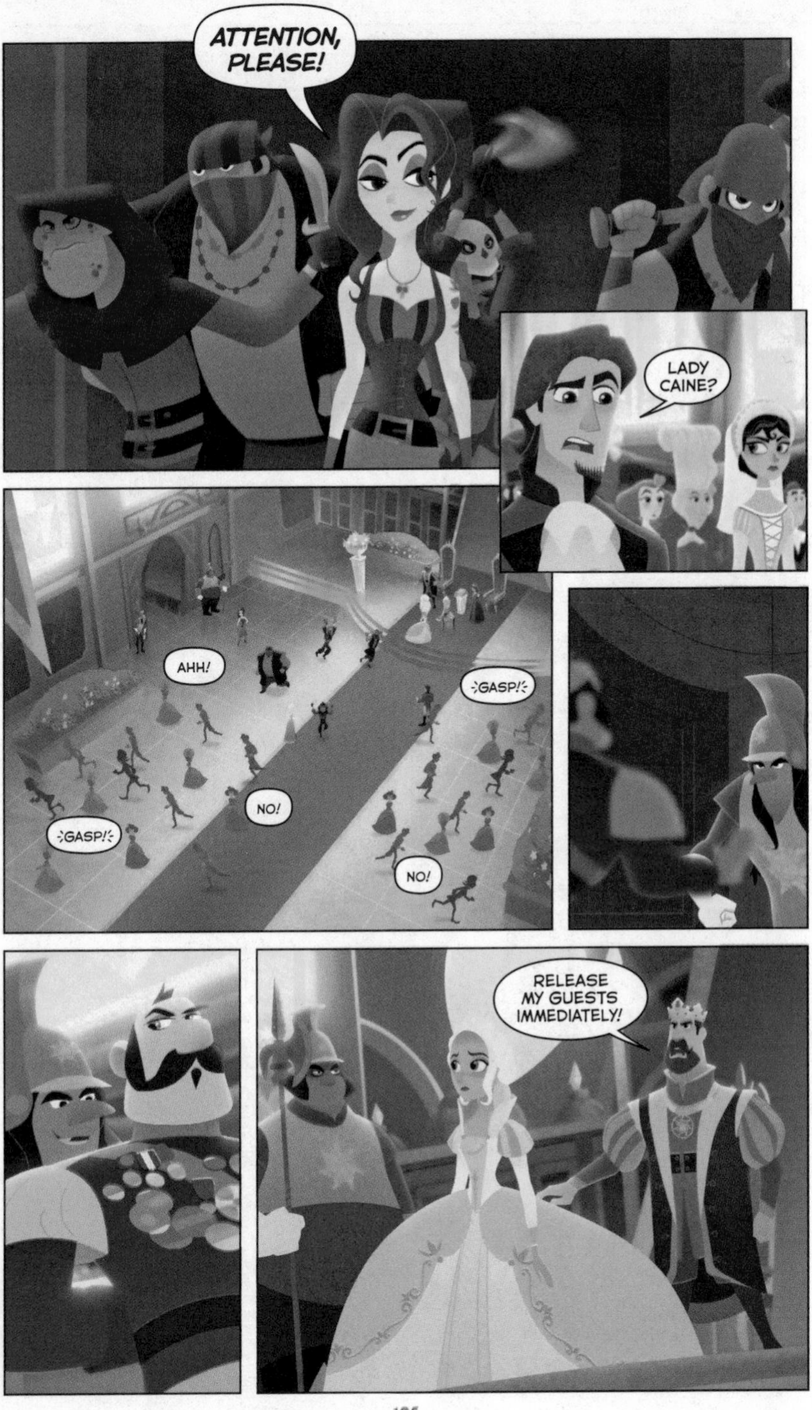
ATTENTION, PLEASE!
LADY CAINE?
AHH!
GASP!
NO!
GASP!
NO!
RELEASE MY GUESTS IMMEDIATELY!

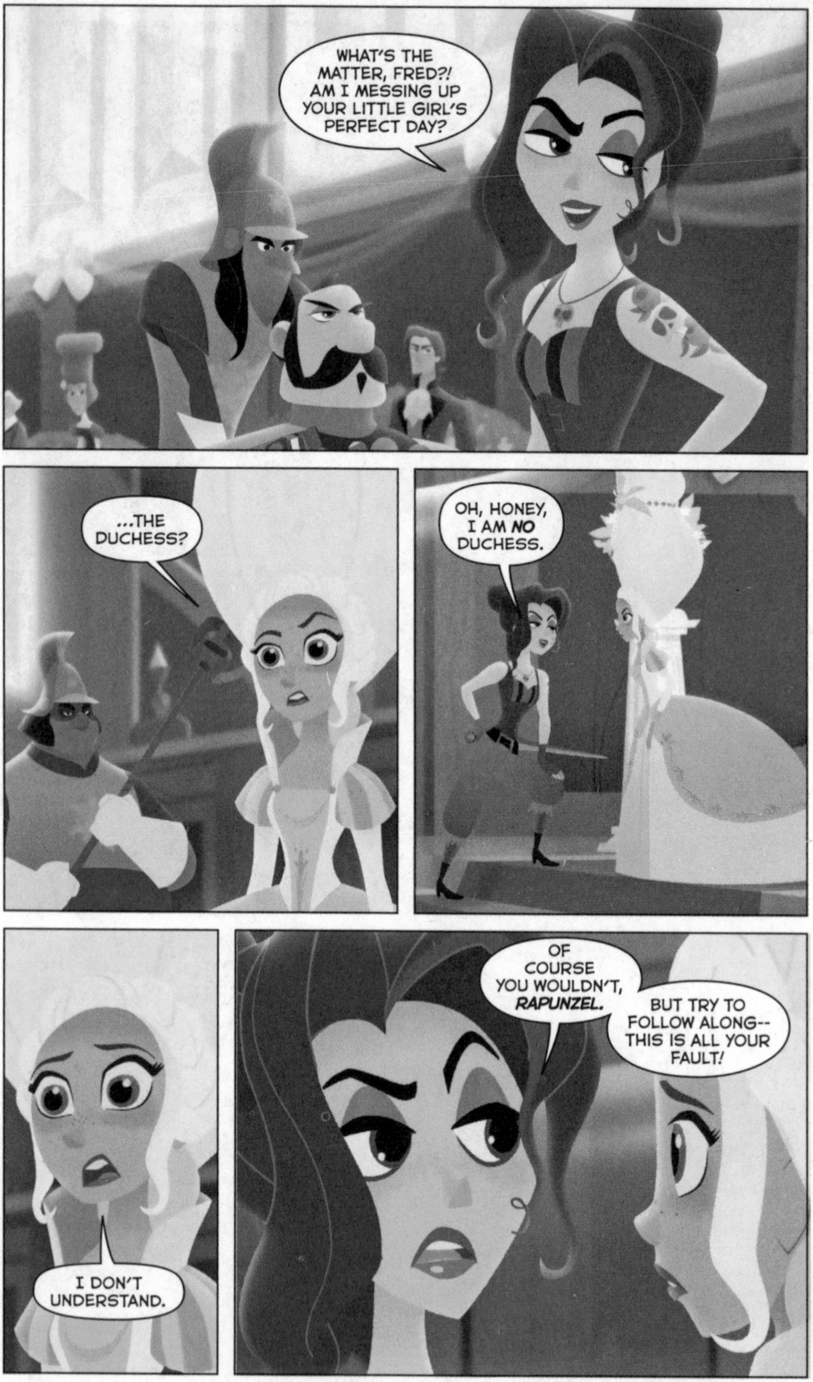
WHAT'S THE MATTER, FRED?! AM I MESSING UP YOUR LITTLE GIRL'S PERFECT DAY?
...THE DUCHESS?
OH, HONEY, I AM *NO* DUCHESS.
I DON'T UNDERSTAND.
OF COURSE YOU WOULDN'T, ***RAPUNZEL.***
BUT TRY TO FOLLOW ALONG-- THIS IS ALL YOUR FAULT!

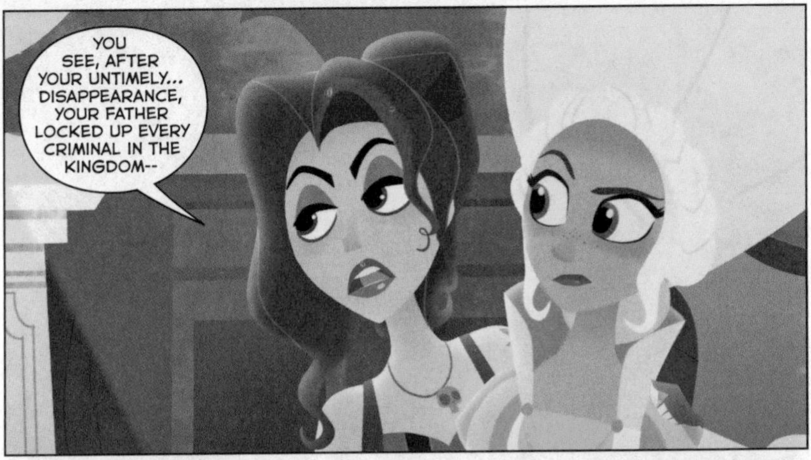
YOU SEE, AFTER YOUR UNTIMELY... DISAPPEARANCE, YOUR FATHER LOCKED UP EVERY CRIMINAL IN THE KINGDOM--

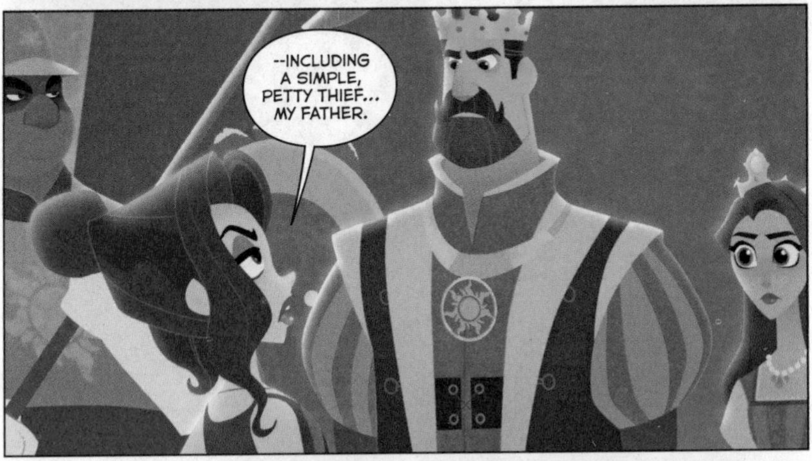
--INCLUDING A SIMPLE, PETTY THIEF... MY FATHER.

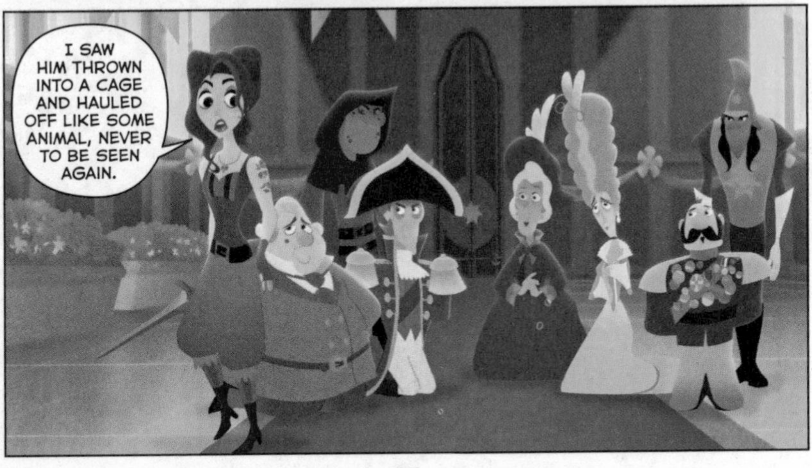
I SAW HIM THROWN INTO A CAGE AND HAULED OFF LIKE SOME ANIMAL, NEVER TO BE SEEN AGAIN.

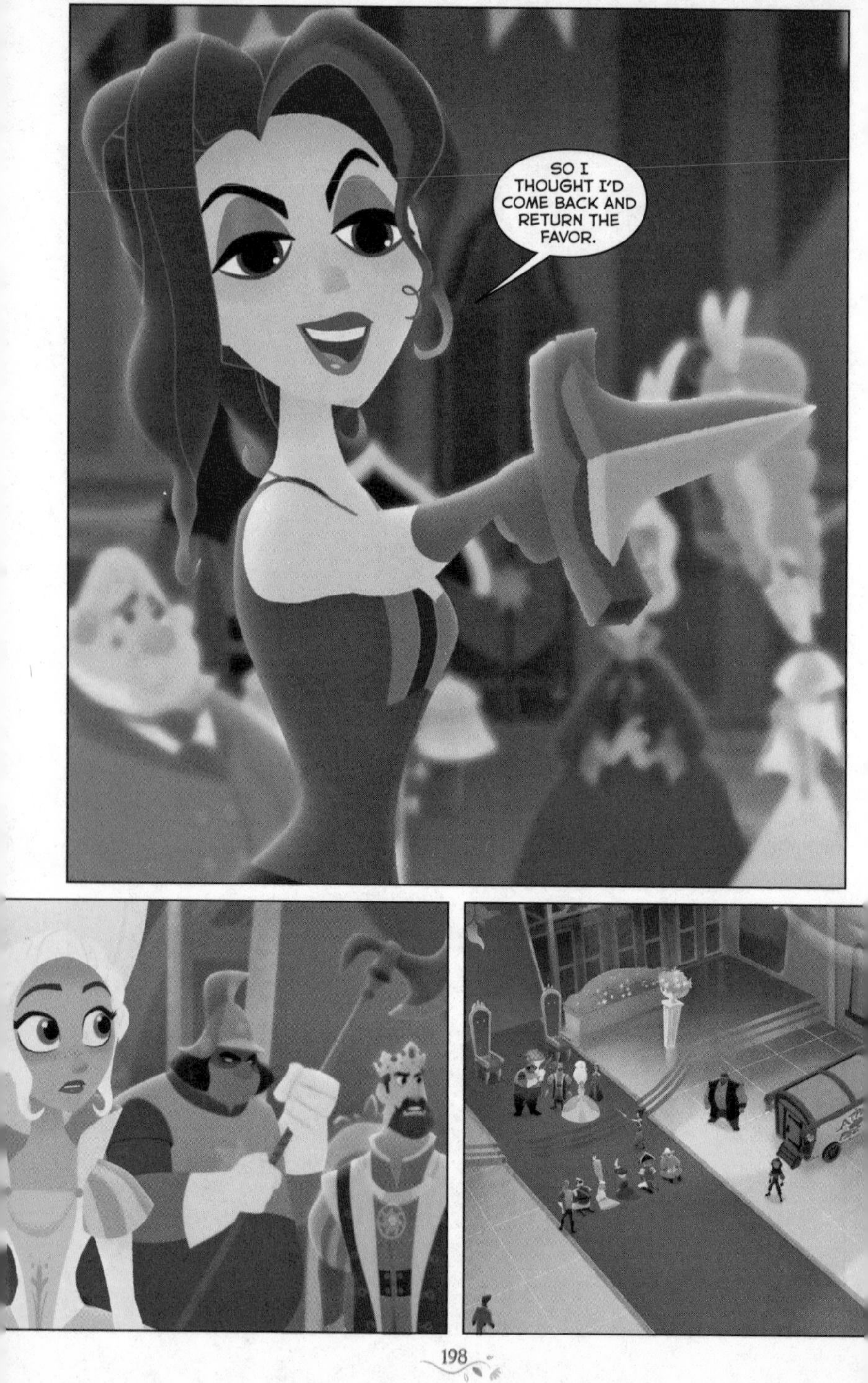
SO I THOUGHT I'D COME BACK AND RETURN THE FAVOR.

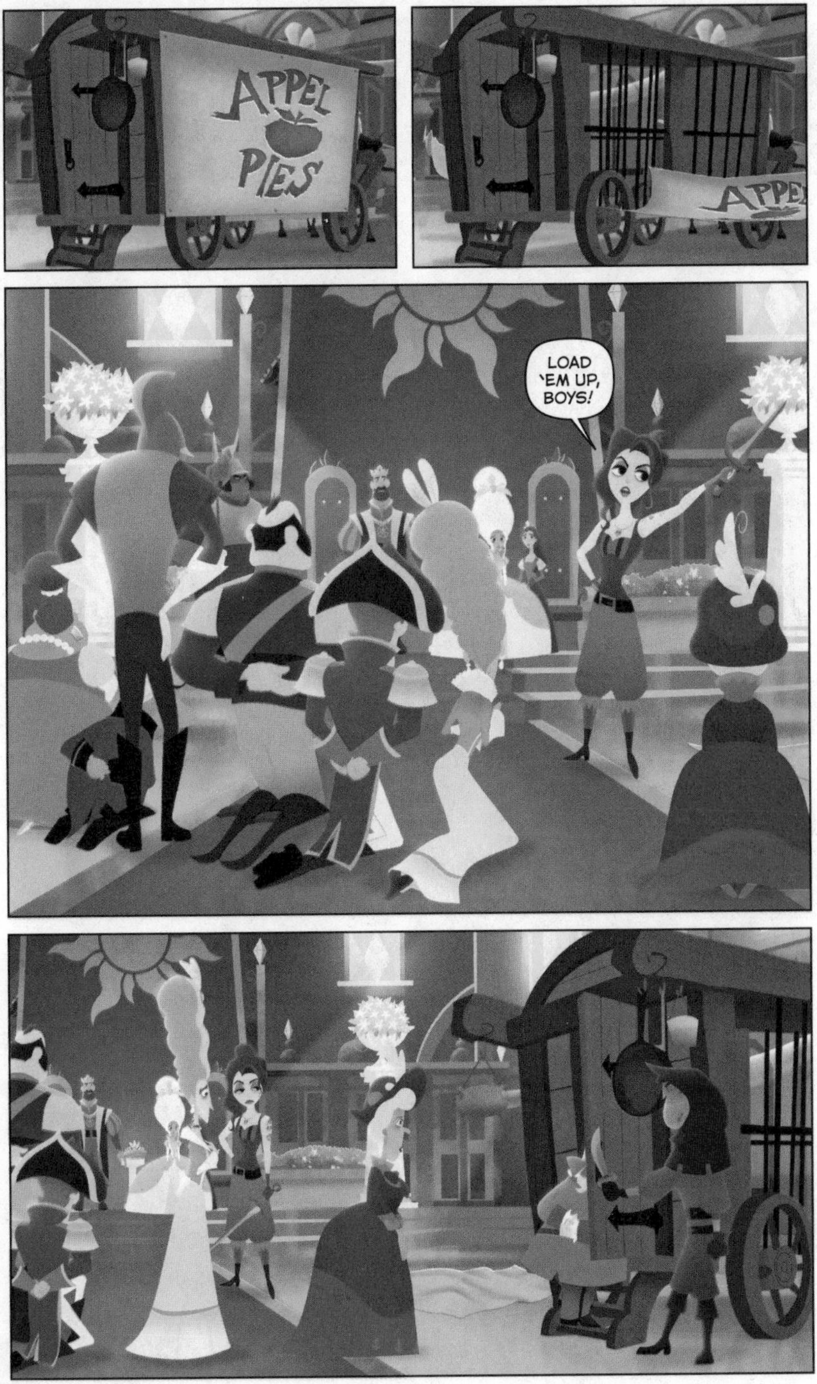
APPEL PIES
APPE
LOAD 'EM UP, BOYS!

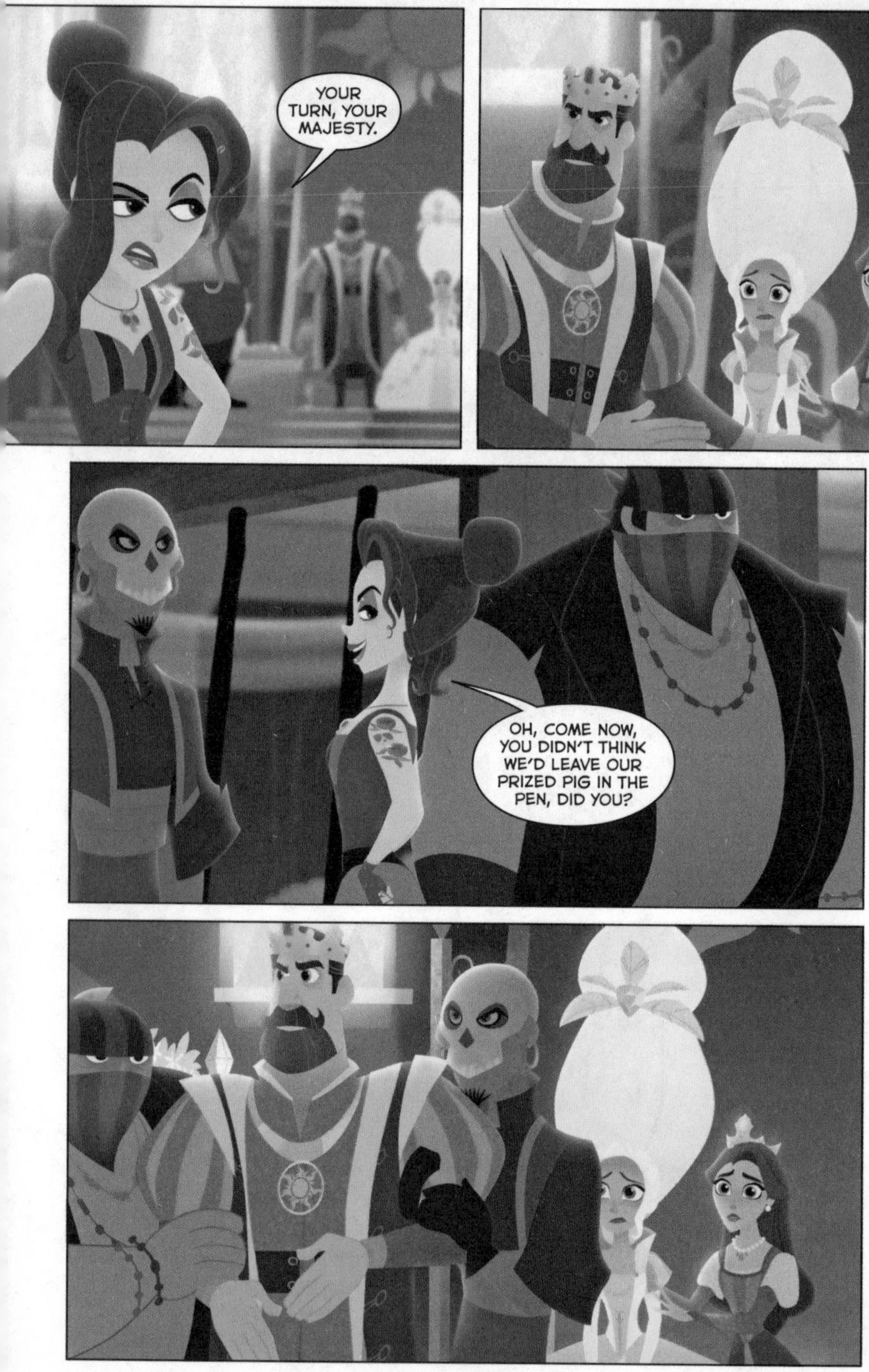
YOUR TURN, YOUR MAJESTY.
OH, COME NOW, YOU DIDN'T THINK WE'D LEAVE OUR PRIZED PIG IN THE PEN, DID YOU?

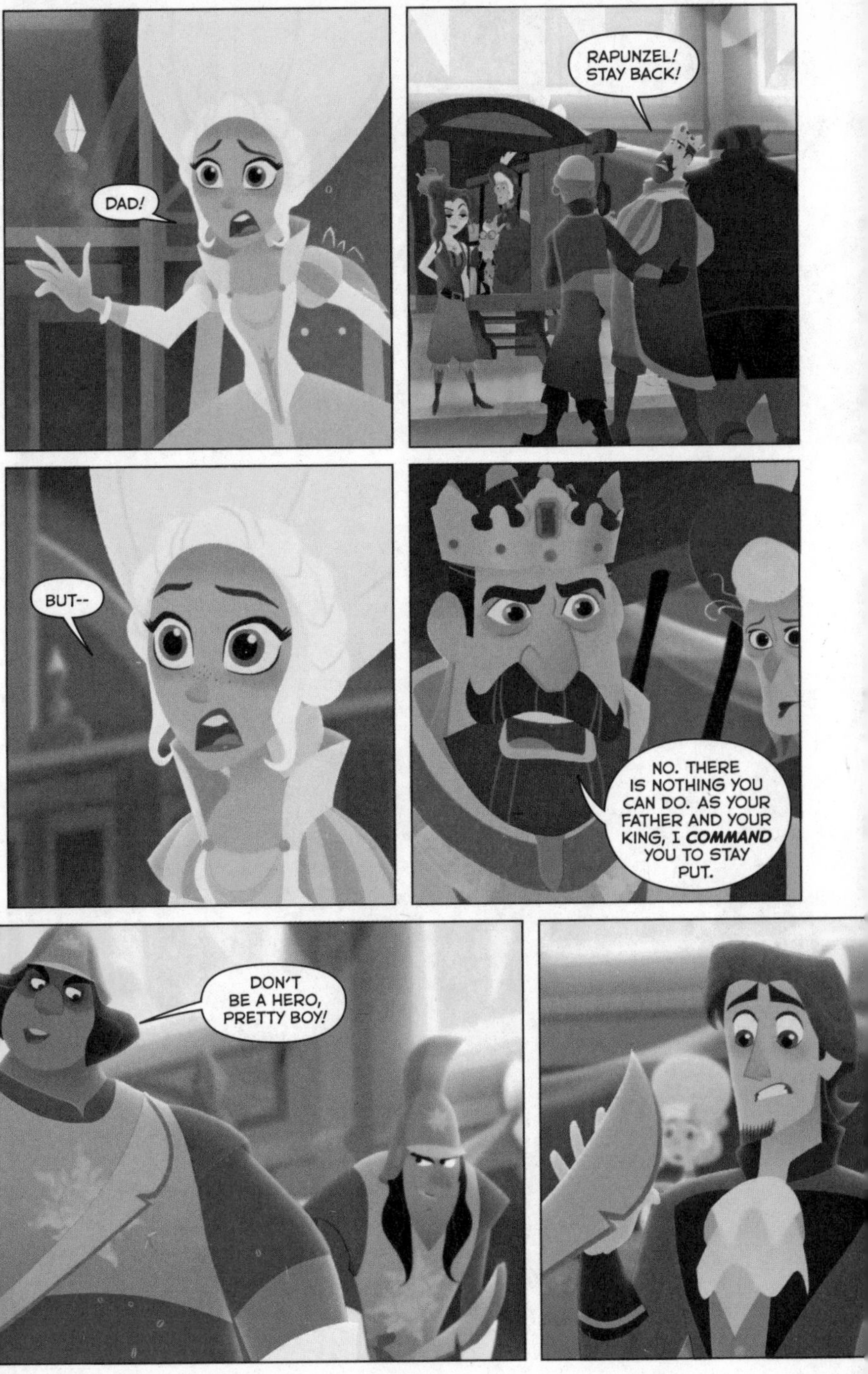

DAD!
RAPUNZEL! STAY BACK!
BUT--
NO. THERE IS NOTHING YOU CAN DO. AS YOUR FATHER AND YOUR KING, I COMMAND YOU TO STAY PUT.
DON'T BE A HERO, PRETTY BOY!

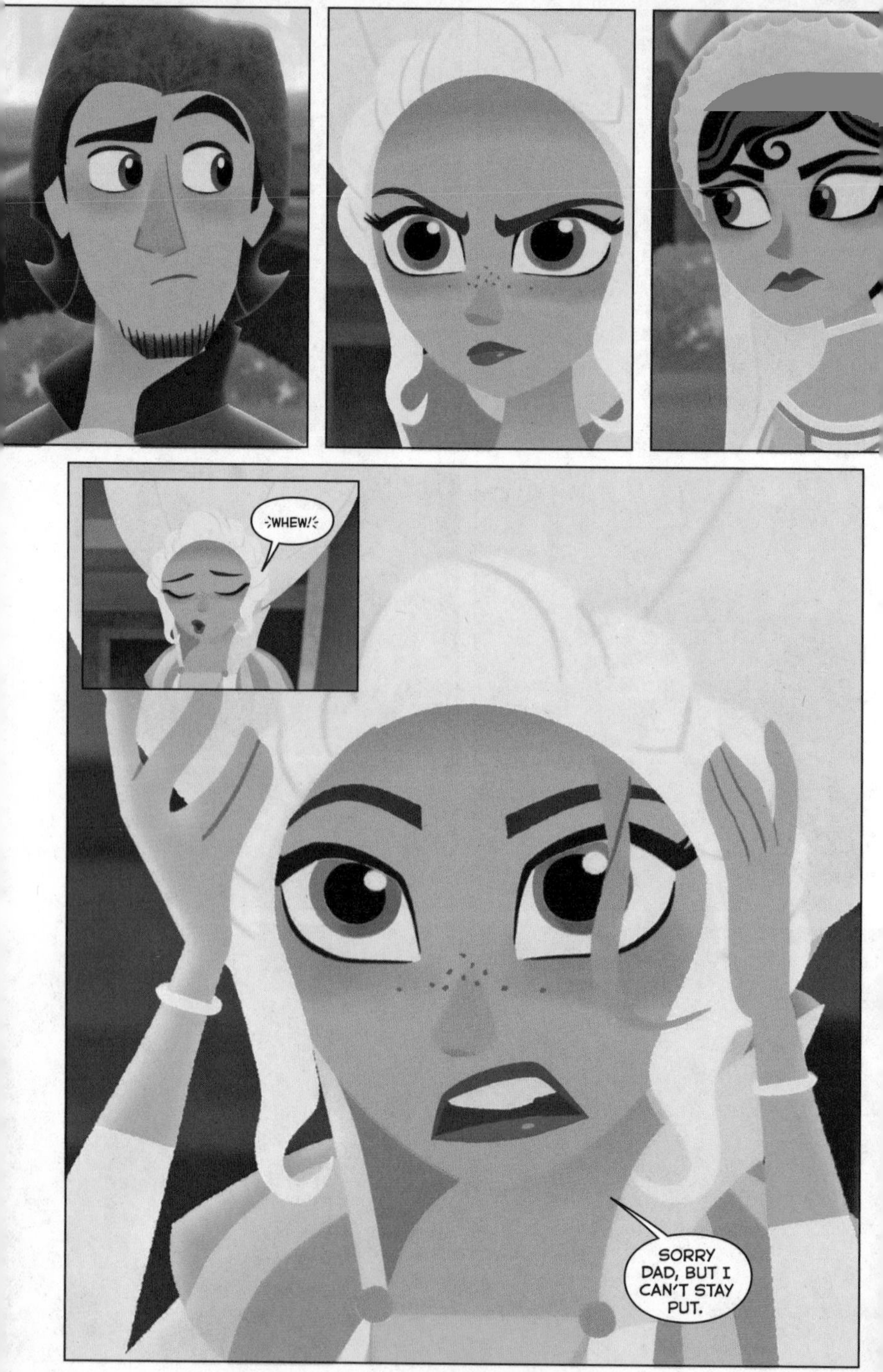
WHEW!
SORRY DAD, BUT I CAN'T STAY PUT.

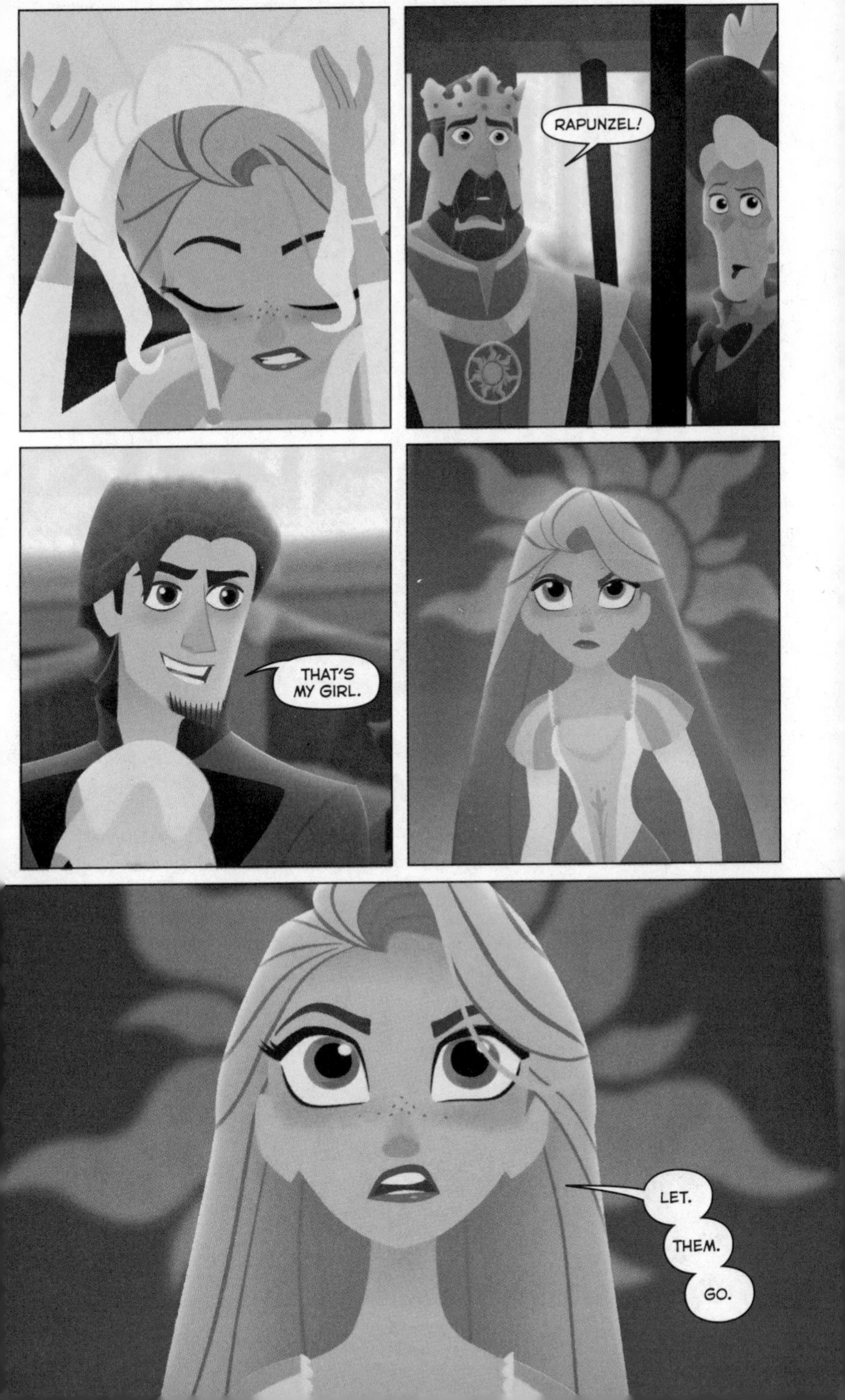
RAPUNZEL!
THAT'S MY GIRL.
LET.
THEM.
GO.

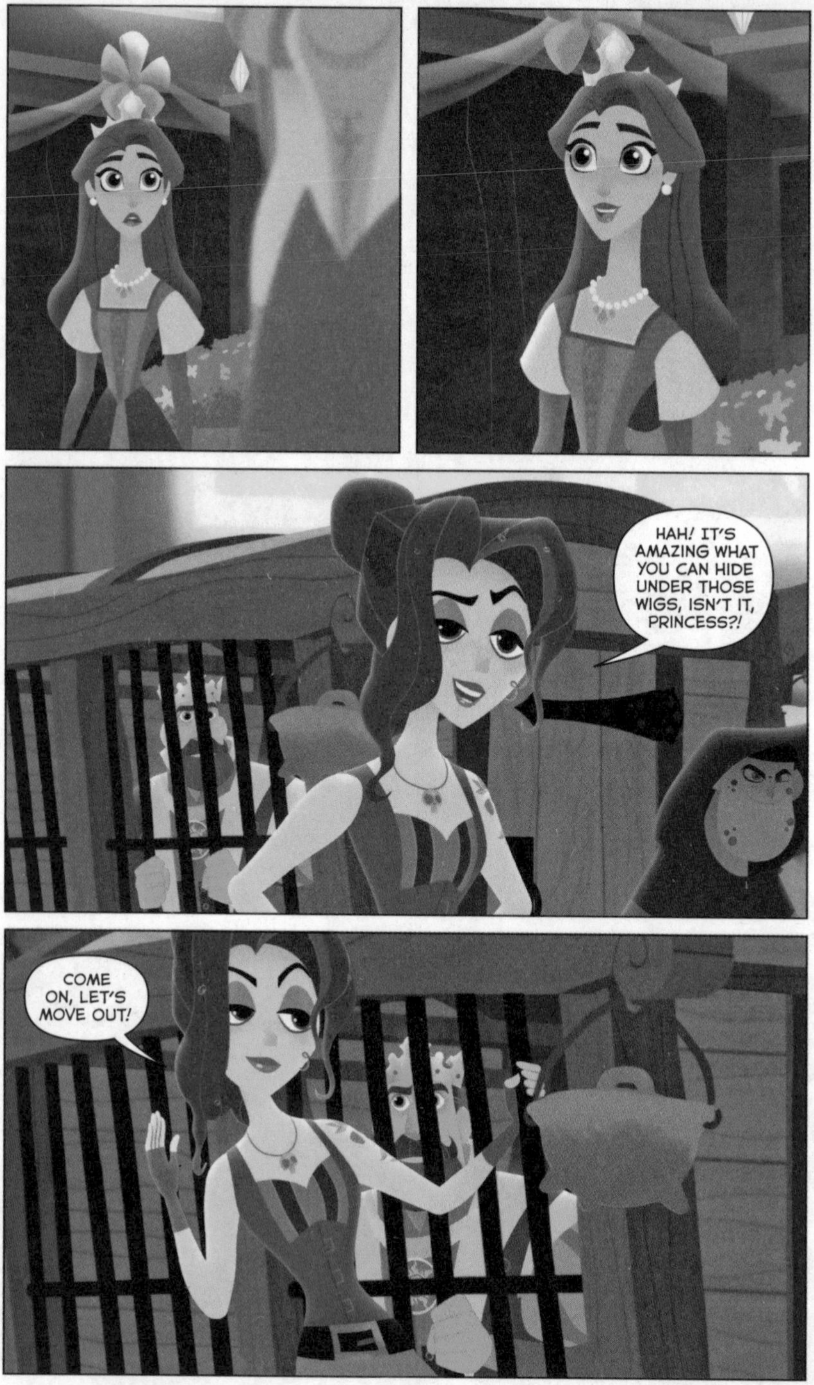
HAH! IT'S AMAZING WHAT YOU CAN HIDE UNDER THOSE WIGS, ISN'T IT, PRINCESS?!
COME ON, LET'S MOVE OUT!

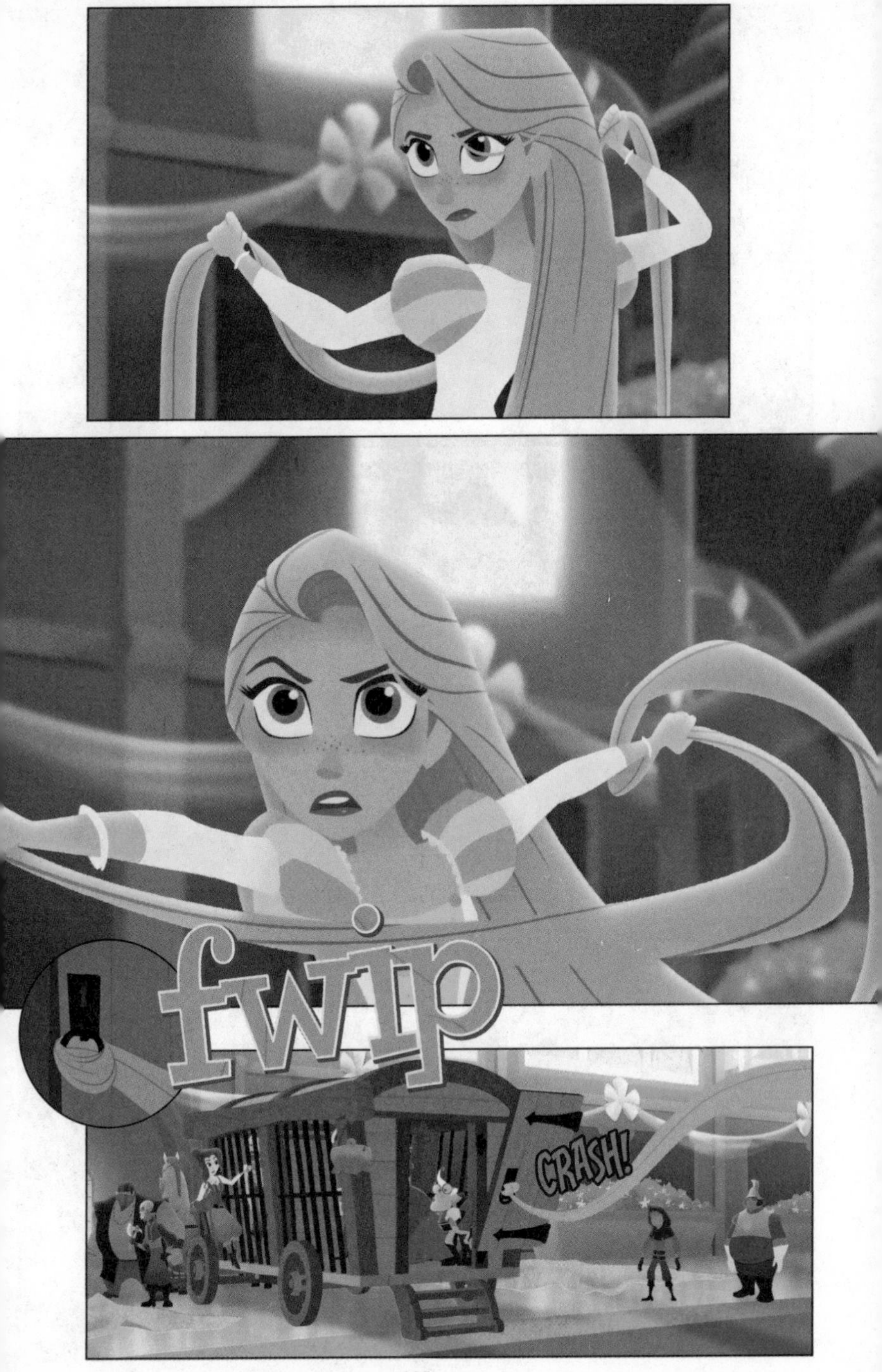
fwip
CRASH!

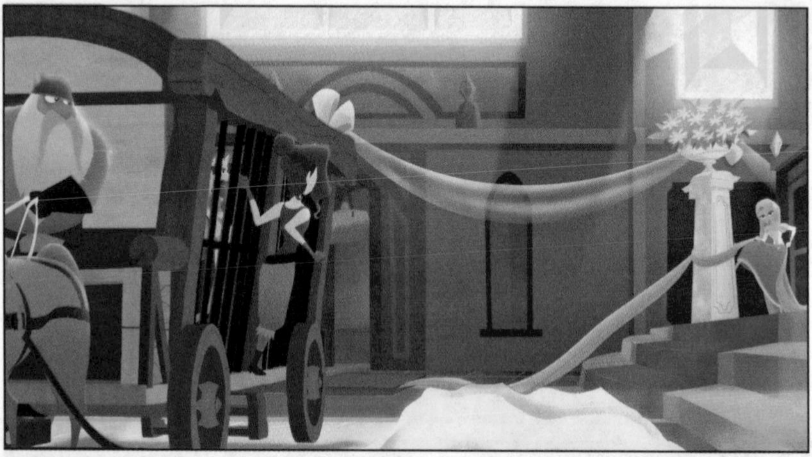

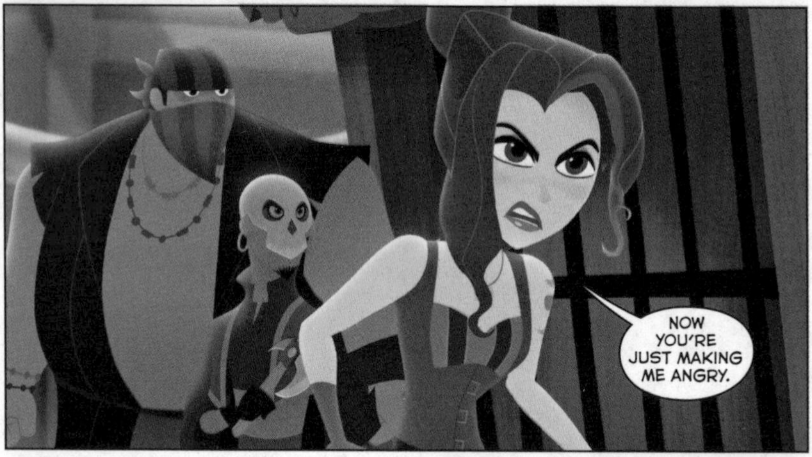
NOW YOU'RE JUST MAKING ME ANGRY.

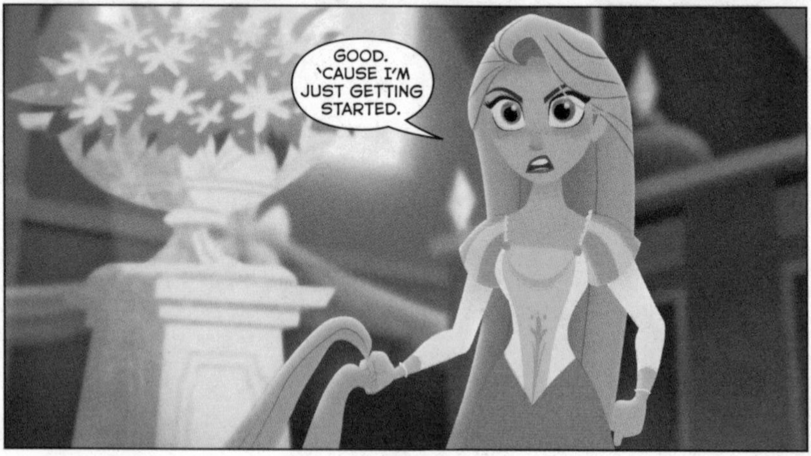
GOOD. 'CAUSE I'M JUST GETTING STARTED.

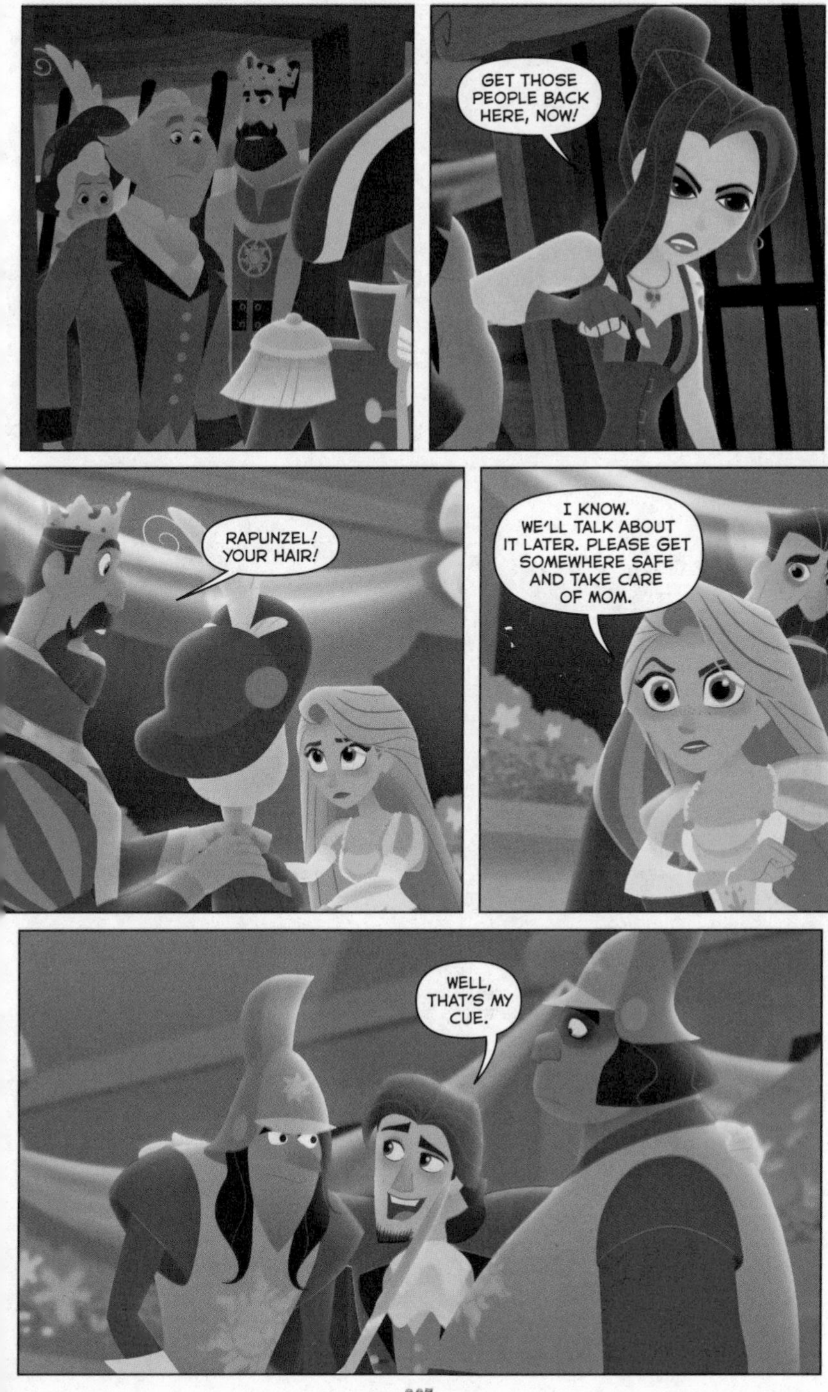
GET THOSE PEOPLE BACK HERE, NOW!
RAPUNZEL! YOUR HAIR!
I KNOW. WE'LL TALK ABOUT IT LATER. PLEASE GET SOMEWHERE SAFE AND TAKE CARE OF MOM.
WELL, THAT'S MY CUE.

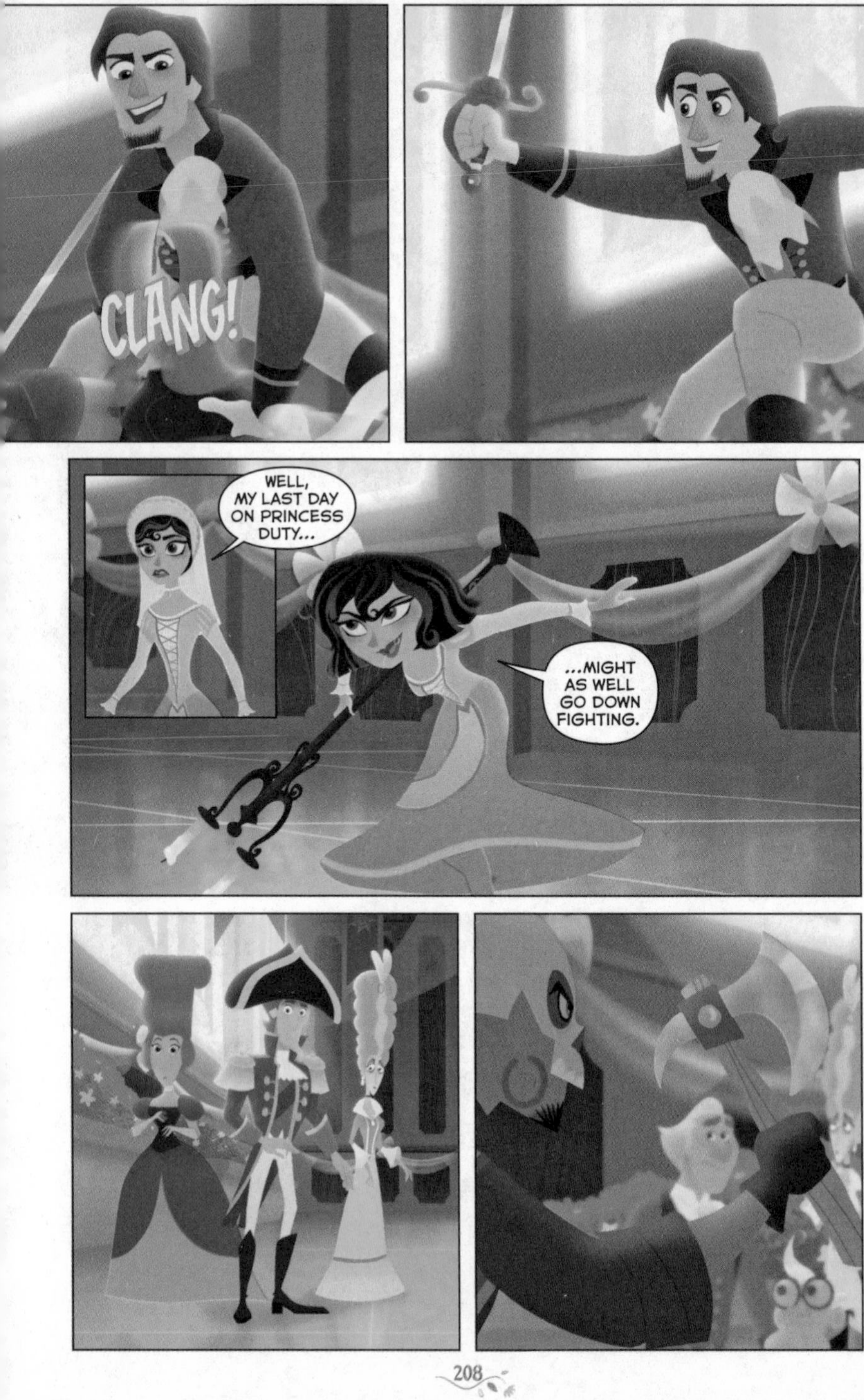
CLANG!
WELL, MY LAST DAY ON PRINCESS DUTY...
...MIGHT AS WELL GO DOWN FIGHTING.

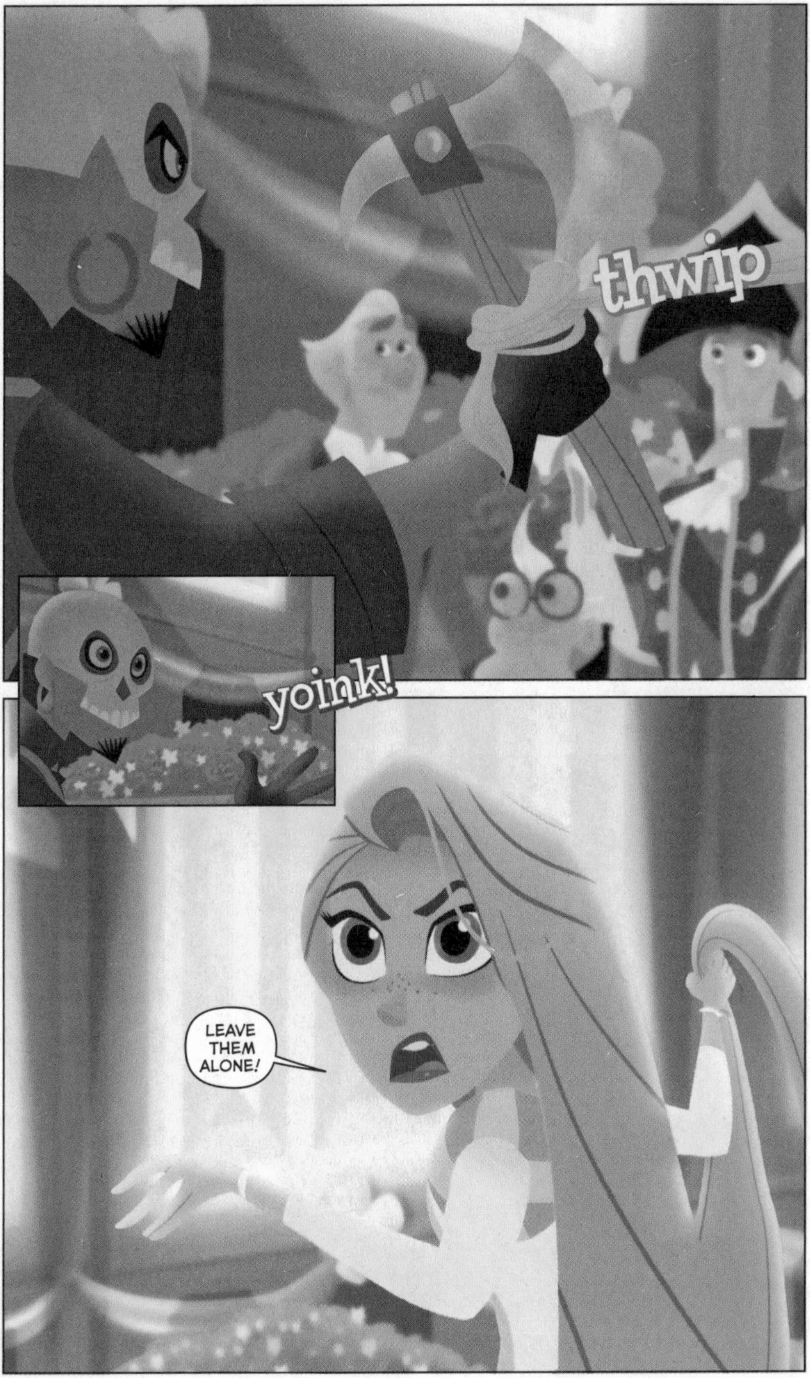
thwip
yoink!
LEAVE THEM ALONE!

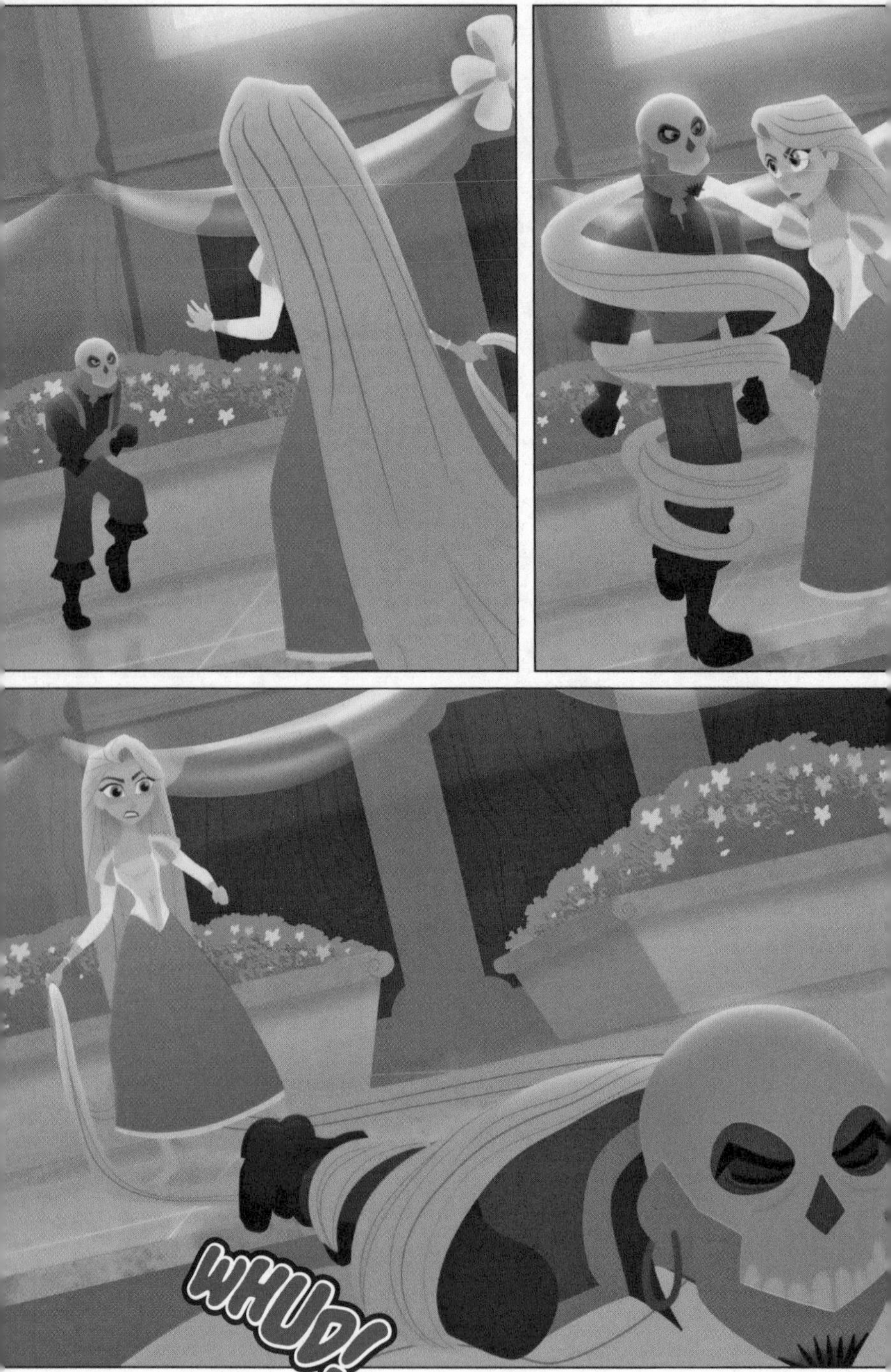
WHUD!

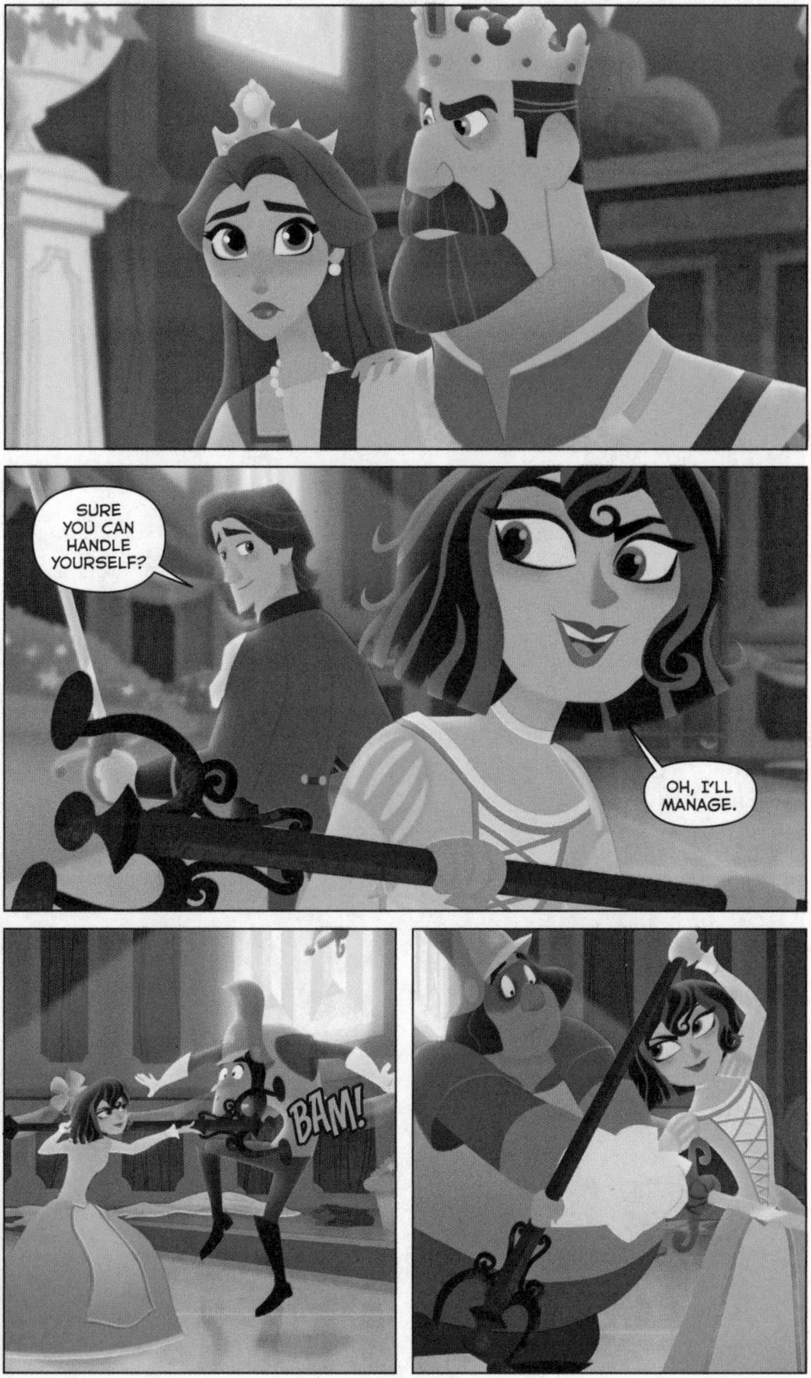
SURE YOU CAN HANDLE YOURSELF?
OH, I'LL MANAGE.
BAM!

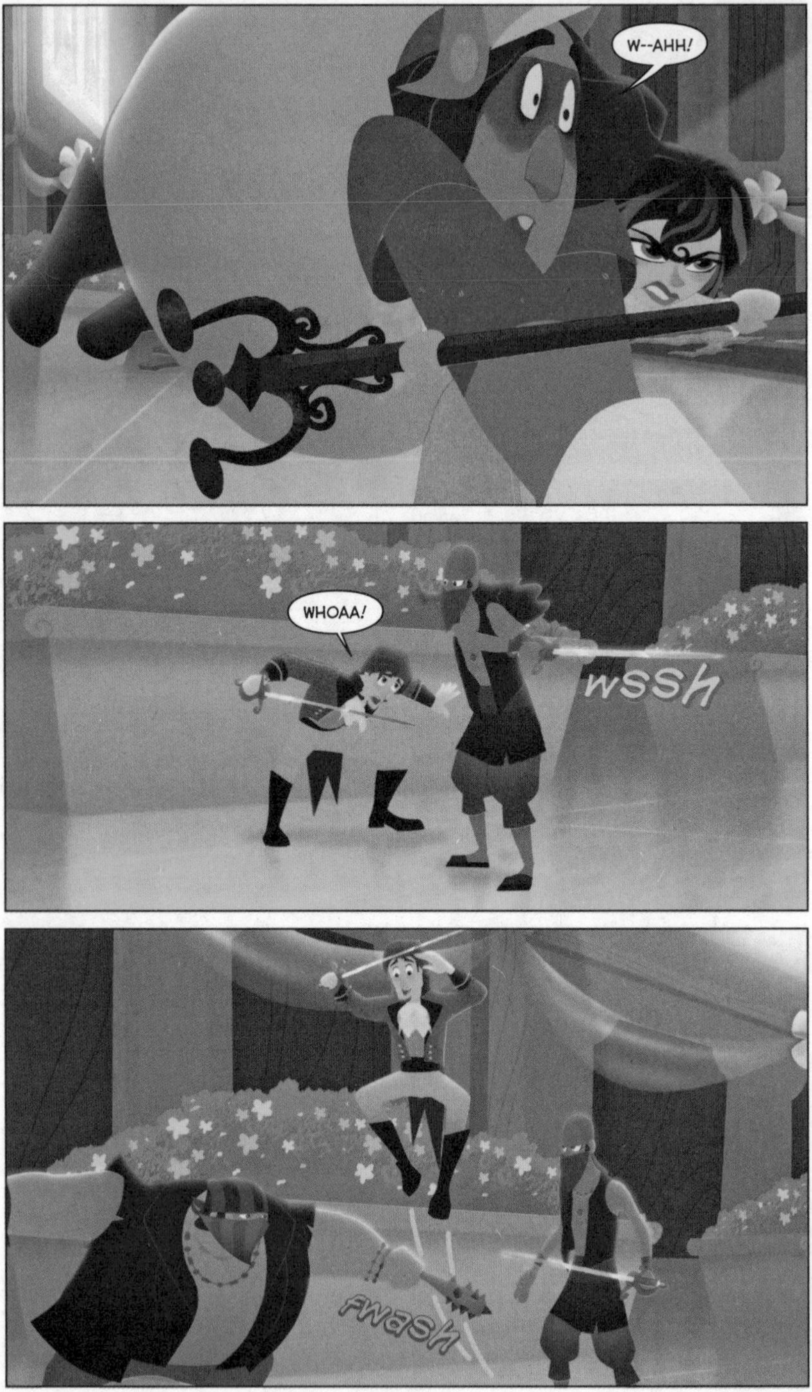
W--AHH!
WHOAA!
wssh
fwash

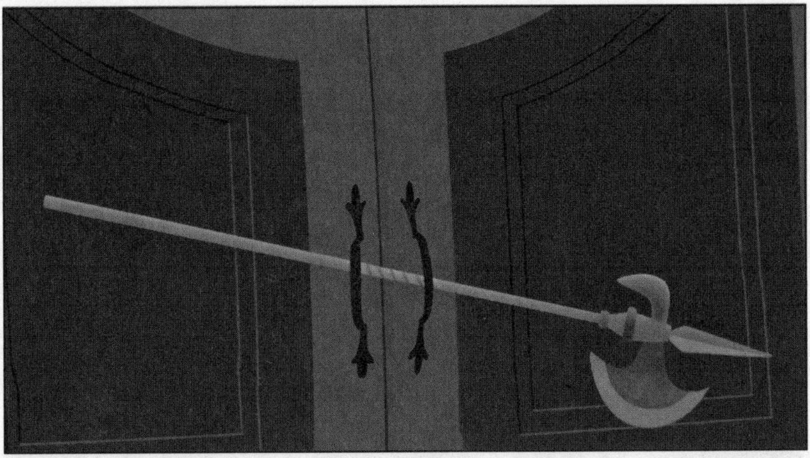

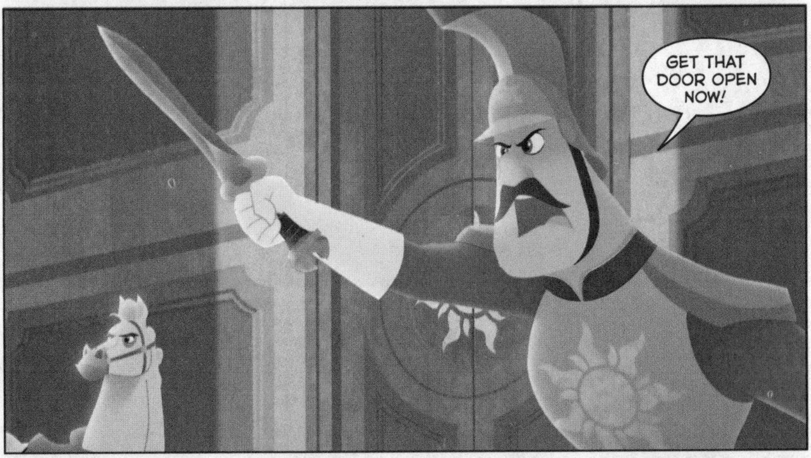
GET THAT DOOR OPEN NOW!

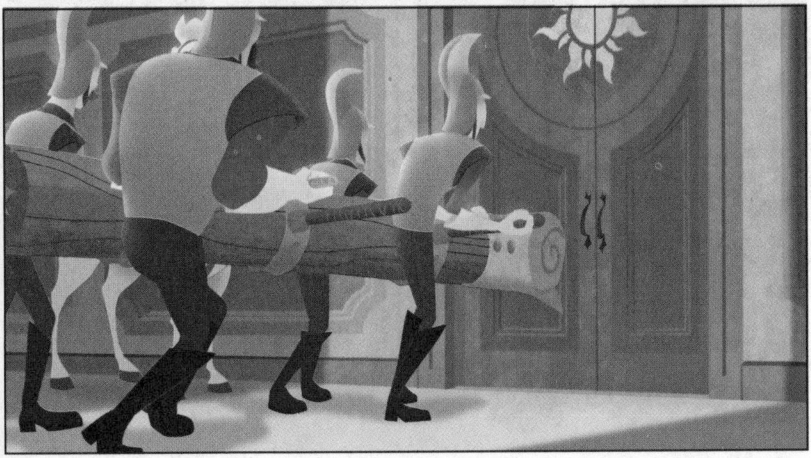

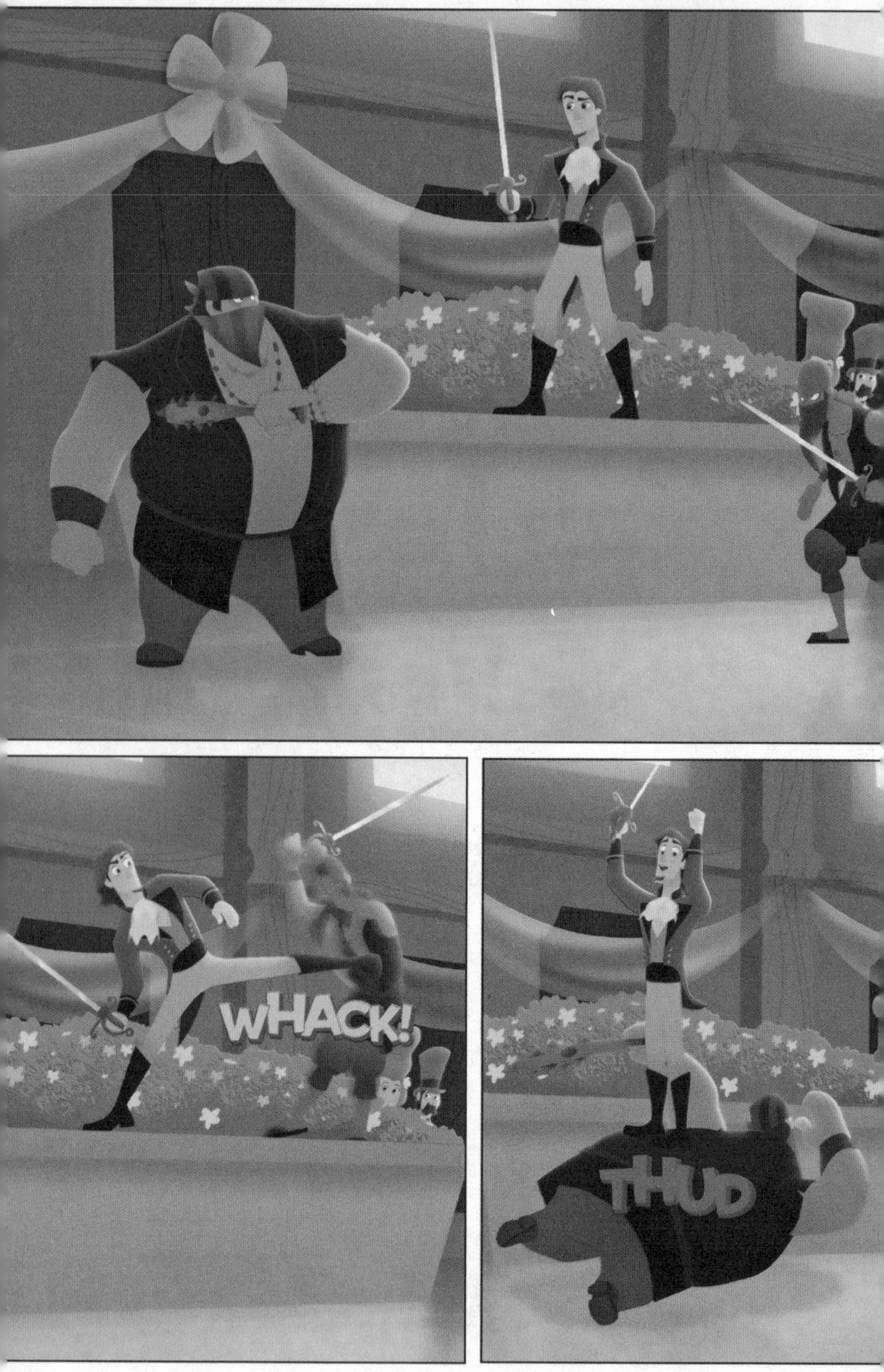
WHACK!
THUD

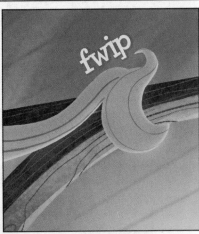

fwip

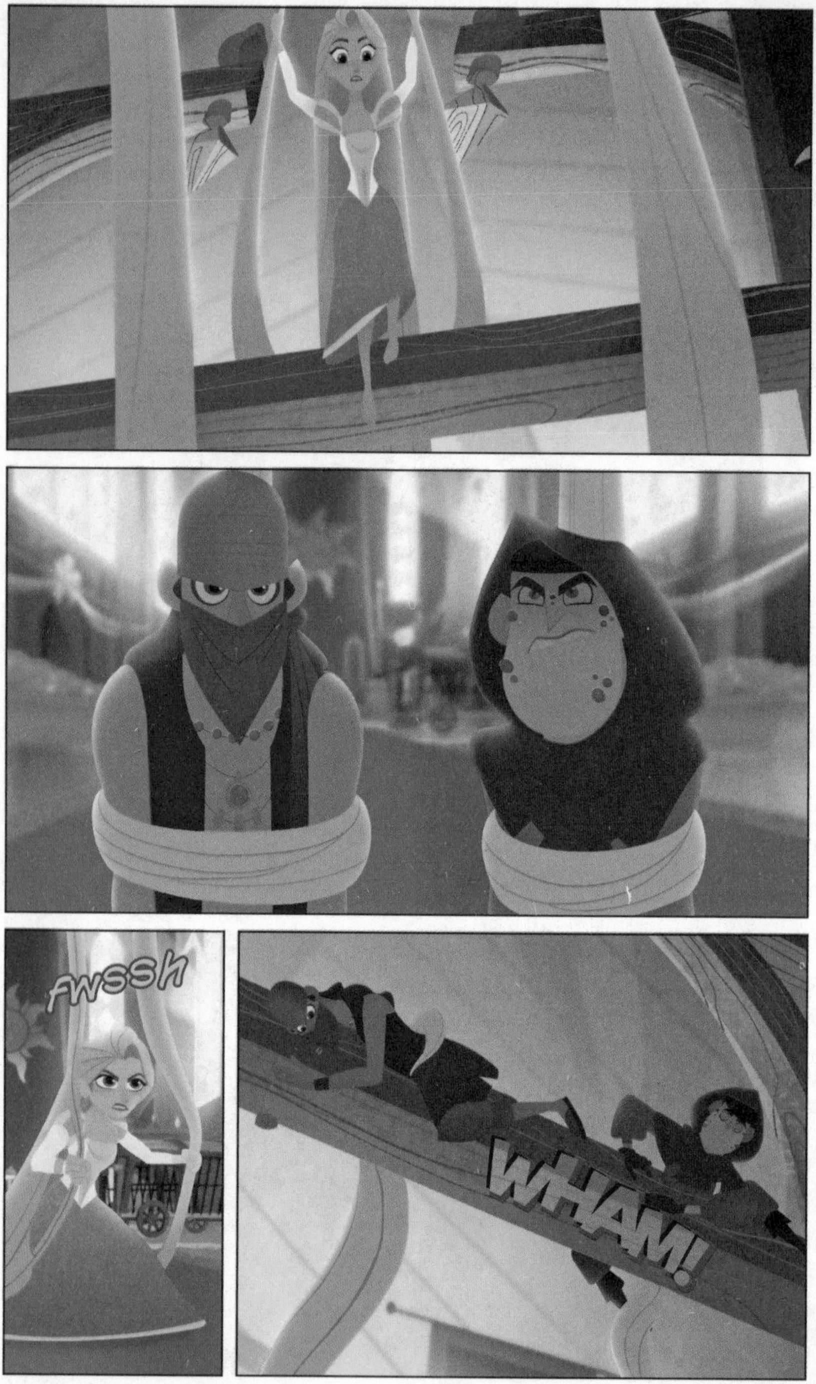
FWSSH
WHAM!

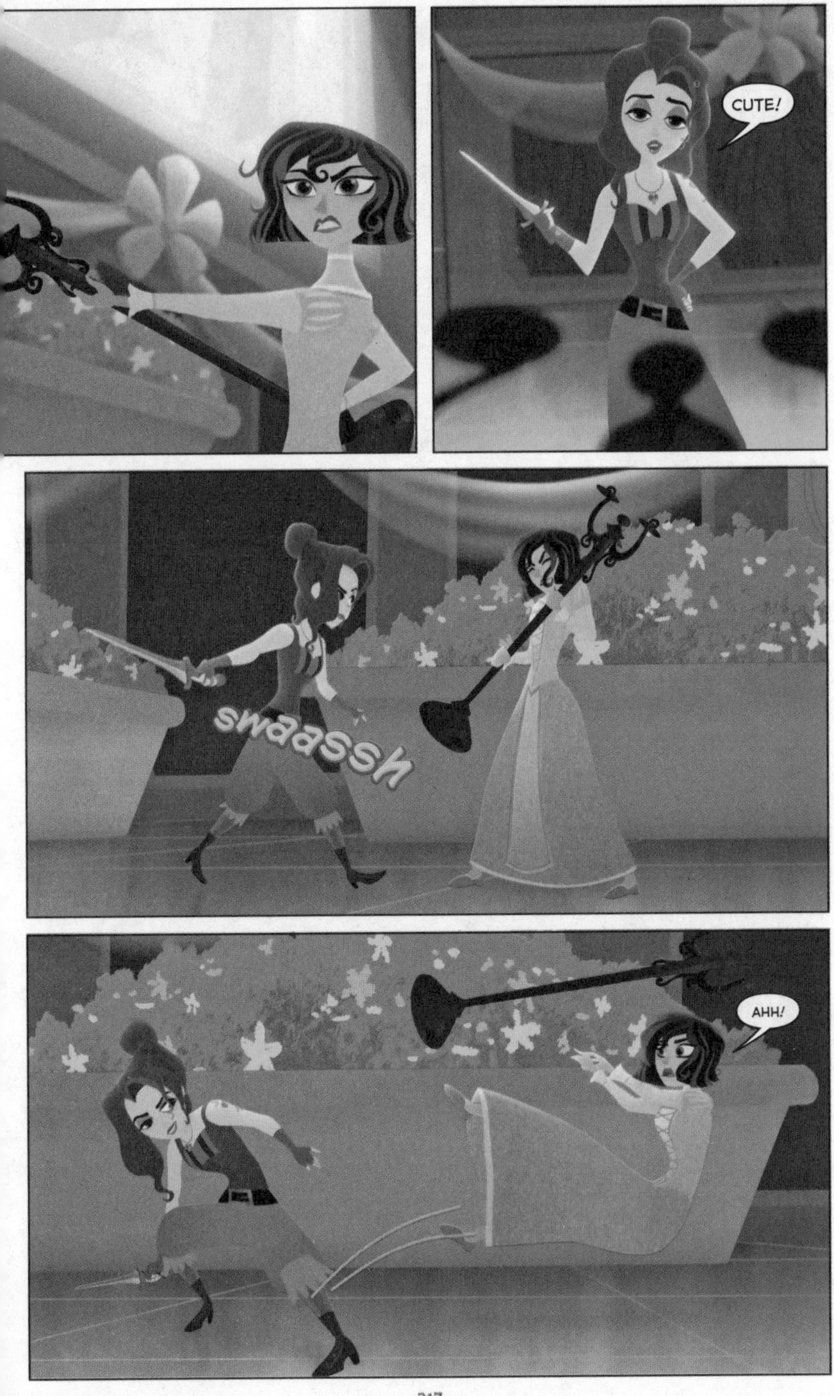
CUTE!
swaasssh
AHH!

shiing

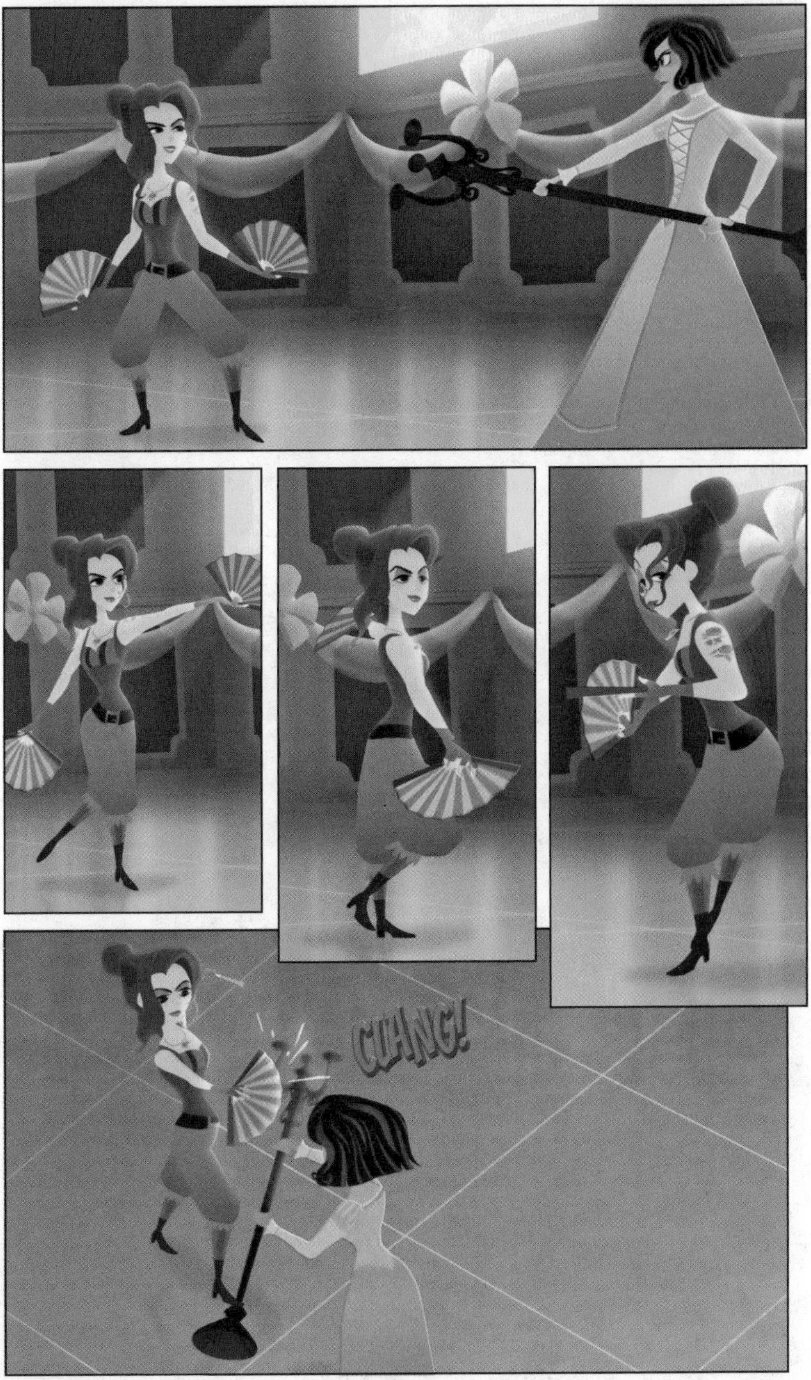
CLANG!

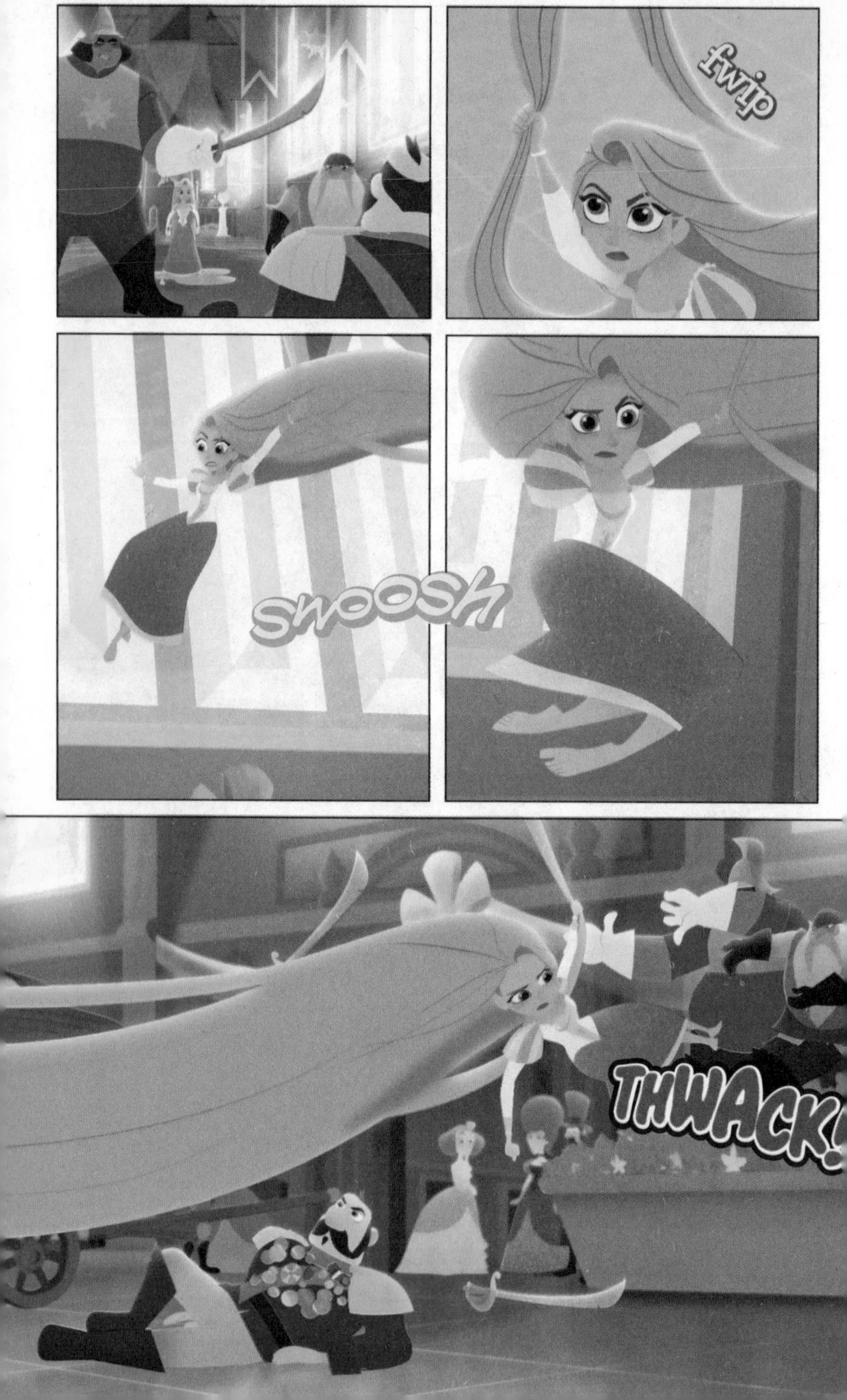
fwip
SWOOSH
THWACK!

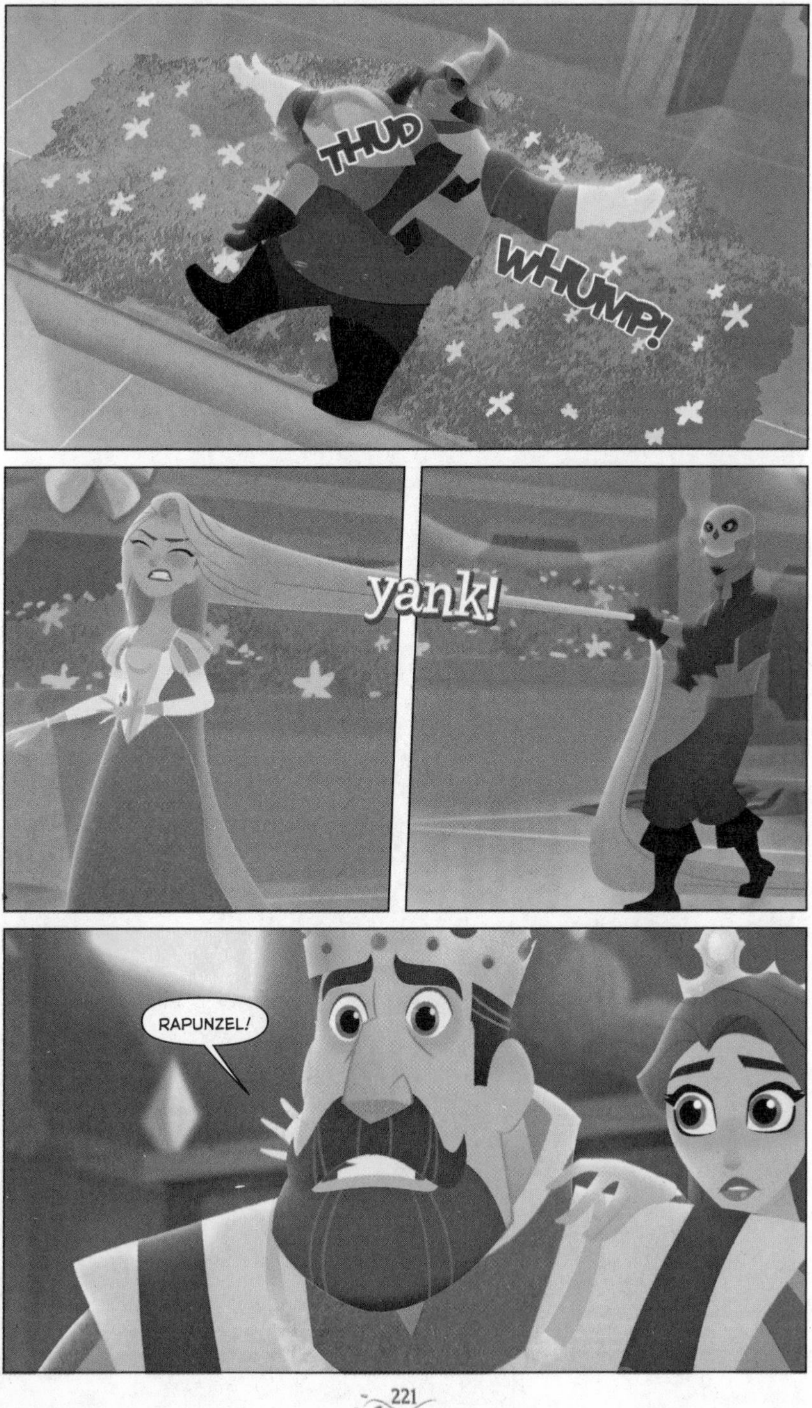
THUD
WHUMP!
yank!
RAPUNZEL!

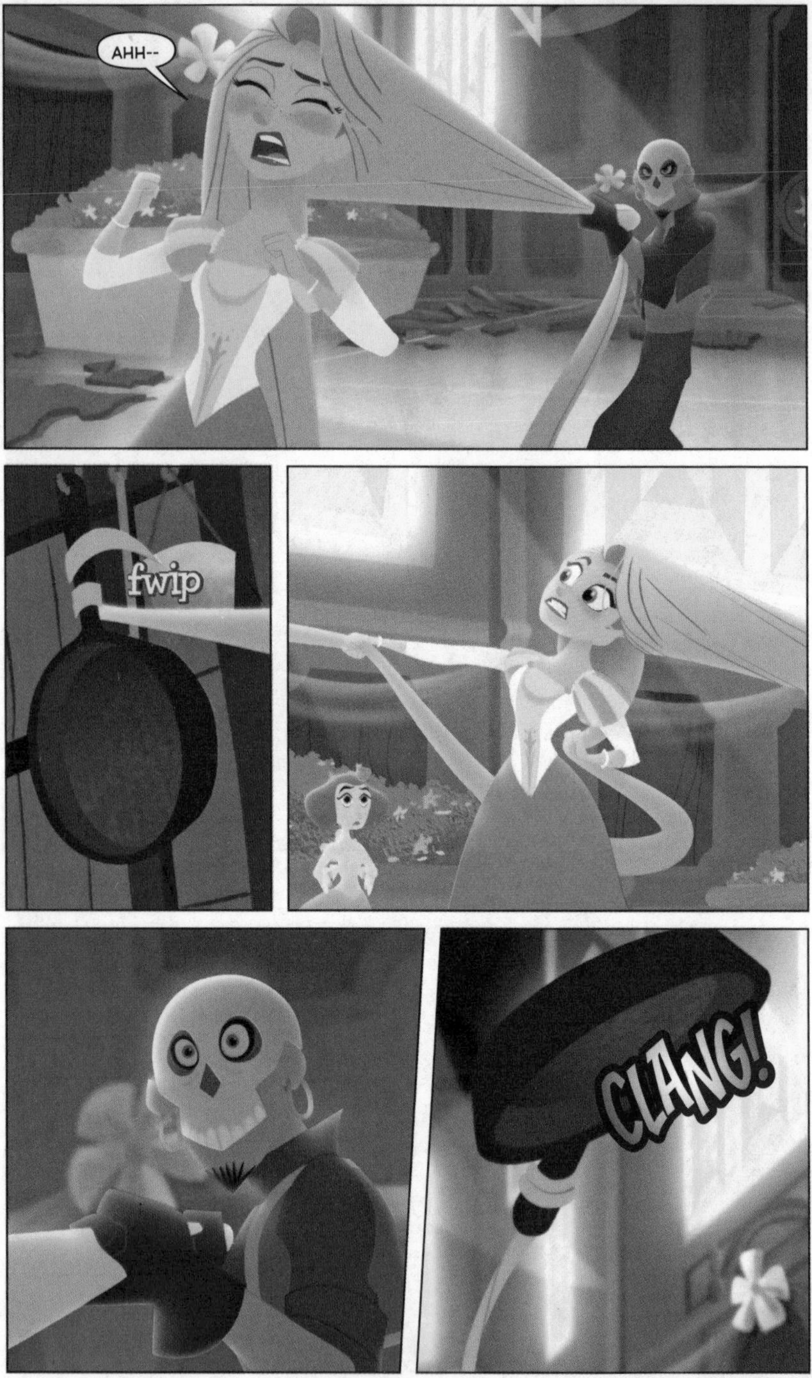
AHH--
fwip
CLANG!

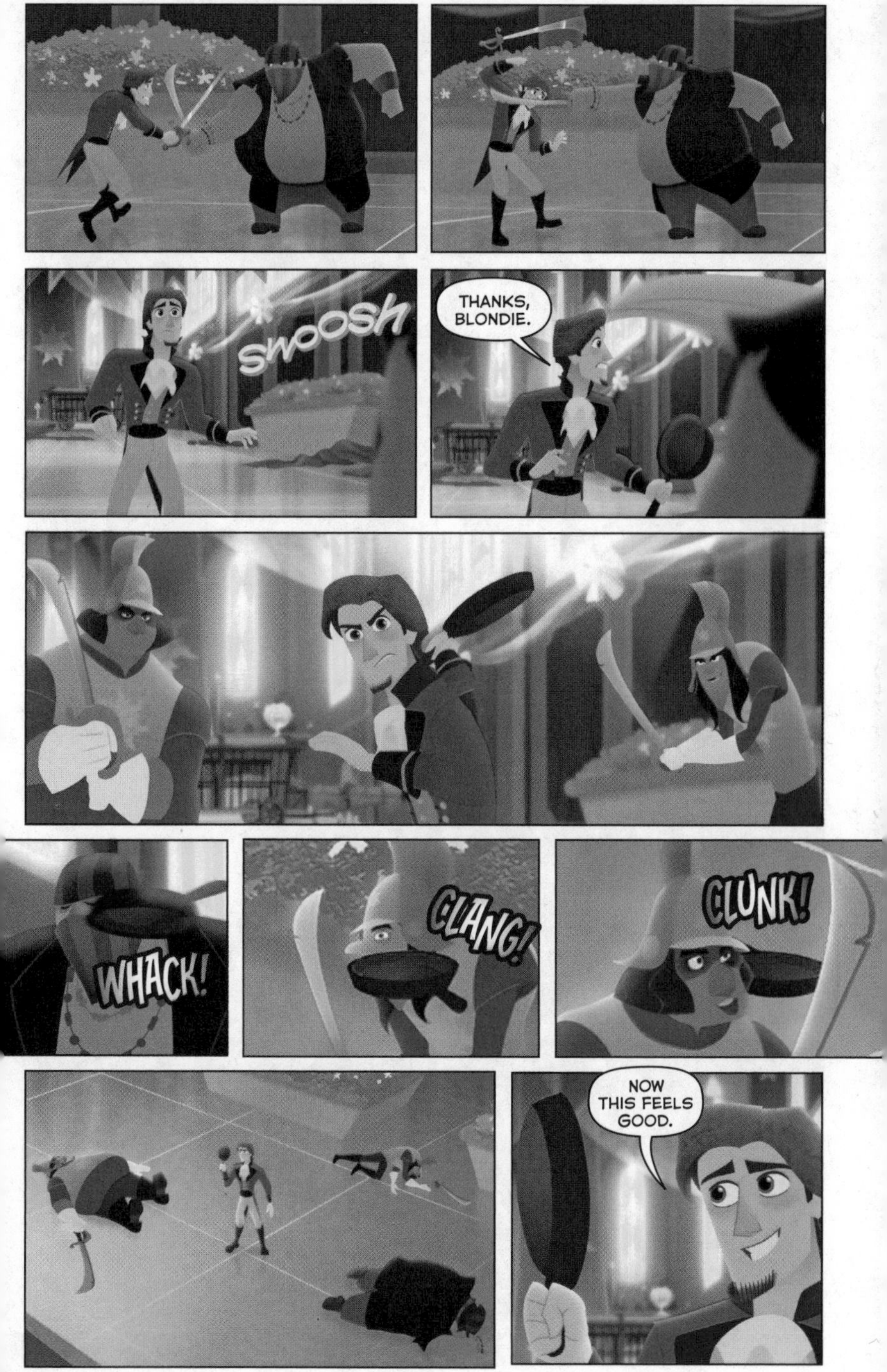

SWOOSH
THANKS, BLONDIE.
WHACK!
CLANG!
CLUNK!
NOW THIS FEELS GOOD.

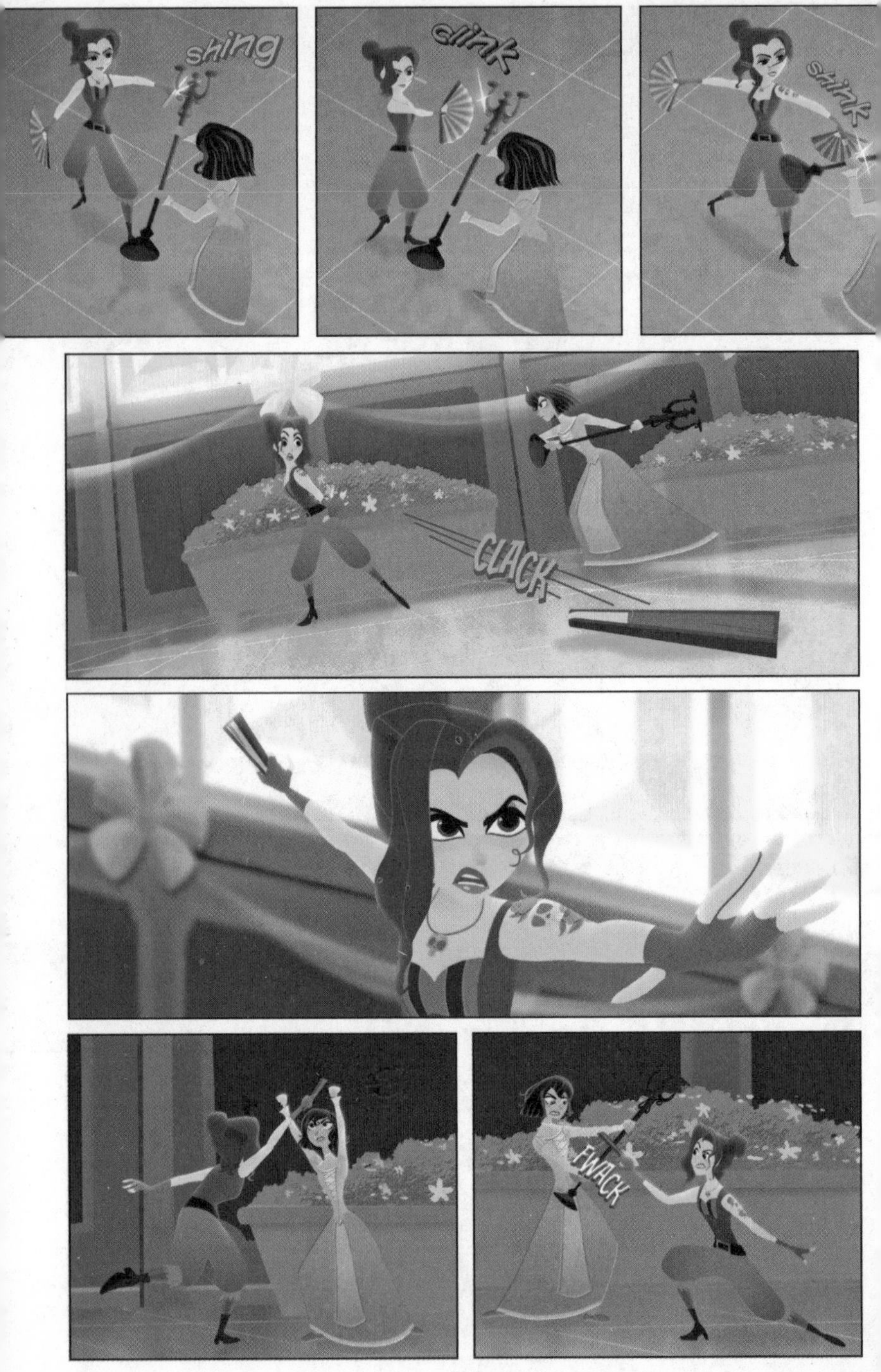
shing
clink
shink
CLACK
FWACK

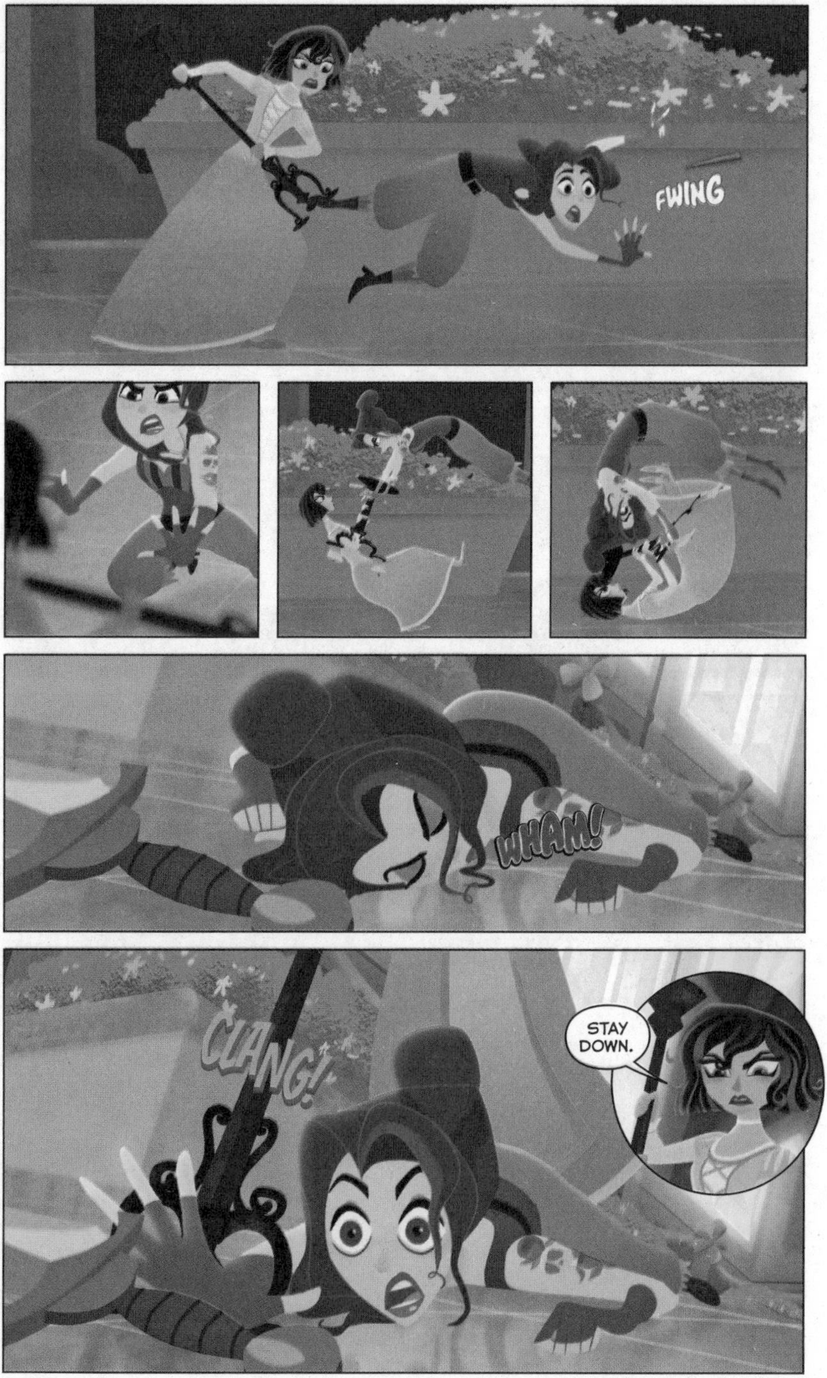
FWING
WHAM!
CLANG!
STAY DOWN.

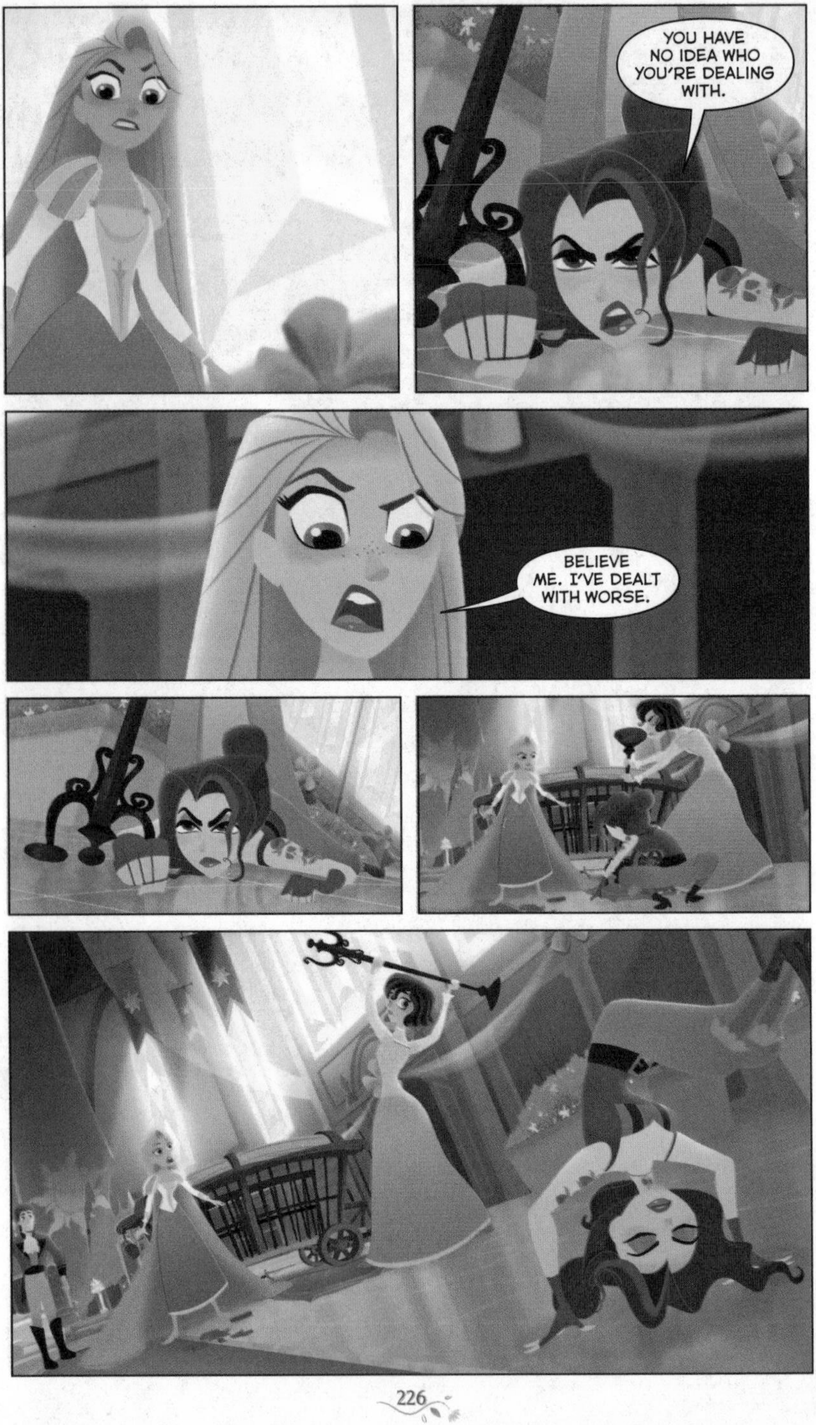
YOU HAVE NO IDEA WHO YOU'RE DEALING WITH.
BELIEVE ME. I'VE DEALT WITH WORSE.

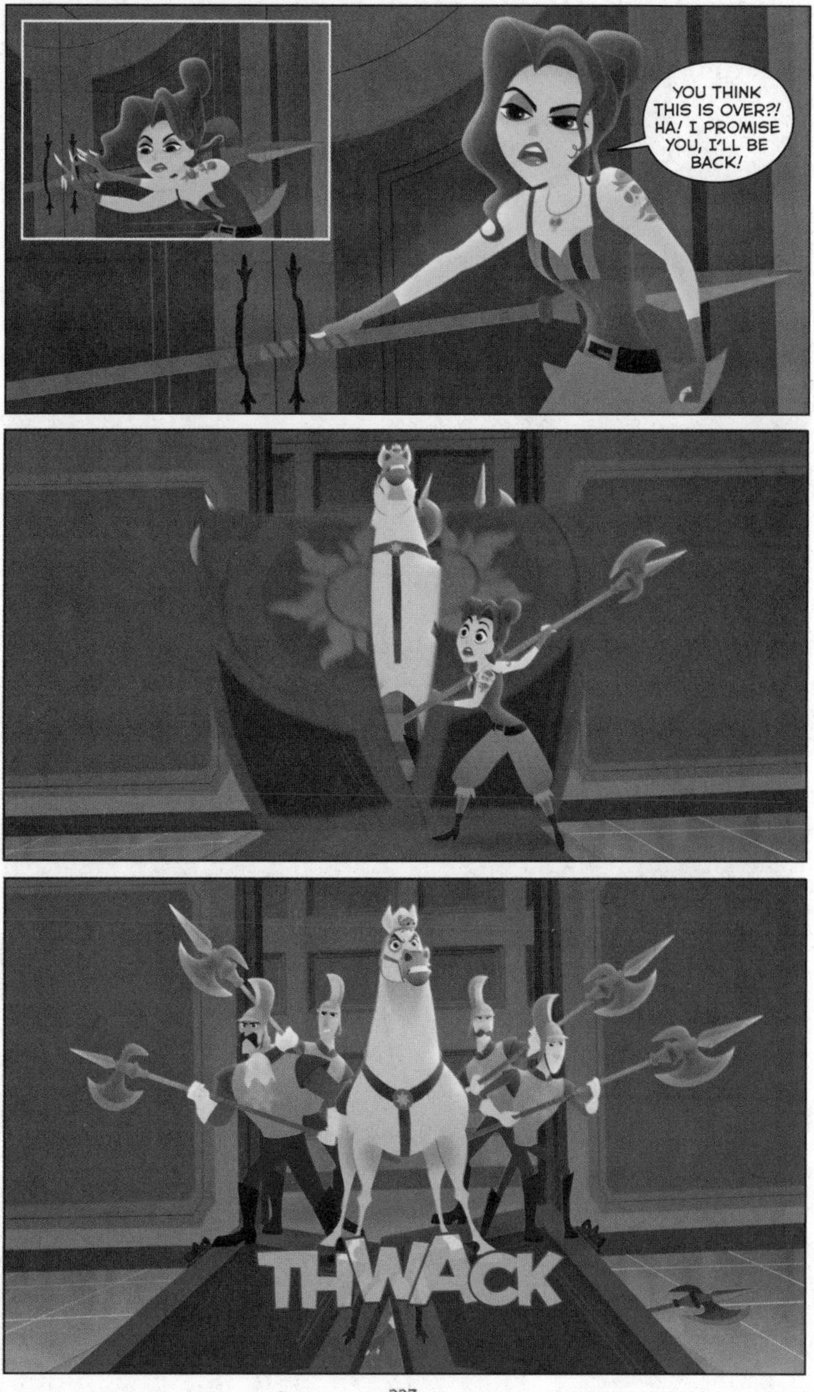
YOU THINK THIS IS OVER?! HA! I PROMISE YOU, I'LL BE BACK!
THWACK

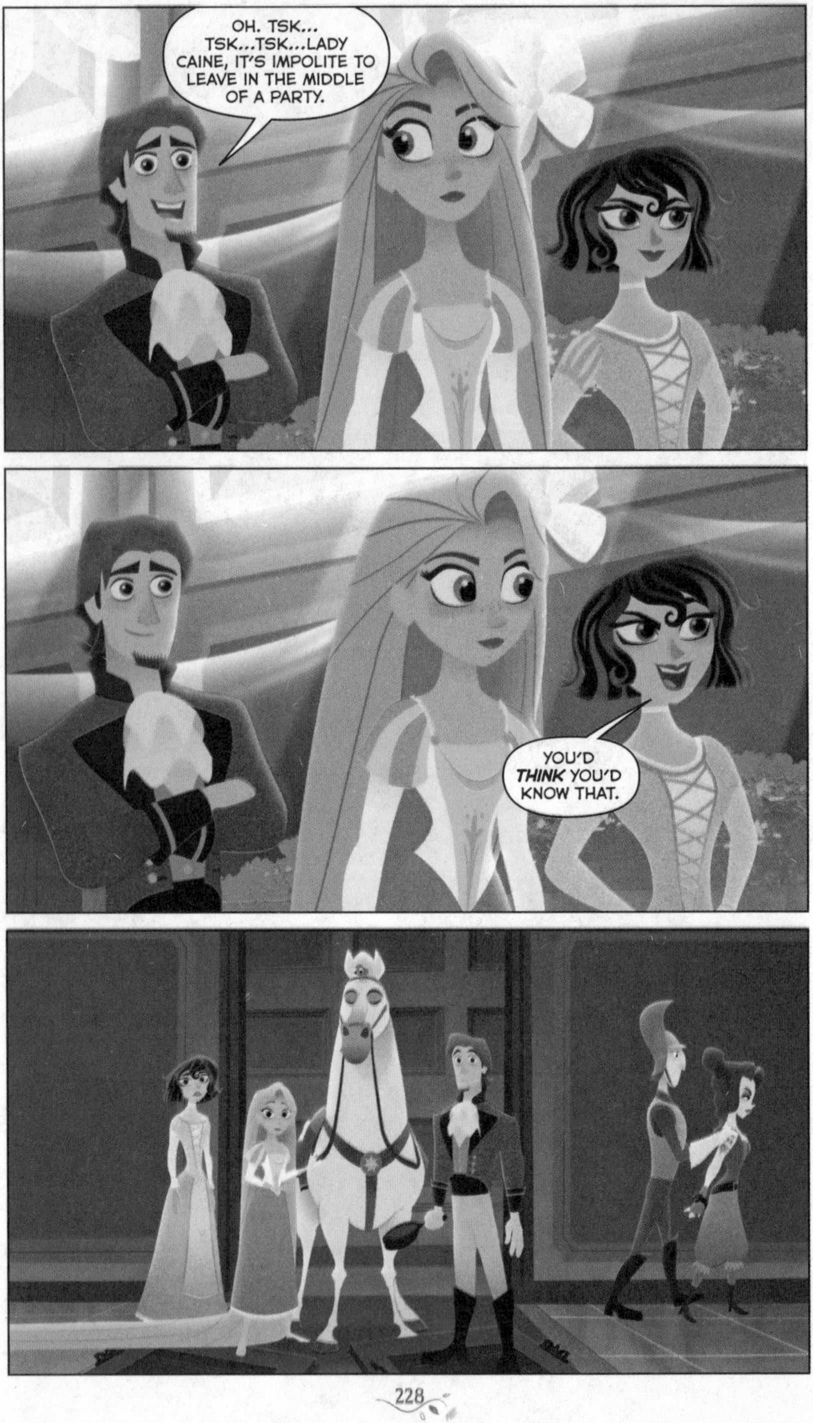
OH. TSK... TSK...TSK...LADY CAINE, IT'S IMPOLITE TO LEAVE IN THE MIDDLE OF A PARTY.
YOU'D *THINK* YOU'D KNOW THAT.

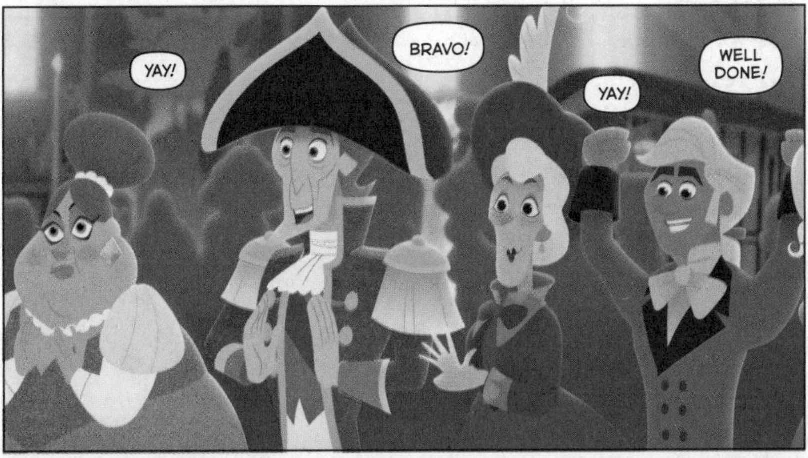
YAY!
BRAVO!
YAY!
WELL DONE!

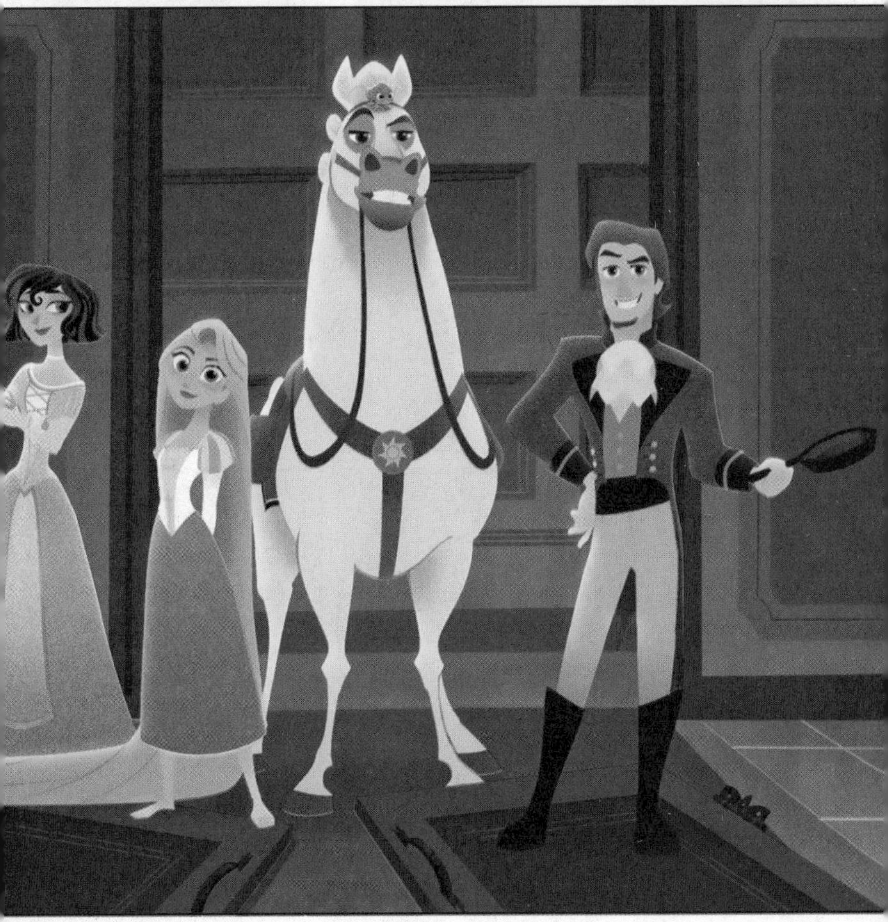

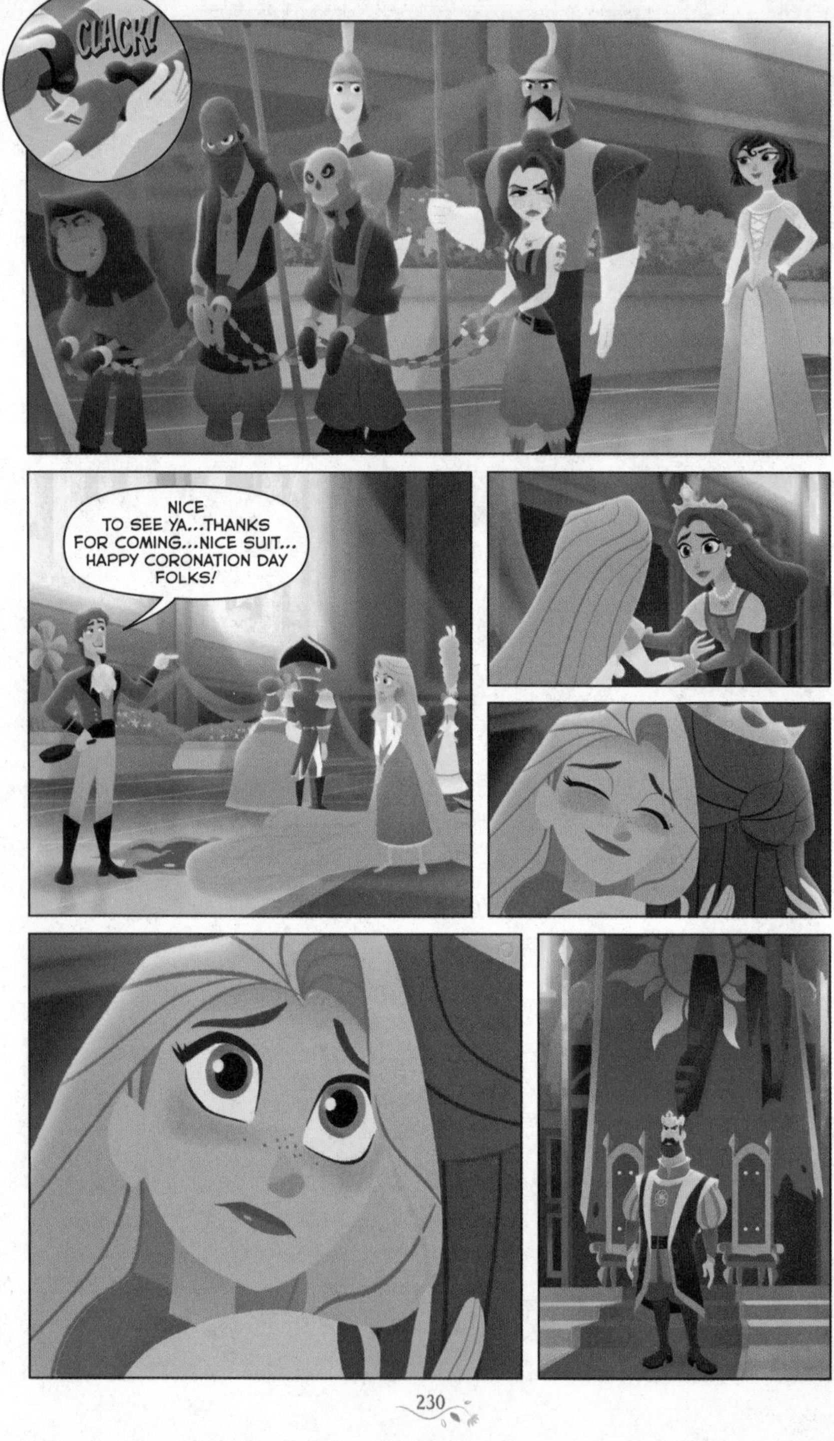
CLACK!
NICE TO SEE YA...THANKS FOR COMING...NICE SUIT... HAPPY CORONATION DAY FOLKS!

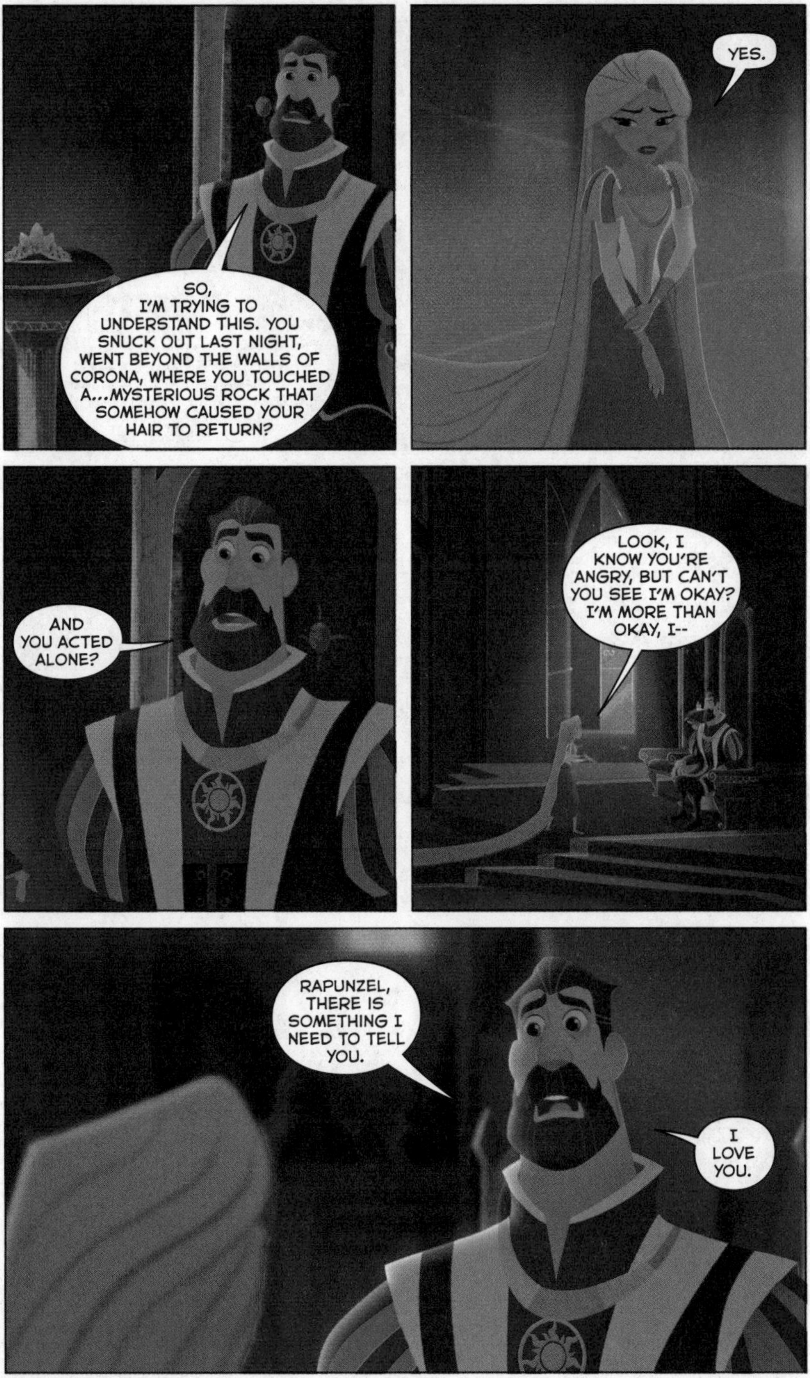
SO, I'M TRYING TO UNDERSTAND THIS. YOU SNUCK OUT LAST NIGHT, WENT BEYOND THE WALLS OF CORONA, WHERE YOU TOUCHED A...MYSTERIOUS ROCK THAT SOMEHOW CAUSED YOUR HAIR TO RETURN?
YES.
AND YOU ACTED ALONE?
LOOK, I KNOW YOU'RE ANGRY, BUT CAN'T YOU SEE I'M OKAY? I'M MORE THAN OKAY, I--
RAPUNZEL, THERE IS SOMETHING I NEED TO TELL YOU.
I LOVE YOU.

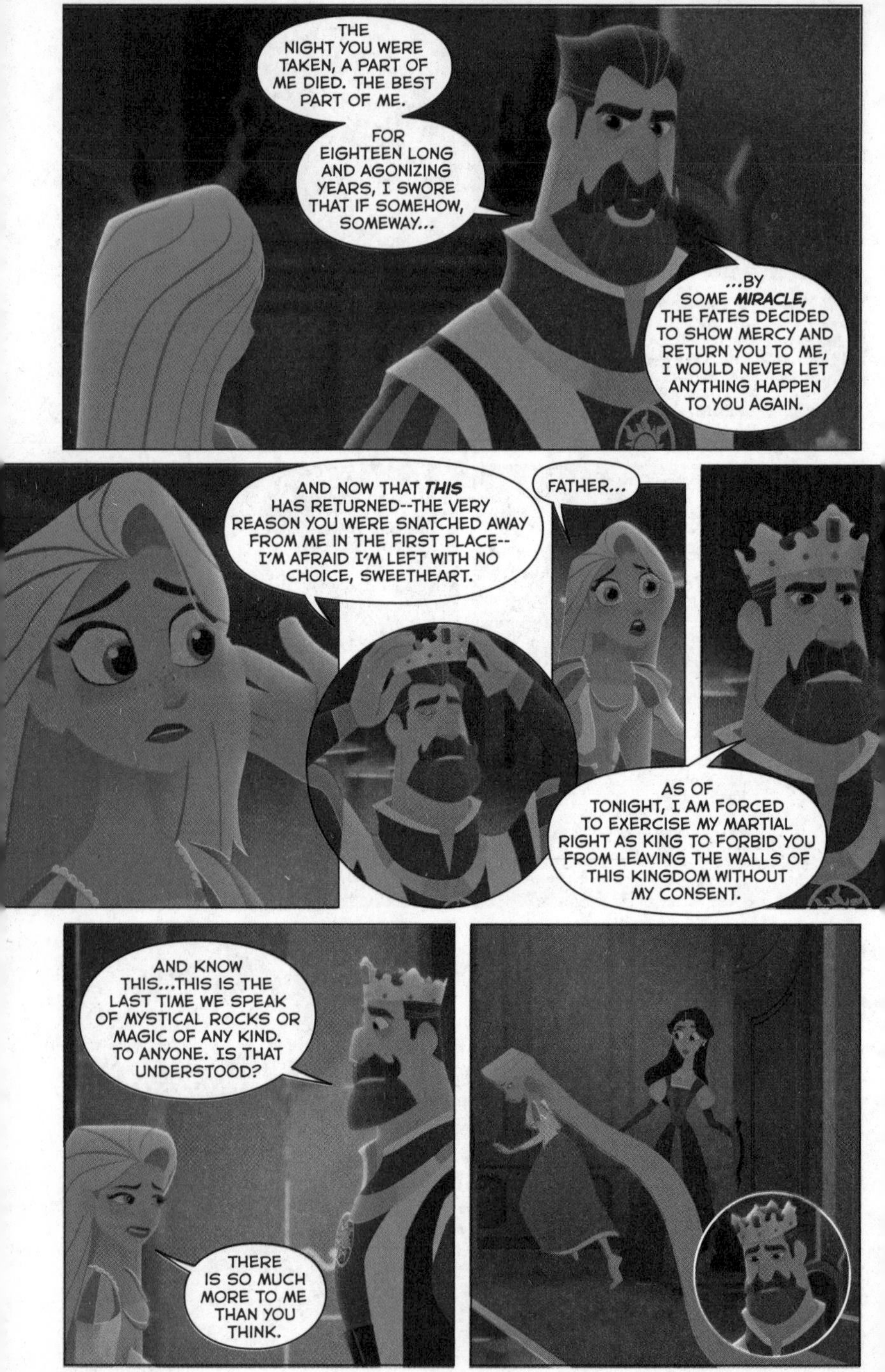
THE NIGHT YOU WERE TAKEN, A PART OF ME DIED. THE BEST PART OF ME.
FOR EIGHTEEN LONG AND AGONIZING YEARS, I SWORE THAT IF SOMEHOW, SOMEWAY...
...BY SOME *MIRACLE,* THE FATES DECIDED TO SHOW MERCY AND RETURN YOU TO ME, I WOULD NEVER LET ANYTHING HAPPEN TO YOU AGAIN.
AND NOW THAT *THIS* HAS RETURNED--THE VERY REASON YOU WERE SNATCHED AWAY FROM ME IN THE FIRST PLACE--I'M AFRAID I'M LEFT WITH NO CHOICE, SWEETHEART.
FATHER...
AS OF TONIGHT, I AM FORCED TO EXERCISE MY MARTIAL RIGHT AS KING TO FORBID YOU FROM LEAVING THE WALLS OF THIS KINGDOM WITHOUT MY CONSENT.
AND KNOW THIS...THIS IS THE LAST TIME WE SPEAK OF MYSTICAL ROCKS OR MAGIC OF ANY KIND. TO ANYONE. IS THAT UNDERSTOOD?
THERE IS SO MUCH MORE TO ME THAN YOU THINK.

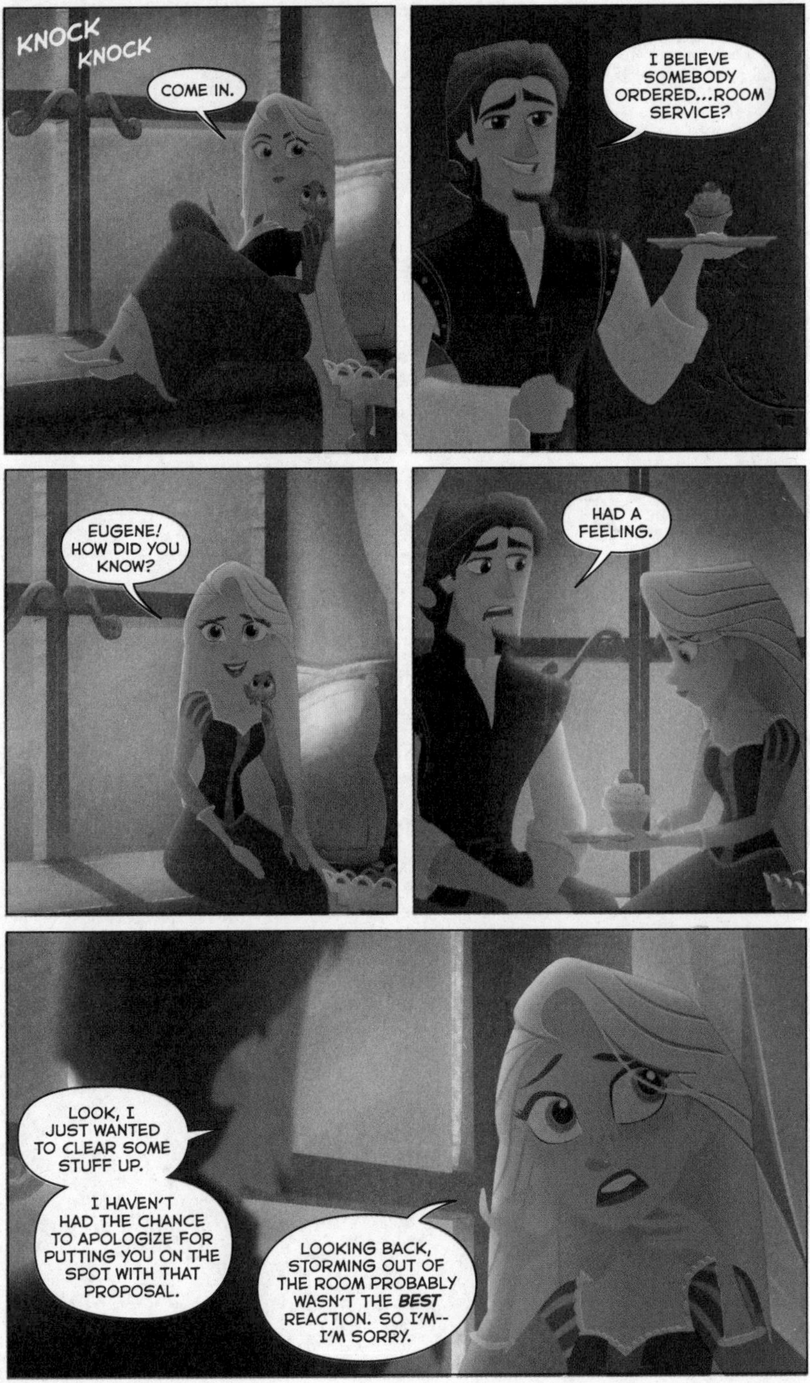
KNOCK KNOCK
COME IN.
I BELIEVE SOMEBODY ORDERED...ROOM SERVICE?
EUGENE! HOW DID YOU KNOW?
HAD A FEELING.
LOOK, I JUST WANTED TO CLEAR SOME STUFF UP.
I HAVEN'T HAD THE CHANCE TO APOLOGIZE FOR PUTTING YOU ON THE SPOT WITH THAT PROPOSAL.
LOOKING BACK, STORMING OUT OF THE ROOM PROBABLY WASN'T THE *BEST* REACTION. SO I'M-- I'M SORRY.

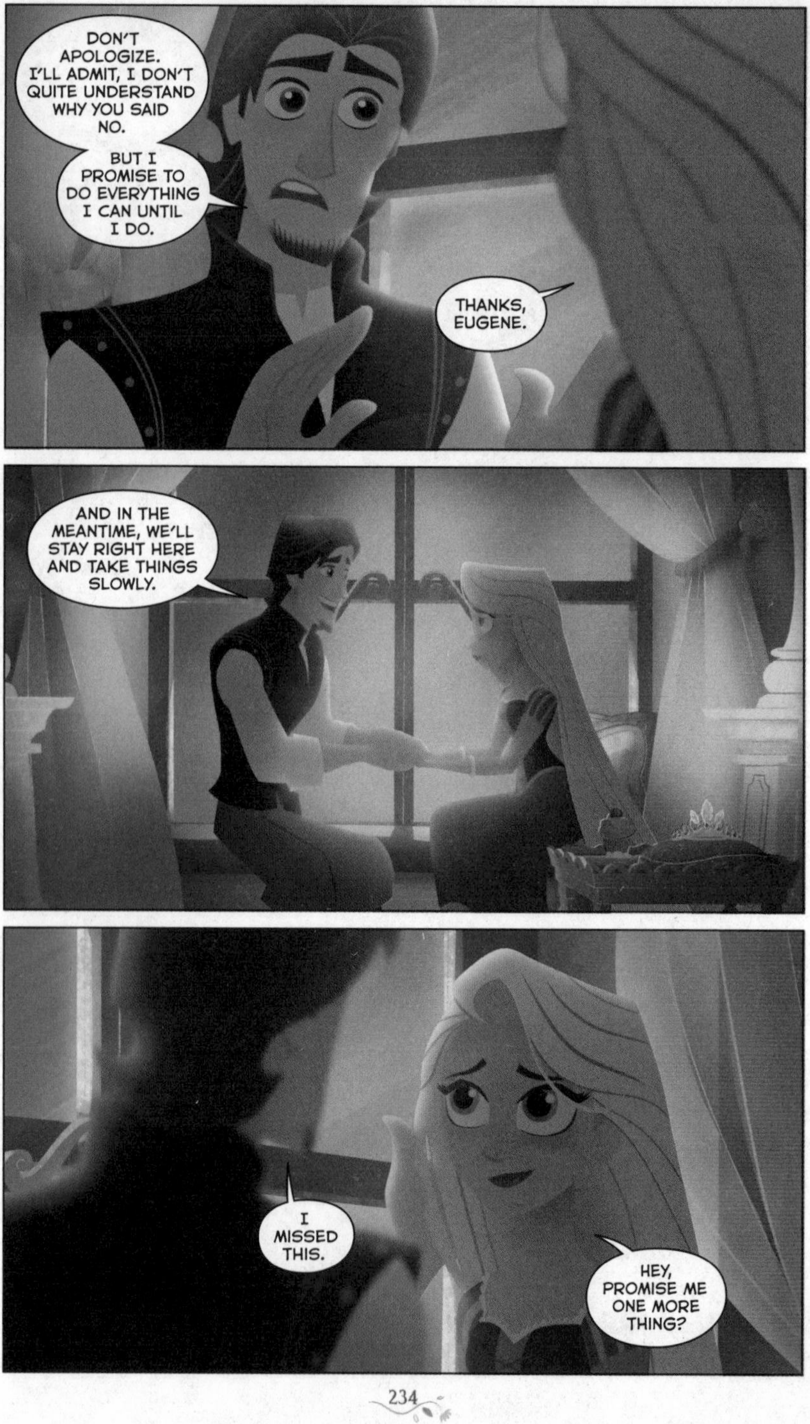
DON'T APOLOGIZE. I'LL ADMIT, I DON'T QUITE UNDERSTAND WHY YOU SAID NO.
BUT I PROMISE TO DO EVERYTHING I CAN UNTIL I DO.
THANKS, EUGENE.
AND IN THE MEANTIME, WE'LL STAY RIGHT HERE AND TAKE THINGS SLOWLY.
I MISSED THIS.
HEY, PROMISE ME ONE MORE THING?

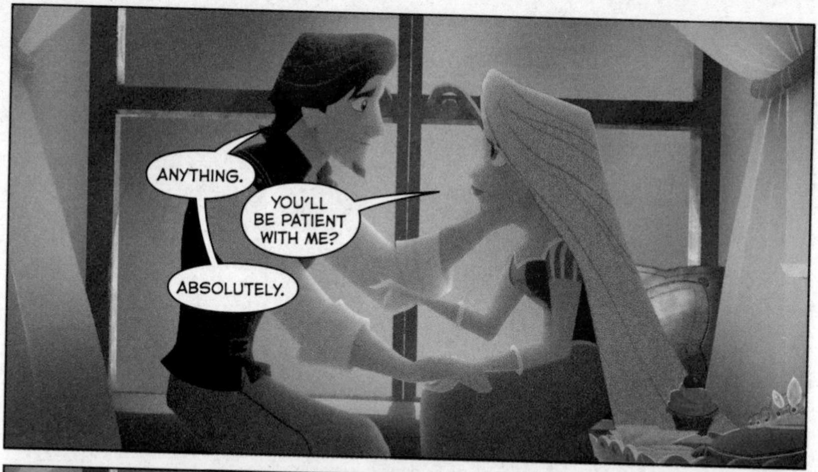
ANYTHING.
YOU'LL BE PATIENT WITH ME?
ABSOLUTELY.

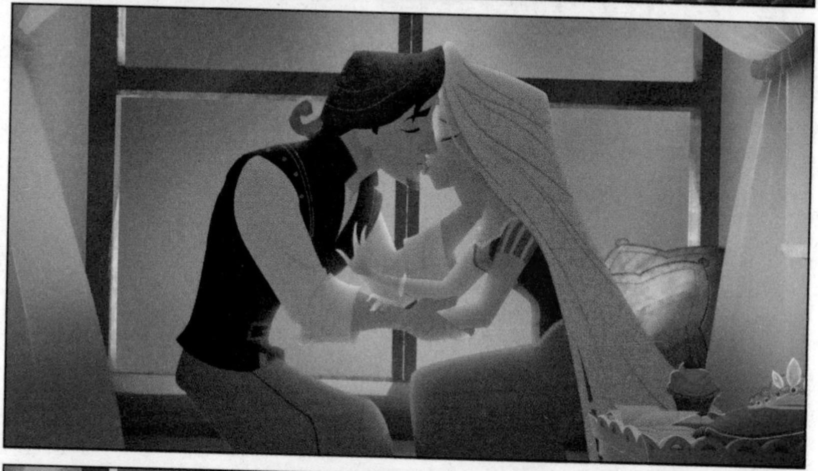

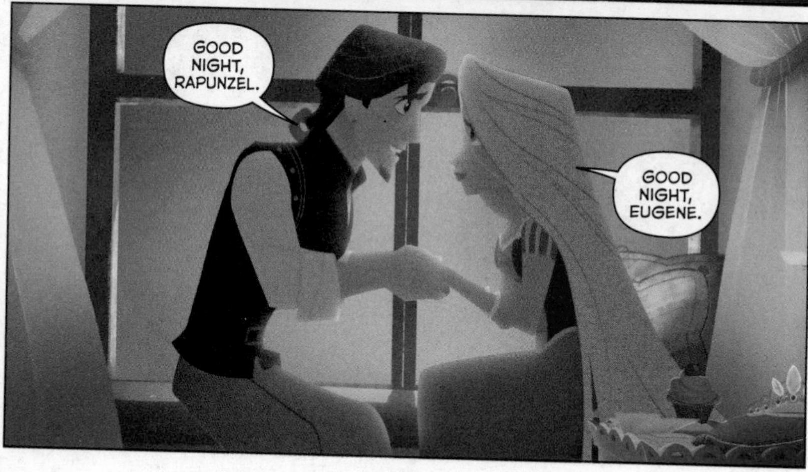
GOOD NIGHT, RAPUNZEL.
GOOD NIGHT, EUGENE.

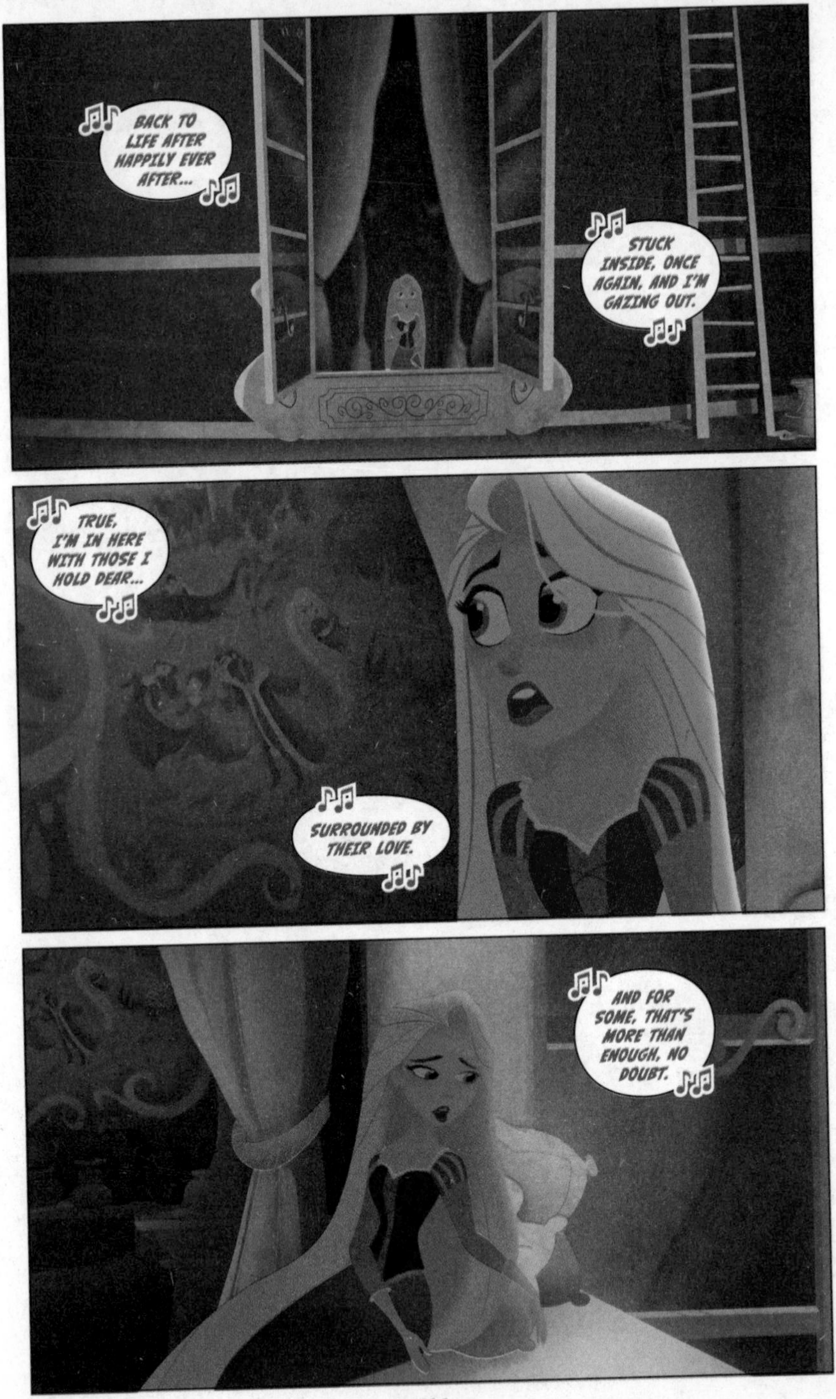
BACK TO LIFE AFTER HAPPILY EVER AFTER...
STUCK INSIDE, ONCE AGAIN, AND I'M GAZING OUT.
TRUE, I'M IN HERE WITH THOSE I HOLD DEAR...
SURROUNDED BY THEIR LOVE.
AND FOR SOME, THAT'S MORE THAN ENOUGH, NO DOUBT.

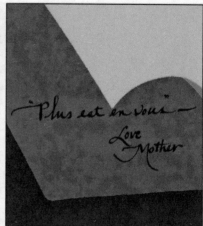

"Plus est en vous —
Love Mother

♪♫ BUT... ♪♫

♪♫ I'VE GOT THE WIND IN MY HAIR... ♪♫

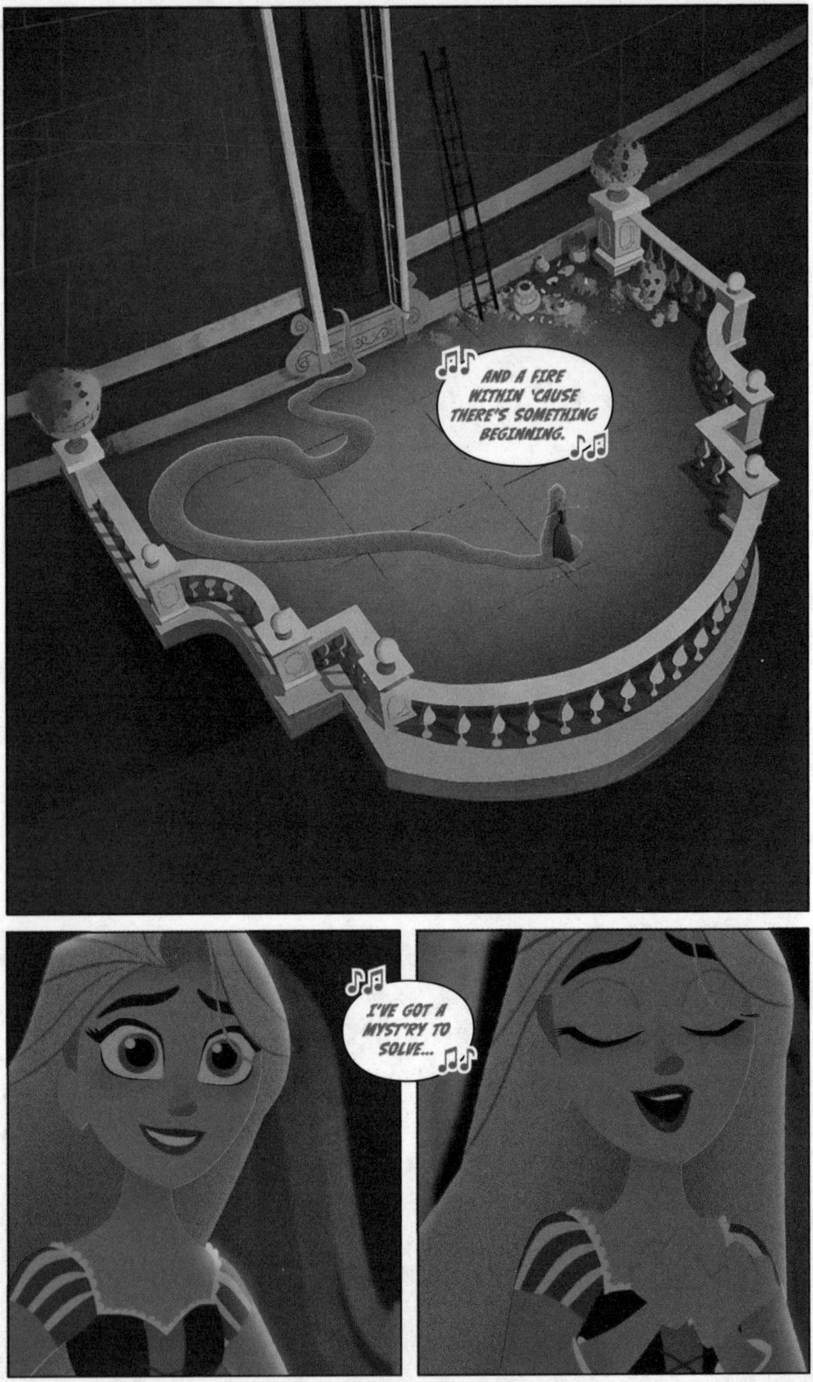
AND A FIRE WITHIN 'CAUSE THERE'S SOMETHING BEGINNING.
I'VE GOT A MYST'RY TO SOLVE...

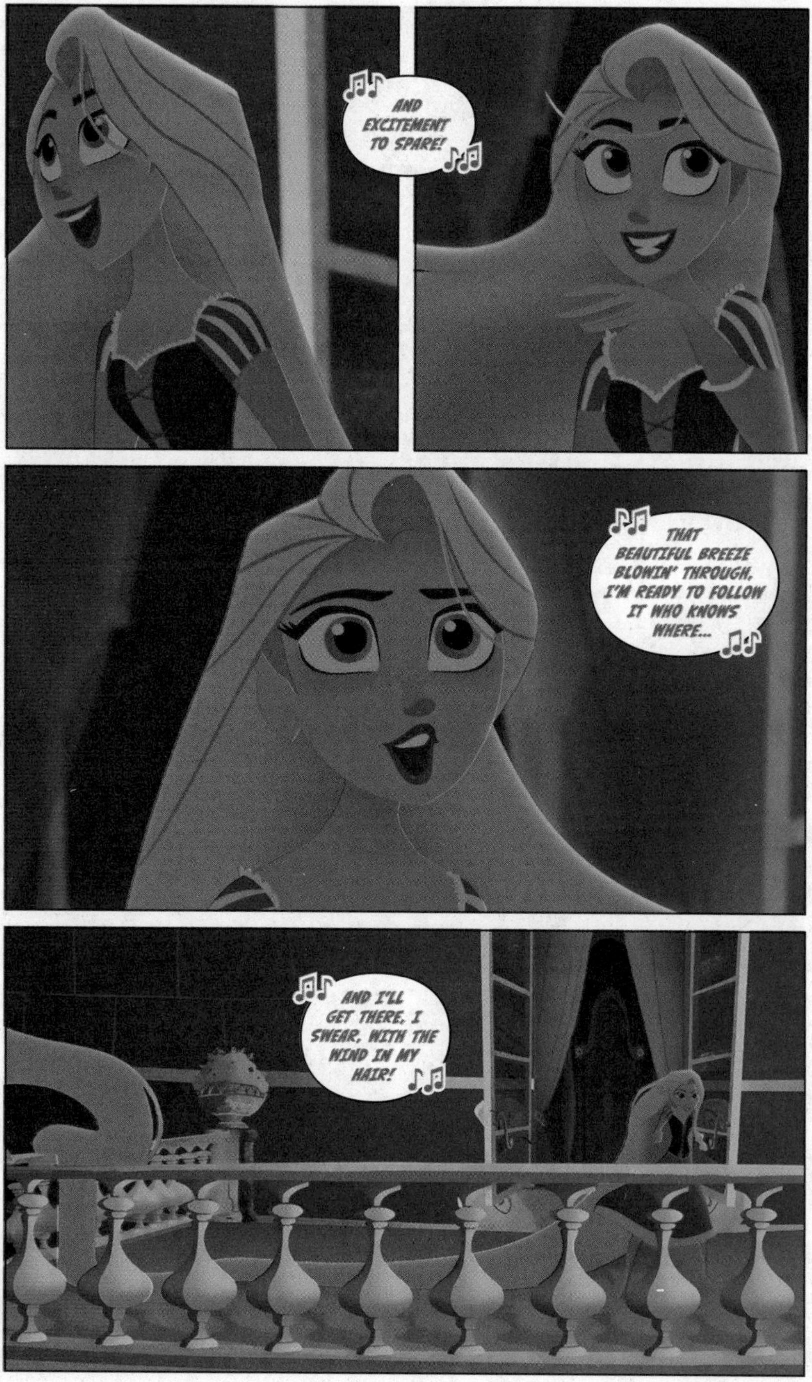
AND EXCITEMENT TO SPARE!
THAT BEAUTIFUL BREEZE BLOWIN' THROUGH, I'M READY TO FOLLOW IT WHO KNOWS WHERE...
AND I'LL GET THERE, I SWEAR, WITH THE WIND IN MY HAIR!

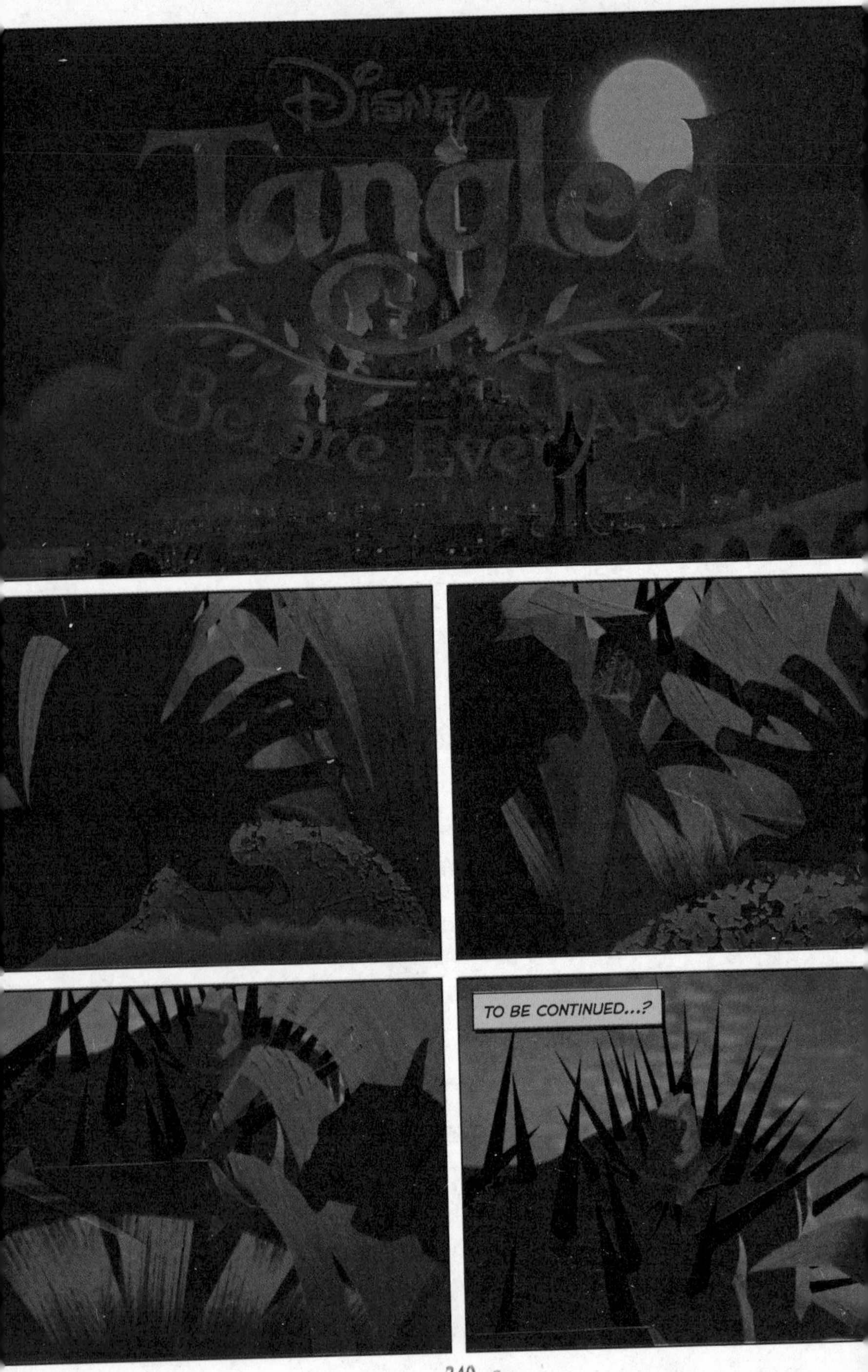
Disney
Tangled
TO BE CONTINUED...?